WHISKEY SUNRISE

By John Turney

Brimstone
Fiction

WHISKEY SUNRISE BY JOHN TURNEY
Published by Brimstone Fiction
1440 W. Taylor Street, Suite 449, Chicago, IL 60607

ISBN: 978-1-946758-08-8
Copyright © 2017 by John Turney
Interior design by Reality Premedia Services Pvt. Ltd.
Cover design by Ken Raney, www.kenraney.com and
Urosh Bizjak, http://uroshb.prosite.com

Available in print from your local bookstore, online, or from the publisher at:
www.brimstonefiction.com

For more information on this book and the author visit: http://www.jturney.com

Brought to you by the creative team at Lighthouse Publishing of the Carolinas and
Brimstone Fiction: Rowena Kuo, Meaghan Burnett, Brian Cross, Eddie Jones, and
Ken Raney.

Library of Congress Cataloging-in-Publication Data
Turney, John.
Whiskey Sunrise / John Turney 1st ed.

Printed in the United States of America

Dedication

It is my honor to dedicate this book to my father who passed before he saw one of my books in print. He was an honorable man who did right for his family. He fought during WWII in the Navy, serving as a gunner aboard a sub-chaser. He saved the USS Missouri from serious damage by shooting down a kamikaze pilot as it closed in on the Missouri's waterline.

And to all the men and women who served and are serving in the US military. Whether on the front lines or in some back-water post, your service is honorable, and a grateful nation can't thank you enough.

PRAISE FOR *WHISKEY SUNRISE*

I had the honor of reading an Advance Reader Copy of *Whiskey Sunrise*, and I can tell you it's a fantastic read. Packed with action. Highly recommended.

~ Linda Swink
Award-winning author of *In Their Honor* and *Life on a $5 Bet*

What starts out as a creepy little story about some bloody murders with supernatural overtones soon morphs into a complex, international high-stakes suspense story that keeps you on the edge of your seat. Strap yourself in—it's one wild ride.

~ David E. Fessenden
Literary agent, publishing consultant,
and author of *The Case of the Exploding Speakeasy*

Acknowledgements

If you've ever read through the acknowledgements page in any book, you find just a portion of the people who have helped in bringing a book to life. It's no different here. I would need to write another book to adequately thank those who lent their assistance to this one. I'll do my best to keep it short so we don't needlessly kill trees or take up too many digital bites.

First off, I would like to thank my editor and friend Rowena Kuo. She saw potential in *Whiskey Sunrise* before anyone else did. She truly is one of those rare people who can bring out the best in others. If you enjoy this story, and I hope you do, much credit goes to her editing. If you don't enjoy...blame me. Next I would like to thank Eddie Jones and Lighthouse Publishing for accepting this manuscript. It was done at the Write-to-Publish writers' conference, and I can never say enough thanks for taking the risk to bring this tale to publication. I would also like to thank Meaghan Burnett, who has played a large role in helping me with the social media side of the writing business.

Secondly, I have been in a number of writing groups. Each of these played a crucial role in my development as a writer. The leaders and members of these groups are too long to mention; I know who you are and cannot say thank you enough. Some of my co-workers have also played an important role in their encouraging me on during the writing. I especially want to thank Cliff Lindberg who provided me details about Arizona to help me get that right.

Thirdly, I would be amiss if I did not mention the writers conferences I have attended and the people I've met there. Especially, Lin Johnson and Jane Rubietta at Write-to-Publish and Vicki Ryan at

Mad Anthony. Great conferences that helped teach me much about this thing called writing such as WTP, where I met Rene Gutteridge while attending her fiction writing classes. One of the exercises resulted in me finding the initial spark that turned into *Whiskey Sunrise*.

And lastly, I want to thank the two most important people in my life. The spouse of an artist has a tough way to go. It takes time away from them for the artist to bring his or her creations to life. Despite the many hours apart, my wife and best friend has stayed by my side. Thank you, Sandy. You are the love of my life. As a Christian, I also want to thank Yeshua ben JHVH who paid the spiritual debt I owed. Without His divine love, I probably would not be alive to have written this story.

Last word: thank you, reader, for picking up this book. I hope you enjoy the ride.

Prologue

Locked in a car trunk, wrists and ankles bound with duct tape, Juan had no doubt this would be his final ride. Gritting his teeth, he pulled against the tape. His arms shook, and his shoulders and upper back burned. Sweat beaded his forehead. The tape refused to budge. Releasing his breath, Juan gave up.

He had tried screaming for help, but the duct tape across his mouth only permitted an elongated throaty grunt. Juan squeezed his eyes shut. The bump on the back of his head pounded in rhythmic harmony with the velocity of his heart.

Bile churned in his gut, and he gagged. *Jesús y la Virgen Bendita, no*. He relaxed, forcing deep breaths until the moment passed.

Hope faded like old blue jeans. He tried to swallow, but without spit, it was like drinking sand.

A metal bar dug into his side. Tire iron? A possible weapon, but it might as well be in Maine for all the good it would do him.

The numbing drone of tires on pavement toyed with his apprehension. From the outside sounds, Juan assumed they had left Phoenix. Probably headed into the desert.

The trunk reeked of oil, exhaust fumes, and the lingering stench of death. Juan wished the stench belonged to furry creatures and not people, but he doubted it. His captors only hunted humans. His captors? Hired gunmen, both of them. He'd seen their handiwork, bloodied victims lying in Mexican streets.

Not good. Stay calm.

During the afternoon, the temperatures soared into the hundred-and-teens, but night brought chilled air. His sweat-soured clothes stuck to his body, robbing him of warmth. He shivered. His own body odor mixed with fear like a Coke and rum. His watch dinged the hour. Midnight?

Time inched. The brake lights lit up his prison, and Juan perceived the car slowing down. The movement of the vehicle rocked him back and forth. Just enough to make his stiff body scream in agony.

After a few seconds of hearing pebbles pinging in the wheel wells and against the undercarriage, Juan figured they now traveled a gravel road.

He had to warn Rye, but how? Then it occurred to him ... the Sharpie marker in his shirt pocket. The one Rye made all his officers carry. If he could only reach it ... He twisted, so his pocket brushed against the tire iron, then using its claws, forced the pen out of the pocket. It landed under him, so he rolled the other way, and his hands found it. After a brief struggle, he fumbled off the cap and wrote in between his fingers. Hands behind him, he could only hope for partial legibility.

By the jolting movements of the vehicle, Juan suspected his captors had turned onto a dirt trail. The car headed up a low grade and bounced like a three-legged horse. The brake lights came on, and the car slid to a stop.

Seconds later, two car doors opened, one after the other. Panic slithered into his psyche.

The doors slammed shut, sending vibrations through the car body. Footsteps approached on either side of the car.

Keys rattled and then were inserted into the lock of the truck.

The car trunk popped open. The desert night rushed in with the scent of creosote bush, cooling rocks, sand ... and booze.

Two men stood like hulking silhouettes blocking part of the starry night. One wore a bandana, and the other's shaved head reflected starlight. No city lights glowed in the skies, and that meant his captors had taken him deep into the desert's heart.

"Juan, time to meet your Diablo," Bandana said, heavy Español-accented English.

Both reached down, one grabbing Juan by the legs and the other by his shoulders, and heaved him out of the trunk. His head banged against the lid, and they laughed. His vision spun in momentary vertigo. Blood trailed down his forehead. He wanted to hurl curses at the two, but only managed weak mumbles against the tape.

They dumped him onto a dirt track. He lay there while they cut the duct tape from his legs and ripped off his gag.

"Get up, dog."

"How?" Juan said, his voice a croak.

Bandana kicked him in the side. An excruciating torrent ripped through his ribs. His vision exploded as if he watched a super nova.

He struggled to get to his feet. Baldy grabbed him by the shoulders and picked him up.

"Get a move on," the man said with a sneer.

One of the men shoved him in the back. He managed small shuffling steps.

"Where're you taking me?"

"Shut up and walk."

He staggered up the dirt trail in silence. He expected to hear the click of a round being loaded into a handgun, followed by an explosion, and then the blackness of death. But no shot came. The moonlight revealed they headed up a washed-out canyon strewn with boulders and gloom. Further up, bleak stone walls cast a shadow across the path darker than the night sky. It would happen there.

Baldy grabbed Juan's shirtsleeve and tore it, revealing Juan's shoulder tattoo of a skull-pommeled dagger dripping blood. A banner across the hilt read *Semper Fi*. "When you're dead, I'll skin them tats off you. Make me a pouch to hold my bad seed."

As his captors taunted him, Juan shot rapid glances at the surrounding area. Icy silver moonlight bathed the open land. Even if he could take down his two captors with his hands bound, there was no place within a hundred yards to run to.

An owl sounded far up the canyon. He shivered. In the Navajo tradition, an owl represented a newly departed soul.

Just then, about a hundred feet up the canyon floor, car lights blazed on, blinding him. High beams. Juan turned his head sideways to avoid the glare. Car doors opened and shut.

"Here comes da man," Bandana said behind him.

Squinting, Juan watched several people approach—shapes distorted by the illumination of the car lights. Boots crunched on the ground. He recognized the tall shadow in front.

Santo polvo. Demonio.

"Amigo," said the Demonio shadow. "I hate to do what I'm about to do, but even more, I hate when an ... asset ... steals from me. In my line of business, the mere appearance of weakness is a ... drawback. I can't have people thinking I'm weak. *¿Comprende?*"

"But ... but ... I didn't take anything ... I promise. Not a thing. Nada."

"I see with my very eyes what you take. The Indian trinket is nothing. A pretty bauble, *si?*" Demonio held up a silver wristband, gleaming in the headlights. "For that you'd lose the tip of your pinky finger. But taking my packets of merchandise?" He shook his head with a downward glance. "Not good. And for this, you must pay. A bullet to the knee. Maybe you never walk again ... but you're alive."

A person in the group behind Demonio handed him something and said, "*Caro petridas es.*"

Latin? There's only one person I know who speaks Latin.

"Then my security hands me photos. Like this one of you watching my wife swim in the natural." He flicked the picture, and it hit Juan in the chest. "Or one with you talking to her while she's in the pool." He flicked another photo at Juan. "You like to watch other men's wives? What are you? A pervert?"

"Wait. I can explain."

"No. No explanations. They are only lies. But there is more, no? I assume you recognize this." Demonio shoved a cell phone under Juan's nose.

Juan blinked, suppressing a wave of nausea.

"I search your room. When guests stay at my home," Demonio shrugged, "I take precautions. A business thing, you understand. I can't be too safe. And I find this cell phone. But it's not the cell phone I provide my associates. So I wonder ... why does he need another cell phone? I supply him the best. So I check. Can you guess what my technician found on your phone?"

"The latest Lady Gaga ringtone?"

Demonio laughed, smashed the phone against Juan's forehead, and dropped it. "You are a funny man. No, I find many calls to a number in America. So I think, 'Who is he calling in the States?' I find this very special phone number. To the police chief in Whiskey,

Arizona." Demonio drove his boot heel into the phone, shattering it. "You're an undercover pig. You have betrayed me. Sold me out to the people who stole our homeland. Sold out my plans for the new Mexico. You steal so much from me. From my associates. From my employees. From our countrymen. So I will take back from you ... slowly."

"Plans for the new Mexico?" Juan licked his dry lips. "Your business is nothing but a bunch of self-serving drug smugglers."

Demonio responded by drawing a knife from its sheath. Juan tried to pull back, but Bandana grabbed him by the forearms. Demonio approached, waving a black-bladed combat knife.

"You delude no one," Juan said, calm masking his fear. "Our ... countrymen know what you are."

Juan glimpsed the arc of the blade, followed by a searing sting across his chest. A downward glance showed him a sliced shirt and a crimson line from nipple to nipple.

Bloody minutes passed like eons before Juan could take no more. He opened his mouth and screamed. He didn't stop for a long time.

CHAPTER 1

WEDNESDAY, 6:42 AM

I hope the desert's in a good mood today.

Rye Dawlsen strolled to his police Tahoe. Fingering the dog tags under his uniform shirt, he hummed an Enemyway chant—*"Anaa'ji"* in the old tongue—meant to excise evil from the land. Something his Navajo mother had taught him as a child. *Why do I even practice this stuff? Except that the wicked have crept into this land like a plague of locusts.*

His white father taught him real men drink. *Now that's a habit I can glide along with.*

In the quiet dawn, his western boots crunched upon the gravel driveway. Steam rose from the coffee travel mug he carried. Goose bumps formed on his arms from the morning chill, but the cool wouldn't last long. Not this time of the year.

He rested his forearms against the top of the SUV doorframe, peered over the roof, and sipped coffee, his attention drawn to the horizon. As the desert morphed from grays into rich colors, he opened the passenger car door, reached into the glove compartment, and pulled out a pair of military issue binoculars.

Sunlight exploded into blood reds on the underside of the plum-topped clouds brooding along the eastern mountains. The weather report warned of a rogue hurricane barreling down on the Baja coast. *Hopefully, we'll get some rain from it.*

He raised the binoculars to his eyes and focused the field glasses. The distant landscape of thorny vegetation, rocks, and sand jumped in close as he performed a slow pirouette. A realm of precarious life and easy death. Days of boiling temps and frigid nights. Now, with all the recent activity of the drug cartels—the shooting of a Phoenix school official and the kidnapping of a state senator's daughter—Rye spent several minutes each morning searching for any signs of cartel or immigration activity.

Seeing nothing besides arid desolation, he returned the binoculars to their place in the glove box. Once behind the steering wheel, he laid his white Stetson on the passenger seat, crown side down. He keyed the ignition and kicked up the air conditioning. Giving his postage-sized piece of desert a final once over, Rye made sure no one lingered around his doublewide, southwest-styled mobile home. He checked to ensure he had closed the gate to his chicken coop. Didn't want his birds running loose in the desert. He slipped the Tahoe's gear into reverse and backed onto the gravel road SR01, a small lane with several lots feeding from it.

The dusty haze he created hung like cheesecloth in the air. He drove past several trailer homesteads resembling his: a mobile home, a shed and a small sandy yard. Tiny rectangles of humanity hacking inroads into a sparse land.

His vision blurred.

An image of a knife dripping blood filled his mind's eye. He shuddered, chills flowing down his spine. A moment later, the vision vanished. The desert ebbed back into sight. Grunting, he yanked the steering wheel to get back on his side of the road.

"Crud," he blurted, slapping the steering wheel. These visions had been gifted to—or cursed upon—him from his mother. A gift he never wanted.

He drove past Johnny Batts' land, the last driveway before meeting the main road. The recluse owned several dozen acres of rock and sand. Rye realized he hadn't seen Batts for a couple of weeks. Later today he'd check up on the man.

At the end of SR01, Rye slowed when he reached the line of mailboxes. He stopped and waited until the dust cloud generated by his vehicle dissipated. He got out and checked his mailbox, a black number nine clearly stenciled on its side. Empty. He pulled the *Arizona Republic* out of the newspaper bin underneath. Sliding back into the Tahoe, he tossed the paper in the passenger seat next to his hat.

The urge for a shot of bourbon rolled over him. He licked his lips. *Just a sip.* He closed his eyes, drowning in the desire for a drink. Trembling hands gripped the steering wheel as if he grasped a lifesaver.

You're the police chief of Whiskey, Arizona ... focus.

Yet the desire intensified. He could taste the burn. His eyes drew open, and he studied the door to the glove box. Reaching over, he opened the compartment. Behind the binoculars, the empty flask awaited him, a bitter reminder of how easy it would be to find a place to fill it. His hand went for the flask, but his fingers brushed the photo of his wife and son, a photo he had tossed in there when they separated. *When she left,* he corrected himself. *I never wanted her to.*

Instead of the flask, he grabbed the photo. An unsmiling Dee stared at him. He could almost hear her reproving tone—imploring him leave the booze alone. Rye returned the photo and slammed the glove box shut. Anger welled inside him, uncontrolled. He punched the dashboard. Jerking the gearshift into drive, Rye stomped the gas pedal. Gravel spit from his tires; the back end squirmed, and the Tahoe shot forward.

His cell phone sounded with Darryl Worley's *Have You Forgotten*. That meant dispatch. He unclipped the phone from his belt holder.

"Yeah, Gabby, whadda ya got?" He took a deep breath. "Anything good?"

"Morning, Chief. Ready to start the day? Zach called. He's having some problem—"

"Just the facts, Gabby."

"Right-o, Chief. Anyway, Zach's at the Drivin' Diner. I love that name Drivin'. Drive in. Get it? Oh, never mind." She sighed. "So we got a call about this disturbance there, and Zach took the call. Zach gets there, and this Mexican fellow is disturbing the breakfast club."

"Disturbing, how?"

"He's waving a gun around. I think Zach said it's a big saucer, although I've never heard of a gun by—"

"He probably said a SIG Sauer." Rye rolled his eyes. *Women.*

"Yeah, that's it. And this Mex fellow is yelling all kinds of Spanish. And, you know, Spanish is like my second language. So Zach holds his phone up for me to hear. And, who woulda thunk, the Mex is like nuts! Spouting stuff about guns, and revolution and ... and walking skins. Or something like that. So I tell Zach to keep an eye on him while I phone you."

"You did good, Gabby, so tell—"

"Zach then phones again. Seems this Mexican gunman tried to escape. Zach's got him cornered in the parking lot. It's got to be hot on that blacktop. I mean, with the sun coming up, that parking lot is going to fry his—"

"Gabby," he interrupted, "call Zach and tell him I'm there in five. Less if I don't hit the ten-car rush minute in town." He ended the call before she could reply. He switched on the Tahoe's police lights. He started to re-clip his cell when Worley's ringtone interrupted.

"Yes, Gabby?"

"There's a personal message for you, Chief. But I kinda hesitated to give it to you before you took that disturbance call. Knowing how this might upset you ..."

"I'm a big boy."

"Well, if you're so sure and all ... I guess I can tell you. But don't say I didn't try to warn you. I mean—"

"Gabby?"

"Okay, okay. Dee called. Gotta go." The phone went dead from her end. Rye snorted once and shook his head.

He pushed Dee's number. After a couple of rings, her voice began a sultry introduction. "Leave a message at the sound of the ..." *Beeeeeep.*

How did she make such a mundane message sound sexy?

"Dee, I got your message. From Gabby. Looks like we're doing the phone tag thing. I'm on a police call now. Later." He returned the phone to its clip.

Minutes later, Rye pulled up to the Drivin' Diner. The 50s-styled greasy spoon resembled a silver tube the size of a train car. A dozen dust-covered vehicles baked in the lot next to the restaurant. Mostly cowboy-wannabe pickups.

Officer Zach Reese stood like a Frederic Remington statue about ten feet away from a pickup painted in beat-up and rust. A Hispanic male sat on the ground by the tires. His long, stringy hair hung down to black, ferret eyes. Rye had seen his kind before ... a coyote or a mule.

Rye parked his Tahoe, but kept it running for the air conditioning. He went around to the back and lifted the hatch door. After slipping into his vest, he picked up his Browning Illusion hunting bow and a Grim Reaper broadhead arrow. After shutting the hatch, he nocked an arrow and walked over to Zach. A trickle of sweat rolled down Rye's spine.

"Glad to see you're wearing your protective vest, Reese. What'cha got?" Rye smiled when the Mexican's eyes grew large at the sight of the bow. It had that effect.

Zach knuckled the Kevlar vest. "The suspect thought he could come into our town and start some trouble." Zach took off his Stetson and swiped sweaty grit from his forehead with a sleeve. "Waving a gun all over the place. Botched robbery. I got him handcuffed, but he put up a fight. He escaped the diner, headed to this piece of junk pickup, when he tripped. He scooted over to the tire and sat there. He won't come willingly, and when I approach, he starts to kick and spit. Didn't want to taser him just yet."

Rye pulled the bowstring a couple of times, enjoying the stretching creak, an ominous sound of pending death. The Mexican stared at the bow with narrowed eyes.

"I see," the prisoner said. "The Lone Ranger arrives to help his little Tonto ... sí?"

"Why you little ..." Zach bunched his hands into fists and started toward their captive.

Rye grabbed the officer's arm. "I'll handle this." Rye sauntered over to the prisoner and knelt down to invade the suspect's space.

"What's your name, amigo?" Rye asked.

"Go stuff yourself, pig."

Rye nodded as if he would consider the idea. "Interesting name." Rye smiled like nothing was wrong in the world. "Sun's coming up. You'll be gettin' mighty thirsty. Think about that." He patted the door to the truck. "Metal's already hot."

Rye stood, and his damaged knee nearly gave out. Nonetheless, he managed to get to his feet without a groan despite the shot of pain. *Nothing a couple of beers wouldn't dull.*

"Don't Move. *¿Comprende?*" he said.

Rye limped back to Zach. *Stupid knee.* Back at his vehicle, he turned around to face the suspect.

"I'll give you a few minutes to decide to give yourself up peaceful-like and get into some air conditioning. Or, you can fry here on the blacktop. Doesn't matter to me. I'd just as soon watch you fry as make the effort to take you to jail. Since you seem to think I'm a pig and all."

The Mexican's eyes flashed hatred.

"Think about it." Rye fished a handkerchief from his pocket and wiped his sweaty face.

Moments later, one of the waitresses strutted out of the diner carrying two glasses. Auborne Day, Rye recalled her name. The sound of ice clinking in the glasses carried across the parking lot. With her high-heeled clogs clicking on the pavement, her whole body moved with a sexual swagger.

"Hey, fellows," she said, winking at Zach.

Rye shot a glance at his officer and twisted his lips to suppress his surprise.

"Here's some lemonade, Chief," she said. "Compliments of the Drivin' Diner."

"Mighty grateful." Zach touched the brim of his hat and took the two lemonades. Leaning in so his lips brushed her hair, Zach whispered, "Aub, you can come over to my place and play with my lemons anytime."

Rye pulled his hat lower and averted his gaze at Zach's lack of decorum.

She threw back her head and laughed as if he just said the funniest joke. The highlights in her hair danced in dawn's glow. She touched Zach's arm and raised one foot. She leaned forward to whisper into Zach's ear, causing her short skirt to rise higher on her thighs.

"If you ask nice, I'll bring the glasses," she said in a silky tone and stood upright. Louder, she added, "Gotta go back to work. I'll come 'round later to fetch the glasses. See y'all soon." She hurried back inside the diner.

Rye took his glass from Zach and downed a long swig of the lemonade, grateful for its sweet replenishment. By now, his prisoner had to be feeling the effects of the heat. He smacked his lips with a satisfied, "Ahhhh. They make the best lemonade here."

Zach downed a large gulp. "Yep."

Rye took another drink. "Mighty nice of them to bring these to us."

"Yep."

Rye shook the glass to make the ice clink against the glass. "That's one crazy good sound. Wouldn't you agree, officer?"

"Aren't many sounds purtier than that."

"Especially with the heat index getting close to what ..."

"I'd say it's over 100 ..."

"What do you say, hombre?" Rye displayed the glass of lemonade. "Ready to give up?"

The suspect dropped his head and nodded. Sweat dropped from his chin to sizzle on the pavement. The swagger left him like air from a flat tire. Zach and Rye set their lemonades on the hood of the Tahoe and sauntered over to him. They lifted him off the ground and walked him over to the SUV. Rye gave the man a sip of his drink while Zach held his handcuffed hands.

"Gracias." The man licked his lips.

Rye nodded towards Zach's Ford Crown Vic. "De nada. Now get in the car. You better have a legit ID, or I'll deport your hide outta my state. And fast."

Rye held the car door open. Zach assisted the prisoner into the vehicle, putting his hand on top of the man's head to prevent him from banging it against the car frame. Just before the prisoner went into the car, he looked back at the diner. His eyes opened wide.

Rye followed his gaze. A Latino male stood in the shadow cast by the diner and a grove of palm trees. Rye noted the man's attire: black jeans, black western shirt with sleeves rolled up to the elbow, black Stetson, and black cowboy boots. Tattoos decorated his left forearm. Rye stared at the man's mirrored sunglasses, unsure of what he saw. Did the sun reflect off the sunglasses, or did the guy's eyes glow behind the sunglasses? The man in black turned to leave.

"Hey! Wait up. I want—" Rye hurried toward the departing stranger as the car door slammed shut behind him. Rye glanced at the prisoner, who stared out the back window, face drained of color, eyes fixated beyond Rye.

Rye followed his gaze, but the man had vanished. In his place, hidden in the shadows, a black dog squatted staring at him with dull, yellow eyes and a fanged snarl.

Thump!

Thump! Crack.

"Hey," yelled Zach. "Cease kicking the window now!"

Thump! Crash!

"Crap!"

Rye wheeled to find the prisoner kicking the remaining glass out of the window. Reese crumpled to the ground, hands covering his eyes. Streams of blood leaked from cuts on his face. The prisoner used his feet to pull himself closer to the car door, his legs dangling out the window.

In three steps, Rye stood at the door. He drew back his bowstring and aimed the arrow at the prisoner's chest. "Morning's early, and I haven't killed anyone yet. So try it."

The prisoner then inched his legs back into the car.

"That's right, hombre, stay put, or I'll pin you to that seat like a butterfly."

Rye knelt to assist Zach, who had his eyelid pried open. Rye set his bow on the blacktop.

"Got a piece of glass in my eye," Zach yelled.

"Let me see," Rye yelled back.

Someone behind him cleared his throat and said, "Excuse me, Chief."

Rye jerked his head around as his hand went for his sidearm. Expecting the Latino in black, Rye stared up at the silhouette hovering over him. The blinding sun behind the speaker rendered his face invisible. Shading his eyes, Rye squinted at the shape and recognized the familiar Golden Gate Del Mar straw hat.

"Hey, Doc." Rye released a sigh of relief. "Can you lend us a hand?"

"Yes, sir." Doc knelt next to Reese. The man looked more like an aging biker with his graying ponytail pulled tight, skull and crossbones bandana, and sleeveless denim shirt revealing hairy arms. Rye had borne witness to the many wounded bodies stitched up by the man. "Let me look, son."

He took over holding open Zach's eyelid. After a brief examination, he said, "Appears to be a couple shards of glass in there. Try not to blink." The doctor opened his knapsack with one hand and withdrew a red plastic box. From the box, he extracted a pair of tweezers.

"Be as still as possible," Doc ordered, "I'm going after them pieces of glass." With a few deft movements, he removed one glass particle after another. Then he reached into the knapsack and withdrew a bottle of sterile contact solution. "This might burn."

The doc squirted the eyeball with the solution and leaned in close to get a good look at the eye. Satisfied, he released Zach's eyelid.

"How's it feel?" Doc said, head tilted.

"I don't feel nothing in there, but my eye hurts like a bad sunburn."

Doc pulled a clean handkerchief out of his sack and handed it to Zach. "Keep that on 'til I can git you fixed up right." He stood, helping Zach up. Rye followed suit, grunting.

"He's going to be okay?" Rye asked, worried.

"Chief, I dressed worse wounds in 'Nam, and the men turned out alright. So I think he'll be okay." Doc patted Zach's shoulder. "I'm heading into Yuma to pick up some supplies. I believe he lacerated his cornea. I don't have the facilities in town to treat this. As a precaution, I think Zach oughta go with me. I can drop him off at the Yuma Regional Medical Center and bring him home on my return. He's going to be out of commission for a few days."

"Whatever it takes." Rye looked for the dog. It had vanished.

CHAPTER 2

WEDNESDAY, 7:33 AM

Dan Olberlein's dirty-white Freightliner M2 box van idled in traffic at the Nogales Mexican/Arizona border on I-19. Car by car, traffic crept towards the arches marking the Mexican boundary. Brushing stringy sandy hair from his eyes, he checked his watch again. *This is taking too long.*

He rubbed the tightness gripping the back of his neck. To ease his jitters, Dan thought about the money he'd earn on this trip. Enough to pay off his gambling debt, finish college, and buy that engagement ring for his girl.

Traffic inched forward.

He looked out both side mirrors, worried that the pet store image painted on the side of his van would smear. Would the guards detect the fake?

Though he tried to focus on the money, he couldn't erase the memory of the men who loaded the truck. He never would have believed that *ragheads* were helping the cartels if he hadn't seen it for himself.

The air conditioning in the cab struggled against the heat. As soon as he got paid for this job, he planned on spending a week with his girl in the Apache-Sitgreaves National Forest. Just the two of them.

After what seemed like hours, Dan finally reached the Mexican/US border. The meticulous border agents, dressed in their stupid green uniforms, cleared the vehicles ahead of him, one at a time. His hands grew clammy. The dusty red Pontiac in front of him pulled away in a cloud of blue smoke. With a tightening in his gut, he inched his truck forward.

Showtime.

A border patrol agent strolled over to his cab. Scrunching lower in the seat, he rolled down his window. Despite being in the shade provided by the bone-white, two-story offices above him, the desert heat blasted his face.

"Sir," the agent said, peering under the bill of his green ball cap. His no-nonsense military stance reflected in the tone of his voice. "May I see your papers?"

Dan glared at the man's nametag. "Sure thing, Senior Patrol Agent Chuck Stevens." He handed the necessary documents over to the agent without another word. Agent Stevens scrutinized the papers.

"Your manifest says you're carrying tropical fish and handcrafted Indian pottery." The agent flipped between pages of the manifest.

"Yes, sir. My store's displaying at a convention of fish aquatics, and I'm bringing in some new specimens. We're using the pottery to *feng shui* our booth."

Dan caught movement in the side mirror. Another agent strolled between the cars, leading a German Shepherd on a leash. A drug-sniffing dog. *This is going to turn ugly. And right now.*

Two cars back, the dog stopped and sat down facing the trunk of the beat-up Impala. Dan closed his eyes for a couple of seconds.

Let the games begin.

The dog handler spoke into a mic clipped to his shirt.

"Stay put," Agent Stevens said and handed the manifest back to Dan. "There might be some trouble."

I'm counting on trouble. Dan eased his window back up.

In the reversed images of his side mirror, Dan watched a dozen agents surround the Impala, aiming Remington 870 shotguns at the vehicle. Stevens walked up and tapped on the driver's window, ordering the persons in the car to exit immediately. Six Mexican males emerged from the car.

The Impala driver yanked a handgun from his waistband and fired point-blank into Stevens' chest. The agent fell to the pavement. The other five Mexicans opened fire on the remaining agents. Two more border agents collapsed. Agents returned fire, dropping one of the Mexican gunmen and wounding another. Screams from surrounding cars blended with the shouts of agents. Glass shattered. Bullets plunked off cars.

The four Mexicans moved out with military precision. They maintained a barrage of firepower.

Someone pounded on Dan's window, and he jumped. A short, dark-skinned woman in uniform stood at his door. "Sir, move your vehicle! Now!"

He waved a two-fingered acknowledgement. Shifting his truck into gear, he sped through the border crossing. Agents poured out of glass doors like gas out of a can. The four remaining shooters continued to lay down withering gunfire.

With the sounds of war diminishing behind him, Dan punched the truck into high gear.

Out of Nogales, the road cut through low hills of scraggly brush. A mile later, he came to an exit with a carwash.

He hurried the truck into the farthest slot, glad no one else was around. He had the place to himself. Dan fed quarters into the spray-washer and hosed down the truck.

The water-soluble paint bled away in streaks of colored suds, and in its place, a vanilla-hued box van emerged. He turned the hose on the lingering pools of water, hastening the last of the paint down the drain. After returning the sprayer to its containment housing, he opened the cab door and reached under the driver's seat to extract two magnetic signs. Dan held them out and inspected the blue logo of an artsy roadrunner beside the name *Ablo's Fast Delivery*. He attached one to each side of the cab.

It's working. The plan is freaking working like a charm. I'm in the money.

He climbed back into the driver's seat, fired up the truck, regained the expressway, and headed north.

After several miles, he came upon an abandoned gas station/restaurant. A cold shiver rolled down his spine as he stopped at the rusted gas pumps.

A man dressed in jeans, a sleeveless shirt, worn-out boots, and a white Stetson with a tooled leather hatband emerged from the dark shadows inside the building. The newcomer swaggered over to the truck and climbed into the passenger side of the cab. Dan instinctively distrusted the newcomer. Swallowing nervousness, he smiled and nodded a "hello." The newcomer returned the gesture.

"Ready?" Dan asked, reaching for the gearshift.

"One more thing," the man said, pulling out a .22 handgun.

"Demonio will award your excellent work ... in hell."

He fired three shots into the driver's head.

The reek of blood, urine, and feces filled the cab.

"I'll take it from here, amigo." He opened the driver's door and kicked the body into the dusty lot. Gaining the driver's seat, he shifted the van into gear and pulled out onto the highway.

He speed-dialed a number on his cell phone. When a voice responded, he said, "Another safe crossing. The plan is coming together."

Iona Haulke stared out the window through the backwards-arching logo of her newspaper business, *The Whiskey Spill*.

She returned her gaze back to her computer monitor and raised one hand off the keyboard, pivoting from the elbow that rested on the arm of her chair. She shook her hand, rattling a dozen or so bracelets of Navajo turquoise and copper. Her favorite colors. The copper matched her hair, and the turquoise complemented her eyes.

"Ms. Haulke," came the muffled cry through the glass door. The door clicked open, followed by the ding of a bell. "Ms. Haulke?"

Despite the early hour, the air conditioner rattled full-time, converting dry desert heat into semi-cool office air. When the visitor entered, a wave of seething air surged past her and into the room. Iona rubbed her sweaty hands on her skinny flare-leg blue jeans. Size 4—thank you very much.

"Yeah, Missy, what is it? You and your twin having more problems with the local cowboys?"

"It's the museum," said the breathless blonde, pushing her hair out of her eyes. She smoothed the piece of cloth meant to be a skirt. Then she twisted back and forth to view her handiwork.

Iona cleared her throat. "Missy, what about the museum? You know, that place where you work?"

Missy's words gushed out. "Helen sent me over. Someone broke in last night."

"Did you call the police?"

Missy shrugged. "Helen doesn't want the police to muck things up. Well, that's not exactly how she put it. So I thought of you. You, like, investigate stuff."

Whatever. "Okay. Let's check it out. I do hope no one's contaminated the crime scene."

"You think someone, like, stole something?"

"I'm going to go out on a limb here, but I'm assuming no one broke in just to see the displays." Iona lifted her turquoise-banded straw hat off the desk and plunked it on her head. "Ready?"

Iona opened the door and stepped outside. Turning the corner, they headed towards the museum's parking. Alligator junipers shaded a few dust-covered vehicles, and heat waves radiated from the metal even this early in the morning. No cars yet in the visitors area.

They entered the museum and stood in the foyer for a moment, allowing their vision to adjust to the dimness.

Old photos of Native Americans and paintings of desert landscapes decorated the walls. The bookstore, off to one side, was dark. A "Closed" sign hung in its window. A full-scale display of a

Navajo Hogan and the life surrounding it occupied the room ahead. Hallways went off to either side.

"Follow me," said Missy.

The girl turned to the left and scurried down the tiled hallway. Raised voices bickered at the far end. *Helen and Terrance. Arguing as usual.* Iona followed at a leisurely pace. She glanced into every room she passed to determine their status. They all appeared to be undisturbed. The thieves probably knew what they were looking for. Missy scampered into the last room on the right, the one displaying supernatural relics of Navajo past.

"Terrance, is y'all gonna fiddle with that broken glass or is y'all gonna clean it up?"

Iona recognized the smoker's voice of Helen, the curator and owner of the museum. Though the woman sounded like some back hills Easterner, Helen shared her love and respect for the Navajo people. Intelligent. Compassionate. Reasonable. Kind of described both Helen and the Navajos.

"Will you just shut up and leave me to clean this mess?" That'd be Terrance, the maintenance man and Helen's husband. A drunk with a mean streak. Iona had seen him numerous times staggering down the streets of Whiskey, gripping a bottle-shaped paper bag. But Helen wouldn't leave him.

"This is just, like, so horrible. Who'd do such a thing?" The final canary voice could only be Missy's twin sister, Mel.

Missy paused under the arched entrance into the room, and Iona stopped alongside her. Terrance hovered, broom in hand, next to the shattered glass case in the room's center. Despite her age, Helen sat, legs crossed, on the floor. Tears marred her heavy makeup, and

31

her presence gave the room the acrid odor of stale cigarette smoke. Mel rambled on, saying nothing in particular, staring at the displays remaining in the case.

"Stop," Iona shouted, holding up her hands, palms out. "You're destroying forensic evidence. All of you, out of the room. *Now*. Has anyone called the police?"

"Awww, Iona," Helen whined. "Can you believe someone stole the Skinwalker feather?"

"We'll talk about it later. Now, please, come out of the room."

"This ain't one of them mystery books yer always writin' about," said Terrance. "This here's real life. And I got to clean this mess up before the museum opens. Someone gets their foot cut on glass, they'll sue us fer sure."

"Chief Dawlsen will probably arrest you if you go messing with his crime scene. Let's go to your office, contact the WPD, and let the professionals do their job."

In Helen's office—a narrow affair with everything arranged in neat order except for the ashtray mounded with ashes and squashed butts—Iona dialed 911. When Gabby answered, Iona reported the break-in, detailing what little she already knew. After Gabby shared the incident at the Drivin' Diner, Iona hung up.

Helen took a pack of cigarettes off her desk and lit one.

"You really should stop smoking those things," Iona said, blinking away tears.

Helen started to speak but erupted in a phlegmy cough. "Yeah. Doc says the same thing. Cigarettes can't be as bad for y'all as what some of the town's residents smoke." She cast an accusing look at Missy, then at Mel, who turned away from her piercing gaze.

"Don't tell me." Iona held up a hand and looked away. "I don't want to know. Gabby said Rye's at another call and will get here when he can. In the meantime, tell me what happened."

Helen, Terrance, Mel, and Missy looked at each other. Silence thickened like Helen's cigarette smoke.

"Don't everyone start talking at once." Iona folded her arms.

Helen coughed some more then said, "Me and Terrance get here at our regular time to open up. Missy pulls up seconds later in her Jeep with Mel. We don't see nuthin' different like strange cars in the parking lot or a busted down door. I unlock the door, and Terrance here goes to turn on the lights and do his rounds. Mel goes to our acquisitions prep room, and that's when she discovers the theft."

"Mel, what did you see?" Iona turned her gaze upon the girl.

"When I, like, come to work, I have to walk down this hallway," she said, pointing to the corridor, "to get to my workstation. You know … I like to look at the exhibits … well, because I like Indian stuff. It's cool. Everything's just like when we closed up last night until I get to this room. The first thing I see is the case is broken. Glass is, like, everywhere. I … I …"

"Go on." Iona prodded her on with a nod.

"I walk over to the case, and I see the Skinwalker feather is gone." She paused. "It's a major display, being it's important to the Indians and all. That's when I called Helen."

"Yep, she did," Helen interjected, smoke leaking from her mouth as she spoke. "And I get here and freak. You know, seeing the place trashed. Pissed me off. Mel told me that the feather was missing, so I checked to see if anything else was gone. Sure enough, the deerskin shield's also missing." She took a long draw on her cigarette. "Piss-ant thieves."

"Anything else stolen?"

Helen shrugged. "After we found out we got robbed, I sent Missy to find you, figuring you'd know what to do and all. Being one of them ex-cop mystery writers. Don't want no cops in here tramping around my exhibits. The place was a mess, so I wanted to clean up the glass before anyone got hurt. We just started when you arrived."

Iona coughed into her hand. *I hate cigarette smoke.* "Good thing I stopped you from destroying the evidence." She nodded at Terrance. "What about you, Ter?"

He scratched his head and looked at his wife. "I reckon that's how it went down."

"What about …"

Before Iona finished her question, the front door opened, and a voice called out, "Hello? WPD."

Iona smiled. "Rye, we're back in the office." Then she stared at Helen. "Maybe now I can get some straight answers."

CHAPTER 3

WEDNESDAY, 8:27 AM

After observing the crime scene for several seconds, Rye set his evidence collection case on the floor, and then removed the lens cap from the Nikon D-80 DSLR camera hanging around his neck.

"I need to document the scene," he told Iona.

"Nice camera," she said, her eyes on him and not on the camera.

"This?" Certain that something must be wrong with the air-conditioning, Rye longed for a nice, cold drink. "Oh, some famous author donated several to my department after her book was made into a movie."

"Only the best for WPD," she said, smiling.

Sudden heat infused his face, and Rye was grateful when Iona averted her eyes.

"Do me a favor." Rye nodded at the evidence case. "Fetch the logbook from the case and start a log of who entered this room and when."

"Sure thing. I'd do just about anything for Whiskey's Chief of Police."

Rye cleared his throat, searching for a distraction. "And phone Gabby for me. Have her send someone to assist." He gave Iona a half smile. "And check to see if I've received any calls from the office. I'm expecting a call from a … um … a colleague. Police business."

Her hand rested on his shoulder for a breath too long then flitted away. Strutting up the hallway, she looked over her shoulder and winked. "I'll get your log going and call Gabby."

Rye took a deep breath to help refocus his attention on evidence-gathering. Forget the diner incident. Forget the phone call. Forget Iona's backside. Work the scene. Flipping open the case, he pulled on booties and gloves.

Let's do this.

Rye stalked the room, clicking pictures. After snapping photos of an object, he jotted the particulars of the picture in his notebook. More photos, more notes.

He stopped, tilting his head as he stared at the wreck of the display case and lowered the camera. Something about the glass case piqued his attention. His gaze roamed the debris and his investigative instinct took over, absorbing the details, allowing his mind to free associate. It'd come, but …

"Got everyone signed in," Iona said, standing at the room's entrance.

Rye turned away from the mess. "Did Helen and Terrance identify how many items are missing?"

"Yeah … a leather shield and a Skinwalker feather. Why?"

At the mention of the Navajo legend, the skin on his arms turned to goose bumps. Ever since his Navajo mother had whispered tales of Skinwalkers into his young ears, he hated Skinwalkers. Hated the legends. Hated the influence it held over his people. Hated the witches who laid claim to the power.

"Just take off your shoes and come here."

"Can I at least have a pair of those cute little booties?"

Rye nodded toward his CSI case. "I got any kind of shoe cover you want as long as it's white, and one size fits all."

After donning on a pair, she knelt next to him—a little too close. Not that he minded. The light scent of her perfume reminded him of lilacs in the spring. She held onto his shoulder, and it felt good. Ever since he and his wife separated, he missed a woman's touch. Even if it was only a hand on his shoulder.

He pointed to the lower shelf. "See the darker square spot. Now, I might not be the sharpest arrow in the quiver, but I'd say something that wasn't a feather or shield was there."

"Appears that way."

"There's nothing here that resembles that shape. Have you any idea what it might be?"

"Can't say as I do."

"Did Helen mention a third item being taken? Being in this room, it had to be something important to the Skinwalker mythos."

"No. She didn't." Iona pointed to the ceiling. "There are security cameras. Maybe Helen or Ter can pull us a copy. I'll check." She rose and hurried from the room.

Rye snapped a dozen shots of the square spot on the shelf. He zoomed in on the debris pattern and the various items that had fallen during the assault on the case and took more photos. Added more notes to his book.

Lowering his camera and covering the lens, he stood, studying the pattern of the glass shards, the damage done to the case, and the collapse of the displayed items. He imagined several approaches the thief could have used to attack on the case. Casting aside scenarios not matching the evidence, he decided on the path of the assault.

"The thief came at the case from this angle," he said aloud to no one, inserting a mental note with a downward chop of one extended hand. "They would have taken a heavy item like a steel bar and smashed the glass right about here." He took a few steps to his right and looked down. "What do we have here?"

In the debris of glass particles, two faint footprints were visible as if someone with dirty shoes had stood there. Rye turned his feet to match the stance depicted in the prints.

"Someone small." He took a dozen pictures and wrote several lengthy descriptions. After fetching a rectangular-shaped evidence lifter, he peeled away the white backing, pressed the clear material onto the footprints, and lifted the material. He held it aloft, scrunching his nose while he stared at the debris.

Satisfied he had taken all he could from the footprints, Rye walked around to the undamaged displays in the room. One case contained several vases—circa early 1900s according to the display plaque—with Skinwalker designs painted on them. Those had to be worth some money, why not take those? Big market for Native American artwork. Another case contained objects of a Skinwalker murder investigation from 1932. A third case showed a dozen pieces of jewelry made of silver and turquoise stones. Nothing missing from them.

Why take a feather, a leather shield, and this third item, yet leave the more expensive stuff alone? Most thieves take items of monetary value. But not this one. Why?

One by one, he studied the large shadowboxes mounted on the walls. Each presented a diorama of a certain Skinwalker. Sepia-toned photos depicted aged Navajo males, dressed in traditional clothing. Each display included artifacts from their lives. A plaque mounted next to the display gave a brief bio of the Skinwalker. He stopped at the fourth one and stared.

Fingerprints smudged the front of the case as if someone put their hands on the glass and then rubbed downward. Rye leaned in close and could see no definable ridges. Nonetheless, he dusted the smudged prints and photographed them from several angles before recording them with transparent lifting tape. He dropped these into his case.

Iona stomped back into the room and snapped, "They claim the cameras don't work. Yeah, right! They're lying. I can feel it." She stared up at the camera. "You're lying, and I know it," she yelled at the lens.

Rye waited a few seconds before responding. "Don't worry about it. If needed, I can get a search warrant." He pointed with his camera to the fourth display. "Come here and look at this case. What do you see?"

Iona peered at it for a microsecond and said, "Fingerprint smudges. You could have figured that one out."

Rye rolled his eyes. "Thanks for the detailed input. I'll remember to look for that next time. What's in the case?"

Iona looked at the nameplate, then at Rye. "Dear, are your eyes going bad that you can't read? It's a display of the only known Mexican Skinwalker. Come on, Rye. Spill it. What's on your mind?"

"For one, it's the only case on the wall with fingerprint smudges."

Rye's *Have You Forgotten* ringtone sounded. He freed his cell phone from its belt holster. "Dawlsen, here."

"Are there any bodies at the museum," began Gabby, "because if there is then I need to contact the coroner—"

"Whoa, girl. This is a burglary not a murder. What do you got for me?"

"Two calls just came in. First, the mayor. He sounded like his shorts got twisted up his fat—"

"Enough, Gabby, I don't need any more detail." *Mayor Richard List. Comes from old Arizona ranching money. Lives in that four story glass monstrosity built into the side of a cliff. A self-serving politician if I ever saw one.*

"Yeah … well … I wouldn't want to be the one returning his call. That's why you get paid the big buckeroos, Chief."

"And the second caller?"

"Johnny Batts. He sounded … upset, but failed to give me any reason for why. Just said, quote, 'I want to talk to the Chief. ASAP.' Unquote. I think he's been out in the sun too long. Town gossip is that he isn't completely right in—"

"Thanks, Gabby. Bye." He shut off his cell phone.

Both calls promised a bad day. A twinge of a headache forced his left eye closed. *Yep, the desert's gonna play ugly.*

"Mayor? Chief Dawlsen here. You called?"

"Chief Dawlsen?" Richard List's fake sincerity leaked through the cell phone like a slow sewer. "Glad you got back with me."

Whatever. "I always do. What is it?"

"All business. I like that in the chief of police of my town."

His town! Yet, Rye hated to admit the veracity of the mayor's statement. The List family owned most of the bars, some of the stores, and much of the ground the city was built on. And the mayor let everyone know it. Rye pressed his lips together. Silence made people antsy to fill in the quiet. Seconds ticked by.

The mayor cleared his throat. "I called because I heard you threw a Mexican citizen into jail this morning. I want to know why."

News travels fast. "Yes, sir. This particular Mexican male threatened customers in a local business, causing panic, and then he resisted arrest."

The mayor's restrained sigh came over the phone. "Don't stonewall me."

"Excuse me?"

"You heard me." The mayor's fake sincerity vanished, replaced by an arctic tone.

Rye didn't reply. Instead, he scanned the shadowbox using a grid pattern similar to investigating a crime scene.

A sigh. "Chief?" A pause. "Is it too much to ask for some detail?"

"Mayor." A pause. "I'm currently investigating a break-in at the Navajo Museum."

"Stop screwing with me," the mayor spat. "No one gives a hoot about that outhouse."

"Look," Rye snapped back. "To maintain the integrity of an investigation and not lose the case on a technicality, I have to maintain control over a case's information."

The mayor cursed. "Just tell me what you got."

"If you insist ..." Rye replied in a deadpan monotone. "Officer Reese responded to a call this morning about a disturbance at the

Drive-In Diner. The Mexican male in question had shown a gun to the girl working the cash register. In the process of Officer Reese's effort at detaining him, the alleged robber escaped to the parking lot where he was apprehended. He carried no ID, and has refused to give us his name."

"That's it?" Rye thought he heard relief in the mayor's voice. "Your officers do Whiskey proud. May I call you Rye? I think we got off on the wrong foot with this conversation."

"Yeah … about that … this conversation started off on the wrong foot months ago. And may I call you Dick?"

"I'd prefer you called me Richard." The brief pause between each word added to the sudden icy tone in the mayor's voice.

"Okay, Dick. I'll call you Richard, Dick. And I prefer you refer to me as Chief."

There was silence on the phone. A smirk formed on Rye's lips as he imagined the mayor struggling to control his anger.

The mayor cleared his throat, waited a second, and said, "I want that Mexican prisoner released. This morning. Consider it a favor." List paused. "One that will allow you to keep your job."

Rye's jaw twitched. *How dare this pompous douche bag threaten my job.* "The man stays under arrest pending further investigation."

More silence.

List cleared his throat and said in a frigid tone, "Come to my office. We will negotiate a release."

"No deal. No release. No way." Just then, a detail in the Skinwalker photo caught Rye's search.

"Listen, Dawlsen." Something shattered in the background on List's end. "I need this man released. I'll make it worth your while."

"No, you listen … Dick. As Chief of Police, I have a sworn duty to protect the good people of Whiskey. I intend to perform that task. Whiskey will be off limits to criminals. I have reason to believe your man's tied to a Mexican cartel. Officer Reese is on his way to Yuma Medical due to injuries received during the apprehension of your … acquaintance."

"Nice speech," List sneered. "Just release the man into my custody."

"Forget it."

"Chief Rye Dawlsen, are you listening to me?"

"Mayor, I'm investigating the scene of a crime. I have to go."

With the mayor's protests ringing in the phone, Rye ended the conversation and returned the phone to his belt clip. *What is it about that photo?*

Then he spotted what nagged his subconscious.

CHAPTER 4

WEDNESDAY, 9:15 AM

"Look carefully. Give that photo a good once over," Rye told Iona.

In the sepia-tinted picture, a man stood on a rocky ledge, snow-covered Superstition Mountains behind him. That meant winter or early spring. The subject wore all black clothing and a duster. Cold, detached eyes peered out from under the brim of his worn-down western hat. A feather jutted from the hatband. Wrinkles like canyons lined his Aztec facial features, indicative of Mexican lineage. One hand carried a shield close to his chest. The other hand held up a square amulet.

"What is it?" she said, her eyes moving while she scanned the words. Her gaze returned to the photo. "Besides the smudges, what's so important?"

"I saw that man this morning."

"Youuu ... did?" she said, her inflection rising on the second word. "According to the plaque, a Navajo medicine man discovered that this man was a Skinwalker and called him on it." She pointed at the Skinwalker. "The guy died three days later."

"I can read, thank you. But I did see this man this morning at the diner. Look close."

Iona leaned in to study the photo. "Oh my ..." She glanced at the shattered case then back at the picture. She pointed. "Could that be the missing feather that's in his hat. And ... and that's the shield."

"Right on both accounts. See the amulet in the man's hand?" He pointed at it. "It's hard to tell in the photo, but it appears to be the same size and shape of our third missing item."

With one eyebrow raised, Iona studied him for several seconds. Doubt tinted her words. "You saying we got ourselves a real live Skinwalker?"

"I'm not saying any such thing. Right now, I'm just turning over some rocks to see what crawls out from underneath them." Rye tapped the glass over the photo. "But this man was at our crime scene this morning."

Iona sighed. "This'll make great copy. I can see the headline." She motioned with her hand. "Dead Skinwalker Haunts Arizona Town."

"Forget the tabloids. He's not dead, and he's not haunting." Rye shrugged. "Ugly maybe, but definitely not dead."

"Perhaps I oughta kick over some journalistic rocks of my own."

"Just be careful. Something about this whole business reeks of donkey dung."

"What did List have to say?"

Rye detailed the conversation while she shook her head, fists on her hips. "Perhaps I oughta kick over his rocks," she said

Rye laughed. "Now I have to return Johnny Batts' call. Gabby said he sounded agitated."

Iona patted his back. "A heck of a morning so far."

"Yeah. Things are just getting warmed up, and it's not even 10:00 yet. I can't hardly wait to see what the afternoon brings."

"State your piece," Batts' drawl came through Rye's cell.

"Hey, Johnny, this is—"

"Yeah, I know. Seen your number pop up on the screen. Chief, you got a problem."

After a few seconds of silence, Rye rubbed his forehead as if probing for a headache. "Go on, Johnny, I flunked mind-reading. Perhaps … a few more details …?"

A spit of hesitation then Batts said, "Discovered a body up one of them washes on my property. It ain't a purty sight. Cut up and all."

"Did you get a look at who it might be?" Rye touched his dog tags. *Just what I need. A murder.*

"I ain't stupid, Chief. I watch CSI. I know better'n messin' with a crime scene." Rye couldn't miss the agitation in Johnny's voice. "So can you get up here? I got some sheep I need to take to pasture, and that body's blocking the way."

Rye stole a glance at Iona.

Batts rambled on about trespassers getting their just rewards, and Rye turned his attention back to the call.

Batts concluded, "Nuthin' I can do 'bout a dead body. But my sheep are alive … and thirsty. That I can do sumpthin' 'bout."

"Okay, Johnny, I'll get there as soon as I can."

Rye disconnected the call and speed-dialed Gabby.

"Whiskey Police Department," she said.

"Gabby. Dawlsen, here." Rye tilted his head, watching Iona bend over. Using tweezers, she picked up a hair from the floor and held it aloft to study it. "Listen, I need you to send someone over to the Batts' place."

"Whitewolf just walked in. I'm sure—"

Rye cut her off. "Send him. This takes precedence over anything else. I'm heading there now. Any more phone calls?"

"No. Just what I told Iona 'bout—"

"Sorry, Gabby, I'm not trying to be rude, but I gotta git." He disconnected the call. "What do you got?" Rye asked Iona.

She turned the tweezers back and forth. "Just some hair. I'll bag it. You okay? You're sounding stressed."

"Stressed? Me?" Rye pointed both hands at his chest. "Let's see, an attempted armed robbery. A museum break-in. And now ... a potential murder. Dee's calling me for some reason. I had to talk to the mayor. And I still got a ton of paperwork waiting for me back at PD. No stress at all."

"When it haboobs, it gets dusty. Now, you done venting? If not, I can recommend a good shrink."

"There aren't any good shrinks," Rye said scrunching his face. "The very idea of someone tinkering inside my cranium makes me want to puke. Besides ... we're done here."

She shot him a coy look under the brim of her hat. "So, I guess that means you're heading off to Batts'?"

"Yep. Let's rope off the scene of the crime." Rye said. "I want to be at Batts' when Whitewolf arrives."

"You know," Iona said, fixing one end of tape to the wall. "Helen and Terrance won't appreciate you roping off their most popular exhibit."

"Can't be helped." Rye finished tying off his end.

"So now ..." She shrugged.

"A trip to Johnny Batts' place. Care to join me?"

"Are you asking me out on a date?" she asked, one eyebrow raised.

"We're going to a murder scene. I don't take dates to crime scene investigations." He took her by the shoulders and turned her to face up the hallway. "However, I can use an extra set of eyes, your detective mind, and that mystery writer's intuition of yours."

With Iona in front of him, they headed towards the front door. Rye couldn't help but admire her backside. *She's putting a little extra swing into her step just to tease me. I bet that'll be the best thing I see all day.*

Twenty minutes later, Rye pulled his Tahoe onto Batts' drive, twin lines of packed dirt going up a small grade. Gravel pinged in the wheel wells. A dusty haze hung above the creosote bush-covered hill, shimmering in heat waves. Rye slowed the SUV to a crawl.

"Looks like someone got here before us," Iona said.

"Appears that way." Rye leaned on the steering wheel and stared at the sky through the floating grit. "You know, if there's a body, then why aren't there any buzzards? A fresh kill should've brought 'em circling."

"Yeah," Iona said, drawing out the word. "That's a bit odd."

Rye eased the Tahoe up the rutted path. "And as a former investigator who now writes mysteries, what do you make of that?"

"I write romantic whodunits," Iona said, slouching in the passenger seat. "That genre would preclude I should know something about the feeding habits of vultures." She paused. "However, the absence of them is like ... X-Files weird."

"Don't go all sci-fi vampire nuts on me, Twilight Twinkle toes." He poked her in the arm.

"Something's keeping the birds away." She looked at Rye. "There's got to be a logical explanation."

"Perhaps the birds evolved into vegans."

They topped the hill, and Rye eased the Tahoe to a stop. Batts' property spread out in front of them. In the valley an SUV, surrounded by a cloud of dust, weaved through the valley towards the far side. There, a log cabin and a couple of weathered outbuildings squatted on the flat summit. The hill jutting up behind the house contained the Batts' mine.

"That's gotta be Whitewolf," Rye said, recognizing the WPD car.

Minutes later, Rye pulled his SUV in front of the cabin. The smell of sheep touched the air. He stepped out of the car's AC chill, and the desert's heat desiccated his body, dispelling any comfort he had enjoyed in the vehicle. Fetching his crime bag from the backseat, he watched Johnny Batts slide out his cabin, its door creaking loudly in the quiet. Arms folded, Batts waited on his rickety porch.

Rye studied the man. Batts folded and unfolded his arms while he shifted his feet back and forth like a bulldozer scraping topsoil. The man muttered whether he spoke to anyone or not. His thin frame hunched over from years working his mine. He wore a beat-up, sweat-stained western straw hat that saw better days years ago. Long, gray hair sprouted from under the hat like shrubby coldenia. Gray stubble coated his jaw. His sunburnt, snake-like arms swung from his sleeveless denim shirt, and the jeans he wore had more patches than denim.

Batts ambled over to them, puffs of dust kicking up at his boot heels. "Chief," Batts acknowledged him with a mumble.

"Johnny."

Noah Whitewolf got out of his patrol car and approached them, carrying his own crime scene case. The officer wore a pristine western hat of the WPD, and his shiny black hair spilled out to his shoulders in a perfect stream. The officer's shirt and jeans had been duly cleaned and ironed. A silver bracelet with turquoise stones and his Chiricahua moccasins hinted at his Apache heritage. He walked with precise steps and stood with a Marine's "at ease" stance.

"Hey, Chief," Whitewolf said, stopping alongside Rye. "Morning, Iona."

Iona hugged Whitewolf. "How's your sister?" The Apache towered over Iona by at least six hand widths.

Twice, Batts spat out a sodden wad of chewing tobacco.

"She does well," Whitewolf answered. "She's teaching young girls our dances and—"

"Ain't got no time fer chitchat." Batts cut off further discussion. "I got me a ranch to attend to. Foller me."

Rye raised an eyebrow at Batts' brisk demeanor, but said nothing.

The miner led them with his lumbering gait as if he still walked a narrow mine tunnel. They passed a sheep pen full of bleating animals. Spits of dust kicked up with each animal's movement.

"I need this cleaned up quick so as I can pasture my sheep," Batts said over his shoulder.

"And I have a crime scene to attend to," Rye snapped. "It'll take as long as it takes."

Muttering about losing his animals, Batts led them down a trail that crossed another valley similar to the first. They crossed a dry creek bed and headed up another incline. At the top, a canyon opened to their view. In the distance, Rye noticed metal reflecting sunlight.

"That's List's place," Batts said. "An ugly building fer one ugly man. This way."

For several hundred yards, Batts escorted them along a path skirting the canyon rim. Rye peered over the ledge. A straight drop of seven stories into more of the rocky Arizona desert.

He clenched his eyes closed as a shiver iced his spine. An impression of a bloody dagger occupied his mind's vision with its gory image.

"Chief? You okay?" Whitewolf gripped Rye's shoulder. "Chief?"

"Yeah." He licked his lips again. "I'm okay. Let's keep going."

The path led into a split in the wall.

"Body's up thatta way some." Batts pointed up the canyon. "I did some investigatin'—without disturbing the scene mind you—and there's tire tracks down the hill some." Batts took off his straw hat and ran a hand through his wire-brush hair. "Stupid sheep wouldn't come out of the cut. Stood there just bleatin' their complaints. That's when I noticed the body."

"We appreciate you leaving the crime scene intact," Rye said. "The three of us will take it from here. Go back and take care of your livestock."

"Good." Batts rubbed his stubbled chin. "'Cause I ain't waitin' out here bakin' in this heat like no fool."

"If you could, I'd like you to stick around your cabin for a little while." Rye took off his hat and swiped his forehead. "I have to ask you some questions about last night."

"Am I under suspicion or somethin'?"

"Do you have a reason to be?" Rye watched the man's reaction, but Batts seemed more put out about his sheep than being a murder suspect. "Look, in any investigation we find the guilty by ruling out the innocent. I'm more interested in establishing your innocence than trying to nail you."

"I'll be at my cabin or in the barn." Batts nodded up the cleft. "I gotta get my sheep some water." With that, he headed back up the cut in the rock.

"That went well," Rye said. "Nothing like pissing off a neighbor. Noah, you examine the tire tracks."

"Sure thing, Chief," Whitewolf answered and strolled down the wash, sticking to the shade whenever possible.

Rye checked his watch. "Yuma's ME should arrive in a half hour or so. Iona, let's do a grid search on the way to the body. We can't process the body, but we can cover the area."

They started up the slope, side by side. In the canyon, the temperature skyrocketed. Anything at a distance shimmered in the heat. The glare ricocheted off the rocks and hurt his eyes despite his sunglasses.

Not more than a dozen feet up the wash, they discovered the car tracks had stopped.

"What're you thinking?" Iona asked.

"When the vehicle came to a halt, someone was in a lot of trouble. More 'n likely," he nodded uphill towards the body, "our victim."

"I can't be sure of the exact make of the car," Iona said. She pointed at the tire tracks. "Safe to say it wasn't an RC Cooper."

Rye started walking toward the body, but stopped. "We have three sets of prints. If I had to make a guess, I'd say the middle one was coerced. See the drag marks."

"Think we're looking at a drug deal gone bad?"

Rye tilted back his Stetson and rubbed his sweaty forehead. "That or gang violence. Let's check it out."

They headed up the canyon, eyes searching the ground for evidence. Though he mostly maintained his investigation, Rye stole several side glances at Iona. She looked good in tight jeans.

Using her forefinger like a speed-reader, Iona scanned the ground in search of clues. She stopped. "Are you staring at me, Rye Dawlsen?"

"No, I'm just … ummm … looking your way."

She nodded once with a half smile. "Sure you were."

Pain stabbed his heart; Dee used to smile at him just like that when they were being silly—before he started drinking heavily and lying to her about it.

And how did he respond to Dee? How many times had he watched disappointment spread across her face? Ignored her tears? Ridiculed her anger? Returned her outbursts? Mocked her religion?

And missed her after she left.

But Iona was a good woman, as well. She dropped hints like breadcrumbs to get his attention. *She's got a tough spirit but a soft heart. She knows I struggle with the bottle. Perhaps, she offers redemption. Among other things.*

"What's wrong, Rye?" Iona's voice cut through his reflection. "You having one of those vision things?"

"No. I'm just thinking about the scene." *About you. About us.* "You know, this is a curious place to dump a body."

She gave him a one-eyed look of skepticism.

"What?"

"No. I agree," she said. "They should have taken it to The Whiskey Burial Grounds. Much nicer option than dumping it on someone's property."

"That's the writer in you. You know, with these footprints, I ought to have Whitewolf cast them before they deteriorate anymore."

Iona peered upward at the pale blue sky, a hand shading her eyes. "Still no carrion birds."

"Yeah, maybe human flesh is out of season." He held up a finger then got his cell phone. When Whitewolf answered, Rye said, "Listen, we have three sets of footprints here. Cowboy boots. Hiking shoes. And dress shoes. Can you cast them?"

"Sure thing. Once I've finished with the one I'm making of one of the vehicles."

Rye disconnected and met Iona's gaze. "Whitewolf'll take care of preserving the footprints."

"Then, let's check out the vic."

They inched their way to the victim's body, on the lookout for other clues waiting in the desert ground to be found. Rye noted the area around the body had been disturbed by a number of people as testified by all the prints covering one another. A lot of blood had been spilt at the site. The victim's clothing appeared to have been ripped to shreds by some kind of razor device.

"Iona, I don't think this is a dump site." Rye made a note to compare the vic's shoes to the prints.

"I agree. This is looking like the scene of the crime." She rubbed a hand across her mouth and squinted. "And it looks to be a bad one."

Rye agreed. He set down the crime kit and got out the camera. Holding it out, he asked, "Could you take some photos?"

She shrugged and took the camera. "Sure."

He took his notebook out of his shirt pocket and began sketching the position of the body, scribbling notes. He had always considered a murder scene to be some sort of sacred ground. A place where a soul departed this life in a violent way. With things left unfulfilled. A place of tragedy, of suffering.

What if this had been Dee? Or his son, Manny? He stole a glance at Iona. His heart felt conflicted over the two women. He still loved Dee, but—looking at Iona's profile—he realized the stirrings of feelings for her as well.

Rye forced his gaze to the ground. *Focus,* he nodded once, sharply. "Johnny won't be able to take his sheep through here. Not today. We're gonna need backup on this one." He reached for his cell phone in its belt holster. "Gabby. Get Yuma's CSI and the Sheriff's Department over here at Batts' ranch." He finished and disconnected the call. He peered at Iona.

"Ready to tackle the body?" he asked her.

She nodded, lips pressed together.

"Let me write a few notes here." Rye continued his scribbling. "Vic is male, probably of Latino descent. Can't tell from this angle, but his neck has the skin tone. No apparent wounds in the back. Body is in a fetal position as if trying to protect against being kicked. He's dressed in blue jeans, black t-shirt and jean jacket. The jacket has been lowered as if to aid in restraining the victim. His shoes are scuffed." He closed his notebook. "Let's circle around and take a look at our victim's face."

They walked around the body.

"What the ..." stammered Rye.

Death by a thousand cuts. The eyes stared sightless, the lids having been severed with some sort of sharp cutting instrument. Dozens of bloody cuts had rendered the vic's face unrecognizable. Rye closed his eyes and shook his head. Without an ID, dental records, or AFIS match, they might never get a name. The front of the body had been shredded as well; the skin, a map of crisscrossing slashes. The victim's clothing lay in strips, stiffened by coagulated blood. From knees to forehead, the male vic had been sliced hundreds of times. The bloody skullcap indicated the victim to be alive when the killer inflicted a scalping. A wicked slash across the vic's throat had nearly decapitated the man. Probably what finished his suffering.

"The killer has to be some kind of evil," Rye said.

Iona slipped away from Rye's side with a hand covering her mouth. She ran several steps before she stumbled to her knees, retching.

"Sorry," she said between gagging sounds.

"I understand. You gonna be okay?" Rye called, not wanting to invade her privacy. He'd embarrassed himself more than once at crime scenes by puking. Rye sketched the body into his notebook. This poor guy suffered one horrendous death.

"I'm okay," she said with a weak voice. "Better'n our vic."

"I hear that. There's some gum in my crime bag. It'll take the nasty taste out of your mouth."

She waved her hand.

A profile of the killer began to form in his mind. A psychopath. A person without a conscience or a sense of guilt. A male with violent tendencies. Probably cartel. And he had assistance. So a leader or someone in a position of power who likes to get their hands dirty.

Pale, but upright, Iona stood by the bag.

Best to keep her busy. Rye tossed her his notebook. "Stay over there. Write down anything I say." He started taking photos. "A large patch of skin has been cut away from the shoulder."

He zoomed in on the face. It seemed vaguely familiar. The multitude of cuts and the swelling made recognition difficult. Yet, he couldn't shake the feeling he knew this person. His mind raced through possibilities while he snapped photo after photo. If he had to, he'd max out the memory card.

"From his haircut, I'd say he's probably ex-military."

While photographing close-ups of the wounds, Rye noticed the absence of insect activity. *That's odd. If the killing took place last night, the mouth, nose and ears should have been filled with blowfly eggs. A major maggot neonatal care unit.*

Rye spotted the corner of an Android phone peeking out from under the body.

"I found me a phone," he called to Iona. After photographing it, he reached down to brush sand away from the device. Holding a surgical glove, he eased the cell out from under the corpse. The phone's screen had been smashed, and blood stained the keypad. He pushed the start button, not expecting anything. It flickered and died.

Rye shrugged, figuring the CSI guys could work their magic on it. He dropped it into a bag and turned his attention back to the victim. The vic's hands were untouched. Something was on the fingers. Using the camera's zoom, he found letters. Some between each finger. Not very legible. Put together, they read, "gs—ds—DHL—DA."

Glad it isn't cryptic or nothing.

The phone nagged him. It wasn't some cheap disposable cell. The kind used by your local neighborhood street corner dope dealer. He opened the evidence bag and stared at the phone for a moment ... then he recognized it. And the writing on the fingers from a Sharpie marker. He fingered the marker he always carried in his own pocket. But that couldn't be. He looked down at the body; then back at the cell. It couldn't be ... but it had to be. He had etched the three x's into the lower back of the phone before handing it to ...

Chills raced along his spill. All energy left him, and he collapsed to the ground. His eyes never left the phone.

"Rye?" Iona's voice filled with a sudden concern. "Are you okay?"

He stared at the victim's face. Despite the damage suffered—the cuts, the swelling, the bruising—and the pooling of blood and skin discoloration, Rye identified the body.

"Juan." His voice stammered over that single syllable.

"What?" Iona hurried over. "No. It can't be." Sinking to her knees next to Rye, she rested her head against his shoulder. "This is horrible. I am so sorry. He was a good man."

"And a great cop."

"I haven't seen him around Whiskey for a couple of months ..." her voice drifted off, leaving their conversation hanging in quiet.

"He went undercover." Rye paused, unsure of what to say. "He went into the newest cartel on the block. We knew its power was growing. There was some tie to Whiskey, but we couldn't find it. So ... Juan volunteered. The Federal alphabet soup of agencies gave their blessing due to their own budgeting issues and corruption investigations by Congress. Last message I received from him claimed he located a definite connection between an Arizona citizen and the cartel."

"Who is it?"

"Juan ended the call before he would say."

"Who do you think it is?"

"Don't know," he said, turning his head to look into Iona's eyes. Those beautiful eyes that shone with her intelligence, wit, and creativity. "But I have my suspicions."

"Pray tell."

Rye shook his head. "Not until I have more facts to back up my suspicions." Though Juan's death tore at his gut, Rye determined to finish this investigation. If nothing else, for Juan's sake. That's what he would have wanted. He sealed shut the evidence bag. "Maybe we'll find something on its SD card."

Iona took the bag from Rye and placed it into the kit. She looked out over the canyon then flinched. "Hello? What's this?"

She used Rye's shoulder for support as she stood. She walked over to a nearby brittlebush and bent over. "Don't you be looking at my butt, now, you hear?"

Rye smiled despite the heaviness of his heart. "What do you got?"

"It's a picture. Some pervert's looking at the backside of a woman swimming naked in some swanky pool."

"What's it doing out here?"

"Wait. That's Juan in the photo."

"Let me see that." Rye pushed off the ground.

Iona handed Rye the photo. "From the looks of it, I'd say this was taken at some wealthy hacienda."

He bagged the photo and set it next to the cell phone. He twisted his lips looking at the bags. *Not much to go on.*

"Oh my ..." Iona said. "Rye, you've got to see this."

Her voice caused him to look over at her. Trembling hands covered her mouth. Something on the ground captured her attention. Rye hurried over to her.

"What is it?" he asked.

She pointed to the ground, past the brittlebush, and leaned into him.

Rye put an arm around her shoulder. "What?" he asked again, this time with a softer tone.

"Look at the tracks."

Footprints and tire tracks covered the area.

I don't see ..." And then he did. One set of footprints headed away from the crime scene only to end abruptly. Like the owner of the tracks simply vanished. Or flew away. No other tracks—human, vehicular, or animal—were anywhere near.

"That's ... strange," said Rye.

"It's worse than strange." Iona paused as if afraid to say the next words. "It appears a Skinwalker legend visited your crime scene."

With arms folded, Rye waited outside Batts' cabin. Its weathered boards, plastic windows, and rusting tin roof appeared to be on their last leg.

The area reeked of sheep, much preferable to the stench of decaying flesh they left behind in the canyon. He never developed an insensitivity to putrefying flesh. The stench and taste lingered in the nose and throat, sometimes for days. It lingered in the mind much longer. The desire for a beer washed over him, just to remove the taste of death from his mouth.

Iona sat on the edge of the porch, head hung down, looking wilted. He told her about the water cooler in the back of the Tahoe. She shook her head as if that very act drained her of the last of her energy.

"Hey, Johnny!" Rye yelled. Nothing. A fly buzzed past his head. *So if they were here, why not at Juan's body?* It made no sense. "Johnny Batts! WPD! This is Dawlsen!"

Silence.

Rye looked to his right and left. *Where did he go?*

Then a stream of curses burst from the house followed by Batts coming out the door, buckling his belt and tucking in his shirt.

"Don't be getting yerself knotted into an uproar. I was detained. Eggs don't agree with me this morning," Batts explained. "Hope that's 'nuff detail."

"Yeaaah." Rye swatted at the fly. "No, I don't need any more information regarding that particular event. Hey, Iona," Rye called to her: "You want in on this discussion?"

She pushed off the porch to join them.

Batts said, "Gotta do some work over at the barn. Care to interrogate me there? I got some camo duct tape and a chair you can restrain me with." A grin broke out on the man's whiskered face. Batts leaned to the side and spat a stream of brown juice. "And I like to chew."

They started across the open yard, and Rye said, "This interview is informal right now. Have no real reason to suspect you. If and when I do, it'll be time to pull out the water-boarding. And the camo duct tape." Rye's turn to smile.

Batts glowered at him for a moment but then broke into a laugh.

"You got me good there."

Rye continued. "But I do have to ask you this: did you kill our John Doe?"

They reached the barn, and Rye muttered a word of gratitude for the shade. Batts slid open the barn door and turned to regard the Chief. "Naw. Got me no need to kill no John Doe." He stepped into the barn and headed for the stack of feed.

Rye followed him in. Despite its outward shabby appearance, the inside revealed the meticulous hand of a master carpenter and a careful organizer. Tools and tacking hung in their proper places. Feed stacked in precise rows on wooden pallets.

Batts concluded by saying, "Time's I get trespassers, but mostly they're kids looking fer some secluded spot to drink beer or get some from their girlfriends."

"You are a little secluded out here," Iona said, emphasizing "are."

"Jest the way I like it." Batts grabbed a 100-pound bag of feed and slung it onto his shoulder in one easy move. "Foller me."

"Sorry, I have to ask you this, too," Rye said. "But what were you doing last night?"

"Well, 'cept for my sheep and a wild animal every now and then, I'm pretty much on my own out here. So, no matter, whatever I tell you, I ain't got no witness to back me up. After sundown, I read fer a while and went to bed. Got up before dawn. Took my sheep to pasture and … well … you know the rest of the story. It's the truth, I just can't prove it by no witness."

"Johnny, you read?" said Iona.

"Yep. All kinds of things. History. Biographies. Religious and political stuff. Fiction. Classics. Shakespeare: 'Away, and mock the time with fairest show: false face must hide what the false heart doth know.' Macbeth. I've even read all yours, Iona. I liked the line, 'Punk, you got two choices, and they both end in your death.' Can't wait for the next Charlie Spikes book. Will it be out soon?"

Rye blinked in disbelief. "Okay, then. Did you hear or see anything out of the ordinary?"

"Not 'til I came upon that there dead body. And the way it spooked them sheep gave me the heebie-jeebies. I ain't never seen nothing like it."

Rye touched the dog tags under his shirt. For some reason, Johnny being spooked didn't sit well with him. He'd never seen the man frightened. Yet, for the briefest of seconds, he watched fear peek around Batts' façade.

"So there's really not anything you can tell me about last night?"

Batts looked skyward in thought, his mouth twitching back and forth. "Nope. Not last night. But yesterday 'bout noon, Richard List drives up here in his purty white limo and wants to know if my property is for sale. I told him no, and he acted all put out. Offered me twice what it's worth. But I ain't selling. This land has been in my family since before the Civil War. Told him to get lost."

Rye waited for Batts to continue.

"List had some other dude with him. A Mexican fella. Thought it odd …"

"Why odd?" Rye asked.

"Well, he's dressed all in black. Had these tattoos on one forearm. His eyes spooked me. Dead eyes, void of human decency. And he had a couple of passengers in the back section with him."

"Go on."

"Didn't see much, 'cause of the angle of the car and all. But I heard voices. Women. Young girls really, you know how they giggle."

"Are you sure of that?"

"Yep. I hate that fat pig. Him and his flunky, Jilt, threw my brother in jail. The next morning, my brother turns up dead. Yeah, I hate that mother. And I don't cotton to him using up them little girls. Just ain't right."

Rye tapped his lips with a forefinger. *Something stinks bad. Real bad.*

CHAPTER 5

WEDNESDAY MORNING

Rye closed his office door and leaned against it. Not the morning he envisioned when he woke up. *The kind of morning that makes you age fast.*

His cell phone ring-toned, *Only God (Could Stop Me Loving You)* by Emerson Drive. His mind flashed to the morning he had his son program that ringtone into his cell. "So you'll know when mommy calls," Manny had told Rye, handing back the phone. *So I could ignore her calls when I hit the bars.* He regretted that notion now.

He unsnapped his cell from its holster. Rye stared at the number and caller name on the screen. *Dee.*

Rye turned his gaze on the stack of three boxes in the corner, his personal effects still unpacked. He resented them as a symbol for his failed marriage, preferring those memories remain boxed.

The phone's ringtone died. A second later, the song repeated. His heart ached to talk to her, yet his finger refused to push the green answer button. He closed his eyes. *Just to hear her voice again. Just to know that she and Manny are okay.*

Before the ringtone silenced, Rye pushed the answer button. "Dawlsen here." He walked over to his desk.

"Oh. Rye."

He sighed with relief. *It's the sweet Dee.* The girl he fell in love with before he ruined things between them.

"I thought we were going to play phone tag."

He ached to tell her how good her voice sounded. "Sorry. It's been a tough morning. What'cha need?" He winced at the coldness of his voice.

"Just wanted to give you a heads up. Manny has a karate meet this Saturday. He's going for his green belt. Manny would really like you to be there. The meet is at the Phoenix Convention Center. Starts at nine." Despite her gentle tone, he heard the ever-present accusatory tone. "Furthermore," Dee continued, "we'd both appreciate it if you could manage to...uh...come sober for once, Rye ... please. Just this one time, come sober. For your son. He misses his father something fierce. He talks about the times you took him to the shooting range as if they happened yesterday. I don't want him remembering the come-home-falling-down drunk dad."

Suspicions confirmed. She couldn't get past his drinking.

"Email me the directions."

Silence oozed from her end of the connection. Seconds dragged by. Rye began to think she'd hung up. *Wouldn't be the first time.* Then she sighed and said, "Okay."

"I want you to know, Manny comes first—"

"He hasn't in the past," she snapped back.

"Dee, we've been through this. I admit it. I'm a big-time screw-up. I know that. You know it. Manny knows it 'cause you drive it into his skull. All our friends in Tucson know it."

"Rye, that's not fa—" she tried to interrupt.

"Let me finish, will you?" He went silent, clenching the phone in a fist. "I will do my dead-level best to be there. Sober. But—things just happened around here. Last night we had a break-in at Whiskey's museum. Then an attempted armed robbery in our diner put one of my officers out of commission for a couple of days. Finally, I just got back from investigating a brutal murder under suspicious circumstances."

"What suspicious circumstances?"

Rye smiled. *Ahhh, the reporter in her smells a story. If I play my cards right, I can use her interest to open the door to reconciliation and ...*

No.

In a heartbeat, guilt heated his neck straight up to his cheekbones. Despite their issues, he could never play her that way. Even if it made things more difficult for him, Rye would be straight with her. If he ever hoped for a reunion, she deserved that much from him.

"Sorry. I can't go into details now, only because I haven't had time to review the crime scene data." He reached across his desk and scooted the lone-framed photo—of Dee and Manny—so he could view it better.

"Okay," she said, resignation in her voice. "I don't have to like it, but I won't press you for details ... at least not right now. But three crimes in Whiskey in 24 hours? That's beyond coincidental."

Rye studied the photo, staring at Dee's face. He traced her jaw with the light caress of a finger. "If you were any other reporter, I'd tell you to go pound sand ... okay ... what I am about to tell you goes no further than us." He took a deep breath and released it slowly.

"It's weird, and I don't want to spook folks. I don't rightly believe this myself ... but what do you know about Navajo Skinwalkers?"

"Skinwalkers!" she said with a laughing snort. "That's an Indian myth. Don't tell me the Navajo side of you believes this nonsense. There's no such thing as a Skinwalker."

"Yeee-ah. That's what I thought too ... until this morning."

Rye watched the prisoner through the one-way window to the interrogation room. The Mexican male yanked at the chains connecting him to the metal table. A light sheen of perspiration touched his forehead. He shot wide-eyed glances around the room.

Next to Rye stood Noah Whitewolf, his dark eyes fixated upon the prisoner as well. Without a word, he handed Rye a manila folder. Rye opened it and flipped through pages of various police reports that had nothing to do with their detainee. And behind the reports waited a couple of photos of the diner. A grin cracked Rye's face. Hopefully, the folder would make the perp think they had a lot on him.

"This man's not a happy camper," Rye said, holding up the manila folder. "And with this, I intend to ratchet up his discomfort."

Whitewolf nodded, his mouth a grim crease. Something ate at his officer, and Rye had learned to trust Whitewolf's instincts. The man not only tracked human predators across the Sonoran Desert, he interpreted the human psyche as if they were footprints on a person's face. And he was doing it now.

"What do you read from him?" Rye asked.

Noah turned his eyes upon Rye then stared back at the prisoner.

"He has the face of a man expecting a coyote-like ghost to come back from death and avenge a horrible wrong. He lives in a prison far stronger than any we could put him in." He turned to regard Rye. "This man fears something or someone very much."

"Perhaps he knows our killer."

Whitewolf rested a hand upon Rye's shoulder. "The terror in his heart will keep his mouth from telling you what haunts him. You can only open his mouth by surmounting his fears."

Rye nodded and trudged towards the door to the interrogation room. "Whitewolf, if you hear anything from the Yuma crime scene guys, let me know immediately. It'll probably be days before they get us anything." He shrugged. "But you never know."

Whitewolf tapped a fingertip on the glass, pointing at the prisoner. "While you're doing that, I'll run his tats through FBI's NCIC and Arizona's DPS. I'm thinking he's cartel."

"Good. The tats might tell us which one." Rye took a deep breath and slid into his game face.

A gray metal table separated two abused chairs. The prisoner hunched over in the chair on his side of the table. The temperature bordered on uncomfortably warm. Rye wrinkled his nose at the stench of sweat and panic.

Rye slapped the folder on the table. The prisoner jumped then exchanged combative glances with Rye, who plopped into the second chair and spent several seconds rotating the folder to be perpendicular to the table's edge. The prisoner studied the folder.

"I'm going to record this conversation," Rye said, pulling a recorder from his pants pocket. "If that's okay with you." Not waiting for an answer, he centered it on the table and took a few more seconds to adjust its location. Rye leaned forward and turned on the recorder.

"This is Chief of Police Rye Dawlsen of the Whiskey Police Department. I am interviewing a UDA on the morning of June 30th."

Rye remained quiet, watching the prisoner fidget in the silence. He picked up the folder and leaned back, pretending to read its contents.

"Not good," Rye muttered, flipping back and forth between pages. He stopped and stared over the top of the folder at the man. "*¿Habla Ingles?*"

"*Poco,*" the prisoner said. "Some."

Rye continued the pretense of reading the content in the folder. Whitewolf had included a page of Navajo jokes, and Rye forced himself not to smile. Rye withdrew photos of the diner and slid them across the table for the suspect to see. They were generic pictures of the diner, from a health inspection during the spring. But the suspect wouldn't know that, and Rye hoped his ploy would play into the man's fears.

"*¿Por qué?*" Rye tapped the photos. "*Why?*"

The suspect looked down, finding a sudden interest in the tiled floor.

Rye smacked the table with the flat of his hand. The man started, but refused to look up.

"Look at me!" Rye demanded.

The man raised his head and glared at him.

"You're not a US citizen." Rye's words snapped like canvas in a desert wind. "Nonetheless, I'm going to read you your Miranda rights. Just to cover all my bases." He pulled out his card, read the words printed there, and tossed the card on the table. "And it's on the recording. Now answer my questions, or I'll check out your papers."

The prisoner remained silent.

"Before we go any further, would you like some water? Coffee? Coke? A candy bar?"

The prisoner leaned back in his chair, maintaining a tough guy sneer.

"I'll take that to be a no." Rye locked eyes with the prisoner. "Let's start with something simple. Was that beat-up pickup yours?" He set the folder on the table for the prisoner to ponder its contents. Rye stood to loom large over the sitting man.

The prisoner maintained his silent glare. Rye strode to the solitary door and leaned his back against it, lifting one leg so the sole of the boot rested against the door. Rye folded his arms, never taking his gaze off the prisoner. Rye did this to suggest to the prisoner that WPD provided the only way to freedom. To himself, Rye counted off a hundred "cold beers" before he proceeded.

"Just to let you know, we've seized that truck as part of this investigation. The Yuma crime scene people will conduct a rigid investigation on that vehicle. Are there things you don't want them to find? Like, hidden drugs; old bloodstains; DNA from a pre-teen girl? They'll search for soil samples … easy enough on that rolling rust bucket. You want them to locate where you're from and where you've been? Care to answer any of those questions?"

Silence.

Rye gestured. "Hey. Feel free to jump in at any time. It may make all the difference to whether we send you home as a prisoner. If so, I'll make sure the Mexican police know you squealed like a rusted bearing."

More silence. However, Rye thought he detected a hint of worry in the man's eyes. *Let's raise this up a notch.* He pulled the photo from the murder scene out of his pocket. Holding it by the edges, Rye held it out for the prisoner to see it. He walked it over to the table and set it before the man.

"Do you know these people?" Rye tapped two fingers twice on the picture.

The prisoner lifted a casual could-care-less glance at the photo. His eyes twitched open, and he jerked back violently in his chair as if to escape from the print. He paled for a brief second, and his hands shook. The prisoner began tugging at his chains in a wild-eyed attempt at escape.

A chill seeped down Rye's spine. Supporting himself with one hand, Rye leaned on the table and shoved the photo into the guy's face. "Who are they?"

The prisoner opened his mouth then clamped it shut. He stared into Rye's eyes and shook his head.

A tough nut, but that photo's got him spooked. And he's starting to freak me out.

Raising his voice some, Rye continued, "Here's the deal. I'm sure you've heard all the stories how US lawmen beat the snot out of their Mexican prisoners." Not true, but Rye let the man's mind fill in the blanks. "Soon, another officer will enter this room and join me." Rye hoped Noah had returned from his database search.

"Amigo," Rye said, "you are in some serious trouble. *Serio lodo.* We have you," Rye used one hand to count the crimes on his fingers, "for attempted armed robbery, public menacing, eluding capture, and injury to an officer of the law. And I think I can get the judge to agree that ugly truck of yours breaks some city ordinance. More charges are pending further investigation. However, we have a little hitch.

We don't know your name. You carry no ID. No driver's license. No vehicle registration. Nada. Nothing. And you refuse to speak to me. I can't help you if you don't cooperate. Got that?" Rye paused, and the man refused to acknowledge him. "I. Said. DID YOU GET THAT?"

The man jumped in his chair and scowled at Rye.

"Okay," Rye said, releasing a sigh. "Let's start with the basics. Tell me your name."

The prisoner glowered at Rye. "Americano, you can go to hell and burn your soul there forever." His Spanish accent was heavy and hard to understand.

"Gee, now that is what I call an intelligent response." Rye put his fists on the table and leaned forward. "Let's try this again. What's your name?"

"You can't scare me—"

"If that's how you want to play this, then I'll choose a name for you. I bet when your madre first saw you she said, 'I have given birth to an idiota.'" The prisoner started to come out of the chair, but the chains around his waist and feet restrained him.

Rye remained outwardly calm at the man's outburst. Inside, he knew he got to him. *Finally.* "So I'll call you ..." Rye paused glancing at the ceiling as if the answer waited in the yellowing acoustic tiles. Rye snapped his fingers. "Got it! Idiota. I dub you Idiota. Whenever you care to tell me your real name, then I will discontinue using the nickname. Besides, we're running a trace on your fingerprints. If something turns up, like an earlier deportation to Mexico or a prior arrest—I will know your given name."

With his lips curling in a snarl, the detainee spat out, "You're a dead man, cop. When he finds out—"

Rye smacked the table. "WHO IS 'HE'? Care to elaborate, Idiota? I don't know this individual. Give me his name. I can pay him a little visit. Work things out. You know, drink a little beer. Chat a little bit. Tell him you're singing like a scalded canary."

The prisoner shrugged his shoulders again, but not before dread flashed through his eyes. "No. I'm just an—"

The door swung, and Whitewolf stood in the entrance. His western hat hung low, and his mirrored sunglasses hid his eyes. It never ceased to amaze Rye how imposing the Apache could be when he wanted. Whitewolf stepped into the room and closed the door behind him with a resounding click. Scowling, Whitewolf ambled over to the open chair, turned the chair backwards—metal screeching against tile—and eased his frame into it. He leaned forward to invade the Mexican's space.

The prisoner leaned backwards as far as the chains would allow.

"This creep is here illegally," Whitewolf said, his voice low and menacing. "I say let's turn him over to I.C.E."

Idiota shot rapid glances between the two cops. "I want a—"

"I don't care what you want," Rye snapped. He walked around behind the man. "You tell us what we want before I give a rat's tail about what you want. What's your name?"

The Mexican shook his head.

Rye leaned in closer and said, "Okay, Idiota, try this one on. Did you steal from the museum? Did you kill someone last night? ANSWER ME."

The man's brow wrinkled. He looked confused. "I ... I ... I kill no one."

"So you were at the museum?"

The man hesitated. "Wh … what museum?"

Rye circled around to the front of the man and folded his arms across his chest. "Here's what I think. You broke into our museum, stole a couple of artifacts, tried to sell them to your mysterious friend. You know, in the canyon where we found him butchered. When the deal turned bad, you killed him. Then you went to the diner to enjoy a breakfast. I think you're here illegally. Am I right?"

"I didn't steal nothing from no museum. It was the crazy woman. A lawyer. I want—"

"I don't care. Lawyers are for US citizens." Rye had just stretched the truth again but figured the prisoner wouldn't know American jurisprudence. "You're one scrawny dude. I bet there's more than one bubba in the penitentiary who'd love to make you his girlfriend."

"No, no. That won't happen. Demonio Amo won't—" he stopped for several seconds, his eyes darting around the room. Then, Idiota continued with a defeated voice, "Allow it."

Rye wheeled on the prisoner. "And who is Demonio Amo? ANSWER ME!"

The prisoner lowered his head and sobbed. He shook bodily from crying. When he looked up at Rye, tears stained his splotched cheeks and ran off his chin. "Please help me. Demonio is one very evil man. I fear him more than God. He sell drugs north of border and buy guns from some Americano gringo and bring south into Mexico." Resignation filled the man's voice. "Okay, my name I tell you. I am Rod Valdez, and I am now one dead man. Can I see a lawyer now? For my son, I need to make out—how do you Americanos say—my last will and testament."

CHAPTER 6

LATE WEDNESDAY MORNING

"We're done here. Do the pre-book," Rye told Whitewolf. "Escort Mr. Valdez to lock-up."

"Chief, we need to talk—" Whitewolf started to say.

"Start the deportation process," Rye said, glaring at the prisoner one last time before turning on his heel and stalking out of the room. He slammed the door behind him and measured his strides down the hall, his footsteps squeaking on the polished tile floors. The desire to punch a hole in the wall would have overwhelmed him had he not pushed it deep down into his soul. Finding Juan's killer took precedence, gnawing at Rye's gut like a coyote gnawing at a rabbit carcass. A handful of Tums sounded good, but it'd have to wait.

He pushed through a door on his right labeled *Squad Room* where six desks lined the walls. Teetering piles of paperwork buried Reese's desk, whereas Whitewolf's desk waited with neat stacks of paperwork arranged in OCD perfection. Two desks sat vacant, one used for collecting overflow papers and file folders. The other had been Juan's. Neat stacks of paper and files awaited his return. Rye swallowed and shifted his focus toward two officers huddled around a monitor at the desk across the aisle from Zach's.

"Uh-mm," Rye cleared his throat. The two spun in their chairs like teenagers caught looking at porn. Rye leveled his gaze at the monitor.

The face of the young male officer reddened. "We're just looking at the new surfboard I bought. It's, like, a Channel Islands ... I got it in the back of my SUV. If you'd like to take a look."

Rye shook his head. "Right now I'm not interested in surfboards. I know you officers just finished your watch, but we've had several incidents this morning, so consider yourselves on overtime. Officer Heilo?" He nodded to the Latina female officer.

She stiffened and grabbed her notepad and a pen.

Rye said, "I need you to check for any deaths in southern Arizona where mutilation with a sharp instrument was used. Start by going back for the last two years."

"Got it." She clicked on an icon, typed in a password, and connected to the state criminal records. "Is this related to the crime scene out at the Batts' property?" she asked over her shoulder while her fingers clacked away at the keyboard.

"Yes. The vic died hard. It involved ... mutilation."

"Is crazy Batts a suspect?"

"He's just an interested party at this time. We'll keep him in the suspect pool until we clear him. However, I don't see him as doing this."

Rye turned to DePute, a fresh recruit who looked like he should be surfing off Maui. "DePute, search for any illegals caught dealing drugs in surrounding counties. Correlate that with any previous record of deportation. I'm particularly interested in a Rod Valdez." He removed the photo from his pocket. "See if you can find the name of the woman in this photo. Send an electronic copy to Yuma if necessary."

"Dude, I am so on it." DePute stood and took the photo from Rye's hand.

Rye clapped a hand on the officer's shoulder and squeezed. "Don't call me dude," Rye said, voice deadpan. "It's not professional."

Whitewolf entered the Squad Room and went to his desk. "I'm on the unsub ... Chief," he said.

No. Not that joke again.

Whitewolf chuckled. "My ancestors would cringe if they knew I called a white man Chief." His laugh sounded hollow and strained in the silence from the others.

"Dude," DePute said. "That joke was like old before your ancestors were born."

"Okay, people, you've got your assignments," Rye said above the ensuing chuckles. "Get me that information ASAP." *While I untangle a cryptic message from a dead man.*

Whitewolf leaned over his chair, palms on the desk, a blank stare at the keyboard.

In two steps, Rye stood next to him, a tentative hand on his shoulder. "Noah?"

"You have yet to tell them." The statement, though level and quiet, sounded like a shout to Rye.

He winced and glanced at the younger officers, whose lighthearted banter had evaporated the moment Rye had addressed Whitewolf by first name.

"You OK, Whitewolf?" DePute said, his gaze flickering between Rye and Whitewolf.

While Rye searched for words, Heilo said, "Tell us what?" She had swiveled her chair to face them.

Rye eased himself onto the edge of Whitewolf's desk while Whitewolf straightened, standing at attention just behind Rye's left shoulder, his face a stoic mask, unreflective of the grief in his eyes.

Rye took a deep breath. "This morning, Sgt. Juan Martinez was found murdered out on Batts' property." He held up a hand to forestall any questions.

Water welled in Heilo's eyes. DePute stared at him, the color draining from his face.

"Right now, we don't know much, but we're cops, and we're going to conduct a professional investigation. We will find whoever did this and bring justice to Juan's memory. But I need all of you to back me on this. Can I count on you?"

At first, no one said anything.

Rye, seconds away from tearing the room apart, gripped the edge of Whitewolf's desk. "Heilo. DePute. Can I count on you?"

Heilo jumped to her feet. "Yes, Chief."

"Yes, Chief," DePute echoed as Heilo rolled the chair behind him, grasped his arm, and sat him down.

"Good." Unable to say much more, Rye pushed himself off the desk. "Let's get to work." And without meeting anyone's gaze, he left the squad room and paused in the hallway.

He thought of the enigmatic letters scrawled on Juan's fingers: gs ds DHL DA. So what was Juan trying to say? His last words. Probably knew he was going to be killed. So he had to get a message out.

Gs ds DHL DA. Rye dropped his head. The letters of the puzzle jumped around in his mind. *DHL? Did he mean the airfreight company?*

Doesn't feel right, but I suppose we need to check it out.

His cell phone rang. "Dawlsen."

"Doc and Zach just pulled up out front," said Gabby. "Thought you'd like to know."

"I'll be right out." *Now I'll have to tell them.*

At the exit into the front lobby, Rye pounded his password—four of the same number—into the keypad, and the metal door swung open. The painted theme of the lobby was administrative gray. The outside wall of smoky glass revealed Whiskey's main street where Doc had parked his Dodge Ram pickup. A single door led outside. The lobby's lone wooden bench waited to be used.

In the Dispatch Room, surrounded by computers and a phone system, Gabby smacked gum with a phone perched on her shoulder. Cute though on the heavy side, she wore her dye-aided red hair in Cher style, bangs hanging over darkly lined eyes. She held up a finger to tell Rye to wait and ended her conversation.

He spoke into the slatted hole. "Gabby, call one of the local law firms. See if any of Whiskey's fine lawyers would represent our latest guest." Rye held up a hand as Gabby started to protest. "I know it's not procedure, but he wants to make out a will. Thanks."

Doc and Zach stood outside the front entrance, talking. Zach sported a white oval eye-patch and was staring at his reflection in the window. He rubbed a gentle finger across the patch.

When the two of them entered, Rye asked, "Hey, how's the eye?"

"Scratched cornea. Just like I figured," Doc answered. "He needs to leave the patch on for twenty-four hours. He's got some antibiotic drops if the eye bothers him. It should be fine within forty-eight hours."

"It hurts like a—" Zach started to peel off the patch.

Doc slapped Zach's hand. "Leave it alone, son, you'll only make it worse." Doc turned to Rye. "You got my permission to handcuff him if he starts rubbing it. After the patch comes off, his vision may be impaired for a little while."

Rye folded his arms. "What about work?"

"Give him the day off," the doctor said, pulling his ponytail.

Zach gestured with his hands. "Doc, really, I'm fine."

Doc ignored him. "He should be okay to work tomorrow. No heavy lifting. When it hurts, he needs to rest. Gotta go."

"Wait," Rye said. "Gabby," he called over his shoulder. "Can you come out here?"

When she joined them, Rye had them sit on the bench while he paced the room for several moments.

"I have some bad news. Gabby received a call this morning from Johnny Batts. Seems he found a dead body on his property. I took a team, and we investigated it." He stopped mid-stride and faced them. *I hate doing this.* "Turns out to be Sgt. Juan Martinez."

Tears filled Gabby's eyes. Doc lifted his head as if praying to heaven while Zach lowered his head as if a giant weight pressed down on him.

Zach looked up at Rye. "Do we know who?"

Rye shook his head. "But we've started the investigation. Now, Zach, you go on home 'cause I'll need you. I don't want to see you until tomorrow."

"I'm good enough to—"

"No," Rye emphasized, his decision, final. "Go home, Reese. We also had a break-in at the museum, and I'm assigning you to the case. If you want, call Helen and Terrance. From home. Resting on the couch. Talk to them, and get up to speed. You can check out the museum tomorrow before you come in."

Zach sighed, exasperation obvious.

Rye added, "And stay out of the bars tonight."

Zach grunted and put his hands over his chest. "You really know how to hurt a guy."

Rye pointed at the door. "Go." *I wish I could visit a bar right about now.*

He rested a hand on Gabby's shoulder. "I know this is hard, but I need you to pull it together and finish your shift. I promise you; we will find Juan's killer."

An hour later, Whitewolf walked into Rye's office and dropped a folder on his desk. Rye looked up from his monitor.

"This is what I found out so far," Whitewolf said. "Not much, but it's a start. What about Juan's family?"

"His mother died several years ago. His father was killed by one of the Fast and Furious rifles. His little brother is in jail for working with a cartel."

"That's pretty tough. Something in that folder might provide a clue."

"Thanks." Rye's fingers tapped out a drumbeat on the folder. "I'll take a look at it. Keep digging."

Whitewolf nodded once and departed.

Rye looked at his Android waiting on the desk. He had called

Chee, leaving a message at the food mart close to where his uncle lived. Chee had no phone, and the food mart served as a community-gathering place.

C'mon, Uncle. Call me.

Rye loved his uncle, but the Navajo sense of time often grated on his nerves. It seemed like they wasted a lot of it. After a noisy exhale of irritation, Rye turned his attention to the folder. He opened it and began to flip through its pages.

Colonel Demonio Amo. One grainy photo. *Could be the guy I saw.* A former officer in the Mexican army turned rogue, Amo had disobeyed a direct order. The commander threatened court martial, and Amo shot him in the head. Amo then assumed command of the company, engaged a small-time cartel, and wiped them out. Took over their territory and grew to be a well-oiled, albeit murderous, cartel. *El Àguila.* The Eagle.

Rye leaned back in his chair and closed his eyes. *So what does this have to do with our perp? If Mr. Valdez is an associate of Amo's, then why is he here in Whiskey? Was he involved in the murder? The break-in? And what did he mean when he implied a woman stole the museum's artifacts?*

Rye sat forward and grabbed one of many Sharpie markers from the pencil holder Manny had made for him—black spray-painted soup can with a paper sheriff's star glued on it. From a desk drawer, Rye took out a clean steno book. He began doodling free-associative thoughts and what ifs. Circles and squares with tags and lines connecting them.

He started with what he knew. When he finished, he read what he had written.

Museum Break-in. Occurred overnight. Activity confined to a single

86

room of Skinwalker displays. Broken display case. Three items taken: 1) Leather shield; 2) Feather; 3) Amulet.

Evidence:

- *Fingerprint smudge*
- *Length of hair. Whose?*
- *No footprints outside. How did they enter?*

Have Reese re-question everyone from the museum. Were the thief/thieves looking for Indian artifacts to sell on the black market? Check with FBI and the Federal Bureau of Land Management. Murder at Batts' property. Vic was Juan. From decomp, he was killed overnight. More accurate TOD?

Evidence:

- *Smashed cell phone found near Juan. Check phone for addresses, etc. on memory card.*
- *Markings on Juan's fingers. Looks like a Sharpie pen was used. ds. gs, DHL. DA. ????*
- *A photo. Juan with a woman. Who is she? Where was the photo taken?*
- *Have several tire tracks. At least 5 sets of footprints. Whitewolf casted all.*

Things to do: Send evidence to forensics at Arizona Criminal Investigation. Contact Juan's brother.

His cell phone rang, and Rye jumped, banging a knee on the underside of the desk.

He grabbed the phone, recognized the food mart phone number, and pushed the answer button. "Dawlsen."

"How is my nephew who refuses to walk the way of the *Diné*?"

"How is my uncle who refuses to acknowledge his nephew walks in two worlds?"

They chatted about family, events concerning the Navajo people, pow wows, dancers, and the weather. When the conversation faltered, Rye figured they had finished with the Navajo niceties and cleared his throat.

"I have some questions to ask you," Rye said. "It has to deal with an investigation. What do you know of ... Skinwalkers?"

Chee laughed and started coughing. "Cigarettes, the white man's curse."

"Actually, Uncle, Indians originally sold tobacco to the white man."

"Glad we got something over on the round eyes. Getting back to your question, the white man doesn't believe in ... *Yeenaaldooshii*. Navajo myths, they claim."

"No." Rye's voice grew quiet. "What I need to know is ... what do the Navajo believe?"

Chee's voice became a whisper. "We don't talk about them when night approaches the *Dinetah*. It's not safe."

"It's daytime," he reminded his uncle.

Several seconds of empty air passed between them. Rye waited for him to say more. From the times he spent with his uncle on the Res, Rye knew Navajos never rushed in to fill silence like a white person would. He tapped his fingers on the desk, waiting.

The silence drew on.

Rye rubbed his forehead and tapped his foot in rapid fire. With a tskking noise, he broke the silence. "Look, I'm investigating a murder, and I need some info on Skinwalkers."

Chee's end of the phone remained quiet. Rye opened his mouth to prod his uncle into talking, when Chee whispered, "*Yeenaaldooshii* walk the witchery way. To gain the power to travel in animal form they must kill a family member."

Rye rubbed his chin. "What do these Yeen ... all ... Ye-nay ... um ... Skinwalkers do?"

"They curse people to sickness. They attack or scare people in their hogans or in their cars. If they lock eyes with you, they can steal your skin." Chee paused, and his words came out like a wintery hiss. "They are evil, nephew. How do Skinwalkers enter in to your non-*Diné* investigation?"

"Can't go into detail right now. But Iona suggested it."

Chee laughed, breaking the tension. "Iona is a good woman. She's a friend of the *Diné*. I read her books. I think she writes about you."

"Get outta here. They're just stories." Rye felt the blush rise on his cheeks. "Don't get off topic. Anything else you can add?"

"Yeah. Don't make yourself so scarce, nephew. Visit me. And bring me a new pair of jeans when you come." He paused. His voice dropped again. Fearful as if he thought someone might be listening. "There's trouble in Navajoland."

"What kind of trouble?"

Chee's next words came out as a strangled plea. "Eight *Diné* have died in the last few weeks. People have been attacked." A long pause. "By a Skinwalker, nephew. A Mexican Skinwalker. Now listen to your Uncle Chee ... if you pee outside, cover your water with dirt, or the Skinwalker can hurt you. Real bad." His voice became an urgent whisper. "Nephew, please be very careful. This is one bad witch."

CHAPTER 7

WEDNESDAY EVENING

Rye swung the Tahoe into his driveway and slammed on the brakes. The vehicle slid for several gravel-spitting feet, coming to rest in a cloud of dust. He glared at the glowing numbers on the dashboard clock.

8:45.

"Juan, why did you have to go and get yourself killed?" Rye yanked the keys from the ignition, allowing heat to saturate the interior. Closing his eyes, he leaned back against the headrest, a long sigh escaping his lips. "Dee says that all things happen for a purpose, so what purpose did Juan's death serve? Huh?" The tears Rye could not allow until now overwhelmed him, and he swiped them away. "God, if this is your purpose, then just leave me alone."

After feeding his chickens and gathering a few eggs, Rye stumbled up the front steps, dragging one aching foot after the other. He unsnapped the holster from his belt, set the weapon on the dining room table, and headed to the kitchen. He traded out the eggs for a beer in the fridge and threw a pizza in the oven.

Taking the beer with him back into the living room, he reached over the couch and cranked down the window AC unit. He plopped onto the couch, remote in hand, relishing the brace of chilled air. Taking a long draw of the beer—promising himself just one more with dinner—Rye turned on the TV.

"And in today's local news," said the dark-haired news babe, "this morning, a badly mutilated body was discovered outside Whiskey."

Rye sat up, listening intently. The story led with some footage from the top of the first hill showing Johnny's cabin before cutting to a shot of Batts.

"Weren't nuthin' you folks need to see out there," Johnny drawled. His close-up was worse than most mug shots Rye had taken over the years. "Let the poor fella rest in peace." Batts finished with the sign of the cross.

Then Rye's own image peered back at him. "At this time," he had said because the newswoman had shoved the microphone into his face, "the Whiskey Police Department is not releasing any information."

The screen showed a picture of the front of the Whiskey PD.

Then the newscaster mentioned the myth about Skinwalkers. *Crap. Where'd they hear that? Just what I need.* He took another swig of beer. He relished the liquid softening his parched throat. With a final guzzle, he emptied the can.

The timer dinged, and he fetched the pizza using a towel. Rye put his hand on the door of the fridge and thought twice about a second beer. His Dee-consciousness told him to have water.

Naw, I'm okay. I can handle another.

Between thirsty gulps of beer, Rye wolfed down his meal, licking the grease off his fingers.

After dinner, he surfed through the news channels before turning the TV off. To his relief, he had found nothing about Juan, giving him more time to conduct a detailed investigation. With night now fully descended, darkness dominated the room. He fumbled at the lamp, turning it on.

Licking his lips, he returned to the kitchen for another beer. Sitting on the kitchen counter, Iona's book peeked out from under the towel. Rye picked up the book and thumbed the pages. *Did she really write about me? She wouldn't.* He didn't care all that much for reading ... but Iona wrote it, and she helped with some investigations. It wouldn't hurt to look at the first chapter.

Returning to the couch with his beer, he kicked off his western boots and scooted them under the coffee table. After taking another drink, he settled back and started to read.

> *"The killer waited alongside the desert road, facing the east. His knife dripped blood onto the dry dusty soil. Though his appearance rendered him into the image of an American cowboy—hat, jeans, pointy-toed boots—he just killed his first American GI in his personal jihad. More would die soon, he swore to Allah."*

Rye startled awake. Confusion washed over him until he saw the beer cans on the table and the paperback opened facedown on his belly. He must have fallen asleep while reading Iona's book.

So what woke him?

His mobile home shook, creaking, and he noticed the winds for the first time. Gusts buffeted the windows, whistling through the cracks. Did a storm front come in? They tended to ride through like a bronco shot in the butt. He started to push off the couch when something struck the outside of his house.

"What the ..."

He hurried over to the table, retrieved his handgun, and tiptoed to the kitchen window. Pulling the slats apart, Rye peered outside, into a world turned coffee-hued with blowing dust.

Two luminous eyes stared at him.

For a moment, they held him prisoner, drained his strength, and froze his mind, as if he had dropped into the nether-existence of limbo. Lost. Drifting. Petrified. The eyes blinked, and their power over him vanished.

He stumbled backwards a few steps and dragged a hand over his lips. It had to be an animal. It just had to be. But there was no creature in the desert tall enough to be the owner of those eyes. Except for one ... man. *People's eyes don't glow unless they're a ...*

No sane white man believed in Navajo myths: however, his Diné mother believed and had warned him. Maybe he should go search for the thing, but before he could decide his next move, the power went out, plunging the interior into darkness. Rye stood still until his night vision allowed him to see shapes. The AC had stopped, no longer masking the screams of the raging desert hurricane.

He parted the slats again, only to discover the twin luminance had disappeared. Blowing dust limited vision to a few yards. His Tahoe, the chicken coop, and the fence had vanished in the whirling sands. Rye cocked his head to one side. Was there another sound hidden in the winds? Faint, but it sounded like ... the haunting howl of a wolf. He fished a police flashlight and safety goggles from the junk drawer in the kitchen.

Thump! Something else smashed against the outside of his house.

He slipped on the eye protection, chambered a round in his gun and hurried to his front door. The wind blew so hard, he had to lean a shoulder against the door to force it open. He stepped out onto the porch, legs wide apart to withstand the buffeting. Grit pelted him like stinging bees, clogging his nose and ears and creeping down his shirt.

Another thump against his house provoked him to shine the flashlight in the direction of the sound. A chicken had splattered against the outside wall, and he watched it slide to the ground.

Shielding his face in the crook of his arm, he battled through the sandblasting winds towards the chicken coop. He played his flashlight over the pile of torn planks that had been his coop. The hut's tin roof rattled, and a loose board beat against a structural support. A few chickens scrambled about squawking in terror while others lay dead in the dirt. The wind grabbed one of the chicken bodies and pitched it away into the gloom.

A ghostly wail howled above the winds. Rye wheeled, shining his flashlight into the wall of churning dust. At first, all he saw was the circle of light reflecting back off the dust. Squinting, he spotted a shadowy form, staring at him. It looked to be a large canine. A wolf? Except this one wasn't like the one at the diner. Its eyes did not glow when struck by light. Frozen, Rye faced a Skinwalker in its animal form.

A resounding crash from behind made him jump. Wheeling around, he saw several boards from the coop fly against his house.

Scowling, he turned to face the wolf. It sat unfazed.

"You!" Rye shouted at the beast. "I know what you are!" He raised his handgun and pointed it at the animal. The wolf opened its mouth in a soundless howl.

Before Rye could pull the trigger, a strong gust bowled him over. He landed hard on the ground, and the wind rolled him several feet. Managing to hold onto the gun, he scrambled to his knees and pointed in the direction where the wolf had been.

Instead of a wolf, a beautiful Native American girl stood in its place. Naked with only a wolf skin wrapped around her to offer a modicum of modesty, she stared at him, head tilted to one side. Her black hair, unaffected by the wind, flowed straight over her shoulders to her waist. When he centered her in the circle of brightness from the flashlight, her eyes glowed with animal luminance. He recognized her.

"Sunflower?" *How—what—huh?* The woman standing before him, calm despite the winds, resembled a grownup version of a girl he knew in high school.

Take care, Rye Dawlsen. Her voice spoke in his head. Not with audible words, but like thoughts she placed in his brain. *You walk a dangerous trail. Evil stalks your land. A Nakai. I cannot warn you again.*

A sudden blast of wind forced him to look away. When the twisting air settled, she had vanished.

Helen woke, emerging from a dreamless sleep into a dull awareness. Night lay thick in her bedroom. Outside, gusting winds rattled the bedroom windows and whistled through cracks. She reached over to her husband's side of the bed finding the covers undisturbed. He hadn't come home from his bowling night. She squinted at the clock to read the neon blue numbers.

1:32.

The lanes closed hours ago. But the bars hadn't, she realized with a spark of anger.

She reached for her cell phone lying on the nightstand. The screen remained dark. *Outta juice. Stupid battery.* She slammed it back on the stand.

With a snort of disgust, she threw back her covers and creaked her way into a seating position. The AC chilled her through her oversized t-shirt and gym shorts. She coughed to clear her throat and noticed that their Jack Russell wasn't on the bed.

She heard the pondering clicks of a dog's nails on the floor.

"Puddles?" she called.

The clicks stopped.

She reached for the pack of menthol slims on the chest of drawers and withdrew a cigarette. She tucked it into the corner of her mouth, her fingers fumbling along the top of the dresser, searching for her lighter.

The tick of dog's nails on the floor resumed, approaching her bedroom. She paused before her fingers found the lighter. It didn't sound like her Puddles' frantic pace. The noise stopped outside her door. Helen bit her lip, alarmed. Then it dawned on her. How did Puddles close the bedroom door?

"Puddles?" Her voice sounded like that of a panicked little girl.

Chill bumps raised on her arms. She yanked her pink bathrobe off a chair and slipped into it. She grabbed the aluminum bat standing in the corner by the door. With a deep breath, she flung open the door.

Nothing.

Helen peered down the hallway. Releasing her breath, she laughed at her skittishness. *You paranoid old woman.* She lowered the bat.

"Puddles. Come to mommy."

She expected to hear the dog running to her. Except for the wind, the house stayed quiet, as if it held its breath.

"Puddles?"

Helen walked toward the kitchen. The familiar hallway now felt like a claustrophobic tunnel caving in on her. Nothing. A soft padding sound came from behind. She spun to face the noise. For the briefest second, she glimpsed a dark shape before it smashed into her, cracking her ribs. The bat flew from her hands as she thudded on the floor, her head bouncing on the surface. Darkness swept over her among the eruptions of starry color. The scent of a wild animal filled her nostrils.

A hand gripped the front of her terrycloth robe and lifted her bodily from the floor. Struggling on the edge of consciousness, Helen felt herself half-carried/half-dragged down the hallway. Her side felt as if a razor slashed at her lungs.

Whatever held her tossed her through the kitchen doorway. Her shoulder slammed into the corner of the cooking island, shooting torment down her arm. She landed on the tile floor face down, grateful for its coolness. With a moan, she turned her head. Blood soaked her robe from the gash on her shoulder.

A large animal walked behind her, its nails clicking on the tile. The stench of wet fur overwhelmed her. She gagged, and then gasped at the torture in her side. She gritted her teeth against the throbbing anguish.

A new scent tickled her nostrils, and she turned her head to find the source of this smell.

A scream gushed from her throat, raw and inconsolable.

Her husband sat at their breakfast nook, hands and feet bound to a chair. His head leaned back, exposing his opened throat. Or what was left of his throat. Blood soaked his bowling shirt. Claw marks sliced his arms and face. Blood had pooled on the floor around his chair and had spattered the window and wall.

Shrieking, she rolled on her back. She stared at the ceiling without seeing it, tears sliding down the sides of her head.

"Noooo," she moaned. "Not my Ter."

She wanted to go to her husband. Her poor, dead husband. The only man she loved, murdered by someone, her kitchen saturated in his blood. She tried to sit up, gasping, unable to succeed from sheer agony. She looked away from Terrance.

Puddles lay on the floor, chewing on a meat-covered bone. The dog paid her no attention. Several bowls of water sat on the floor. A bag of dog food had been sliced open, spilling its contents.

A wolf with fur the color of a starless night shuffled from the other side of the kitchen island. Looming over her, it sniffed her for several long seconds before disappearing from view. Helen thought its gait odd, like it had an injured hip or ... or ... *no, it couldn't be.*

Her whole body trembled uncontrollably, and her heart pounded, her skin clammy. Panic throttled her. She had to tell someone. How? If she could only leave a message. She spotted the pen jar by the wall phone. Too far away. Her side pulsating, her shoulder burning, she writhed toward Terrance. Then her hand touched a rivulet of Terrance's blood, and she recoiled.

Wait a minute. Terrance's blood ...

Forcing down a gag, she dipped her finger into the sticky liquid and began to write on the floor. A low growl emanated from the hallway, and Helen flopped onto her back, unable to do anything more.

A man, Mexican by Helen's estimation, stepped into the kitchen, naked except for animal skins draped over his shoulder and around his loins. His eyes glowed with a honey color, like a wolf. He wielded a black-bladed knife.

"Where is it?" he snarled, pushing the point of the knife under her chin. "I want the amulet from the Skinwalker display in your museum."

"You stole …" her moan of a question went unfinished.

"Wrong. The break-in occurred before I got there." He stood over her and pressed the point of the knife into her forehead. "It's the amulet I want. Where is it?"

"Stolen," she sobbed. The point of the knife cut into her skin. "Pleeease, I don't know."

"That's too bad, chica." He pulled the knife back so she could see it stained with her blood. "Last chance."

He paused as her gaze fixated upon the blade, and sobs racked her.

"Where's the amulet?" he yelled.

She shook her head and choked out, "Really, I don't know."

He spat a curse and slashed downward. The searing raked across her throat was the last thing she felt.

CHAPTER 8

THURSDAY MORNING TO EARLY AFTERNOON

Rye moaned. From a far away canyon, a woman's voice droned. He wished her voice would disappear into the fog. Several heartbeats passed. A man's voice mumbled. The two voices sounded like a conversation, but they weren't talking to each other. Rye pried open one eye. He lay on his couch in the living room, and the morning news played on the TV.

Rye forced himself into a sitting position, wishing he didn't have to. With his butt on the edge of the couch, he bent over, resting his head in his hands. His tongue, swollen like wet wool, and the nasty morning-after beer breath turned his already-sour stomach into a flash-flooded gulch. A wave of nausea crashed upon him. With another moan, he leaned against the back of the couch, head resting on the top. He draped one arm over his eyes.

How much did I drink last night?

His cell phone began singing.

He swiveled and winced at the pinpoint explosions that raced across his forehead. Muttering, Rye pushed off the couch and stumbled toward the ringing cell.

"Dawlsen, here."

Zach rushed past a good morning and began a rapid fire sermon about the museum break-in. Rye winced at the officer's loud voice, managing to catch every third or fourth word. Holding the phone away from his ear, Rye rubbed his forehead at the maelstrom accelerating between his ears.

"Ho, slow down, cowboy." Rye took a deep breath and continued. "Is the museum even open by now? Have either of the two Visser girls arrived?"

Rye listened for several moments, and then said, "Remain there for a half hour. If no one arrives, go over to Helen and Terrance's ranch. I'll have Gabby send Whitewolf over to the twins' home. They like to go danc—"

Zach cut him short, and Rye returned the favor. "No, Reese, I will not send you over to talk to the girls. Stay at the museum, and keep me in the loop." He ended the call.

"What's that about?" Iona stood peering through the screen door. When Rye raised an eyebrow, she added, "Covering last night's storm damage. Seems like this area got hit the worst. Strange it concentrated here." She frowned. "Are you okay?"

Rye rubbed his mouth. "Had too much to drink last night." He motioned her to come in.

"So what's up?" she asked, setting herself into the single recliner.

"Zach's at the museum this morning. He arrived, but neither Helen nor Terrance made an appearance. That's odd 'cause they're always there early."

"That *is* odd." Iona pointed toward the back of the house. "Take a shower. I'll brew some coffee."

"Knock yourself out," Rye said and headed towards his bedroom. "Thanks," he called over his shoulder.

After the shower, Rye stepped out onto the deck, wearing only a pair of jeans. Leaning on the wood railing, he closed his eyes, enjoying the morning's warmth.

"Feeling better?" Iona said, joining him. She handed Rye a cup of steaming coffee.

"Dunno," he said, glancing at her. "Ever get the feeling you were being watched?"

"Sometimes."

"I'm getting that feeling now." Rye gave the surrounding area another look-over. "Act normal."

"I'm standing next to a man with bulging muscles who's practically naked. What's normal about that?"

Sipping his coffee, Rye plied a cautious gaze over the landscape. "Keep talking like nothing's up. Anyway, I promised a special kid I'd be in Phoenix for him this weekend."

She put a hand on his shoulder. "Manny? How's he doing with the separation?"

Her touch sent shivers down his spine and into his loins. His thoughts shifted into being with Iona. He studied her profile, surprised he found her attractive. And not by a little bit. She radiated the beauty of a Hollywood actress. He had to rip his eyes away from her low cut active-wear thin-strapped shirt. *How did I miss that earlier?*

"It's tough on all of us. It's ... nice to have a friend like you." Rye patted her hand. "Ever since Dee joined that church, she's been on my case about my drinking." He took a sip of the coffee, all too aware about all the empty beer cans inside. He shrugged. "Perhaps she's right."

Iona withdrew her hand from Rye's shoulder. "I suppose that's a wife's prerogative."

Rye closed his eyes, flinching at his stupid comment about Dee. *Dawlsen, sometimes you're dumber than a mentally-challenged mule.*

Rye's phone began playing. He dashed inside and grabbed his cell. "What 'cha got, Gabby."

"You know how you told Zach to go to the museum this morning? He called in and said he stayed there for a while, and no one showed up. Which is really odd because Helen loves that place and—"

"Gabby, I've talked to Zach. Just tell me why you called."

"Well, if you don't want all the details. You know it's important I supply all the intel I can. The former police chief …" she stopped.

"Can we have this discussion later?" Rye snapped. "Just give me the facts."

"Humph." Her irritation clearly vocalized. "Zach's over at the Arches' place. He rang the doorbell. But neither Helen nor Terrance answered the door. He hears their dog yapping inside. He wants to know what he should do." She paused, and Rye started to say something when she added. "Something's wrong. I just know it. Helen's in my square dancing group. This is so unlike her. I'm worried about her."

Why Zach went through Gabby to contact him when he had just talked to the officer, Rye couldn't figure out. "Tell Zach to check the outside of the house and look into the windows. If he has visual evidence of a person in danger, then he has my permission to enter the house. I'll be over at the Arches' in about twenty."

Twenty-three minutes later, Rye came to a gravel-spitting halt in the Arches' driveway where two Whiskey police vehicles already waited. The driveway headed through a cactus garden of various agaves, desert spoons, marigolds, and Arizona ash. The Arches' *casa*, a tan adobe box with stone decor, squatted behind the garden. Several Indian pots planted with fish-hook barrel cacti lined the narrow portico covering two sides of the house. A fig vine had wrapped itself around wooden posts that held up the awning.

Whiskey usually saw one or two murders a year, and those generally a result of drunken arguments. Theft was equally as rare. His major troubles had been drugs and gun-running. And most of that had stayed in the desert. Without warning, trouble had strolled into Whiskey and plopped in the middle of the town. Now this with the Arches. He hoped they were okay. Something told him they were not.

He studied the rugged terrain spread out behind the Arches' lot. Sand, rocks, and spiky desert vegetation led to some rocky escarpments. About a mile away, the only Baptist church in Whiskey perched atop a lone hill. Its spire shone pallor white against the further distant mountains.

Leaving the engine idling, he stepped out of his Tahoe, adjusting his hat and sunglasses. Hitching up his Sam Browne belt, Rye started kicking gravel on his way past the other two cars.

Iona pulled up behind his police vehicle in her Firenze red Land Rover LR2. No mistaking that vehicle. She hopped out, giving the car door a push with her hip to close it. She waved a manila folder. He waited for her, and together they headed for the back of the house.

"What'cha got?" Rye asked.

"Photos from the museum. I swung by my office. Any word on the Arches?" A hint of concern graced her voice.

"Zach phoned to say he got no response. This might not be pretty."

Iona shrugged. "I'm a big girl. I can handle it."

"Yeah, that's what they all say."

She punched him in the shoulder. "Get out of here." She studied his face for a second. "You're serious. Okay. If I'm right, you take me on a romantic dinner to Yuma."

"Deal." He paused. "And if I'm right, and you lose it, what's in it for me?" Rye stared into her eyes.

"I'll think of something ... rewarding."

From inside the house, the Arches' dog barked incessantly. Zach leaned against the back door, face pressed against the window and one hand blocking the sunlight. In the back yard, Noah ambled head down in a back and forth pattern.

"What's the situation?" Rye said to his two officers.

"Can't see into the windows," Zach said. "Someone spray painted them from the inside. Why would anyone do that?"

Noah joined them at the house. "I searched the area, boss. Got nothing."

Rye went to the back door and pounded on it. "Helen! Terrance! This is Rye Dawlsen. Open the door!" He held up one hand for silence as Zach started to speak and listened with his head slightly cocked. The dog's yapping drowned out the house's silence. Concentrating, he rubbed his chin.

The Arches took their dog everywhere. He remembered seeing it in the pen behind the museum. How many times had he seen them driving through town with the Jack Terrier sticking its head out the window. Now the animal was protecting its domain and Helen and Ter were nowhere to be found. What was the dog's name?

"Puddles?" Rye cooed through the door. "It's okay. You know me. We won't hurt you." He went on for several minutes muttering this nonsense before the dog calmed down.

"Hey!" Iona yelled, standing in front of the detached garage. "The Arches' car is still in here. I don't like the way this looks."

"Stay there, Iona. This isn't one of your mystery stories. I'd say we got ourselves an emergency." Rye said after a few more seconds, "Noah, you got that door buster?"

The Apache hightailed around the corner of the house. Moments later, he hurried back, the black metal ramming device over his shoulder. "Stand back," he said.

Whitewolf stood on the top step while Rye held open the outside door with one hand and drew his handgun with the other. Noah started swinging the battering ram with two-handed swings. "One … two … THREE."

When the metal head connected with the wooden door, a shower of splinters and ruined timber exploded inward.

"Police," Rye yelled.

Rye stepped through the ruined door and moved to his left. The stench of death—rotting meat and piss—rushed into his nostrils, making him gag. He cupped a hand over his nose and mouth.

"We got two bodies in the kitchen," Rye managed to say over his shoulder.

Two torn and headless bodies lay in a lake of blood. The sliced remains of Helen and Ter resembled meat in a butcher shop. Ter looked to have fallen from a kitchenette chair. Helen appeared to have met her fate lying on the floor.

Similar MO to Juan on Batts' property. Decapitation meant the killer was escalating. The thing that shook Rye was the pile of dry dog food and several bowls of water that had been left for the animal.

"Oh, that's just …" said Zach, pushing past Rye. The young cop covered his mouth.

"Don't puke and ruin the crime scene, Reese," Rye snapped. "Go outside."

Whitewolf came in behind and growled something in Apache. "Who'd kill and mutilate yet take time to feed the dog?"

"Someone with a demented mind," Rye said, trying not to be overwhelmed by the amount of spilt blood. "We got a crime scene to process, but we also need to secure the house." His gaze traveled across the carnage, fighting off the shiver of death's cold hand down his spine.

"We can sweep the house," Whitewolf said. "Then exit out the front. That'll help maintain the integrity of the scene."

"Let's do it then." Using hand signals, Rye directed his officers how to proceed. "Be careful. The killer may still be here."

They passed through the house with handguns pointed toward the floor, fingers poised alongside trigger guards. They exited the kitchen into the living area and saw no one. Rye pointed to the lone hallway. Sweat trickled down his forehead and stung his eyes as he paused before the hallway's dark maw.

This is it, then. If anyone's here, they're down there. Taking a deep breath, Rye stepped into the corridor.

At the first bedroom door, Rye peered in and figured it to be

Helen and Ter's bedroom. He pointed at Whitewolf, who followed on his heels, and then at the bedroom. Noah nodded and entered the bedroom.

Rye moved on, and he sensed Zach's presence closing in behind him. At the next bedroom door, which appeared to be a home office, Rye indicated for Reese to examine it. Zach nodded and proceeded into the office.

Rye continued down the hall, suddenly feeling alone and stranded. He swiped a sheen of sweat off his upper lip. At the third doorway, he paused and stared at the closed door. His hand reached out to take the doorknob. *I'll be an easy mark.* He flung open the door. The room was bare as if the Arches never used it. Not even carpet or a throw rug. Rye lowered his gun and examined the closets. Empty.

He breathed out a tension-releasing sigh.

One more room. The bathroom.

Back in the hallway, Rye moved to the restroom. The half-opened door revealed a white tub with a Navajo inspired shower curtain. Entering the bathroom, nothing appeared suspicious. The sink supported two toothbrushes and toothpaste. A rack over the toilet contained towels, shaving supplies and whatnot. Last thing to check, the tub.

"Clear," Noah yelled, a distant voice in Rye's ear.

"Clear," Zach yelled a heartbeat later.

Rye focused on the shower curtain. He pointed his gun, touching the curtain with the barrel. That's when he heard the droning flies. The stench of death flooded his nose, burning into his lungs. He drew the curtain open. In the bottom on the tub, the heads of Helen and Terrance stared up at him with blank eyes.

CHAPTER 9

THURSDAY AFTERNOON

The smell of death lingered in Rye's nostrils.

Sitting in his Tahoe typing a report on his in-car laptop, Rye glanced out the windshield to observe the coordinated swarm of Yuma's forensics. The coroner stood beside a white van directing his two assistants as they loaded the two bodies.

Despite the AC, heat leaked into the vehicle, and Rye swiped a bead of sweat running down his cheek. The sun hovered, white-hot, in a colorless sky.

Standing in the meager pool of shade offered by the garage, Iona snapped photos of the investigation. When she noticed him watching her, she raised a hand to wave, a smile spreading across her face.

She's one fine looking woman … Now write your report.

A Yuma County Sheriff pickup parked alongside him, crunching gravel and stirring up a dust cloud. Heat waves shimmered off the white truck. Sheriff Anne Oakmann stepped out, adjusting her black uniform. Dark hair cut short, mirrored sunglasses hiding her eyes, a curt attitude that took no BS. Deadly shot. Yet despite her granite demeanor, Anne tended to exhibit a softness toward kids and animals.

She slipped on her western-style hat, adjusted her Sam Browne gun-belt, and sauntered over to Rye's vehicle.

Before she could tap on his window, Rye pushed the button to lower it, heat smacking him like a bomb blast.

"Hey, Dawlsen," Anne said, standing gun side away from him. "What's up? Anything good?"

Rye looked at the flock of law enforcement encircling the house. "Well, Oakmann, yeah, if you consider a double homicide under ... um ... inexplicable circumstances good. Pretty gruesome stuff."

"Don't tell me. Wanna form my own opinion."

Rye nodded. He knew that about her ... very hands on.

"Mind if I have a look around?" She twisted around, taking in the activity.

"Go ahead, just sign the log book. I'm in no mood for territorial spats. This one creeps the snot outta me." She continued to observe the scene. Rye added, "Go, have a look-see. Then let me know your thoughts. I want to finish this report."

"Something making your Navajo blood nervous?"

Rye forced down the flash of anger. Anne didn't mean anything racist by her Navajo comment. That's just the way she operated—didn't pull any punches. "Go inspect the scene, and tell me if it doesn't make your European blood nervous."

"Will do." She pressed her lips together into a firm line, failing to hide the smile. As she walked away, Rye raised his window. He turned back to his laptop, grateful for the cool air.

The passenger door opened, and Whitewolf climbed into the front seat. "Good and cool in here," he said, closing the door. "I must've lost ten pounds from dehydration. Got anything to drink?"

"Yep." Rye reached into the cooler on the back floor and fetched a bottle of water submerged in the half melted ice. "Here. Get anything?"

"Not a whole lot." Whitewolf held the plastic against his face, ice water dripping off his chin. "Apparently, the Arches didn't spend much effort getting to know their neighbors." After taking a long draw on the water bottle, he fished his notebook out of his shirt pocket and perused his notes. "You know Joel Pinner? He's a contractor at the Army Proving Grounds in Yuma."

Rye nodded, noting Whitewolf's meticulous script in thin-tipped permanent marker upon the page. He forced the sudden image of dead Juan's ink-stained fingers from his mind and concentrated on Noah's words.

"Says he saw Mr. Arche at the bowling lanes last night. Claims to have witnessed an argument last night between Mr. Arche and a Mexican fella. Said the guy walked in like he owned the place and found Mr. Arche at the bar. They had a hush-hush discussion, which escalated into words." He flipped the notebook closed and took another drink of water. "Sounds like we got ourselves a person of interest."

"Good. When Reese gets back, go down to the bowling alley and talk to the owner." He glanced at the dashboard's clock. "They should be open." His hand strayed to his dog tags. "Did Mr. Pinner describe this Mexican fella?"

Whitewolf scrunched his mouth. "He did, as a matter of fact. Said the man wore all black. Cowboy hat. Shirt. Jeans. Boots. And mirrored sunglasses." Noah looked over at Rye. "Who wears sunglasses near midnight?" He re-opened his notebook. "Mr. Pinner mentioned the fella had tats on his forearm." He turned to the correct page. "Like these."

Rye studied the crude renderings. "Gang tats, no doubt about that. This guy's showing up in interesting places."

Whitewolf nodded. "You know the letters that Helen spelled out? S-K-I. I think she was trying to ID her killer. That means she knew him." Whitewolf turned his head to study Rye. "She knows your uncle. Chee Skinner. There's been problems on the Navajo res." Whitewolf raised a hand to stall Rye's protest. "I'm not accusing your uncle of anything. Just kicking a blanket to see what crawls out. If nothing else, clear his name."

Rye pushed an index finger against his lips. "Let me handle it."

Zach slipped into the back seat behind Noah. "Whew, it's frigging hot enough to make the Devil sweat," he said, reaching for the cooler. "You mind?"

"Help yourself, that's what they're there for. Get anything?"

"A few things. First, several witnesses said they saw a suspicious pickup truck in the neighborhood last night. Older model. Like the one that Johnny Batts drives. And they're pretty sure it was Batts driving. That puts him in the vicinity of two murders."

"Yeah. It's not looking real good for Johnny ..." Rye shook his head. "I just don't see him doing this. Batts and the Arches weren't enemies. What else?"

"One witness claims he saw a stretch limo following Batts. Didn't get the license number, but said it was definitely an Arizona plate."

Rye rubbed his forehead. "A limo? There's only one person in these parts I know owns a limo. Richard List. What would he be doing in this neck of the desert? I'll have to mull that one over and take it around the block a few times. Anything else?"

"Welllll. Mrs. Julia Martin, Arches' next door neighbor, made an interesting observation. After midnight she claims to have seen ... how'd she put it ... a big old wolf that looked like it was drunk. Or sick.

Or sumpthin'. Snooping around the Arches' house." Zach pushed his hat back off his forehead. "Weird, huh?"

Despite the heat, Rye shivered. They had another Skinwalker sighting.

Amalia huddled in the back of a shallow cave, willing herself to sit still while she baked in the afternoon heat. She closed her eyes. *Conserve your energy*, she repeated to herself. With nightfall, she might have enough strength to climb down this gray granite spine jutting from the desert floor.

She whispered a Hail Mary—cracked lips barely moving—for protection of her and the dozen girls with her. *Blessed Virgin, help us. Go to your Son and plead our case.* Amalia knew she would not survive another day. Not without divine intervention. Or water. She hummed *Ave Maria*, recalling the comfort it brought her as a child.

Three nights ago, a coyote—a Mexican man with a whisper of a mustache and cold dark eyes—had smuggled them across Mexico's Northern border. The way he eyed her had made Amalia nervous. But something went wrong. The sounds of helicopters and the pounding hooves of horses from that night still filled her heart with terror. Somehow, they'd evaded the US Border Patrol. The young man refused to explain what went wrong. Instead, he led them to these mountains.

They had reached the cave at daybreak.

The coyote left after assuring them the patrolmen did not know of this place. He promised to bring water and food the next night. He never returned. Now, the sun lowered in the afternoon sky, baking the grotto.

Amalia wished for water and a bit of food. Her stomach grumbled. This wasn't the first time she had gone hungry. Her uncle—offering her shelter after drug gangs murdered her parents—often withheld food when she refused his advances. One night, he came home drunk with some streetwalker and told Amalia he found her a job in America. His promise brought her to this cave of death.

With her forehead propped on her knees, she listened to the whispers of the girls sitting close to her. They spoke of leaving tonight. Or staying. From the panic in their voices, they had no plans beyond getting down the mountain. No idea of where they were. No idea of how to avoid the border patrol.

If they left and the coyote came back, he'd hunt them down. All of them. She figured if he returned and found them gone, his ego would force him to hunt them down like dogs.

Or the *bajaderos* would get them. Predators that would rape and kill them.

That's all we are. Esclavos. Slaves.

One of the girls rocketed to her feet and pointed a finger at another girl's nose.

"I say we go tonight. All of us. No one stays."

"No," said the other. "Each must make her own decision."

"If any stay," said the first, "then they can reveal our escape."

"And you don't think," said the second girl, waving her hands with darting gestures, "an empty cave won't?"

The argument grew more heated, and other girls joined in the argument. The two girls started shoving each other.

Amalia sprang to her feet. "Càllate!" *Shut up! Shut up! Shut up!* The echoes from her shout died as all eyes turned in her direction. "We are in a bad situation, no? We stay, we die of thirst. We go, evil men kill us. If we argue among ourselves? They win."

The first girl who started the fight wheeled upon her. "How dare you! You sit back there sobbing like my little sister. Now you yell at us. How—"

A man's voice cut through the crowd. "Perhaps you should listen to your hermanita." *Little sister.*

A hot breeze ruffled their clothing. Silence choked the cave. This was not the voice of their coyote, nor of one of the Americanos. Amalia turned to see the speaker.

A man dressed in black blocked the exit of the cave. Dust coated his clothes. He removed his black Stetson, lightly brushing it with his fingers to remove the offending dirt. The yellowing sky framed his black silhouette and hid his face. He stank of evil. The newcomer donned his hat, precise in its placement.

"Okay, ladies, your plans have changed. Your miserable little guide won't be returning. He—shall we say—dug himself into a hole." The man laughed at his own joke, but Amalia clenched her jaw. She cared little for the coyote, but he was not born evil.

The man pointed out the cave. "Take the trail down to the base of the mountain. I have some *compañernos* waiting for you. They have water and food for you." A grin, cold like winter snow, snaked across his face. "Afterwards, we will talk about what you can do for me."

The first girl who started the argument wheeled to face the man. "Who are you," she said, "to tell us what to do?"

Like a striking rattlesnake, he drew a handgun from a shoulder holster. He aimed it at the girl, and Amalia realized she stood in the line of fire. Her skin goose-fleshed. The man in black shrugged.

"Who am I?" he returned the question. "I am your executioner."

The gunshot roared in the confined space. The girl's head jerked back. Amalia screamed as the body dropped, twitched once, and went still. The smell of gore and gun-smoke filled the cave.

"Any other questions?" He pointed his gun at the crowd of girls. Amalia closed her eyes, hoping he would go away. Next to her, a girl sobbed. Amalia smelled the ammonia of someone wetting herself.

"No?" said the man with a self-congratulatory tone. "*Bueno*. Now get to your feet and follow my instructions. Except for you."

Amalia opened her eyes, fearing the worst. The enormous crater of the gun's barrel pointed her way, commanding her attention.

"I have special plans for you."

He lowered the gun, and Amalia felt her skin go cold despite the heat. What had her uncle gotten her into?

CHAPTER 10

THURSDAY EVENING

Rye leaned back in his office chair, feet propped on the desk. He stared out into the darkened hallway, relishing the quiet. Gabby, gone for the day. Noah and Zach, reports done and on his desk. DePute, on patrol now. Later, Heilo would take the graveyard shift. That left him alone at the station.

He took a swig of beer and set the can atop the same water ring forming on the chair's arm. Five more beers, cold and wet, waited for him in the break room fridge. He would need them tonight. Weariness set in like drying concrete, and his eyelids drooped. His mind drifted in darkness until a white spot rolled his way. No. Not one, but two, and growing larger as they approached. When the dots bumped into his feet, he recognized the Arches' heads, sightless eyes staring accusations at him. Helen's blue lips moved when she said, "Never a cop around when you need 'em."

Rye bolted upright. "Holy puke," he gasped.

He raised the beer can to his lips and downed half of it. He shook his head to clear his mind of Helen's talking dead head.

Rye snatched up the top report—Whitewolf's—and began to read.

The buzzer to the front door went off, indicating someone entered the building. Rye set the beer on the floor then reached for his gun resting in its holster on the desk.

"Rye?" The voice echoed in the empty halls.

His shoulders relaxed. "Iona," he yelled. "I'm back in my office."

Rye holstered his weapon.

The delicious scent of diner burgers blitzed his nostrils. Seconds later, Iona strolled into his office carrying two takeout bags. She lifted them for Rye to see.

"Din-ner," she said in a sing-songy voice. She plopped in a chair across the desk from him. "Garcon drove past when I parked out front."

Rye arched a brow at her.

"DePute. He let me in."

"You're a long distance mind reader." Rye eyed the bags spotted with grease smears.

Iona dropped the two sacks of food on the desk. "I saw your light, so I thought I'd grab us a bite. She checked the bags and slid one to Rye. "A double-decker taco burger for you."

"Thanks," he said, lifting his meal out of the bag. "Let me get you a beer."

He returned moments later with two cans.

Iona nodded at the reports. "Learn anything new?"

He grinned. "I like this. Discussing cases with a famous mystery writer is kinda like us being Castle."

Iona waved a hand. "Hey, having a Masters in Criminology, a

Bachelors in Forensics, and half a dozen years on the force in Phoenix doesn't hurt." A flash of pained memory crossed her face.

Rye understood. "Did they ever find the lowlife that shot you in the hip?"

She closed her eyes and gave an almost imperceptible shake of her head.

"And all those months of physical therapy ..."

"Just to walk again. Hoping I'd return to the force."

"Yeah, I know. Just like my knee. I wanted to re-up for another tour, but the Army wouldn't let me."

"Phoenix PD offered me a desk job or early retirement." She stuffed several fries into her mouth. Rye took that to mean she was done talking about her early retirement.

Halfway finished with his burger and working through a mound of cheesy salsa and fries, Rye asked, "Hip bothering you?"

"No more 'n your knee."

"That's the reason I like the desert. Hot dry air doesn't bother it. Not as much as cold rainy weather, anyway." He left unsaid it also started him on heavy drinking. He had discovered booze numbed the pain that enflamed the joint. He tapped the reports with his index finger. "Read these while you eat." He rotated the two reports and pushed them across the desk towards her.

She reached out and drew them closer. After taking a sip of her beer, Iona held up the can. "Go easy on this stuff. Remember last night."

The three remaining cans of beer loomed strong in his mind. They waited for him on the right side of the fridge on the second shelf down. The colden golden. Cut the desert dust from his throat. He pursed his lips as guilt tinged his conscious. Perhaps two beers would be enough for tonight.

When Iona finished the reports, she slid them back across to Rye. "Interesting."

"What do you think?" Rye tapped on the reports and took a sip of beer.

"Looks like you got a couple of leads. That's a start. Forensics uncover anything at the Arches'?"

"They pulled the usual evidence, and they'll be processing that. But it takes time. It may be weeks before we hear anything. Nothing jumped out and screamed, 'Hey! I'm the mac-daddy of clues.' Except for the bloody boot prints and paw prints."

Iona sighed. "It appears someone is trying to play on the Skinwalker fears of us desert folks. What about the guy you got in the slammer?"

"He won't talk. Wants to lawyer-up. To do a will. Go figure. I think he wants to stay in the cell. The man's terrified."

"You got any idea why?" Iona leaned back in her chair, munching on some fries.

Rye looked up at the ceiling then laughed. "He freaked at the arrest when he spotted the black-clad Latino male mentioned in the reports."

"Sooo ... watch'ya going to do with the prisoner?"

Rye shook his head. "I can't get over the idea he wants to stay in jail. Most folks can't wait to get away."

"Perhaps you ought to charge him room and board. Can't imag—"

"What the—" Rye blurted and half stood.

Gunshots, from outside, mixed with screeching tires.

"Stay put," he told Iona as he grabbed his holster.

When Rye reached the front door, more gunshots ripped apart the dusk's calm.

Burnt rubber fouled the air.

People screamed.

Standing on the sidewalk and strapping on his holster, Rye watched as a half dozen trucks and a rusty El Camino squealed tires in demonic clatter while they drove in crazed circles at the three-way intersection of Yuma Street and Whiskey Drive, the town's major intersection.

Rye absorbed the commotion within heartbeats of exiting the police HQ. The evening's twilight had settled upon the town. It'd be dark soon.

He dashed between the vehicles parked in front of the Police Department and peeked over the hood of Iona's Land Rover as people scrambled to flee the chaos.

Gunmen stood in the beds of the trucks, pointing rifles in the air and firing. The traffic light at the intersection had been shot out, pieces left to swing on sparking wires.

He raced over to the Tahoe, threw open the back hatch, and grabbed the first weapon he had ever learned to use—his bow. Opening a secret compartment, Rye withdrew the quiver hidden there and slipped the strap over his head. He yanked his cell phone from its belt.

Come on, pick up.

"Depute here."

"We have a situation in town," Rye said. "I need you here now. Rápido."

"Chief, me and Heilo are investigating a report of approximately twenty female mules crossing Tucker's ranch out on 8. We're here searching for them."

A sudden burst from about a dozen weapons erupted at the intersection.

"Dude! What's that?"

"Gunfire. Someone's shooting up the plaza."

"We're—"

"Getting here ASAP." Rye spotted Zach sprinting up the side street towards him. "I see Reese. But we need your backup."

"Roger that," Depute said. "Our TOA is fifteen minutes."

Rye disconnected the call and sped two blocks to the first intersection. At the corner, in front of the Cowboy's Cyber Café—a yuppy coffee bar—he hunkered down behind a square adobe column supporting the awning over the sidewalk. He counted some fifteen Latino males in the truck beds firing various weapons. Their drivers circled the plaza like Indians set to attack a wagon train.

Zach knelt next to him. He wore a black wife-beater shirt, jeans, and moccasins. He carried a Glock.

"Looks like we got ourselves a real mess, huh, Chief?" His words rushed over each other, a half octave higher than normal.

One of the shooters leveled his weapon and fired. Windows from several stores exploded in showers of glass.

"Can you shoot with that eye patch?"

"No problema." Zach nodded to Rye's weapon. "So what, you bring a bow and arrow to a gunfight?"

Rye shot him a dirty look. "You a freaking comedian now, or what?"

Zach cleared his throat. "How do you want to handle this?"

"Let's walk down the street. Maybe a show of force will scare them off."

"Say what?" Zach said, his voice rising even higher in pitch.

"Maybe with an aggressive police presence, they will cease their firing at innocent civilians." Rye glanced again at Reese, who stared back, speechless. "Let's do this."

"Roger that."

As they stepped out onto Yuma Street and started walking towards the violence at the intersection, Rye figured this had to be one of the dumbest ideas he ever had. He was about to say something when Zach raised his handgun and aimed at targets down the street. Determined to stay the course, Rye nocked an arrow and pulled the string taut.

"Now what, Chief?"

"You take the twelve guys on the left, and I'll take the twelve guys on the right. DeFute and Heilo are on their way. They can have what's remaining."

"Now, who's the comedian?"

They passed by stores, small businesses, bars and restaurants, all familiar to Rye. He knew the owners. Faces full of worry and fear peered out from behind drawn curtains. Several shop owners lifted rifles or handguns and mouthed, "Need help?"

Rye shook his head at each in turn, mouthing, "No."

Other citizens hid behind cars, pickups, and SUVs parked along the street. Mothers with children. An elderly couple. A teenager had removed a rifle—a Remington, Rye noted—from the back of a pickup, and, though scared, appeared ready to begin returning fire. Rye shot him a glance and said, "Stay put."

A bullet pinged the street a dozen yards in front of them and ricocheted away with a whining noise. Another window crashed, shot out from the sound of it.

They reached the next intersection. The shooting stopped, and the trucks came to a halt, facing them like an offensive line. Their Spanish and laughter filled the void left by the silent guns.

From the bed of a blue '63 Ford with black fuzzy dice hanging from the mirror, a man wearing a straw cowboy hat pointed a rifle at them. Rye tensed. Straw Hat fired a shot, striking a car parked nearby.

Zach squeezed off a round, striking the center of the grill. Steam swarmed over the truck's front. A steamy green puddle formed under its front bumper. The expended shell clinked on the pavement. Straw Hat and his friends ducked.

"You missed the shooter," Rye said.

"No way. I aimed for the radiator. Consider it a warning shot."

"Shooting the gunman would've been better."

"There's a critic in every crowd."

The driver of the Ford sprang out of the truck when the cloud of heated antifreeze flowed over the windshield. He raced to the front of the truck and stared down at the expanding pool of antifreeze before hurling hot curses in Spanish in their direction.

"Sir, lay down on the ground," Rye yelled back. "NOW!"

The driver gave Rye the finger and scurried back into his Ford.

"Now, that's one impolite hombre," Rye said.

A dozen guns from the men in the truck beds pointed at them.

"Time for cover?" Zach's voice shook.

"Noooo," Rye said, drawing the bowstring taut. "Tell them to stand down."

Zach shot him a questioning glance. Several shots rang out from the trucks. Bullets hit the pavement or struck cars. *The way these morons shoot, maybe standing in the middle of the street IS the safest place.*

"Whatever you say, Chief." Aiming his gun at the Ford driver, he bellowed, "This is the police! Lay down your weapons! NOW!"

They laughed, elbowing each other as if they shared a big joke. They sounded drunk.

With a tremor in his voice, Zach said, "I don't think I persuaded them."

"I'd say you gave them ample warning to lay down their weapons." Rye sighted down the arrow.

"Yeeeeah?"

"They've broken several laws, wouldn't you say?" Rye aimed the arrow at a truck.

"We got enough to hold them until Armageddon."

"And they most certainly have put our citizens and guests at risk." Rye compensated his aim for the heavy, odd-shaped arrowhead.

"No doubt."

"They damaged property?" Rye asked. He took a deep breath.

"Sure, Chief. But ..."

"And I believe they gave the wrong response to your command," Rye said. "Let's see if they think this is funny."

"What kind of arrowhead is that?"

"Watch."

Rye loosed the arrow. It struck the front right fender on a pee yellow '69 Toyota Hilux truck. The Hilux exploded in a ball of fire and flipped, sending men sailing from its bed. The truck slammed into the

'63 Ford next to it. Rye resumed walking toward the line of trucks. Orange tongues of flames crawled along the torn metal, and thick black smoke billowed into the sky.

Zoned in on the scene unfolding before him, Rye observed the minutiae, the shooters scrambling from the trucks, the drivers grinding the transmissions to get their vehicles in gear, a passenger struggling to get his handgun from his shoulder holster. A horseman galloped towards town, cutting across open land. Whitewolf. Zach trailed a step behind.

"The! Officer! Said!" Rye shouted while he withdrew another arrow. "Lay! Down! Your! Weapons!" He nocked the arrow and lifted the bow. "DO IT NOW!"

When one of the gunmen in the bed of the El Camino aimed a rifle at him, Rye sent the arrow into the vehicle's headlight. The front on the car exploded in a shower of fire and metal. Flames licked at the ruined car, the twin stacks of black smoke joining together. Rye readied another arrow should the shooters want to engage further.

That's when he heard the sirens.

Thank you, DePute.

Men stumbled away from the burning trucks. Those in the undamaged vehicles jumped from the beds to assist their injured and load them into their trucks. With the drivers spewing curses, they fled the scene, tires squealing.

Rye lowered his bow. "Let's check out our crime scene."

Sheriff's Deputy April Cruze parked her cruiser along State Route

23, angling it to block the two lanes. She sat in her car a moment, staring at the red slash on the western horizon. Already, the temps had started to drop.

Sheriff Oakmann had ordered her to this section of the highway to set up a roadblock in response to a BOLO. Something about a cartel shootout in Whiskey.

This spot she had chosen, with the angle in the road, would force any driver to slow down. Just in case the shooters came this way.

Unlikely. Not on this back side to nowhere. The road only led to the houses of some rich people.

She took off her Stetson and set it upside down on the passenger's seat.

Why do I get all the rotten details?

Then she glanced out of her side window. About a half mile away, a convoy of headlights raced towards her position. She retrieved her cell phone.

"This is Deputy Cruze near the interchange to Whiskey on State Route 23. I have multiple fast moving vehicles coming from Whiskey. Please advise."

A few seconds later, Oakmann replied, "Try to halt the lead vehicle using your Stop Stick. Consider the convoy to be armed and dangerous. Backup is on its way."

"Roger that."

"What's your 10-40?"

Cruze relayed her location then signed off.

She flipped on her lightbar and exited the car. The blues and reds splashed over the desert. She hurried to the trunk and opened it. First thing, she checked her vest, unhooked her holster, and grabbed extra mags. Satisfied, she fetched the Stop Stick from the underside of the trunk lid, and with one easy throw, deployed it onto the road. It looked like a black snake lying across the pavement. She made sure the wire attached to the tire deflation device was taut.

The lead box truck drew within a hundred yards. Staying within the flashing lights, she stepped into the road—glad for the absence of civilian traffic—and waved. The trucks did not slow down. She continued to wave. When the headlights from the lead truck highlighted her, it shot forward. In a microsecond, she noticed the dent on the driver side fender, the crack in the windshield, the male driver wearing a straw cowboy hat, the male passenger chambering a round in the handgun he held in front of him.

Not good.

She dove into a nearby ditch and prepared to yank the Stop Stick.

With the truck barreling down on her, April saw the driver aim a handgun out the window too late. She activated the stop stick. Heard the pop of several shots. Jerked her gaze at the driver. The sound of angry hornets flew past. She felt a tremendous kick in her chest above her left breast.

She spun around and rammed her head into her car. She heard the truck tires blow and squeal. Coming out of her momentary blackout and lying on the ground, she witnessed the box truck swerving right and left then toppling over. In a spray of sparks, it skidded along the road, dipped into a ditch, and turn upside down. Several others raced past.

Her upper chest blazed. A wet, sticky substance spread under her shirt. Her left arm failed to move. The bullet had just missed the vest.

She fetched her cell phone off her belt and dialed 911.

"What's your emergency?"

"This is Deputy Cruze ... on State Route 23 ... officer down. I repeat ..." Sudden nausea swept over her. "Officer down ... I'm shot."

"Please stay on the line, Deputy Cruze. I have units responding to your location. Where have you been shot?"

"Outside my car."

"Where on your body have you been shot?"

In the swirl, she recognized her mistake. April laughed and then coughed. *Man, that hurt.* Breathing became increasingly difficult.

"Left ... upper chest. I'm going ... to inves ... tigate the truck." Her body screaming, April pushed herself off the ground.

"Deputy, please remain calm and don't move. You'll only aggravate your wound and increase your loss of blood."

"The truck is upside down in the ditch." She began what seemed an endless trek to the box truck. Her vision spun like a DVD. Her left arm hung useless at the shoulder. She felt the blood flow down her arm and drip off the ends of her fingers. The cell phone suddenly felt too heavy, so she lowered her arm. Though she tried to drop it, her hand refused to let go of the phone. The dispatcher's voice continued to plead with her. She stumbled towards the crashed vehicle.

The back door to the truck had opened during the crash, spilling several boxes. One had broken open. Dozens of handguns lay scattered in the ditch.

April mumbled nonsensical sentences, her mind refusing to string together meaningful words. She fought to focus on the situation in front of her. The entire left side of her shirt felt sticky now.

She reached the ditch and stared at the truck. In the driver's mirror, she saw the reflection of a badly injured man. *I hope the SOB dies.*

She heard the dispatcher's plea. April glanced down, surprised to see she still carried the phone. Straining against its weight, she lifted the phone to her mouth.

"Tell the units ..." she breathed, "we have ... multiple wounded."

"It's April, right?" said the dispatcher. "Your name is April. Stay with me, April. Tell me what you see."

"I'm looking ... into the cargo ..." She took a breath. Now, she heard the sirens of approaching rescue. "Cargo area ... Boxes ... Stenciled ..." She didn't want to die, and sadness sapped at her dwindling strength. "Guns ... military issue. And C4. Repeat. Cargo ... Guns and C4. Lots of ..."

Sirens sounded close and far away at the same time. She heard car doors open and slam close. Voices. Thirsty, she wanted a bucket of ice-cold water. Blackness took her as she fell and slid into the ditch.

Rye's cell phone rang while he surveyed the damage at the plaza. *Now what?* He unclipped his phone and saw Iona's name and number.

"Hey, what's up?" Perhaps she had experienced one of those mystery writer moments when a clue jumps out and leads to the killer.

All the commotion around him swallowed Iona's shallow whisper.

Reese had moved into the crowds pouring out of the local businesses, taking notes from witnesses, his notebook out and Sharpie scribbling at a furious pace. Riding hard into the town, lights flashing, DePute and Heilo squealed to a stop at the intersection. They parked their cars to cordon off the area and opened their doors in unison. Whitewolf halted his horse next to the cars.

"I can't hear you. You're going to have to speak louder."

"Can't. Just get back here ..." The phone went dead. He stared at it for a microsecond.

"Protect the scene," Rye hollered. "Keep towners away from the burning wrecks. Something's going on back at HQ."

Rye sprinted towards the station, passing more rubberneckers coming out of the buildings. Something had frightened Iona, but what? The more he thought about the sound of her voice, the faster he ran.

The faux old-west street lamps came on sending pools of light to the ground. Rye dodged people in the street mumbling hasty "excuse me"s.

I can't barge into the place. Have to trust the darkness to keep me invisible. How to approach? No real cover. He focused on what Uncle Chee taught him when they hunted. Think like the prey, Chee often told him. *But I have to know what I'm hunting.* Assume a male. The worst-case scenario? *He's got Iona.*

He slowed as he approached the police station. Reaching back to the quiver, he realized he only had the explosive arrowheads, and that wouldn't work in this situation. He took a couple of deep breaths and raced to the corner of the building.

Stowing his bow and the quiver along the foundation of the station, he drew his Glock. A set of sirens out on I-8 headed away from town. A car honked down the street. His pounding heart sounded too loud in his ears. He stood outside his office but could not see through the blinds.

Go for the back door. Three. Two. One.

Ducking under the windows, he hurried to the rear entrance.

Leaning against the door, he took a few deep breaths and stepped inside.

Dark. The only light came from the emergencies. Quiet, no sound save for the undertone of the AC. Typical smells: stale coffee, sweat, disinfectant. And something else?

His eyes adjusted to the deeper darkness with aching slowness. He moved one quiet step at a time, looking for anything out of order. He paused at the Locker Room door and listened. Nil. He eased open the door on silent hinges and removed the flashlight from his belt. Shielding its light, he swept through the rooms, the locker area, the bathrooms, and the showers. Good places to hide, but no one was there.

Rye turned off the flashlight and stepped outside the locker room. A few steps brought him to the main hallway. The holding cells were to his right where Mr. Valdez awaited legal proceedings. Rye turned left, inching around the corner, and proceeded toward his office.

The peculiar scent was stronger. *A wild animal? In the station?*

Off to his right, a hallway led to the bathrooms. No one. Next came the break room. He peered through the window. Light from the vending machine lit the room. Empty.

Rye tiptoed to his office, paused, and listened. Quiet. His office door stood partially open. Watching in all directions, he pushed the door until it bumped the rubber stop. At least no one waited for him behind the door.

"Iona," he whispered.

Nothing.

"Iona," he said a tad louder.

Was that whimpering? He hurried to the backside of the desk. In the open area between the drawers, Iona scrunched down in a fetal position.

"Iona? You okay?" He holstered his gun.

"Rye?"

She rushed out of hiding and hugged him, tears soaking into his shirt.

"I saw it," she said, drawing back, staring into his eyes.

"What?"

"A Skinwalker ... headed for the cells."

CHAPTER 11

THURSDAY EVENING

Rye eased open the bottom desk drawer and took out his moccasins, slipping them on in exchange for his boots. Motioning for Iona to stay put, he hurried to the door, making all the noise of a prowling mountain lion.

Gloom enshrouded the hallway. With his Glock pointed in front of him and slightly downward, Rye tiptoed down the corridor. Finger tapping the trigger guard, he shivered from the cold air *whishing* through the AC ducts. Sweat slickened his palms, so he gripped the gun so tight he thought he could crush the magazine. He sniffed and caught the lingering musky scent of a wild animal.

Halfway down the hall, he noticed someone had left the door open a crack to Pre-Booking. None of his officers would be so foolish to break that protocol. So who …?

Rye touched the toe of his shoe against the bottom of the door and pushed. Silence permeated the darkness. The room reeked of wet fur, blood, feces, urine, and fear. Bile rose in his throat. The stench of death. But whose?

He played the beam from his flashlight across the room. Detainee benches lay on their sides. A laptop and a printer had been smashed on the floor. Paper carpeted the floor. The door leading to the cells yawned open.

"Oh no," Rye muttered.

He inched forward, gun ready to fire, and shone his light down Lockup. The door to the prisoner's cell leaned open. Shining his flashlight, he peeked.

With arms folded across his chest, the prisoner, Valdez, lay on the bottom bunk. He appeared to be in peaceful slumber ... except that his throat had been torn out. Blood splattered the cell and pooled on the floor. Bloody canine footprints marred the cell floor, yet there were none outside the cell.

Rye tried to imagine how the scene unfolded. In his mind's eye, he pictured the destruction of Pre-Booking. The thing had searched for something ... what ... the keys to Lockup and the individual cells. Then the creature savaged his prisoner and ... then ... vanished?

Rye swept through the remainder of the building, searching each room. The lingering scent of wild animal had dissipated. No bloody footprints, human or animal, appeared anywhere outside the murder scene. His Navajo half wanted to engage a native shaman. His white half urged a logical police procedure. Was this what his uncle was trying to warn him about?

Locating no further clue to the whereabouts of the killer, he returned to his office to find Iona perched on the edge of his desk. He plopped down into his chair, and she scooted close to him. She looked pale and nibbled at one fingernail, staring blankly at the wall behind him. He took her other hand and in a rush she collapsed into his arms. Minutes passed in silence wrapped in each other's hold; she, sitting on his lap and he, caressing her back.

"Oh, Rye, what is going on?"

"I don't know. But I intend to find out."

"Nobody will believe what happened here." She loosened her grip and pulled back. She studied his face, and Rye drank in her evocative stare.

Before he could stop himself, he leaned forward and kissed her. Sudden heat flooded him at the touch of her tongue, stopping time itself.

Until Iona pulled back. "I can't do this. Not while you're still married. Some women would say, 'Forget that.' I'm not like those women. I won't be a home wrecker, even if it's on the verge of collapse."

Rye rubbed his forehead, stammering, trying to find a response.

Iona stood up abruptly. "I want some coffee. I'll brew us a pot."

With one hand playing with her hair, she departed.

His chair scraped across the floor as Rye rose. "Iona."

"I'm fine," she said in a tone that told Rye she wasn't.

He glanced down at his desk pad as if it held the answers to his problems. They had always been nothing but friends, and the kiss had rattled her When she had pulled away from him, it lay bare on her face, coloring her movements. And sealing her lips. He couldn't blame her. On top of that, she'd witnessed real evil stride by her.

Rye called Yuma's Medical Examiner. Someone answered the phone after the seventh ring. He explained the situation, and the contact on the other end said the ME would get back with him. *This is one the coroner will want to see.*

Iona came back with coffees for both of them. She set one in front of Rye and returned to her spot on the desk. She blew on her coffee but didn't drink it. Rye glanced at her, but she didn't say anything.

"The ME is going to call shortly." Rye tried to steer the situation away from the precipice they stood on. "So let's cover tonight's events. What exactly happened here?"

He wasn't sure if he meant the Skinwalker or the kiss.

Rye leaned back in the chair. It objected with a long creak. He stretched out his arms and, interlacing his fingers, rested his hands on the back of his head.

Iona stared at the ground between her feet, arms folded across her chest.

"Let me postulate for a minute," he continued, emphasizing me. "I'm trying to think outside the box. Trying to make sense of this. Why would a group of Mexicans come into an American town and shoot the snot out of it? If they were trying to kill people, they did a piss poor job. Cartels have no qualms about killing innocents and do so often. So why this stunt?"

Iona shrugged, still not looking up.

"And why this acting like a Skinwalker and sneaking into a police department to murder a prisoner. The killer had to know the risk was high."

Iona shot Rye a look. "It was all a distraction."

Rye nodded, considering her comment. "But a distraction from … or … for what?"

Rye's cell interrupted the quiet with a jangling harshness. He and Iona shared stares as he reached for the phone.

Rye looked at the caller ID. "List." He pushed the answer button. "Police. Dawlsen speaking."

"Dawlsen, what the blazes is going on in my town?" Rye imagined the rank smell of the caller's cigar smoke oozing through the phone. He touched his dog tags.

"Mayor Dick, nice to talk to you too."

"Name's Richard, you half-breed."

"Did you call to discuss something, or did you just want to diss my heritage?"

"Dawlsen, you know what? You're a real piece of—"

"Coming from you, I'll take that as a compliment. Why'd you call?"

"My associate tells me a bunch of Mexicans shot up my town tonight. And I want to know what you're doing about it."

"Your associate is correct. We did have an incident in town. A few trucks blocked the plaza at Whiskey and Yuma. Shots were fired. We are now assessing the damage."

"Did you arrest those ignorant wetbacks?"

Rye closed one eye and frowned. List's racial slur had a tone of what? Not bigotry, though List excelled in that department. What then? Disingenuousness? He wasn't concerned about the damage done to the town. So why was he calling?

"No, sir," he answered in the clinical tone of reciting a report. "They fled town before pursuit could be engaged."

"Don't screw with me, Dawlsen. You're not telling me something."

"With all due respect, Dick, this is an ongoing investigation. I do not feel it appropriate at this time to release any information which would lead to useless speculation."

"Dawlsen, if you don't—"

"If I don't what?" Rye rubbed the solitary vein dividing his forehead like a mountain range. "Run this town like it's your private kingdom? Take your money under the table and look the other way? Kiss your fat pahtouy like your flunky former Chief of Police Bare-butt Jilt?"

"That's Barend Jilt, you miserable—"

"Mayor, you got exactly three seconds to make this discussion meaningful, or I'm going to hang up."

"Don't you threaten me, you bas—"

Rye slammed the phone back into its cradle. He snatched his Styrofoam cup off the desk and gulped down what remained as if he could extinguish the burning in his gut.

"I hate cold coffee." He grabbed the can and finished it. "I hate warm beer." He held out a hand to Iona. "I need some fresh air. Let's check out our crime scene."

The gunfire had ended about an hour ago, yet, the rain of explosions still echoed in Missy's mind. With hands over her head, she cowered in the dark between her bed and the wall. The very thought of turning on the lights made her want to vomit. Though she had to pee, she refused to move. She swiped at the latest trickle of tears.

Sometimes, during periods of raw emotion, Missy sensed what her twin experienced. And it worked the other way as well. Maybe Mel sensed her fear right now. Maybe Mel had left off dancing and even now rushed home. Maybe …

Mel, I need you. Come home. Por favor.

Her life had recently gone downhill … when? A shudder racked her body. *The mal Mexican tio dressed in black!* Ever since he visited the museum last week. Missy pressed her hands tighter against her skull, hopelessly trying to force away the images that flooded her mind.

He had stalked past the museum's ticket booth without so much as a hello, or a ticket, and stormed down the hall. Like he owned the freaking place. His boot heels clicked on the polished floor like gunfire. His smell reminded her of a wild animal. Snorting, she had chased him down the hall to get the admission price from him.

By the time she caught up to him and blocked his progress, he had paused outside the Skinwalker exhibit. With his nose twitching like a dog's, he removed his mirrored sunglasses and turned a gaze upon her. His ghastly yellow eyes glued her on the spot. He had shoved her aside and snarled, so she figured it best to leave this one alone. He left shortly thereafter, after visiting only the Skinwalker exhibit.

Afterwards, she had been followed everywhere she went. Sometimes it was the guy in black. Other times it was the Mexican guy with the junky pickup truck, kinda cute if not so creepy. The worst was the mayor's flunky dude. Stalking her out in the open like it was okay or something. And now ...

A car backfired, and she jumped, banging her head against the nightstand behind her. She laughed at herself, foolishly allowing her imagination to get the best of her. She heard the puttering of the backfiring car. A car door opened. Then the puttering stopped.

Thinking that odd, she scooted to the bedroom window and parted the blinds a quarter inch to peer out. The same beat-up pickup sat halfway out of a parking spot, mostly blocking the lane. The driver's door yawned open, but she spotted no movement. The faint strains of a country-western song cried out to her.

Then, like a feral beast, the man in black rose from the far side of the truck. He stared at something at his feet. Suddenly, he looked up at the window. She gasped and ducked. Her breath caught in her throat like a swallowed chicken bone.

She waited several moments before risking another peek. The pickup hadn't moved. But she saw nothing of … him.

She sensed his presence outside, biding his time. She didn't know him, didn't want to know him, and just wanted him to leave her alone. *Call Mel.*

Huddling on the floor, Missy took a deep breath and jumped atop the bed. Snatching her purse, she rolled off the side.

She dug into her purse, found her phone, and punched in Mel's number. The phone beeped for her to leave a message.

"Mel, be careful. Some creep followed me home from the club. He may have seen us together. Call me." She pushed the "end call" button and peeked out the window again. Her motorcycle waited at the far end of the lot to whisk her away.

If she didn't go now, her trepidation would destroy any stirrings of resolve. Steeling herself, Missy swept up her purse and headed for the front door. She passed Mel's room and staggered. A bloody image of Mel's face passed before her vision. Ice shivered down her spine.

Then she heard scratching at the door. Like fingernails against dry wood. She whiplashed vertically and held a hand over her mouth to blockade the scream forming deep in her throat. She took two steps back from the door.

Her cell phone rang, playing *Cowgirls Don't Cry* by Brooks and Dunn.

She jumped. A stifled shriek leaked from her mouth.

Looking at the screen, Missy sighed in relief. "Mel, I am so glad you—"

A strange scratching noise came over the phone. She pulled the phone back, staring at it as if she held a rattlesnake. The scratching over the phone matched the noise at the door. The cell dinged, indicating she had an email. With trembling hands, she checked.

From Mel?

The email contained no message, but did have a jpeg attachment. The photo displayed the bottom of their front door with its ceramic Gila monster covered in gore ... and Mel's bloody face, the blank stare of dead eyes.

She dropped the phone and screamed. And screamed until her voice disappeared.

Johnny Batts startled out of sleep, jerking his head upright. *I fell asleep on watch!* Sitting on the steps to his porch, his neck ached from the awkward sleeping position he had slumped into. He reached behind him for his rifle and grasped empty air.

He stared at the spot where his rifle should have been propped against the stairs. But it wasn't there. By the pale blue moonlight, Batts scanned the area for the weapon, thinking he may have misplaced it. However, it was nowhere to be found. He rubbed his chin, fretting over the weapon, when something else hooked his attention.

A stench in the desert night congealed like the thickening air before a storm. Batts sniffed, wrinkling his nose at the putrid air.

That smell ain't right.

With a sick wrench in his gut, he turned his head and listened, recognizing the silence.

No.

He began to walk over to the sheep pen. In three steps, his pace quickened.

No. No.

The rotting stench of death rolled into his nostrils.

Noooooo.

Dark shapes lay on the ground in the pen as if all the sheep decided to fall asleep simultaneously. Except their heads lay at odd angles to the bodies. Black pools surrounding the animals reflected the moonlight.

"Nooo!" The scream tore from his throat.

Batts pounded a fist against the top rail of the fence. Every last one of his sheep had been slaughtered. And he'd been less than a hundred yards away … sleeping.

Rye and Iona stood side-by-side at the intersection. Not as close as Rye wanted, but closer than mere friends. *Did he want to be more than friends with Iona?* Though he still had feelings for his wife, he and Dee had to decide upon a direction. However, that discussion would have to wait until after his son's karate demonstration.

Power to the shot-up streetlight had been disconnected, and it no longer sparked. Fires had been extinguished from the blackened hulks of metal. The air reeked of the violence done.

Lights from the Whiskey Plaza on the other side of the intersection lit the statue of the Chiricahua Apache warrior protecting his family. It was at this spot one such warrior had mooned the approaching cavalry and gotten away on his desert pony. Rye cracked a wry smile. The story behind the statue never ceased to amuse him.

Halogen work lamps lit up the intersection with midday brilliance. Insects buzzed in the pools of light. Firemen examined their fire hoses and started to roll them up. Sheriff's deputies had blocked off and yellow taped the intersection. FBI agents wandered through the crime scene, handkerchiefs covering their noses and mouths. Outside the taped section, crowds watched the proceedings.

Rye spotted Whitewolf standing beside a WPD crown vic on the driver's side. Whitewolf closed his eyes a moment, lowered the phone, and dragged himself over to join them.

"Bad news?" Rye could tell from his officer's normally stoic face, something bothered him.

Whitewolf stared at the ground for several seconds before looking up. "I just received word about the deputy that had been shot."

"One of Oakmann's people?" Rye asked.

Iona covered her mouth with the tips of her fingers.

Whitewolf nodded. "She didn't make it ... DOA." He paused and spotted Heilo working the scene. "It gets worse. It appears that the deputy was friends with one of our own." He nodded in the direction of Heilo.

Rye turned to look. "Oh, no."

"You want me to tell her?" Iona offered.

Rye took a long breath. "No. I'll tell her."

"No, sir," Heilo interrupted Rye's attempt at offering her time off for the next several days. "April wouldn't want that, and I want to stay busy and keep my mind off her ..." Heilo's voice faltered.

"Do what you need to do." Rye touched a finger under her chin and eased her head upward. "We're all friends here. If you need anything ..."

"Thank you, Chief. I think I'll continue processing the crime scene." She looked down and returned to her investigative duties.

Iona slipped her hand under Rye's arm and drew close to him. He breathed in the scent of her hair. Rye said, "Poor girl. Lost a friend and a fellow officer."

"Yeah. It sucks, doesn't it?"

"There's a lot in life that sucks."

Iona pulled away and stared over his shoulder.

"Rye, look." Iona pointed towards an aged pickup, alone in the gravel lot next to the Plaza. By all appearances, the truck looked abandoned.

"Stay here while I check it out." Rye unlatched the leather strap on his holster and rested a hand on the grip of his gun. He dashed across the street and approached the vehicle from the blind spot of the driver. Nothing moved inside the cab. Rye inched forward.

"You in the truck," he called out. "Put your hands on the steering and do not move." He repeated the instructions in Spanish. Silence greeted his demand. Drawing his weapon he stepped towards the driver's door. No movement. After peering through the cracked window, he loosed a sigh of relief. The truck had been vacated.

Rye motioned for Iona to join him and gave the inside of the cab a once-over. Nothing of any real interest. Keys were still in the ignition. Probably could get prints off of those.

Rye moved to the bed of the truck and peered into it. No bodies. No blood. Among the spent casings, garbage, and empty beer cans, several paper-ream boxes lay neatly wrapped in brown shipping paper.

That's odd.

After testing the strength of the mud-stained back bumper, he stepped up on it and into the truck bed. He took out his cell phone and snapped several photos of the boxes.

"Time to see what's in these boxes." He slipped on a pair of latex gloves.

He fetched a box off the truck and set it on the street. Kneeling next to the box, he stared at it, his curiosity building with each passing second.

"What do ya got?"

He looked up at Iona and suppressed a budding smile, not wanting her to know how pleased he felt about her presence.

"This box. It's wrapped in brown paper as if it's going to be shipped. But this wasn't some rush job. Someone took their time with it. There's more in the truck."

Heilo and DePute hurried across the street and flanked Iona.

"Find something?" Heilo asked.

Rye produced his switchblade and released the blade with a click. "Let's find out."

White Styrofoam peanuts fell like water droplets to reveal an old Navajo water pot, gray and clay-toned with a ropelike pattern on its rim. Iona whistled long.

"That's ancient," she said. "Looks like there's dirt still on it. I'm thinking a soil test is in order."

Rye set the pottery on the pavement next to the box. "We might have someone involved in the theft of Navajo artifacts. I have no idea how much something like this is worth."

"Is there more?" Heilo asked.

"I think so." Rye sunk his hand back into the peanuts and moved his hand around, discovering two more pots. Iona turned over the pottery, spilling plastic peanuts on the ground. Rye opened his mouth to comment about littering when a rectangular package fell out of the clay pot and landed at Iona's feet. The four traded glances.

"There's more than stolen pottery going on," DePute said.

"You think?" Heilo replied and took several photos of the package.

Rye's cell phone rang. "Dawlsen."

"Nephew, it is good to hear your voice."

"Uncle Chee?" His uncle rarely contacted him. "How's Navajoland?"

"Filled with Navajos. What did you think?"

Rye laughed. "Okay, you got me. I'm at a crime scene now, so I have to keep this short. What's on your mind?"

"You will be in Phoenix on Saturday?" He turned his statement into a question.

"Yeah," Rye said, drawing out the word. "How did you know?"

"I talked to Dee." Rye's back stiffened when he heard her name. Chee continued, "She said you'd be watching your son at karate meet. It's good for a father to care for his son."

"I guess," Rye said. He walked away from the group. "My father wasn't the best of role models. Great community leader, lousy father." He stopped at the truck's cab and peered into the window. He spotted Iona staring at his back. "Why'd Dee call you?"

"Can't go into it now. I'm using the phone at the food mart. Listen, I'll meet you in Phoenix. We have things to talk about, you and I. Things are moving through the land that are seen only when they want to be seen."

"Is this more of your Indian mumbo jumbo stuff?" Rye shook his head. Uncle Chee always tried to sound like some shamanistic mystic. *Especially to tourists when they bought his "authentic" Navajo jewelry made in China.*

"Your words wound my heart, nephew," Chee said, sounding genuinely hurt. "When will you leave for Phoenix?"

"I was planning on leaving early Saturday morning. But if you want, I can meet you Friday night. Maybe we can do dinner and talk some. I'll be at the Wyndham."

"Sounds good. Eat and talk." Chee now sounded pleased. "I will be in their lobby at seven o'clock, white man's time. I'm bringing a friend … if that's okay."

"Sure." Rye dragged out the word. "Do I know this mystery guest?"

"See you then, nephew." The phone went dead.

Rye lay on top of his bed, hands under his head, staring at the ceiling. He wore only his boxer shorts and a muscle t-shirt. Cool night air from the window caressed him. Weariness weighed heavily on him, as if his mind were sheathed in iron. Yet sleep failed him.

Tomorrow afternoon, he would leave to go up to Phoenix. Though he disliked the idea of leaving a murder investigation, he really wanted to see his boy. Perhaps, he and Dee could move forward one way or the other. Get back together or divorce?

His phone rang.

He swiped his cell phone off the shelf of his headboard. "Dawlsen."

"Chief? Heilo." Her tone chased away any sleepiness Rye might have felt. "Looks like we got ourselves another murder. And it ain't pretty."

They never are.

CHAPTER 12

LATE THURSDAY NIGHT

"Uhmmm ... where's the body." Rye stifled a yawn behind a cupped hand. Weariness weighed at his shoulders like anvils. If he weren't so numb from lack of sleep, the ache alone would keep him awake.

He fixated upon the blood-spattered apartment door and the puddle at its base. Lots of blood. Directional splatter higher up. He tore his gaze away.

These apartments had been remodeled from an old 50s two-story hotel. The redesign maintained the décor of an old west hotel. The second floor balcony, complete with a rustic wooden railing, led to stairs at each end. The parking lot was half empty. The lightbar on Heilo's car flashed its alternating red-blue-red-blue on surrounding objects. Rye yawned again and shook his head.

"Good question, huh, Chief?" Heilo brushed back a disobedient strand of hair. She looked as tired as he felt, though she probably pushed herself to keep her mind off the death of her friend.

"Who called it in?"

"A neighbor."

"Interview 'em yet?"

"Just the basics." She opened her notebook. "He'd been out drinking, so he was low on the coherent scale. Says he just moved in, so he didn't really know who lived here. And he's got an alibi."

"We can follow up tomorrow when he's sobered up. Whose apartment is this?" Rye nodded at the door.

"Don't know." Heilo shrugged then tugged on her vest. "I contacted the manager. He should be here any minute." She pointed to the blood pooled at the doorstep. "I put up the tape as soon as I got here, so I don't think the scene was contaminated. Especially that."

For a moment, Rye's sleep deprivation prevented his mind from registering to what Heilo pointed. He stared at the dark stain, lights glistening in its moisture. The fresh blood hadn't coagulated yet. He rubbed his eyes with the heels of his hands and looked again. Then he saw the tracks of boots.

He knelt on his good knee and bent over. The right footprint had the same strange nick in the heel as the boot prints at the Arches' death scene.

He rose with a grimace.

"Knee bothering you?"

"Right now, everything hurts." Rye adjusted his belt. *A beer sounds good.* "Did you check the apartment?"

"I tapped on the window. Nobody answered. I stayed away from the door ... didn't want to disturb the crime scene. So we don't mess up any evidence, it's probably best we go in through the back whenever the manager gets ... Ahhh, here he comes."

A balding man approached, head down and arms pumping, his bulky beer-drinker's paunch jouncing. In his 40s, Rye guessed.

"Chief," Heilo said, "this is Geoff Anderson. He's the manager of the apartments."

"Mr. Anderson," Rye said, holding out his hand to shake, "can you tell us who rents this apartment?"

He took Rye's hand and gave it a bone-crushing grasp. "Yep." Anderson fumbled with a ring of keys numbering well over a dozen.

"Aaaaa ... Mr. Anderson, who ..." Heilo said.

"That'd be them Visser twins—"

"Missy and Mel, if I remember."

"That's them. Work at the museum. Terrible thing 'bout that there break-in. Nice gals, jist not too bright. I had to kick more'n one cowboy outta their apartment. Party girls, if you catch my meaning. They in trouble?"

Rye pointed to the blood at the doorstep. "You tell me."

Anderson's face blanched. "Awwww, no. *Esto es muy malo.* They's mama's in the hospital dying of cancer and all. They don't need this." He held up the key ring to catch the light from streetlamps. "Aha." Flourishing one key up like an obscene gesture, he worked it off the key ring. "It'll open the entrance here and the back door to their apartment."

Rye took the offered key. "Thanks. We'll return the key as soon as we're done here. Now if you'll kindly ... wait a second." Rye held up an index finger. "You're just the manager, right?" Anderson nodded. "Let me ask you, who owns the complex?"

"That would be Mayor List. Been owner for going on ten years now. Why'd you ask?"

"Just curious. Never can tell when a piece of information will solve a case." Rye pointed with an open hand toward the edge of the parking lot, indicating that the man should leave.

Muttering about losing his sleep, the manager waddled down the balcony to the stairs.

They walked around to the back, and Rye noticed every back entrance had a shower stall-sized square of concrete. The breeze stilled as if the darkness held its breath. Sounds of the town's nightlife mixed with the buzz of the insect nightlife. Rye unlocked the door and pushed it open, its hinges squeaking. Heilo found a light switch and flipped it on. A single uncovered light bulb dangled from the second floor ceiling, casting the stairwell in a soft gloom.

Rye pointed to the light. "I'm not up on my rental property laws, but I'd say that unprotected light bulb represents a violation of the building code. I'll just have to bring that to the good mayor's attention next time I have the displeasure of talking to him."

They went up the stairs and found the apartment number to the Vissers' back door.

"Got your vest on, Chief?" Heilo had her gun aimed and her flashlight poised.

Rye tapped his chest, so she could hear it. With that sound, adrenaline flooded into Rye's system, and his weariness faded. He saw the same in Heilo's eyes.

Rye slipped on a pair of latex gloves and tried the door handle. *Locked.* He inserted the key into the lock and, as quietly as he could manage, unlocked the door. The click sounded too loud in his ears. He drew his gun and turned on his flashlight, then nodded to Heilo. She returned his nod. He shoved open the door, and they swept into the apartment.

"Police!" yelled Rye. "Don't move."

"WPD! Anyone here?" hollered Heilo.

No answer.

"Police!" Heilo moved in one direction.

"Whiskey Police!" Rye headed the opposite. He passed through the kitchen, noticing all the knives were in the knife block. He hurried into the living room, decorated in southwestern furnishings.

"We have signs of a struggle," Rye yelled out.

Magazines lay helter-skelter beside the overturned coffee table. A lampshade hung off kilter. Several pieces of furniture pushed aside. But no bodies. And no bad guys.

"Clear!" yelled Rye.

Moments later, from a back room, Heilo returned his yell. "Clear."

Rye played his flashlight along the floor. He hoped to find evidence the girls were okay, yet it didn't feel that way. The preliminary evidence indicated a struggle. Violent. Perhaps fatal.

Rye glanced up from his search to see Heilo standing in the exit from the living room to a hallway. She nodded down the hallway.

"Chief, you gotta see this."

The hallway had three bedrooms and a bathroom leading from it. The door to the last bedroom had been left partially open. A bloody boot print decorated the center of the door, the frame splintered at the catch.

Rye nodded, raising his gun. Heilo pushed open the door with the toe of her shoe. She shined her flashlight around the room. It contained shelves filled with what appeared to be Navajo and Hopi pottery. It took a couple of seconds before the brunt of what he saw revealed itself.

"Yeah," said Heilo, "my thoughts exactly."

"This is ... stuff ... from the museum?" said Rye.

"Without checking the records, it's hard to say for sure. See the twirled rope, look? Resembles what we found in the back of the truck."

"What are they doing here? The Vissers probably don't have that kind of money. It's expensive to start an extensive Navajo pottery collection."

"Perhaps we found a black market dealer in Indian antiquities."

"And motive for murder. I wonder …" He shone his light on a blank spot on a shelf. Dust had gathered on the shelves, but a couple spots indicated things had been removed recently.

Rye picked up a pot next to a blank spot, shining light into the interior.

"Hello. What do we have here?"

Holding the pot with one arm, he swiped a finger of the other hand along the bottom of the inside. He eased his hand out of the pot and held up his index finger. A white powder coated the tip.

"Wanna bet that's Cocaine?" he said. "Instead of antiquities theft, we might have part of a narcotics ring. But the Vissers? Doesn't sound right."

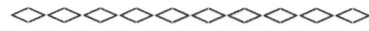

Rye leaned against his Tahoe. He felt like he'd just gone through a marathon weight training session. He closed his eyes as his mind drifted off to sipping on a cold beer in a cheap honky tonk.

"Chief," Heilo said. "Chief, you okay?" A hand shook his shoulder.

Rye opened one eye, yawned. "Yeah. I'm fine. Just tired."

"Fell asleep standing up, huh? I've like done that before." DePute stood beside Rye. "In Afghanistan. I was on patrol and we took 5. I'd leaned up against whatever was handy."

"Not me," said Heilo. "I have trouble falling asleep." She stifled a yawn.

A black SUV pulled into the parking lot. The coroner from Yuma slid out of the vehicle and called out a greeting. The man's shoulders slumped like someone accustomed to violent death. He fetched his medical bag from the back of the vehicle and made his way over to them.

He held out his hand. "Rye, I wish I could say it's good to see you. But there's always death when you call. And, recently, you've been calling way too often."

Rye took his hand and pressed firm. "Good to see you too, Doc. I hate to call you for the same reason. I think you know these officers."

The coroner shook hands with them then faced Rye.

"Call said this was a weird one. Where's the body?"

"No body, just a big pool of blood. Need your take on it."

The coroner shifted his position and opened his mouth to say something when his head erupted in a shower of blood and brains. The air tasted of coppery death. The report of a rifle echoed off the surrounding buildings.

Rye dropped to his knees. His bad knee cracked, but he didn't feel pain with the adrenaline suddenly coursing through his veins. His gun appeared in his hand. The two officers joined him at the base of the SUV.

"Where did that come from?" DePute yelled.

"Can't tell," Rye said, his weariness gone. "One shot. Efficient." He risked a peek over the hood of his Tahoe. "But if I had to guess, from the angle of the shot, I'd say it came from that restaurant. Or close to it." He ducked back down.

"I think that bullet was meant for you, Chief," said Heilo looking at the coroner. "Is he ..."

"Dead?" Rye finished her question. "With half his skull blown away, I'm gonna go out on a limb here and say yeah." He peeked through the driver's window. Scanning the area, he spotted movement on the roof of the restaurant.

"Over there. On the roof," Rye pointed. "DePute, take the front. Heilo, with me."

They raced toward the line of palm trees at the edge of the parking lot, guns ready. When they reached the trees, Rye spotted a white Ford F150 fishtailing out of a parking lot. A light from the back of the truck was out. Dust from the tires rose into the air. He cursed. *Too far away for a shot.*

"I see him, Chief." Heilo yelled. "You know who drives a pickup like that?" Her voice said she had the answer.

Two names came immediately into Rye's mind. "Depending on the model year, Batts has an older one. Barend Jilt—List's associate, mind you—drives a newer make. But I didn't get a good enough look."

There it was. A connection to both of his suspects.

He slammed his foot down on the accelerator and sped away. He pounded a fist against the steering wheel while a stream of curses poured out of his mouth. *Why did that fool doctor have to move at the last second? I had Dawlsen dead to rights.*

He got his cell phone and speed dialed the same number.

"Negative," he said when the ringing stopped.

"Our friend will not be happy." The line went dead.

He rolled down the window. Just ahead I-8 crossed over the Mohawk Canal. Slowing down on the bridge over the canal, he reached his arm out the window and tossed the phone over the cab.

Time for Plan B ... in Phoenix.

Chee lay with eyes closed on the beat-up couch. He had said his night prayers and now wanted to sleep. Despite the night's chill, the windows stayed open. A desert breeze blew through the torn screens, carrying the nocturnal harmony. He nodded in the spiritual satisfaction of being connected to the land of the *Diné*, smiling at the call of the coyote.

"Sing to me, little brother."

His stomach sated with fry bread, Chee dropped into sleep. In his dream, he saw a young woman standing outside his trailer. She waited for his permission to enter. He owned very little and kept his home clean. No need to make preparations for his guest.

In his dream, he went to the door of his trailer and held it open for the woman.

"Ya'at'eeh.' *Hello.* "Come."

"No," she said. "You are asleep, and I want to speak with you. I will wait."

Chee's eyes blinked open. He pushed up off the couch and crossed the floor of worn boards. Peeking out the door's window, he spotted the real version of the dream woman. The moon bathed her in silvery light. In a white gown, she looked like a spirit. Her black hair hung to her waist, and she stared at her bare feet so Chee could not see her face. He sensed a great spirit power within her.

He opened the door, its hinges squeaking loud in the night.

"Come." Chee motioned to the woman.

"Yes. Now that you are awake, I can speak to you."

She crossed the sandy land between her and his trailer without looking up. At his door, she raised her head and leveled dark eyes at him. Chee recognized her. The witch he was to take to Rye. Chee shivered, feeling her shaman powers wash over him. He swallowed the growing lump of fear.

"Your nephew," she said with a tone of dread, "is hunted by a great evil. We need to go to him sooner. He needs our help, or he won't be alive this time tomorrow."

CHAPTER 13

FRIDAY MORNING

Rye struggled into wakefulness. A glimpse through one bleary eye confirmed his location as his bedroom. Rolling his head back and forth, he cast a glance at the clock. 9:12. Morning? Yeah, from the light coming in through the window.

With a groan, he swung his legs over the side of the bed and pushed into a sitting position. Head hanging low, he stared down at his hairy legs sticking out of dark boxers. With a sigh, he rose to his feet and headed into the master bathroom. Relieving himself, he stared at his image in the mirror over the toilet.

"You need some coffee," he told the reflection.

After splashing cold water on his face, Rye stumbled back through his bedroom, into the hall. He prepared the coffee pot and headed to the living room to wait for it to brew. He stopped.

Lying on the couch under a sheet, Heilo slept, hair spilling across a pillow. One arm protruded from the sheet, hand resting next to her handgun on the table. Beside the gun sat her neatly folded uniform. Under the table, she had lined up her shoes heel-to-heel and toe-to-toe. A slight snore escaped from her lips.

Did we …?

With a snort, she woke and sat up on the couch. The sheet tumbled from her shoulders to reveal a black sports bra.

"*Buenos dias*, Chief." She yawned and stretched.

"Morning, Heilo." He hesitated. Then, pointing a finger back and forth between them, he asked, "Did we … you know …"

"Have sex?" She laughed then coughed. "No. You were so tired, I drove you home and dragged your butt to bed. I straightened up your casa a bit. When I went out to my car, I found all four tires slashed. I figured I'd stay the night."

He held out his hands as if to stop someone. "Someone slashed your tires?"

"Yeah. Pissed me off royally, but I was too tired to do anything."

"We could have been killed in our sleep." Rye paced, rubbing the top of his head.

She shrugged. "Don't sound so disappointed."

Rye pointed his thumb over his shoulder. "Take a shower. I'll round us up some breakfast. After we eat, I'll get someone from the garage to come out and fix your tires."

She stood, unabashed in her bra and panties.

Rye turned his head. "Towels are in the cabinet."

After finishing a breakfast of scrambled eggs, coffee, and conversation, Rye stood in the shower enjoying the lukewarm water.

In the bedroom, toweling off, he heard the crunch of tires. Peering through the venetian blinds, he observed Iona exiting her Land Rover.

Great. Just what I need.

Before he could do a thing, he heard Heilo fling open the front door.

"Welcome to Rye Dawlsen's trailer," Heilo said in a sing-songy voice. "The sleeping quarters for exhausted cops."

Iona froze at the bottom of the stairs, her eyes wide. "Cora?"

Rye shoved on a pair of pants and a gray WPD t-shirt. He rushed to stand behind Heilo. "Who?"

"Corazón Heilo." Hand on a hip, Heilo tilted her head at him. "You don't know my first name, Chief?"

Iona turned a gaze on him, and he felt the heat rise on his face. "It's not—"

"I don't want to know," Iona said, raising a hand to silence him. Pounding up the wooden steps to the front door she shouldered her way past them, a sneer crinkling her lips. She stopped as her gaze slipped to the sheets on the couch.

"Nothing happened, I swear," Rye said.

"Are you done with your sleepover?" She crossed her arms under her breasts, tapping a foot.

Heilo pointed at her car and snapped, "Look at my vehicle ..." But when her mouth formed a "b," Rye shook his head no. Heilo huffed then added, "Someone slashed my tires after I got the Chief into his house." She leveled an icy stare at Iona. "How am I supposed to go home with four freaking flats?"

The two women stared daggers at one another. Rye wanted to crawl back to the bathroom and hide.

"Whatever." Iona broke the silence flinging her hands in a frustrated gesture. "Don't just stand there like a pair of goons. Finish getting dressed." She turned her narrowed gaze upon Rye. "I'll take you both into Whiskey."

165

Minutes later, they got into Iona's Land Rover. Silence hung like an ice cloud inside the car. Even the desert heat failed to provide warmth.

Near the end of SR01, Rye asked Iona to stop her vehicle. She stared straight ahead and didn't slow down. Several sarcastic remarks came to his mind, but he thought it best not to say any of them.

"I want to get my newspaper." He pointed to the mailboxes with the newspaper tube underneath.

Iona sighed and pulled over to the row of dust covered plastic boxes, refusing to look at him. She pressed her lips together to signal her unwillingness to talk. He closed the car door a little too hard and went over to his box. Looking skyward at the darkness gathering in the southwest, he reached for the newspaper tube when a sudden pounding on the glass halted him.

"Chief, don't move!" Heilo screamed, both fists striking the window.

That's when he heard it, the sinister rattle icing his blood. He caught the scent of cucumbers and glanced down at the tube. Instead of the day's paper, a rattlesnake lay inside, coiled and ready to strike, its tongue flicking like lightning strikes. It pulled its head back. Taking a deep breath then holding it, Rye eased his hand out of range in slo-mo and stepped backwards.

"Nice snake," he whispered to the animal. "Nice stupid snake hanging out in my newspaper tube." He hoped the soothing tone took away the snake's combativeness. "I'd wanna bite someone too if some moron stuck me in a tube."

He slid back into the passenger's seat and grabbed its edge to steady his shaking hands.

"Thanks, Heilo. I owe you one."

"Don't mention it." Looking at the window, she rattled off a string of profanity in Spanish at the snake.

"I hate to state the obvious," Iona said. "But snakes don't hang out in newspaper tubes." Turning to Rye, she added, "Looks like someone wants you dead."

Iona hit the brakes and squealed to a halt outside Heilo's tiny homestead.

"Get out," Iona said. She gripped the steering wheel with white-knuckled firmness and stared out her side window.

Rye clenched his teeth so as not to say something to aggravate the tension. He and Heilo exchanged glances. Rye nodded once. Without a word, she slipped out the car and slammed the door shut. Rye turned at the tapping at his window, and Heilo stood there, motioning for him to open his window. He lowered it.

"I'm gonna grab a few hours of sleep and come into HQ," she said. She didn't look at Rye, but stared at Iona. "I'm not ashamed of what happened between us."

"But I thought nothing ..."

"That's right. Nothing happened, so I have nothing to be ashamed of." She saluted and scuffled away, shoulders slumped.

Rye risked a glance at Iona. She stared straight ahead, eyes cold.

"Hurricane's coming," Rye said, hoping to break the ice.

She wheeled upon him. "Did you sleep with her?"

Rye sat back, straighter. "No. Heilo? No." He shook his head and laughed nervously. "No. Didn't you just hear?"

"You better not have." She turned to stare straight ahead. "You're still married."

She shoved the gearshift into drive and lead-footed away from the curb. Minutes later, she pulled into the back parking lot of the twins' apartment and pulled alongside Rye's Tahoe.

"Thanks, Iona ... I ..."

"Get out. I might talk to you later."

She pulled away and left Rye staring down at his feet. There were days he just didn't understand women. Iona had made him feel guilty, and he hadn't even done anything to feel guilty.

After driving back to HQ, Rye stopped at the Pre-Booking Room and swept off his western hat. Yellow police tape blocked the door. He stared at the chaos.

"Soooo," he said, tapping his hat against his leg, "what exactly are we dealing with here? What happened, who caused this, why, and how?"

"What happened," Reese said, coming down the hallway, "is that we lost a prisoner. I spent over two hours processing Pre-Book and Lockup. Lots of blood in the cell, but I think it's all from our guest. I took several samples. Got beaucoup photos. How the unsub got to him, I don't have an answer."

"This case just keeps getting better and better. The victim wanted a lawyer to do his will," Rye said. "Did he talk to anyone?"

Zach scratched his head. "I don't think so. But I'll check on it. I was headed to the museum. I'm chasing down a thought."

"Good, just keep me in the loop. And be careful of your eye. Don't push things ..."

Zach waved a hand to say he didn't want to hear any more about his eye and disappeared into the Patrol Office.

Rye's cell phone rang. "Dawlsen here."

"What the ... what's going on there?"

"Good morning, Mayor List," Rye said with a phony sweetness. "How may I help you?"

Curses exploded over the phone. "Don't jerk me around, Dawlsen."

Rye smiled, imagining the mayor's face turning beet red. "Fine. Last night we had a shooting incident in town involving several Mexicans. Drug cartel I suspect. Our prisoner was killed in his cell. That would be your buddy you wanted to spring and, no, I'm not releasing details at this time. The Visser twins are missing and presumed dead. And finally, the Yuma ME was gunned down when he showed up to investigate a crime scene. I got very little sleep, and I need more freaking coffee. How's that for an update?"

"Listen, Dawlsen, if you can't control my town, then I'm going to remove you from office and place my own man back in there."

Rye barked a laugh. "You're joking, right? You're going to put your flunky Jilt back in as chief of police? Don't be a bonehead, Dick." He ran that together to make it sound more like an insult. "After all the corruption under Jilt's stint as Chief of WPD, he has a snowball's chance on the Palomas Plain of running this department."

"At least he didn't have gun battles in the street."

"That's because the bad guys were in his office downing Mexican beers and smoking Mexican weed." Rye felt his gut tighten, and he squeezed the phone until his hand shook. "Mayor, I am getting off the phone before one of us says something we'll regret later. And, Dick ..."

"What is it, Dawlsen?"

"Don't ever. Threaten. My job. Again. You got that?" And he jabbed the disconnect button.

Rye hovered behind Zach, both staring at a folder on his computer.

"These are pictures I took at the museum," Zach said. He clicked open the folder. A dozen pictures were lined up on the monitor. "This is the newspaper article Ms. Haulke wrote about the exhibit." Another click opened a PDF file. Zach opened a third file. "Here's close-ups of the two photos she published."

"Okay, what do you have?" Rye's vision roamed over the various files and nothing jumped out at him.

"It took me a while, but I kept looking at these pictures. Here, this one is from the opening of the exhibit. See all the people standing for the photo? There's the Arches." He pointed to a smiling Helen and a frowning Terrance. "Here and here are the Visser twins." His finger pointed to the two of them partially hidden by the crowd. "In the back row, we have the mayor and Jilt."

Then Rye saw it. The man in black stood behind Jilt.

"I believe," Zach said, his finger touching a face in the monitor, "that is our person of interest."

"You're on to something here. Can you zoom in?"

"I can. But wait … there's more." Zach panned to the other photo from the exhibit. "This is a photo of the Skinwalker exhibit taken the day the exhibit opened. Here," Zach again pointed, "we have something like a Sioux ghost dance outfit. But it's not Sioux. According to the plaque under the photo, it's a Skinwalker shirt meant to resemble a wolf."

"I never heard of such a thing."

"Me neither, but that's what the blurb said. Who knows? Now," Zach said, dramatically dragging out the word, "look at this photo. I took this one the day after the break-in."

"Yeah. I saw the Skinwalker shadowbox. The shirt had been replaced by the wall mounted exhibit of a Mexican Skinwalker." Rye paused. "And the man in the photo is the spitting image of our mysterious man in black."

Zach turned his chair and looked up at Rye. "That shirt is missing. It's not on any list in any museum report I read. I mean they had to store it someplace, right?"

"Okay, Sherlock, I can tell you've got something you're wanting to spill."

"This is in my report, but one of the people I interviewed for the Arches' murder reported seeing a wolf." Zach pointed at the monitor. "Perhaps what they saw was a man wearing that."

Rye ran a hand across his chin. "Okay. Go back and interview those people again. See if you can get Iona to go with you."

"You want me to do what?" Hands on hips, Iona stood in the doorway.

Rye gave her a wary look. "You up for some field work? I need someone to assist Zach, if you can spare an hour or two. He can explain on the way."

She returned his gaze. "Sure, why not. I only have a newspaper to run and a book deadline to meet. Besides, riding around with virile young men ..." she said, a smile gracing her lips, "is my idea of a good afternoon."

CHAPTER 14

FRIDAY AFTERNOON

Rye drove East on I-8, the knobby tires of his Tahoe droning on the pavement. Sunlight bounced off his outside mirror, and he slipped on reflective sunglasses to keep the glare out of his eyes. The AC, at war with the outside temps, blasted into his face.

He passed miles of baked land dotted with creosote bush and cactus, cut by the occasional dry creek beds and intruded upon by desert-bleached towns. Tall hills and mountainous backdrops relieved this realm of thorns and colorless sand.

Country music from the satellite radio filled his loneliness. He crooned off-key when he knew a song and tapped the rhythm on the steering wheel when he didn't. Just then, the song *Drinking My Baby Goodbye* by Charlie Daniels came on the radio.

The song sparked a night he wished never to recall. It started drunk and ended worse. It was the night Dee left him.

The sudden blare of a truck's air horn shattered Rye's retrospection. While daydreaming, he had drifted to the wrong side of the road. He jerked the steering wheel to the right. The semi whistled past like a wall of white rock. The SUV shook. For a minute, Rye's heart pounded in his chest while he castigated himself for letting his mind wander.

A few miles down the road, he spotted a green road sign warning of his exit coming up in two miles.

Rye shook his head. He hadn't been there for Manny for many years. Or for Dee. Then she took drastic measures and had left him.

And what had he done in the intervening months? His answer tasted like bile: nothing. He had just let her go. In the end, he'd run from her just as she ran from him.

He came to his exit and headed north. Just another dusty desert highway. A wasteland.

Just like my life.

Although he preferred one of the small cheaper hotels on the outskirts of Phoenix, he figured he'd splurge this one time and got a room at the Wyndham close to Manny's tournament. Besides, he only planned to stay for two nights.

Tomorrow, he'd be with Dee watching their son at his chosen sport. Manny's progress at his karate lessons made Rye's heart swell with pride. When he talked to him on the phone, the kid sounded ... what ... more self-assured. More confident. It seemed to be doing the boy some good.

At a light, a blue Ford F-150 pickup truck pulled up next to him. The driver, of Hispanic descent, looked vaguely familiar. The man pulled his Cardinal's ball cap low.

Rye turned to face forward. The man's actions raised his suspicion flag. Rye frowned. *Now where have I seen ...?*

The light turned green, and he went to the next block before turning left. The blue F-150 went straight. Rye waited for the truck to pass to get its license plate number. But the mud plastered on it only gave him a partial. He'd check it out when he got home.

The fleeting glance of the truck driver's face gnawed at Rye's memory. The man was wanted for something, and Rye swore he'd find what that was.

Driving through downtown and admiring all the high-rise buildings, Rye found the Wyndham with its half circular balconies resembling a giant beehive.

He pulled into valet parking, fetched his overnight bag from the trunk, and headed into the hotel. A pretty girl with dark hair and tanned skin smiled as he approached the front desk. Behind her, copper squares mounted on the wall burnished in the lights.

"I have a room registered under the name of Dawlsen. Rye Dawlsen," he told her.

While she brought up his registration on the computer, he studied the bar. Dark paneling separated by built-in glass shelves. Several tables of black wood and leather seats. Some occupied. The bartender talked with two forty-ish women dressed in stylish business suits. Several men at one table broke out in drunken laughter. One glanced at him then averted his eyes. *Like he didn't want me to know he was watching.*

Rye stared at the bottles behind the bar as if he were considering a drink before heading to his room. This gave him opportunity to scrutinize the men. Though they were well dressed, Rye noticed one man had a gang tattoo almost hidden by the sleeve of his suit.

"Mr. Dawlsen ..." the girl called him back to finish the registration.

"Sorry," he said. "I'm tired from the drive."

She smiled in faux sympathy.

He took his keycard with a word of thanks and cut a circular path around the lobby's pillars. He passed the table of men, who turned silent at Rye's approach. They glowered at him. Whistling a tune, he headed to the elevators. At the sixth floor, he got off and went in search of his room. Rye found it at the end of the hallway, unlocked the door, and went in. A clean scent dusted the air.

After dumping his stuff on the bed, he gazed out the balcony window. In the street below, traffic inched along and people scurried in and out of buildings. After adjusting the air conditioning to his liking, he sat on the bed and got his cell phone.

"Whiskey 911," said Gabby. "What's your emergency?"

"Hey, girl. Dawlsen here. Anything up?"

"Chief," Gabby answered with a joyous tone, "it's good to hear from you. Did the trip go okay? Of course it did, otherwise you wouldn't be calling and asking if anything happened. But since you've left, things have been good here. At least, no more bodies ... yet." She took a breath, and Rye attempted to say something, but Gabby interrupted him. "Whitewolf's called in. He's investigating the deputy's murder. Claims there's a connection between that and the other homicides. But he didn't provide any details. Least ways, he didn't share any with me."

"Uh, Gabby?" Rye tried to pry in a word. What was Noah up to? Let the Sheriff's Department investigate that.

She hurried on. "Zach's busy doing something with Iona at the museum. Again, he didn't tell me nothing, so I have nothing to report there. Except that he is doing something, I just don't know what it is. Heilo is at the shooting range, practicing her gunmanship—as if she needed to improve. She's already the best shooter in the state.

And Batty called, but won't leave me with any details except to say someone killed all his sheep last night and that a strange truck stopped by the mailboxes this morning. So basically, everybody is busy, and I'm in the dark."

"Gabby," Rye cut her off with a sharp tone, "come up for air. Did Batts give any details about the truck at the mailboxes?"

"Just that he saw two men and a Ford pickup. But other than that he was sketchy on details. I didn't know it was important or I'd've push him for more info."

"No, you did good." Rye motioned with his palm outward. "I'll give him a call. You hold down the fort, and I'll talk to you when I get back. Later."

Rye dropped the cell next to him and remained seated on the bed. A murderer had settled into his town. They had no concrete evidence or even a solid lead. Yet the man in black intrigued him. Rye had not seen him around town until the day he and Zach arrested Valdez at the Drivin' Diner.

Then, there was Batts with his erratic behavior. He'd been spotted in the proximity of the Arches' murder. But then, he did report the Ford F-150 sighting. Could it be the one he had seen a little bit ago?

And what about those three bloody letters at the Arches? Did they implicate his uncle? Hopefully, Chee would have an alibi. Rye checked his watch. An hour to go before meeting Uncle Chee. He needed to either prove or clear his uncle of causing the Skinwalker problems. He'd look into Chee's eyes and ask him point-blank. Then he'd know one way or the other.

Perhaps he should get downstairs early and look around. Rye slipped into his shoulder holster, checked his Glock and its magazine, then re-holstered the weapon. Despite the heat, he slipped on his jacket. Wanted to look good for Chee and his mystery guest. He put on his Stetson and left.

The elevator dinged, and stepping inside, he pushed the button to the parking garage.

The elevator opened and the smell of hot metal and asphalt blew into his face. A car door slammed nearby, and Rye caught up to the Mexican valet, who pointed the direction to Rye's vehicle.

Rye anticipated meeting Dee tomorrow. Did she still wear a trace of that perfume—what's it called—Ralph Lauren Blue? Or did she wear something new? He imagined Manny's smiling face as the boy raced into his arms.

He had just reached his car when a yell exploded close by. In the far corner of the lot, two males in their mid to late thirties argued nose to nose. One sported a ball cap, and the other appeared to be the valet. Ball Cap pushed the other man away. The valet threw a weak punch into the Ball Cap's gut, causing him to bend over double. The valet stood over him with his fists raised in a menacing gesture. He yelled something, but the noise echoed off the cement walls, and Rye couldn't tell what was said.

Rye fished out his badge and held it up. Pulling out his Glock, he walked toward the two, his handgun pointed downwards.

"Hey!" Rye shouted. "What's going on?"

The two ignored him.

"Police!" Rye shouted. "Freeze!"

Moving closer, Rye thought the two sounded drunk. He hated angry drunks. The situation never turned out well for anyone.

"PO-LICE" Rye bellowed. He passed one of the thick cement

columns. A warning surged through Rye's mind. Something didn't look right.

At that moment, Ball Cap stood upright and unfazed. Rye recognized the man. He faced the driver of the blue Ford F150 truck.

"Got you, po-po," a familiar voice said behind him. A hard object crashed down on his head, sending a shower of white sparks whirling through his vision. He felt the cool cement against his cheek and realized he had fallen. A hand rolled him over and grabbed the front of his shirt. Someone raised him off the cement. A familiar face swam into view. Yet, the owner's name refused to surface in his vertigo world. A fist shot like a rocket towards his face. In the next breath, his world went black.

CHAPTER 15

FRIDAY NIGHT

Beep. Beep. Beep.

Rye cracked open an eye. Lights overhead.

Beep. Beep. Beep.

"Rye? You awake?"

A familiar voice.

"Rye." The voice came into his vision, an indistinct shape. "This is your uncle."

"Chee?" Rye licked his lips. One side felt ... enlarged. Tasted of blood. "Where ..."

"You're in a hospital. You got beat up pretty bad."

He heard another familiar voice. A woman's. But from a distant memory. *Who's that?*

Rye opened his eyes, or tried to open both. One eye refused. The other eye found Chee, a worried smile worn on his wind-aged face. Rye couldn't help but wonder if he was looking into the face of a killer. Time for that discussion later. Like when he could talk without pain oozing from his pores.

"We," a shallow breath and a wince, "need to," another shallow breath, "talk."

"Later. How do you feel, nephew?" Chee asked.

"Did someone get the serial number," Rye paused, the words leaking out of his mouth like a weak faucet drip, "of the Abrams M1 tank?"

Chee laughed.

Rye closed his eye. "Don't ... laugh."

"Stop telling jokes."

"How?"

"How to stop telling jokes?" Chee said.

"Find ... me."

"A mutual friend knew you were in trouble. She led me to the Wyndham parking lot. I found three men beating up on you. One had just lifted you halfway off the ground and hit you in the face." Chee laughed silently. "I scare them good. White men fear drunken crazy Indian."

"Then ... you saw them?"

"Yeah. I gave their descriptions to the police."

"Thanks."

"Don't mention it." Chee cleared his throat and shot a look to a distant part of the room. "There's somebody else waiting here for you?"

A beautiful Native woman with long black hair came into view. Despite being much older than the last time he saw her, Rye knew her in a second.

"Sunflower?"

"It is. How are you feeling, Rye Dawlsen?" Her toothy smile failed to mask her concern.

"Seeing you always makes me feel better."

Her smile faded. "I contacted Chee. An evil trouble surrounds you. I see it in my dreams."

Rye did not have time to reply as a nurse, wearing Looney Toons scrubs, walked in to check his condition. She forced him to use her thermometer. Checked his pulse. Checked his fluids. Looked at his IV and turned to leave. "That's all, folks," she said.

"Nurse … wait," he called out. *I can't miss Manny's tourney.*

"Yes?"

"What time is it?"

"It's a little after midnight. You're here for observation. You got a nasty knock on the head. Your ribs are bruised. You have a tiny fracture at your eye socket, probably from a punch. I'd hate to be on the giving end of that. The owner's hand probably suffered significant bruising. You received numerous hits or kicks, which will be sore and bruised. Other than that, I think you'll live."

"I need to get out of here by eight."

"If the doctor—" She cocked her head and frowned.

"No, you don't understand." Rye paused, grunting at the sharp sting in his ribs. "I have to get back to …" The injured ribs forced him to silence. *I have to get back to my family. That's what I have to get back to.*

"I'll check with the doctor." She stared down at him and sighed. "If there are no complications, I see no problem getting you out of here by then. Except, you'll be hurting with every move."

He grinned and then winced. "I'm a big boy. I can handle it."

The nurse smiled and left. Chee leaned over the bed.

"Nephew, I know one of the men who hurt you."

Rye raised one eyebrow. "Go on."

Chee paused and looked around as if to make sure no one could hear him. "He works for Mayor List ... that former Chief of Police ... Barend Jilt."

CHAPTER 16

SATURDAY MORNING AND AFTERNOON

Rye eased out of the cab, every move accompanied by a groan. Though he stood with most of his weight on his good leg, his damaged knee protested any load.

"This hurts worse than sticking a cactus up your nose." Leaning against the cab, Rye looked up at the steel canopies of the convention center jutting out over the street. Sunlight reflected off their beams. His first visit to the convention center, he brought Dee on a date for some event. His memory failed at recalling the event, but he'd never forget their kiss-fest stroll across the glassed-in walkway.

Chee paid the cabbie while Sunflower helped Rye step up out of the street. Their cab pulled away and another pulled to the curb.

Rye hobbled a few steps by himself. Sweat covered his face. His uncle came alongside. "Lean on me, Nephew."

"Thanks," Rye said, putting his arm around Chee's shoulders. He marveled at the strength he felt in his uncle. He took several steps before his injured knee buckled.

Rye glanced at Chee and grunted, "I hate that. I hate when that happens."

"How did those men attack you?"

Rye pursed his lips in consideration. "They set me up. Staged a fight. I tried to stop it. That's when they jumped me."

"Why would they do that?"

Rye studied his uncle's weathered face for a few seconds. "They're List's men. It appears the mayor wants me out of the way for some reason."

"He is one bad round-eye," Chee said.

Sunflower interrupted, "If we want to make the meet on time, we'll have to drag this helpless white man to the auditorium."

Rye said, "Squaw makes joke."

Sunflower punched him on the shoulder.

"Great!" Rye exaggerated a wince. "You've injured the one place I don't hurt."

With Chee assisting Rye, they managed their way toward the doors with Sunflower close behind them. Children dressed in karate outfits and their parents flowed past them like a stream around rocks.

Rye limped his way past the ticket areas. Approaching the glass doors, he saw himself in the reflection: a man barely able to walk with a patch over his eye, a split lip, and a face ripening into a bruise. *That's enough to scare the fur off a mountain lion.*

He pushed through the doors and took a flyer from a teenage girl who stared at his face.

"You should see the other guy," Rye told her.

A few minutes later, they approached the North Room where the meets were to take place. Rye leaned on Chee again. At this point, all he wanted to do was to locate Dee and find a seat.

Out of the swirl of crowd, a man carrying a tray of beers bumped into him, splashing Rye's shirt.

"Hey," Rye yelled, "watch it."

"Hey yourself," Beer Man started to say something else, but when he saw Rye's face, he mumbled an apology and disappeared into the crowd.

At least my ugly mug is good for something.

Sunflower vanished into the swirl of people. Returning seconds later with a handful of napkins, she commenced on daubing the wet spots.

When she finished, Sunflower carted the wet wad to a trash container. Rye glanced down at the wet blot on his shirt. The napkins had done little to soak up the hand-sized spot.

"Rye Dawlsen," spat Dee's voice from behind. "I'm surprised you came. But for God's sake, it's only nine in the morning and already you smell like a brewery. Did you have to do this to your son?"

Rye stiffened at the tone of her voice, that blackboard-scratching sound of reproach.

He lowered his arm from Chee's shoulder. With a limp that must have resembled a drunken stagger to one predisposed toward that opinion, he turned to face her.

With a sharp intake of air, hands going to her mouth, and dark eyes opening wide, she said, "Rye ... what happened?"

"I was on the wrong end of a beating. Got jumped in the parking lot where I'm staying. Sorry about the beer smell, some … umm fellow attendee … just spilled it all over me." He indicated the wet spot on his shirt.

Just then, Sunflower walked up, "I was trying to wipe it away."

"And you are …?" Dee stared at the woman and left the question dangling.

"Dee," Rye indicated his estranged wife then indicated the Navajo woman, "this is Sunflower. The older sister of a high school buddy and an acquaintance of Chee's."

Sunflower held out her hand. With reluctance splashed across her face, Dee shook her hand.

Sunflower held her head high, "I read your newspaper articles. You always write good things about the *Dine*. Thank you."

"Rye taught me to appreciate the Native way," Dee said.

With that, Dee rushed into Rye's arms and squeezed him to her. He gasped. Agony sliced him like a knife blade jabbed between ribs.

"What? Did I …?" She started to pull back, but Rye held her tight.

"No." He twisted her hair with his forefinger and thumb, reliving when they dwelt in each other's arms for stretched-out minutes. "My ribs are bruised a little." She tried pulling away again, but he held on. "No. Don't. I'm okay. Having you in my arms is worth it all."

She laughed and slapped him lightly on his shoulder. "Such a romantic."

"You remember Chee."

She held out her hand to him. "Yeah, he deposited you on the front porch many a night." Rye opened his mouth; she cut him off. "Your uncle only offered sympathy and support for us." She turned to the Navajo. "How are you, Chee?"

"It's good to see my nephew's flower smiling again," he replied taking her hand.

Dee looked at her watch. "Manny will be up shortly. Care to join us?"

Before they could take a step, Chee put an arm out to block Rye. "Don't look. But Jilt is here. I recognize his white hat with the Confederate flag pin and feathered hatband."

Dee shot worried glances between Rye and Chee. "Rye, what's going on?"

"Remember Jilt?"

She nodded.

"It was he and two of his buddies who attacked me. Security's tight, so they won't do anything here. Let's find Manny."

Sunflower leaned forward to speak into Rye's ear. "The one who desires your death is here."

That's when the milling crowd parted to reveal the man in black standing a few yards behind Jilt. The man stared at the ground.

"Found him."

As the words left Rye's mouth, the man in black glanced up and locked eyes with him, shooting a sudden chill through him, so much so, that his breath came in short gasps.

The man in black smiled without any friendliness, touched a forefinger to the brim of his hat, and, turning, disappeared into the crowd.

Rye blinked his eyes open. His head pressed against the passenger window of his Tahoe while one hand held his Stetson on his lap. He remembered Dee driving his Tahoe as she jabbered nervously. She had said something about Chee following them in his uncle's truck and that Sunflower rode with his uncle. South Mountain had loomed off to the right. Then nothing. He must have drifted off.

Now, he watched the heat-shimmering flat lands of I-8 flying past his window. Faint mountains formed the background. For a second, he had no clue as to his exact whereabouts.

Then he heard Dee humming to the tune on the radio, and it didn't matter. He closed his eyes and smiled, concentrating on her voice. It felt good to have her in the car with him.

The Tahoe hit a bump, and Rye groaned and caught his breath.

"Dad," said Manny from the back seat. "You awake?"

"Yeah, bud, I'm awake. The way your mom drives makes it difficult to sleep."

"Get outta here," Dee said, laughing. "I had to turn the radio on because your snoring reminded me of a badly oiled chainsaw. I couldn't hear the music, so I pushed you to get you to face the window."

"You could have turned the radio up."

"I didn't want to blow your speakers."

"Dad," Manny said, "you sounded like a jet taking off." He performed a mock snore imitating his father.

"I was that loud?" Rye feigned shock.

They came to the exit for Whiskey, and Dee took it, heading south. With the sun hanging low over the mountains to the west, the storm clouds to the south lit up in a display of reds and purples. Distant flashes of lightning flickered in the roiling storm clouds.

"Looks like the hurricane approaches," Rye said, brushing imaginary dust motes from his Stetson's brim.

"The radio said it built in intensity before slamming into the Baja

190

coast," Dee replied. She risked a glance out the side window. "It's been awhile since I've been here. The land never changes, does it?"

"Nope. Hey," Rye said pointing to the storm clouds. "Check out that lightning."

"My geography teacher said it's global warming causing all the bad storms," Manny said from the back.

"Just 'cause you put your boots in the oven," Rye said, "don't make 'em biscuits. Same with global warming. The climate and weather constantly change. In fact, it's said to be getting colder."

"If some of my colleagues at the Sun heard that," Dee said, glancing at Rye, "they'd hand your head to you on a platter."

"Well, your colleagues are just plain weak north of their ears."

They drove for a while in silence.

"Rye."

"Dee."

They had started to speak at the same moment. They laughed, and Manny added, "Sheesh."

"Go ahead," Dee said.

"No, ladies first."

"Okay, then. I want to apologize for behaving badly at the convention center. I just ... it's that ... well, when I saw you leaning on Chee, it brought back bad memories. Then I smelled the beer on you ... I didn't realize it was literally on you. Sorry, can you ... can you ... forgive my stupidity?"

Rye stammered, "I ... I wouldn't expect you to react any differently. Not after what I put this family through."

"I won't hide it. It's been tough."

"I won't hide it either." Rye reached over and touched her hair.

"I … I try to stop drinking, but I'm not successful. Yet I'm sober more than I'm drunk."

"Glad to hear it." A smile flashed across her face.

With rising hope, he decided to give it a full court press. *No sense holding back.* "Does that mean we can consider reconciliation?"

Dee shook her head, and Rye could see she struggled not to cry. "Oh Rye. I don't know. I want to, but …" Her voice trailed off. "I can't. Not now. We've had one really, really good day. Let's just have that for now." She looked at him. "We can try to have another one tomorrow and build on it."

He risked a glance at Manny, who was staring out the window, earphones in place leading to an iPod in one relaxed hand. "I need to tell you something, Dee. Something that happened the night you left."

She nodded, keeping her eyes on the road. "OK … go on."

"I'd had a rough and bloody day, so I ended up in some dive reeking of sweat and spilled beer." Rye stared at the road ahead, finding it difficult to stare at her profile. "A juke box played beer-drinking country songs. A couple of girls squatted on barstools close by. Guys played pool in the back room, the clack of balls striking one another. The bartender was talking with a guy at the end of the bar. And me, I sipped rum and coke. Then, the door opens. The bartender shouts, 'Hey, kids, get outta here!'

"Two kids. The older one, a girl, maybe thirteen or so, wearing a ragged dress draped over a bone-thin frame, she says, 'We're looking for our pa.'

"The bartender opens his mouth to say something, but the guy with him turns and looks at the two kids, saying, 'Whadda you want?'

"The girl says, 'Pa, there ain't no food in the house. Me and Jason's hungry.'

"He says, 'Whadda you want me to do? I ain't got no money. It's your mother's fault.'

"The bartender yells, 'You heard the man. Now get out before I call the cops.'

"The boy, Jason, his eyes tear up. A snarl flashes on his sister's face, and she turns him around. She takes his tiny hand and says, 'We'll find something to eat. We don't need his stinking money.' The door shuts and cuts off anything else she might have said.

"The father downs the glass he was drinking, reaches into his wallet, and pulls out a twenty. 'Give me another,' he says to the bartender.

"I was so angry, Dee. I marched over to the father, tapped him on the shoulder, and said, 'You're really something, you know that.'

"He turns to me and says, 'Yeah, well it ain't none of your business, buddy.'

"I say, 'Maybe I should make it my business.'

"The man gets up from his stool, fists clenched tight, and says, 'Try it.'

"The bartender says to me, 'We don' want no trouble here. Scram before I call the police.'

"I open my jacket and flash my badge. I say, 'I am the police. And child neglect is a crime.' I grab a fistful of the man's shirt and say, 'If I ever hear of you doing this again ...' I let the threat trail off and let go of the man's shirt with a shove. The drunk father stumbles backwards, slamming into the bar. Then I head to the door.

"And the father yells, 'Screw you, pig. If you're so righteous, what're you doing here?'"

Rye paused and swallowed.

"Oh, Rye ..." Dee said, swiping at a tear sliding down her cheek.

He turned to look through the side window. Too late to stop now. "So out in the parking lot, I spot the two kids as they passed under a street lamp a half a block away. I dashed after them, yelling to get their attention. They turn around, and I catch up to them. I pull two twenties out of my wallet. I say, 'Get you something to eat, then buy some groceries.'

"The girl looks at me, suspicious, but the brother says, 'Take it, sis.'

"She reaches out, takes the money, saying, 'Thanks, mister.'"

Rye closed his eyes. "I looked at their faces, seen that same haunted look in adult women abused by their men."

"That's so awful, Rye." Dee's knuckles gleamed white, hands gripping the wheel.

"I told them, 'I'm a cop,' and I showed them my badge. I handed the girl my card. Told them if they needed anything, anything at all, to call. The girl turns to her brother and says, 'Let's go get us McDonalds.'"

Rye shook his head. "Seeing those kids hurry up the street made me think of Manny. That I needed to start being there for my family. But when I got home, the house was dark, cold, and empty. You and Manny were gone. Your note said you couldn't handle my drinking anymore. I was too late." Rye's voice cracked. He whispered, "And ever since, the drunk's words never left me: 'If you're so righteous, what are you here for?'"

The car came to a halt, and Rye recognized his gravel driveway. Dee pulled him into an embrace, sending agony down his stiff body, but he didn't care.

"I wish you'd told me sooner," she whispered against his cheek. "But now I see I couldn't hear anything you had to say before today. Rye, I am still gonna need a little time."

Rye took a deep breath and released it with a long exhale. "Okay. Today's fine. We'll do it your way. I lost you once. I don't want to jeopardize the delicate balance we've established."

She pulled back to look at him. Tears left wet trails on her cheeks. She mouthed, "Thank you."

As Rye eased his way out of the Tahoe, Chee drove up in his old pickup. Rye nodded to Sunflower and Chee in the truck.

He gave his son a hearty hug then mussed the boy's hair. "I want you to know you made your dad very proud today." A grin spread across the boy's face. "You done real good getting your next belt. But I also want you to know you don't have to do anything to earn my love. You got that free of charge." Rye hugged Manny again, relishing his son's embrace. Then, Rye gave Dee a long embrace.

She whispered, "Thanks. That means a lot to him. And me. I pray for you, Rye, every night, for you to defeat this demon you face with the booze. I ... I still ... love you."

They held each other for several seconds. *Why not?* He leaned over and kissed her. A light touch of the lips first, then, a deeper kiss. She melted into him.

"Mmmm," Dee murmured, pressing against him.

Manny coughed. "Will you two get a room?"

They broke the kiss, laughing. Rye shot a one-eyed stare at the boy. "Where did you hear that?"

"At school." But he refused to say more. Instead, he pointed at the roiling clouds. "Wow. Look."

An explosion of lightning filled the sky with spidery tentacles. Thunder rumbled.

"Nice," Rye said while he took both of Dee's hands in his. "Y'all best be going, but I wish you would stay. At least 'til the storm passes."

"I've got work waiting for me," she said in a regretful tone. Rye drank in the gaze of her dark brown eyes. "Call me tomorrow."

"Will you answer if I do?" he mumbled.

"Sure."

He released her hands.

Sunflower opened the passenger door, scooted out of Chee's pickup, and drew close to Rye. Over her shoulder, he watched Manny and Dee climb into the truck and work their way to the middle of the seat.

He glanced back at Sunflower, and she stared at him in silence for several seconds. He wondered how his life would have been different had her family not suddenly disappeared the night the two of them shared an intimate rendezvous in the forest. She touched him on the arm, the tips of her fingernails lingering on his sleeve.

"Rye Dawlsen, you take care and watch your back. Remember, a great evil follows you. Even Navajos," her voice dropped to a whisper, "fear this evil Skinwalker." After a quick survey of their surroundings, she added, "He comes for you. This man to the south has great power, and he looks this way." She pressed something into his hand.

A glance at his opened palm revealed a square cut from leather with a glyph of twins made of beads sown into the square. A leather necklace dangled off the side of his hand.

"Did you get this from the museum?" he asked, suspicion rising in his voice.

"You need to wear it," Sunflower urged. "It will protect you."

"Sunflower, answer my question." He gave her a stern look. "Did you or did you not break into the Whiskey Navajo Museum two nights ago and steal this from one of the displays?"

"It doesn't matter," she answered, her voice going cold. "Just ... wear it." She paused and her eyes searched his. "If you want to live, do what I say."

"Stop right there, mister."

Johnny Batts leveled his AK-47 at the approaching limo, aiming it where he assumed the driver's head would be.

The vehicle rolled to a gravel-crunching stop in front of his cabin. The tinted glass prevented Johnny from seeing the car's occupants, but he figured he'd fire a couple of bursts at the window if they didn't stop. *Some SOB stole my Winchester and kilt my sheep. And they're gonna pay.*

"Git outta the car." Johnny motioned with his rifle.

Thunder rumbled in the distance. He took quick notice of the storm moving in from the south.

"I ain't asking y'all again." He fired a burst at the ground in front of the car. Thunder drowned out the echoing gunfire.

The back door opened, and a young Mexican senorita stepped out.

Nice. Johnny eyed her. *For a fourteen-year-old.* She wore a slinky black dress, revealing much of her light brown legs. Johnny spit into the dirt.

"What?" Johnny asked. His AK never wavered from the front windshield.

197

She started to speak and choked on her words. Johnny noted the fear in her eyes. *Go easy on her. Someone's putting her up to this.*

"He wants to buy your land, mister." The girl struggled with her English.

"Who wants my land?"

"He do." She nodded to the open door. Johnny heard a smattering of Spanish coming from within the car. She opened her mouth to speak.

Johnny turned his gaze to the limo. "I know enough Spanish," he yelled at the car. "It must take a real man to kill a poor man's sheep and frighten a teenage girl. I'm keeping my land. Now git off of it."

This time the Spanish from the back of the limo hissed like a snake.

"What did he say?" Johnny demanded.

"He say when he returns, it won't be to kill livestock."

CHAPTER 17

SATURDAY EVENING

Watching as Chee backed out the driveway, Rye's heart staggered under the weight of regret. He wanted to chase after them, stop the truck, and compel Dee to stay. But he didn't. Fear of making the wrong move and ruining today's precarious start froze his feet.

As the truck drove down the street, Manny turned and waved through the back window. Rye returned the wave. When he could no longer see his son, he lowered his head.

Setting his overnight bag down, he slipped Sunflower's amulet over his head despite feeling foolish for doing so. A chill swept down his spine. He fingered the talisman and glanced back to the now empty road.

Winds buffeted him, and he tasted the hint of moisture in the air. Lightning flashed like a rock concert light show. Thunder rumbled. The air turned cool.

"Gotta check the weather radio," he said aloud to himself.

He limped his way up the steps, grimacing and grunting. *Gotta find my knee brace and wear it. Can't afford to be a gimp. Not with all the problems brewing like a bad stew.*

Dee grinned at her son who jabbered nonstop with Chee about Indians this and Indians that. Mostly stories he'd seen on TV.

Her smile faded while she puzzled over the recent events. She had enough difficulty processing Rye's story of the night she had taken Manny and left. Even more so, her mind refused to wrap around the idea of Navajo Skinwalkers in today's modern America. Skinwalkers ... ludicrous. She had started researching what Rye had asked of her ... and held off saying anything about it. He hadn't even asked.

A gust of wind battered the truck, and a squeaking yelp escaped from her lips. She felt her face turn warm.

"Looks like we're in for some rough weather," Chee said.

Sunflower grunted an acknowledgement and said to Dee, "I'm a *Yeenaeldooshi.*"

Dee stared at her. "You're a ... a ... Skinwalker?"

"Don't go there," Chee snapped, glancing at Sunflower. "It's almost night, and a storm is about to sweep us away. You can talk about it tomorrow. When there's daylight."

Sunflower ignored him. "I am not ludicrous," she said to Dee.

"How ..." Dee forced her gaping mouth closed.

"I put my life into your hands to reveal this to you. But I trust you, wife of Rye Dawlsen." Sunflower never removed her piercing gaze. "I walk the path of a Navajo witch." Sunflower lifted her head.

Dee eased herself away from the woman as far as the cramped seating would allow. She began to shake.

"Don't fear. I will not steal your soul."

"Mom," said Manny, "I'm afraid."

"We're okay," Dee told him. "We're with friends and family of your father."

Sunflower continued as if she didn't hear the interruption, "Your husband faces an evil greater than any I've seen. Other Skinwalkers fear this one. It comes from the south."

The truck veered, rocked by the wind. Chee muttered a curse.

"Mommy," Manny said, his voice shaking. There was something different in Manny's voice.

"What, dear?"

"He scares me."

"Your uncle is driving great. We'll be okay." She patted his leg.

"Mo-om. Not Uncle Chee. *Him*." The last word expelled out of Manny's throat like a striking rattlesnake. His hand shook visibly as he pointed out the back window of the truck.

Dee twisted in the cramped cab to look out the back. In the bed of the truck crouched a man-shaped thing wearing a black wolf skin. The skull of the wolf covered his head. He opened his mouth in a grotesque snarl.

Dee screamed.

Rye sat on his bed and strapped on a black knee brace. He walked up the narrow hallway to the living room, testing the brace's support. He turned and grimaced at an arc of hot pain. Except for quick turns, the brace seemed to bring some relief to his knee.

After hobbling over to the kitchen, he opened the refrigerator and studied its near empty interior. Two beers and a six-pack of flavored water. However, with Dee's presence lingering in his heart, the water made a better choice.

While reaching for one, a gust of wind struck his mobile like a blast from a jet engine. Lights inside his home flickered. *Did I close the windows to the car?* He limped over to the front door and peered out the window. Sure enough, the windows were down. He spat a curse and stepped outside.

Winds whipped up huge swirling dust clouds and pelted him with debris. Rye squinted and raised a hand to shield his eyes. He held onto his Stetson to prevent it from blowing away.

Castigating himself for leaving the windows open, Rye limped over to the driver's door and sat in the SUV. He powered up the car and raised the windows. After getting out of the car, he decided to fetch his bow from the Tahoe's back hatch.

He limped to the back of the Tahoe and raised the hatch door. Reaching in for the bow, a gust pitched his hat into the front of the storage area. Grumbling, he leaned forward to get his hat, careful not to antagonize his knee more than necessary. Gritting his teeth, Rye grabbed his hat and turned to sit in the storage area. Pain-induced sweat beaded his forehead despite the cooling temps. He sighed, thinking about the walk back.

Just then, his mobile home erupted in an explosive fireball. The blast smashed into the Tahoe, knocking it sideways. Thrown from the vehicle, Rye struck the ground amid a shower of orange burning splinters, both in and outside his head. Sound vanished into a muffled ring. His vision decreased in a narrowing circle.

What the …

Rye blacked out.

Dee gazed into the pale eyes of the man-creature as it pressed its face against the cab's back window. Its stare fixated her, left her gasping for breath. The creature leaned backwards and raised a fist. Mouthing unintelligible words, its fist smashed into the window. Like a gunshot, the glass exploded inward, glass shards filling the cab.

Chee swerved, nearly losing control of the vehicle. Dee bounced between Manny and Sunflower.

Sunflower grabbed the man by his wolf skins. "Leave us, Skinwalker!"

Her words forced him backwards as if shoved by a giant hand. Snarling, he leapt forward. Grabbing her hair, he pulled her through the shattered window into the truck bed. She shrieked, laying at his feet and bleeding from several cuts made by the broken glass.

"Sunflower, you are a Skinwalker," the creature growled.

"That won't work," she said, pushing herself up from the truck bed. "Sunflower is a nickname and not my true identity."

"Then I will drag your real name out of you."

"Forget it. You're not even a *Diné*." Sunflower sprang to her feet and punched him in the jaw. He shoved her away from him. The woman witch and the Mexican Skinwalker faced each other, fists clenched.

Time decelerated into slo-mo. Sunflower's hair seemed to float out from her head. The combatants traded punches that glided.

"Dee."

Someone called her name. Yet, she could not tear her eyes away from the fight in the truck bed. The truck rocked back and forth like a boat in a storm.

"Dee!"

Who's calling me?

"DEE!"

That broke her away from her dream consciousness. Sunflower's hair whipped in the wind. Their punches came fast and furious, the smack of skin against skin loud even in the maelstrom of noise. Winds buffeted the truck, the gusts trying to push it off the road.

Dee looked over at Chee who said, "Open the glove box. You'll see a brown paper bag."

"Mom!" She flinched at the terror in her son's voice.

"Hang on, Manny," she yelled over the noise.

Dee found a crumpled paper bag stuck between tape cassettes of Native music and a handgun.

"Open the bag and dust us with its contents."

She reached into the bag and withdrew a handful of ash. "What the—"

"JUST DO IT!"

Dee tossed the handful over her son, then Chee, and finally, herself.

Manny sputtered. "Aw, Mom, what is that stuff?"

"Cedar ash," Chee replied concentrating on driving in the near gale force winds with two Skinwalkers fighting in the bed of his truck. "It'll protect us. Try to sprinkle some on that black-hided demon!"

Dee turned in her seat and snatched a handful of the ash. *If this stuff hurts Skinwalkers, I can't throw it. I'll hurt Sunflower.* She stared at the two now lying tangled in the bed of the truck.

Sunflower raked her fingernails across the man's bare neck, leaving blood tracks. He howled and slapped her face. She spun away, putting a modicum of distance between them. He drew a knife from a sheath bound to his forearm.

Dee saw her opening and tossed the ash at the Skinwalker, following it with a second handful. Though much of the ash blew away in the winds, some struck the wolf creature in the chest. His skin blistered, and smoke rose from the wound. The scent of charred skin filled the cab. He snarled at Dee and leapt out of the truck bed.

Sunflower reached a hand through the window in an effort to re-enter the cab. Trying to help, Dee grabbed the woman's arm. Just then, a tire exploded. Dee slammed into the metal of the truck's door. Out of the dust-blown darkness, the Skinwalker reappeared, running alongside the vehicle. Dee watched in horror as he lowered his shoulder and slammed into the side of the truck.

With that, Chee lost control, and the truck spun off into a wash. It rolled once—she slammed into the metal dashboard, dragged her hand along broken glass, smashed a shoulder against the ceiling of the cab, crumpled, then crashed backwards into the foot well—and the truck slid to a stop.

With consciousness slipping, she gazed at the Skinwalker standing next to the truck. The creature lifted his head and howled in victory.

At that, a torrent poured from the skies, the Skinwalker vanished into the sheets of rain, and the darkness took her.

Wanting to make it home before the storm struck, Iona rushed around her newspaper office preparing to leave. She saved her computer files and shut it down. At the door, she gave the office a once over and turned off the lights.

Winds whipped trash-filled dust devils up the street. Thick boiling storm clouds, laced with explosions of electricity, killed the sunlight. The evening turned black as midnight. Streetlights flickered on.

She locked the office door, the winds shoving at her back. Because several cars had been parked on the street, Iona did not see the man until she turned toward her Land Rover. While she fumbled with her keys, she sensed movement in front of her and looked up.

"Oh," she said, "Junior List, you startled me. How's your daddy doing?"

"Get in the car," he said. "The driver's seat." Menace charged his voice. That's when she noticed he had a gun pointed at her. She held up her hands.

"What's going on?"

"Don't make me tell you again." Junior waved his gun at the car. "Just get in the freaking car." He back-handed her across the mouth. She tasted the coppery tang of blood. *The last hombre that did that, I broke his forearm. But he didn't have a gun pointed at me.*

Rain began to plunk on them, sounding hollow on the metal car roofs.

She slid in the driver's seat, jammed her key into the ignition, and started her vehicle. She peeked in the rearview mirror. Junior stood at her back bumper talking on his cell phone.

"You never were very bright," she muttered. She threw the Rover into reverse. With tires squealing, the car flew backwards onto Yuma Street.

"Hey," Junior screamed, jumping out of the way. In her side

mirror, she saw him kneeling on all fours, the rain plastering his hair to his head. He glared at her. His gun lay several feet away in a puddle. Iona rammed the gearshift into drive and slammed on the gas. Once again, the tires spun then caught on the pavement as the Rover leapt forward.

She heard the explosions of gunfire, but only one shot smacked into the car.

At the end of Yuma, she turned and headed for Rye's neighborhood.

Keeping her eyes on the road, she plunged one shaking hand into her purse on the passenger seat and fumbled for her cell phone. Using her thumb, she pushed 911.

"This is Yuma 911. What's your emergency?"

"I'm being shot at," Iona yelled into the phone.

"What's your location, ma'am?"

Iona cursed. "Didn't you hear me? I'm—"

"Yes, ma'am, I did hear you. But I can't help you if I don't know your location. So I'll ask you again, where is your location?"

"Yeah, I'm heading out of Whiskey. Heading south on Pioneer."

Iona heard the clicking of a keyboard. "That's good. Can you describe the shooter?"

"Describe him? I know who it is."

"And who might that be, ma'am?" The background clicking stopped.

"Junior List." Iona paused. "The son of Whiskey mayor ..."

She caught movement in the rearview mirror. To her horror, she watched a pair of headlights skid sideways off Canyon Road onto Pioneer. The lights grew larger. She recognized the car.

"Crap! He's following me!"

"Ma'am?" said the 911 operator.

A sudden gust of wind shoved against the Rover. With adrenaline rushing through her veins, Iona overreacted and yanked on the steering wheel. The vehicle fishtailed, then caught a puddle and spun around.

The last thing Iona saw were the headlights aiming straight for her.

She screamed into the phone, "HE'S GOING TO HIT ME."

CHAPTER 18

SUNDAY MORNING

A constant plinking like hundreds of tiny snare drums filled Rye's hearing. Strange, the noise harmonized with the splashing of water. His legs felt wet. His knee ached. It hurt to breathe. A cool breeze caressed his face. He opened his uninjured eye to see dirt, gravel, and his hat. Why would he leave his Stetson in the dirt? His mind squatted in a morass of confusion. Nothing made sense.

He sat up, a groan escaping from his lips, and grabbed his hat. He scooted into the back of the Tahoe and leaned against the back seat. It was then that he noticed his Tahoe lay on its side.

Like a slow sunrise, he began to remember. Phoenix and the trip back home—with Dee. *C'mon, man, think.*

He stared down at his jeans soaked from the knees down. Why was he lying out here in the rain?

He jerked upright.

The explosion!

He rose, still wobbly, to stare around his vehicle and through sheets of rain. His house was gone. Nothing but blackened timbers and debris jutted from the soaked ground. Wind blew away the smoke from smoldering fires. The pungent smell of burnt wood tickled his nose. Gritting his teeth so hard his jaw hurt, he lowered his head.

Gone. Every freaking thing I owned. Gone.

He glanced into the interior of the vehicle. The glass on the passenger front and middle, the side facing the explosion, had been blown out. Most of the windshield as well.

He searched in vain through his pockets, looking for his cell phone.

A car pulled into his driveway. Rye squinted against the blinding high beams, raising a hand to block the glare. The driver switched to the low beams. Rye stared into the black metal push-protector covering the grill. A Crown Vic cruiser. Rye spotted Whitewolf behind the steering wheel. The officer waved for him to get into the car.

Limping through the rain, Rye hurried to the passenger side of the cruiser. He collapsed into the passenger seat, rainwater dripping from him. Gasping for breath, he stared at the ruins of his home.

"You piss off somebody?"

"An explosion." Rye paused, still unable to process the event. "Someone tried to kill me." He turned to stare at Noah. "This is a crime scene. Unfortunately, the rain will destroy most of any evidence. Hopefully, when the rain subsides, there may be something left."

"What happened to your ... face?" Noah's eyes, already wider than Rye had ever seen them, scanned him head to toe and back up again.

"Jilt and a few of his buddies jumped me. In Phoenix." Rye recognized the look on the Apache's face. "What aren't you telling me?"

Noah looked away. "It's about your Uncle Chee."

"Yeah, what's wrong?" A crushing anxiety lassoed his heart. "Tell me."

"His truck was found on 8. Overturned in the median. Chee's missing. But we did find an Indian woman. Navajo."

"That would be Sunflower. A friend. She and Chee visited ..." He felt bile churn in his stomach. *Noah said they found a woman. Not two. Not Dee. Not Manny. That could only mean ...*

Noah continued with his report. "She had been tossed from the truck. She's banged up pretty bad. Docs say she might not make it. Claw marks from an unknown animal left ugly scratches all over her. They found a suspicious knife close to her."

"Take me to her," Rye said with urgency. "Suspicious in what way?"

"One of the investigators at the wreck also did work at Batts'. He says this knife could be the one used on Juan."

"Sunflower wouldn't—"

"There's no fingerprints on the knife. Zach sent me over to get you. When we couldn't raise you on the phone, we figured the storm knocked down some lines. But this ..." Noah paused staring at the remnants of Rye's house. He rubbed his chin. "Chief, what's going on?"

"I'm not sure, but I got some ideas." He buckled his seat belt. "We need to haul butt to the hospital. I have to talk with Sunflower. She might provide some answers."

Rye peered down at Sunflower, lying in the ICU bed with plastic tubing sticking out from her in numerous places, ending at the various life support systems.

Twenty-four hours ago, that was me laying there.

He took her hand, careful not to move it because of the IV. She looked pale, and her breath came in shallow waves. He wished she would wake. Tears pooled in his eyes, which he wiped with a quick swipe of the back of his hand.

"Sir," a nurse came into the room, "I'll have to ask you to leave."

Rye tore his eyes away from Sunflower and stared at the nurse. He felt her eyes give his battered face the once over.

He pulled out his badge. "Nurse, just give me another moment. I'm involved in a case of multiple homicides along with a possible kidnapping of a child. Your patient may hold key evidence that would help solve these crimes."

"If you don't leave right now, you'll be killing her." She folded her arms, leveling a stern gaze at him. "You can leave on your own free will, or I'll have security haul your backside out of here."

A moan emanated from the bed. Rye leaned over to see Sunflower gazing at him with pain-wracked eyes.

"It's okay," she croaked. "I must talk to him. I'll rest … afterwards. Promise." Her words came weak, a mere whisper just a few decibels louder than the machines keeping her alive.

"Go ahead," Rye said brushing her hair.

"A Mexican Skinwalker," her words inched out syllable by syllable. "Fat white man … with limo … has … your wife … son … Chee …" Her voice drifted off.

Rye stood ramrod straight. Even though he doubted the existence of Skinwalkers, the news hit him like a mule kick in the gut.

"Sir—" The nurse began to speak, her voice like the edge of a razor.

Rye spun around. "I'm leaving. Just do your best to keep her alive." With that, he disappeared through the ICU exit.

Rye spotted Whitewolf's Crown Vic waiting under the pavilion at the emergency entrance. Rainwater streamed over the gutters like a waterfall and crashed on the cement driveway. The vehicle's flashing red-and-blues glared off the wet walls of the hospital. Rye slid into the passenger seat and leaned forward, resting his forehead in the palms of his hands.

He sat there a few seconds, eyes closed. The inklings of a plan formulated in his mind. *Would it work? It had to. Dee, Manny, and Chee needed it to work.*

Whitewolf cleared his throat and said, "Chief." He waited a couple of seconds. "I got more bad news." Rye raised his head and turned to meet Whitewolf's gaze. The officer continued, his words spilling slowly. "Iona's missing. State patrol discovered her Land Rover crashed on Pioneer and abandoned. Before the crash, Ms. Haulke called 911. I heard the replay of the call. Someone had been shooting at her. And she ID'd the shooter."

After a few seconds of quiet, Rye prodded, "Go on."

Noah leaned his head back against the headrest. "Once I say the name, the whole ball game changes. Just so you know." Another pause.

"If it's who I think it is, then it's already changed." He stared unblinking at his officer.

Noah took a deep breath and sighed. "Okay ... Junior List."

With that said, Rye's plan solidified in his mind like a concrete structure. "You know the storage place on Pioneer close to 8." When Noah nodded, Rye said, his words cold like a winter rain, "Drive there.

I'll call Gabby to have DePute and Heilo meet us there. This ends tonight."

Johnny Batts dashed from the back of his cabin, through sheets of rain, to the entrance of his mine. He stopped inside the cave, shivering and soaked to the skin. Water puddled at his feet. The place reeked of wet stone. He studied the back of his cabin, the place he'd called home for the last dozen years. Maybe for the last time.

He turned and hurried into the blackness. He counted off his steps. When he reached fifty, he stopped and faced the wall. Had it been a sunny day, he would have been able to make out the red plastic knob. But not in this blinding darkness. His hands explored the stone in tight circles at shoulder height. He stretched his hands outward, until his left hand bumped against plastic. Johnny pushed the knob.

The click and hiss of hydraulic pistons sounded loud in the passage. He sensed rather than saw the door swing inward on silent hinges. When fully open, pale-green LEDs blinked on to reveal a square room cut out of the stone.

Johnny stepped into this chamber and pushed a button on the wall behind him. The door swung shut, and another door opened on the opposite wall.

He entered this second room. A motion detector sensed his presence and switched on a row of humming fluorescent lights. On the wall before him, thirty rifles of different types hung on a gun rack. To his left, handguns from dozens of manufacturers covered the wall. Below the handguns, wood cabinets stored ammo. To his right, several types of outfits hung from a clothes rack.

"List, you've done forced my hand," he said to the gun racks. "You've raped your last teenager. You've sold your last ounce of coke. No more gunrunning for you."

Johnny stripped off his wet clothing, leaving it in a pile. He chose a black microfiber rain shirt and pants. He slipped on the pair of black Rocky Miner Boots. Then he paused before the handgun rack. Arms folded across his chest, he raised a hand to rub his mouth. "Which ones?"

In his home office, with stucco walls covered in western art and wooden beams crossing the ceiling, Mayor Richard List leaned his bulk back into the burgundy leather chair and took a draw from his cigar. The end glowed orange. When he blew smoke into the air, the ceiling fan dispersed it. Awed by the storm's splendid violence, he monitored it through the quad six-foot tall windows. Lightning exploded, followed in a heartbeat by a roll of thunder that rattled the panes.

He leaned over for the cut glass decanter on the desk and refilled his drink.

"To our mutual success." He raised his glass—its liquid catching the faint light—to the man dressed completely in black sitting in the dark shadows. He sipped again, the two ice cubes tinkling in the glass.

"Y màs," his guest said, likewise raising his glass. "I bring you drugs. You give me guns. We all—how you Americanos say—happy campers."

"Yeah. We can sing Kumbaya around the campfire." Richard downed his drink.

A shadow moved behind the man in black, and a young, dark-haired girl emerged from the gloom. Though her dress must have cost several thousand, it left little to the imagination. He liked that in a dress. His guest put a hand on her rear and squeezed. The girl started to yelp, but clenched her teeth so not to make a sound.

"Ahhh, Mayor List," the man in black said, "I see you have an appreciative eye for my Amalia. Maybe, after our business is concluded, I will allow you an hour with her to enjoy her ... exquisite charms." He grinned, flashing his teeth—one top incisor plated in gold—but the humor never reached his eyes.

The girl flinched, but Richard couldn't care less. *She'd be one nice* ... "Demonio, I'll take that under consideration." He had trouble removing his eyes from Amalia, but he hid behind swills of alcohol and a cloud of cigar smoke. "Another drink?"

"Sì, I am thirsty. Amalia, fetch one for me. And one for yourself. You may be in need of its blurring comfort later."

The girl flashed a glance at her captor, her hands darting upward to cover her chest.

Richard waved his cigar-holding hand toward the teenage girl. "Not that I mind, but, why the eye-candy? I thought you were married."

Demonio did not respond right away. His gaze stared beyond the room. Finally he said, "My wife is a beautiful woman, no? She lives in a mansion surrounded by servants. She and her family live in safety on my estate. I give her children to dawdle over. But her heart is cold. I need hot woman to warm my bed. Sì. Like my Amalia."

Whatever. Keep telling yourself that crap if it makes you sleep better at night.

As the girl brought a glass over to Demonio, Richard admired her alluring walk; the swaying hips, the long brown legs flowing from under the dress, the bounce of her adolescent breasts, the stream of her hair. Demonio's proposition sounded better with every step she took.

Amalia handed Demonio the glass, and he held it up in toast. "To my new nation of Northern Mexico."

"And to making lots of money," replied Richard, and took a long swallow. *Never forget what's important.*

Just then, the door to the office opened. Jilt filled the doorframe, his large hand on the neck of the Dawlsen woman. Behind them stood her kid, the Indian uncle, and the small town reporter held by Junior. The Dawlsen woman squirmed, and Jilt shoved her. She stumbled, falling hard to the teak wood floor. Rainwater dripped from her, forming a puddle on the floor.

Pushing to a kneeling position, she glowered at Richard through strands of wet hair. He returned a fierce stare until she lowered her head.

"I positioned our men," Jilt said. "They're in strategic points around the property and throughout the house."

"When the cop comes," Junior added, "we'll be ready."

"When which cop comes?" asked Dee.

List laughed and said, "Your fool husband." List pushed out of his plush chair and lumbered over to Dee. Leaning over, he tapped her forehead with a thick forefinger. "He meddles with my business." Tap. "He interferes with my associates." Tap. "The insufferable little man can't be bought, so he's in my way." He slapped her cheek. "But not after tonight. You're here to assure his arrival. I plan to terminate his employment. Permanently."

Lights danced before her eyes, and her face ached from the slap. She shook her head to clear it.

"MOM!"

She jerked a glance at Manny. In that moment, seeing his eyes wide in fear and mouth gaped open, her heart sank. From the corner of her eye, Dee saw the motion. List's raised arm moved like a striking snake. His fist crashed into the side of her face, and her mind went black.

CHAPTER 19

SUNDAY NOON

Rye and Whitewolf waited in the patrol car outside the lone gate of the Whiskey Storage Lot. Through the rain-splattered windows, Rye studied the lot and its security. Titanium chain-link fence topped by barbed wire. Double-walled units. Secured roll-up doors. Cameras set in inconspicuous places. It had been a good choice.

Whitewolf cleared his throat. "I've done some investigating."

"Yeah? About ...?"

"About the shooting of the Yuma Sheriff deputy."

"Really?"

"We've assumed that there was only one truck. The one that crashed. But I've replayed the tape from the event, and Deputy Cruze clearly indicated trucks. Plural. That got me thinking. So I checked out the crash site."

Rye turned away from the window to study Whitewolf's profile. "And?"

"There was more than one truck. I figure there were at least a dozen. And I found out where they went to."

Darryl Worley's song on Rye's cell phone blended with the rain's rhythm on the car's roof.

"Dawlsen, here."

"Chief," said Gabby, "Reese, Heilo, and DePute are about two minutes away."

"Gabby?" He frowned. "What are you doing? You're supposed to be at home."

"Not tonight," she said, "you need me here. Besides, I.C.E and the FBI are here looking for you and found me just as I was leaving. Something big's coming down. And looky here, Yuma's sheriff's walking in right now. This is getting real cozy." Her voice backed away from the mouthpiece. "Should I order out pizza?"

"Hey, Dawlsen," a distant Sheriff Anne's voice came through.

"And guess what," Gabby continued, returning to the phone. "The fibbies brought intel. Though I would have preferred German chocolate ice cream. Even Neapolitan would have been okay. But it is what it is. First, that photo you found on Juan at Batts' property. Their fingerprint analysis reveals prints from you. A set of unreadable prints. And another person of interest."

"Go on," Rye said with growing interest.

"Our very own Mayor Richard Humphries List."

"That's enough for a warrant," Rye said, smiling.

"It gets better. From notes on his phone, it appears our Juan was about to turn an important source."

After a couple of seconds of silence, Rye said, "So the cartel discovered this and killed him."

"Correct-amundo." Gabby popped a bubble with the gum she chewed.

"And he left that message before he died." Rye spoke more to himself than to Gabby. He narrowed his eyes recalling the letters. "It was so important; he used his dying breath to leave us that clue. What's he trying to tell us?"

"Yeahhh." Gabby's voice trailed off like she pulled the phone away. "The Feds want to talk to you. I'm putting us on speaker phone."

"Chief Davilsen," said an unfamiliar female voice. The phone speaker did not improve the impersonal sound in her voice.

"Yes," he said with uncertain caution.

"My name is Emmie Clark, and I am with the FBI. I have a search warrant for the residence of one Richard H. List."

"I don't understand." Rye shook his head. "What's going on?"

Gabby said, "The FBI, ICE, Yuma Sheriff's Department and Border Patrol had planned to raid the List complex tonight. Something about gun smuggling and drugs ... just to name a couple. And jay walking, I believe. However, the storm's grounded them."

Agent Clark spoke up. "The weather forecast calls for the rain to continue for a while. That grounds our operation. By the time the weather clears enough, the transaction of guns, drugs, and money we believe taking place tonight at List's place—"

"Wait a minute," Rye interrupted her. "What did you just say about guns, drugs, and List?" Rye watched the headlights of an approaching car. He freed his handgun from its holster and nodded at Noah, who caught the chief's meaning and readied his own weapon.

"Sir, really, we don't have—"

"Hold on a second." He pulled his notebook out of his shirt pocket and thumbed to the correct page. "Juan's message: 'GS. DS. DHL. DA.' It's guns and drugs. DHL. It's not an airline, it's someone's initials ..."

"Dick Humphries List!" Gabby interrupted.

"Right," said Rye. "That means DA is probably a person. But who? I don't—"

"Demonio Amo," Clark said. "Head of a military group turned drug cartel. He's a real SOB."

Rye peered through the watery traces on the back window as the other car came to a stop behind Whitewolf's Crown Vic. Heilo stepped out of the driver's seat and waved.

Rye said with a throaty sound, "And he's got my family."

Rain streamed off the brim of Rye's Stetson while he unlocked the garage door to his storage unit. Rainwater spilled inside his collar sending shivers down his spine. Rolling up the door, he stepped into the square room, glad to get out of the weather. The smell of gun oil permeated the space. Rain drumming the roof made hearing difficult. His fingers probed the wall until he found the light switch. When the lights flickered on, one of his officers whistled.

In the glaring illumination of a single fluorescent bulb, wooden crates sat on metallic tables or wooden pallets, along the walls and down a middle aisle. Stenciling on each box explained its contents.

"Nice," Heilo yelled over the noise.

DePute nodded his head in appreciation.

Rye said, "You can thank Iona. She provided the funds to purchase these weapons."

Rye took several steps into the storage area, his boots scuffling on the cement floor. Behind him, someone shut the garage door.

"And I think our circumstances require it." He strolled over to a table against the back wall and powered up the laptop sitting on it. "Gather around." He typed in a password, lighting the screen with the WPD logo and two rows of folders on the left side. Rye clicked on one labeled "Photos." A window popped up to show icons. He clicked on the first one.

"This is the front entrance to List's house." He looked at his officers. "This is where we're going in. List has been a project of mine ever since I became Whiskey's chief of police."

The picture revealed a beautifully southwestern-styled home, with a large vehicle turnaround and a wall that opened to a garden in front of the house.

DePute whistled. "Sweet."

"As you know, that's only a fraction of the house. This part sits on top of the cliff.' He opened another photo. "This is the rest."

The picture showed three stories of glass building tucked against a canyon wall. Rye clicked through several more photos showing the large concrete pad for a patio, the back acreage that led down to a dry gully, stables with a curving ramp leading to the middle story, and blueprints of the building's floor plans. The next screen shot showed an aerial view.

"This is List's compound," Rye explained, drawing an imaginary and irregular circle with his finger on the screen. "The back of his house faces this canyon which opens and drops into this creek. His property continues up this hill to this ridge." He pointed at each spot. "Any questions so far?"

Everyone signified a no.

"This is the road to List's place." He indicated a gray line that split the compound into two unequal sections. "That's the road on which Deputy Cruze was shot and killed." He paused, giving his officers the chance to make the connection between the murder and List's location.

"We'll come down this road," Rye continued. "Park at this little turnaround and make our insertion somewhere along this fence line. Notice the thick vegetation."

"Where does a mayor of a Podunk town in the middle of the desert get the money to afford all that?" asked Heilo.

"Good question," Rye answered. "I believe Whitewolf has the answer to that. Tell 'em what you told me."

Whitewolf bounced a glance between the other three. "Deputy Cruze was not killed by a lone truck that crashed. It was a convoy of trucks taking arms and drugs to List's place. He's been trading with one of the cartels."

Silence.

"Son of a—" Heilo stomped over to a wooden crate stenciled with a black "HK." She kicked it then smashed a fist on its top. She tilted her head and read the black markings. Caressing the top of the box with loving fingers, she turned to Rye. "Heckler and Koch?"

"Find out." He snatched a tire iron lying on top of the table and tossed it to her. She caught it one-handed.

She pried under the lid of the box, the nails giving way with reluctant squeals. The lid crashed to the floor.

She closed her eyes and lifted her head skyward. "Thank you, Jesus!" She lifted one of the olive green assault rifles out of the box and cradled it like a newborn. "The HK 21E Shorty Beltfed with a 9" barrel," she said. "Dig the scope. This is sweet. This baby can fire 800 rounds per minute, and it's mine. I trained on it in the Rangers."

Another crate lid fell to the floor, and Whitewolf held up a SIG P226 handgun, the dull black finish looking wicked. "Heilo, check this out."

Heilo joined Whitewolf. "Coo-ool," she said making the word into two syllables. "The 9mm, baby. It holds 15 rounds. Now, we can deliver some payback."

Reese stood next to Rye. "You said Iona paid for these. Where'd you get them?"

"Let's just say, I've got my sources." Addressing the group, Rye said, "You got a few minutes to get familiar with these weapons. I got several assault rifles, Hydra-Shok bullets, various knives with scabbards, tactical armor vests, helmets with tactical headsets, night vision goggles, and special boots." He paused for a breath. "I want everyone armed with an assault rifle, several of the P226s, extra mags, and at least one knife. Plus your service handgun. There's a screened-off area to change clothes. Now all I have to do is figure out how to connect these headsets to the FBI. Let's get ready, boys and girls."

"Hey, Chief," DePute said. "What about that Polaris MV8000 ATV in the back corner. That baby rocks."

"I want this to be a stealth operation."

"I can dig that, but how about a little misdirection. While the rest of the team deploys quietly." DePute nodded to the olive ATV. "With that, I can create all the diversion you'll need."

Rye smiled. "This is supposed to be where I argue with you 'cause I don't want to change my plans. But ... you've given me an idea."

He brought the group over to the ATV. He reached down in the back area and opened a door to reveal a hidden compartment. In there, he had stored some nonperishable food, camping supplies, a couple extra P226s, extra ammo, and half a dozen flash-bangs.

Then he looked at DePute. "Okay … dude … you have your ride." And Rye explained to him what he wanted.

Afterwards, Rye clapped his hands and shouted, "I want to roll in five."

Dressed with vest, helmet, goggles, knives strapped to each leg, handguns at each hip and locking in the ammo box to her HK 21E, Heilo stepped from behind a screen and said, "I'm ready to rock and roll."

Rye studied his officers. "This situation is no longer an investigation. It's a rescue mission."

"Boss?" crackled the voice over the radio on List's belt. Demonio jerked his gaze toward the fat Americano. "There's some moron playing on an ATV a couple hundred yards out from the house. How should I proceed? Over."

Sitting in a chair in the shadows of the room, Demonio steepled his fingers and tapped them together. *I will see how this vaca handles situations. I'll see if our relationship continues after tonight.*

List's face reddened. He struggled to get the radio from his belt while mashing the remains of a cigar into an ashtray.

The hombre struggles to keep his emotions in check.

List put the device up to his mouth and pressed the call button. "Well, idiot, go check it out. If there's any doubt, kill the SOB."

Too reactionary.

226

List returned Demonio's stare. "If he's on my land, he's one dead punk."

It would have been better to try and extract intel from the trespasser. Perhaps, he is more than a kid playing in the rain.

List rose from his chair and stormed over to the window. Demonio trailed him with his eyes.

Demonio grabbed Amalia's hand resting on his shoulder. He did not miss her slight flinch when his skin contacted hers. *This one still fears me. Buena.*

"Do we have a situation?" Demonio hissed at the mayor.

"Yeah," snapped List, "we got some idiot riding his ATV out in the rain. On my property. People think they can come out here four-wheeling or horseback riding. Pisses me off."

"Do you need me to take care of this … situation?" Demonio's voice whispered like a snake through tall weeds. *How easy it would be to fillet this vermin … But not yet.*

"No." List shot him an angry look. "I'm going to my Tech Room and take a gander at the monitors to see what this fool is doing. Dawlsen should be showing up soon. Make sure things are ready for him."

On his way out, List slammed the door behind him. Demonio stood, brushed imaginary lint off the front of his black shirt and returned his empty glass to List's desk. He meandered over to the window and peered out.

In the window's reflection, he watched the girl. She glanced at List's desk and flipped her gaze back to him. A humorless smile passed across Demonio's face. *This one wants to kill me.* The strength of the Skinwalker started to swell within him.

Wheeling, he pounced on the girl, grabbing her by the throat.

One-handed, he lifted her from the floor. She grabbed his arm and kicked at his shins, but to no avail. Demonio's gazed pierced her. Her eyes grew big with fright. She gasped for breath.

"Listen to me," Demonio said in a snarl. "I must leave for several minutes. I want you to stay in this room. Comprendido?"

She nodded the fraction of an inch his grasp permitted. He let go, and she collapsed to the floor, gasping and rubbing her damaged throat. An aching sob escaped her lips as tears rolled down her cheeks.

"Don't screw with me," he warned her and slipped out of the room.

When the door clicked shut behind Demonio, Amalia suspended her tears and snorted a derisive laugh. She made him believe she cried like a weak little muchacha. *Que idiota!* Because of her *pervertido* uncle, she had learned how to cut and shuffle with men's inherent stupidity regarding women. She swiped the faked wetness off her cheeks. In rapid Spanish, she muttered curses upon men. *But, this Demonio's something else … not quite human. A monstruo.*

Amalia's gaze turned to the door. Demonio's absence offered freedom. *Maybe my only chance.* Yet, if he caught her leaving, he'd kill her without reservation. She had witnessed his cold murderous rage at the cave. And overheard his murderous threats against others. Besides, he was going to kill her anyway.

She tiptoed over to the door and listened. No sounds. Cracking it open, she peered into the hallway. No one. *Now's your chance. Correr.*

But she had two things to do before she escaped this crazy casa. She tiptoed to the desk and snatched the sword-like letter opener from the cut-glass penholder. She scratched several long lines into the desk's surface. Then she plunged the letter opener into the chair's leather backing and dragged it through the material. Now, time to find those two girls and escape with them. The uninjured one had been kind to her. Now she could return the favor.

The steely glint of determination crossed her face. *Besides, I need an English speaker.*

She stepped into the hallway and eased the door closed.

Sheriff Anne Cakmann peered over Agent Clark's shoulder, staring at the agent's 17" monitor on her laptop. Two dozen video feeds from List's house played on the screen.

She watched as DePute immersed himself into his role of ATV junkie playing in the rain. The treacherous hills in the background were mere gray phantoms.

One feed showed List exiting his office and heading down the hall until he was out of the camera's range. Her stomach knotted. That man had caused law enforcement untold problems while evading prosecution for the last fifteen years. Slick pony-tailed lawyers always managed to get him off on technicalities. She was tired of him trampling over the people in her jurisdiction. .

Another feed revealed six armed men exiting the house headed towards the back lot.

Anne pointed at the feed, and Clark nodded.

DePute's voice came over the radio. "This is Rider. Eye, tell me what you see. What's going on?"

"Rider," said Clark, "this is Eye. You have six barking dogs headed your way. They just exited the north side of the dog pound. Over."

"Roger that."

Rye's voice crackled over the radio. "Rider, this is Crawler One. We are in position. I repeat. We are in position. Over."

"Roger," crackled DePute's voice. "Time to find the backdoor. Over."

The radios went silent in the dispatch room. Everyone crowded around Clark's monitor to watch the events unfold.

Anne snapped her fingers. "I can put two horsemen on that ranch in half an hour. Give or take. Mostly give. We'll miss the opening of the dance, but we can get there to mop up any wallflowers."

She bounced looks between the federal agents. She held out her hand. "I can take the warrants so no lawyer screws us out of a conviction."

"Do it." Agent Clark leaned forward. "I will inform our team there will be backup. But they are to proceed as planned." She looked at her watch. "Our window to capture List and Amo is beginning to close."

Rye motioned for his group to follow him. They had hidden their vehicles on a muddy trail in a thicket of red barked madroño trees and pine-oaks a half-mile back. Crouched in a single file, guns at the ready, they crowded the fence line to List's property.

"Careful," he called over his shoulder to his officers behind him. He nodded at a sign on the fence. "We have an electric fence. Knowing List, it's hot."

He studied the desert inside the fence and an uneasiness nagged Rye's thoughts. Though dotted with various acacia trees and some hackberry, the landscape exposed him and his people to List's scrutiny. They had no knowledge of what they faced inside List's house. How well armed were they? How many? But his wife and son were in danger, and nothing else mattered. Urgency forced him into playing this hand, no matter the cards dealt him.

Dee, hold on, babe. I'm coming for ya.

Waterfalls of rainwater poured off his helmet and soaked him. Winds drove the relentless rain into his face. Yet the discomfort only added to his resolute determination.

A dead tree, unable to withstand the storm, had toppled over, crushing the barbed wire and providing a route over the fence. A treacherous access, especially with the buffeting winds, but an access nonetheless.

"Eye, we found means to infiltrate the fence."

"Roger. Proceed with caution."

Easy for you to say. You don't have to cross this live electric fence lying in a growing pool of water.

Clark spoke again, "Wait, Crawler One. Voice has an urgent message for you."

What's Gabby want now?

"Crawler One this is Ga ... uh ... Voice. The Yuma ME office just faxed us an update on our ME shooting. It appears the bullet they extracted from his ... from him was fired from the gun of someone we know."

"Who?"

She paused. "Barend Jilt."

Rye whistled. *This just keeps getting better and better.*

"Mom."

The voice of a child whispered into her ear. The child sounded … scared. *Why?* A hand on the shoulder shook her. Dee did not want to leave the comfort of the darkness. Her skull throbbed, and when she tried to talk, her jaw exploded in hot pain.

"Mom."

Still hushed but more urgent. She knew that voice. *Who?* With a shock jolting her to consciousness, she recognized the voice. *Manny.*

"Mo-om, wake up." The hand on her shoulder gripped her tighter and shook harder. Dee opened her eyes to a lighter darkness.

"Manny … where …" her voice croaked. She touched the side of her swollen face.

"The bad men brought us here. It's by the house. It's a stable, I think. But there aren't any horses around."

She wanted to reach out and hug the fear out of him. Then she remembered. "The others?"

"They're in the stall next to us."

Dee rolled over on her back, mostly to escape the dank rotting smell of the ripened straw, dirt, and manure filling her nostrils with every breath. A moan escaped from deep in her throat.

"Mom, you okay?"

She ignored his question. Didn't want to cause him any more stress. Her eyes began to adjust to the darkness, and she could barely make out her son's form. "What …?"

"That jerk-off that punched you. I wanted to rip his heart out, but one of his men knocked me down and put plastic cuffs on me."

Anger colored over her son's fear. *Good. I'll need that Dawlsen determination if we're to survive.* "I appreciate it, son. You did good. It takes a real lowlife to hit a kid."

She opened her arms, and Manny cuddled next to her. She smiled at his nearness, at his smell as she enclosed her arms around him.

"Mom ... I think Dad's coming."

Dee remembered the Mexican's words before he punched her. *That's another one who will pay.* "We have to warn him. This is a trap. They want to kill him." Dee wanted to offer her son some comfort. "I love you," she told him in a quiet whisper.

"Me too. We gotta get out of here," Manny said. Even in the gloom, she could see his face go stone cold with resolve. *He looks just like Rye.*

"Wait," she said. She felt soooo tired. *Just give me a comfortable bed with a thick quilt. But not yet.* "There is one thing we need to do."

"What?" *That voice is Rye all over.*

"Remember at church last week. What did the pastor preach on?"

She sensed more than saw Manny shake his head. "What's that got to do—"

Dee reached out and touched a finger to his lips to quiet him. "Prayer. We need to pray for your father. That God will protect him."

CHAPTER 20

SUNDAY MORNING LATE

Johnny Batts crouched under a rocky outcropping behind List's property. Though rain poured over the overhead ledge, this niche mostly kept him out of the weather and provided decent cover to scout List's property. Using night binoculars, he witnessed DePute's antics below him.

"Be careful, kid." Turning his head sideways, he spat out a stream of chewing tobacco then dragged the back of his hand across his mouth.

Several three-burst gunshots rang out. Jerking the binoculars in the direction of the gunfire, Johnny spotted a squad of List's men heading for the ATV. Crouched over like military, they spread out with practiced precision.

"Dang-it. Pros."

Johnny swung his binoculars back to DePute.

"Get outta there. Now," Johnny said under his breath. As if Johnny's words traveled telepathically, DePute jerked the ATV 180 degrees and dashed for the creek bed. Raging roiled waters attacked its banks.

"Don't do it, kid," Johnny growled. *Them waters'll sweep you away in a heartbeat.*

DePute dodged boulders along the creek's edge, turned right at the creek's edge, and drove into a gully out of sight.

"Why'd you do such a fool thing?" He wanted to spit another wad of tobacco but refused to take his eyes off the unfolding scenario.

DePute reappeared among a tumble of large rocks further up the hill. Moments later, the young cop stopped the ATV, gathered some things and vanished into a crack in the rock. Johnny cackled until he began coughing. The kid cop had just compromised the mayor's escape route.

"Johnny boy," he addressed himself, "it's time fer you to enter this hoe-down. Hoo-rah."

Tip-toeing down a dark hallway, wood floor cool on her bare feet, Amalia heard footsteps coming her way. Panicked glances unveiled her best option. She ducked into an unlocked room and peered through the crack in the door. Moments later, three men with some kind of rifles turned onto her hallway, so she eased the door closed. She held her breath while they marched past her door.

After their footfalls faded, she stepped into the corridor and peered both directions. She gnawed her lip … hesitant for a moment … then hurried in the opposite direction of the patrol.

The hall ended into a living room. Amalia scanned the area, relieved to find it empty. Her mouth dropped at the display of wealth before her. Several large screen TVs. Entertainment equipment. Paintings of cowboys and Indians. Western-styled furniture. She crinkled her nose. The room smelled of stale beer and cigarette smoke.

Americanos are so rich. One of these paintings would feed a Mexican family for a year. And these TVs ... the sale would buy medicine to keep a village of niños alive. She shook her head. This Americano dwelt in luxury she knew came from the sweat and blood of her people. *Señor List, Dios will make you pay.*

Lightning from the storm flashed, illuminating the room like a strobe light, followed by a window rattling roll of thunder. In the silence after the thunder faded, a wolf's howl shattered the storm. Hairs rose on Amalia's arms.

The gringo sisters! She had to get them out of here. They knew of Demonio's smuggling operation. And that equated with being dead.

Leaning on clenched fists on the desk between his two security agents, Richard List scrutinized the monitors in his control center. He chewed his cigar, eyebrows furrowed in concentration. The reek from its acrid smoke filled the chamber.

The cold gray light emanating from the monitors provided the only source of illumination in the room.

A few rain-smeared cameras produced distorted images on some monitors. Curses rolled off his tongue like water from a downspout. The kid on the ATV disappeared from view.

Seconds rolled by.

He punched the table, shaking a couple of monitors.

The security person on his left leaned forward and peered with an intense gaze at one of the monitors. He clicked some keys on the keyboard then grabbed his mouse to control one camera. Scrolling its wheel, he zoomed into a patch of mud.

"There!" he yelled.

"What?" asked Richard.

"In that mud." The man pointed. "ATV tracks."

"Where's that?" Richard put a hand on the man's shoulder.

Scrolling the wheel to zoom out, the man yelled, "He's at the emergency exit."

The image showed the entrance to the square-cut cave.

Curses exploded from Richard's mouth. "Look at the ATV. That's no punk kid. That's one of WPD's pigs."

"Wiley's squad is converging on that spot now," said the security man. "But the rain's making things difficult."

"Send a patrol down the tunnel," Richard said. "Tell all patrols live ammo. Shoot on sight and shoot to kill."

"Sir," said the other security agent, "a satellite will be overhead in about five minutes."

"How's that going to help?" snapped Richard.

"It'll provide live images of heat sources. I will be able to tell where everyone is."

Richard wheeled about and headed for the door. "When you get that, contact me immediately. I have my Nextel. You guys armed?"

"Yes sir," they said together.

"Don't let anyone through those doors unless you hear from me directly." With that said, he rushed out the door, making sure it locked behind him.

"*No es posible*," Heilo said. "I'm not crossing on that tree."

Rye couldn't agree more. The tree that had collapsed on List's electric fence lay half-submerged in a pool of rainwater with the fence under it. Tree limbs jutted out of the water like skeletal arms. But options, like time, were something they were short on. "Okay. You got something better?"

Everyone stared at the growing puddle.

Heilo snapped her fingers. "Got it."

Before Rye could say anything, Heilo dashed back toward their vehicles. Rye looked down at his glistening boots. *Do I even want to know what she's going to do?* He heard a distant revving of a motor and, intrigued, he stepped over to the street. A moment later, she came barreling up the road in her patrol car headed straight for him.

Surely, she's gonna stop. When the car didn't slow, Rye took a step backwards.

She's gonna kill herself. And me with her. He took another step backwards and waved his arms. Still the car sped towards him and he began to wave frantically. Ready to jump, he swore he could see the whites of her eyes.

She stomped on the brakes and the car squealed to a stop, its back end fish-tailing.

The Crown Vic sat perpendicular to the road, aimed straight for the damaged section of the fence.

She looked out the window with a mischievous grin. The window slid down with an electric whirr. She met Rye's eyes. "Welcome to Plan B."

Heilo shifted into drive and stomped down on the accelerator. For a second, tires squealed on the wet road, then caught traction and leapt forward. Before reaching the fence, the car began sliding, missed the puddle, and crashed into the fence. The car finished its errant journey by nose-diving into a tree.

Rye opened his mouth to shout, but said nothing. The car straddled the fence providing a bridge across the electrified barrier.

Heilo opened the driver's door and raised herself to the roof. "As DePute would say, 'I got me a killer of an idea.'" Bent over for balance, she scampered off the car roof onto List's land.

Zach shrugged, climbed on the trunk, and crawled over the car to join Heilo.

"Eye," Rye said into his microphone, "this is Crawler One. We are entering List's property."

Whitewolf swung his rifle on his shoulder, "Crazy Cuban chick." He went up and over the car like a mountain cat. The three moved out into woods, blending into their surroundings.

"Roger that, Crawler One," said Clark. "Be careful. Our intel says he's got a sophisticated security system."

"Yeah," grumbled Rye, "I've been here—" Rye took a deep breath and clambered across on the car. He leaned against a tree and pulled a compass out of his jacket pocket. *Hang on, Dee.*

With two fingers extended, Rye motioned them forward. Whitewolf and Reese snapped their rifles to their shoulders, studying their approach through their scopes. Heilo leveled her HK21E machine gun at her waist. Step-by-cautious-step, they moved ghost-like through the sodden pine-oaks, walking in a tight v-shaped line.

When they reached the edge of the wild growth, Rye held up a fist.

Everyone stopped. He motioned downward with the flat of his hand.

"This is Crawler Three," Heilo whispered over the headset. "Don't anyone move. There are two men approaching. I've got 'em."

"Crawler Three, stand down. Do not engage." Rye did not want to risk exposing their positions with gunplay this soon. "I repeat, do not engage."

Silence. *Come on, Heilo, say something.* Rye held his breath in anticipation of the gunfire. Was she going off the reservation? He needed her to be clearheaded, not driven by her grief to seek revenge, thereby exposing their mission to failure.

"Crawler Three? Come back."

Silence.

"Crawler Three, where the—"

"This is Crawler Three. Two perps are down and will not be attending this dance. We can proceed."

"Crawler Three," Rye's voice sounded like a whispering tornado. "I told you to stand down."

"They were right on top of my position, I had to do something … and you did want us to bring knives."

"Roger that," Whitewolf and Reese said together.

Rye rolled his eyes. "Advance on my three," he said and counted.

As one, they emerged from their hiding places and marched to the roundabout in front of List's house. The house lingered in quiet. No lights. No movement. Rye held up a fist.

They all dropped to their knees.

A white pickup sat parked off to one side of the turnaround. One taillight was broken. *That fits the description of the truck leaving the scene of the ME's murder.*

"It's too quiet," Rye whispered into the mic. "Proceed with caution. Crawler Three, be ready with your HK."

"Roger that," came her hushed reply.

"Crawlers, this is Eye." Clark coughed. "I ... umm ... believe that List has advanced knowledge of your position. We suspect he may have a satellite feed and has the capacity to receive heat signatures."

Great. Just freaking great.

"There's movement behind the wall!" shouted Clark into his earpiece. "Get down. NOW!"

Rye dropped to the wet ground—the cold moisture soaking into his shirt and pants—when several guns opened fire upon them. Bullets whistled overhead, cutting through the vegetation. Leafy debris showered him. Lifting his head slightly, Rye spotted gunfire coming from the wall and openings in the garage door.

"Crawler Three," Rye said. His heart pounded. His mouth went dry. Time snailed. "Respond to our rude hosts. The wall and the garage door."

"With pleasure," Heilo said, her voice a snarl.

A moment later, a wall of sound erupted from her weapon. The 51mm caliber rounds tore into the adobe wall, creating a shower of dust. Holes in the partition evolved into expansive gaps. She turned the weapon on the steel garage doors, punching gaping holes into them with ringing punishment. Hidden cameras sparked out of existence. Wounded men screamed.

And still she poured on the firepower. Expended shells landed on other shells with a musical note. Bullets struck the house behind the ruined fence. Tiled shingles disappeared into dust. Windows exploded. The outside walls morphed into a bullet riddled fresco. The garage door collapsed with a metallic ring.

She stopped, and the silence roared louder than the gunfire. Seconds ticked by with numb ringing in his ears before Rye regained his hearing. Rainfall and screams of wounded men replaced the dreadful racket of hot lead.

"Cover me," Rye said and sprang from the ground. He raced across the open driveway and huddled by a piece of adobe wall still standing. He risked a quick look into the compound. He spotted several forms lying in puddles of red. Most remained still. A few writhed in wounded agony.

One of the wounded men struggled to a kneeling position. Heilo's firing had torn his left shoulder to shreds and blood soaked his shirt. Their eyes met at the same time. Pain and hatred flowed from the man's stare like hot lava. The man glanced down. Rye's gaze followed his. A 9mm pistol lay at the man's knees.

Don't do it, Rye pleaded. *Just be still and survive.*

They exchanged stares again, and Rye shook his head "no." The man grabbed for the pistol, and Rye fired a three-shot burst into him. The man stared gap-mouthed at the bloody holes in his shirt. His eyes rolled back, and he collapsed. *Why couldn't you have just remained still?*

Rye waved for the others to join him. In a hunched-over line, they double-timed towards the remnants of the adobe wall.

"Everyone okay?" Rye asked.

The three officers nodded.

He pointed at Heilo, and Whitewolf then motioned for them to check out the garage. She loaded another box of ammo on her HK and nodded. Crouched over, they hightailed it for the garage.

"It's probably too late to ring the doorbell and ask nicely if we can come in," Rye said.

"As if that really would've worked," Zach said.

Rye peeked around the adobe barrier. The large front window with its glass shot out appeared to be the best way in. The bottom of the frame sat even with the ground. From his previous visit, Rye recalled the sunken living room. *Careful, any number of people can be hiding in there.* Just when he made the determination to enter, a face appeared and fired a shot at him.

The bullet struck his rifle and drove the scope into his face. He cursed at the eruption of pain. Stars circled his head. He heard movement at the window, and he pulled the trigger.

Nothing. *Piss!* He tried a couple more useless pulls of the trigger.

A burst of gunfire erupted next to him.

"Guy started to climb outta the window," Zach said in a low shout.

Muttering, Rye ducked behind the wall. His eye socket throbbed worse than a three-day hangover. Blood blinded him and dripped off his chin. He tossed the weapon as far as he could.

"You're hurt, Chief," Zach said. He fumbled in the pocket of his jacket. Pulling out a medic packet, he tore it open. The scent of medication blew into Rye's nostrils.

Zach dabbed at the wound then pressed the gauze against it before applying tape. Rye turned his face upward to allow the rain to wash the blood from his face.

"That's going to look bad," Zach said. "Don't try out for any beauty contests. You might need stitches."

"Maybe when this shindig is over. You got a flash-bang?"

"Wouldn't leave home without one." Zach grinned, pulling one out of the thigh-pocket of his tactical-pants. He held it up for Rye to see it with his good eye. Rye drew one of his SIG P226s. He checked the magazine and slammed it back into the butt-end of the grip. Cocking the gun, he nodded his readiness. Zach pulled the pin and lobbed the flash-bang through the window. Seconds later, a bright white explosion enveloped the front room.

"Go! Go! Go!' Rye sprang to his feet and raced for the window. "WPD! WPD!" Rye yelled as he dropped into the sunken living room. His boots crunched upon the broken glass. Kneeling, he searched the room down the barrel of his handgun. What he wouldn't give for some aspirin.

Dirt from overturned planters covered the floor. Pillow feathers floated in the still air. The painting of some western mountain range hung in shreds. Bullets had chewed up a cedar column. The room stank from the flash-bang explosion, human sweat, blood, and death.

"Police!" Zach yelled, joining Rye.

A couple of groans came from behind an overturned couch across the room. Rye pointed in that direction. Zach nodded. With guns raised, they converged on the couch.

Two men rolled on the wood floor behind the couch, hands to their ears and tears flowing from their eyes. A third lay still on the floor, blood pooling around his head.

Rye read them their Miranda rights, even though they looked to be Mexican nationals and not US citizens. *With the courts these days, you can't be too careful.*

Zach zipped the plastic handcuffs on them and connected them together, both hands and feet. "I don't think they'll go anywhere." Using cloth napkins from the table in the next room, he gagged the two by stuffing the cloth into their mouths.

Rye gave the room another once-over. *Gotta find my family. Think! Where would List keep them?* His eye socket throbbed. He caressed the injury and found it had started to swell.

"Crawler One," DePute's voice sounded in his earpiece, "this is Rider. I've got company."

Sheriff Anne Oakmann halted her horse atop the canyon. Rain spilled from the brim of her Stetson. She reached back into her saddlebags and fetched her binoculars. Perched upright in her saddle, she focused the field glasses and tried to peer down into the canyon below her. But the rainwater beat against the lens and blurred her attempt.

She snorted in frustration and lowered the glasses, resolved to watch ant-sized men swirl the grounds of List's estate.

Returning the binoculars to the saddlebags, she looked down and spotted water filled human tracks on the ground. *Hello, what do we have here?*

Who'd be out in this mess? Friend or foe? The rain had destroyed any details, but there was no mistaking the outline of a boot print. Some kind of hiking boot, if she had to make a guess.

"Tex, take a look at these," she said to her companion.

The deputy rode up next to her. He slid from his horse and knelt by the tracks. Anne took pleasure in watching his broad shoulders, college-age waist size and 6'-5" frame. Tex hailed from Texarkana and had ridden horses all his life. When she had pulled up to the stables, he already had the animals saddled. Not a Hollywood pretty boy by any means, nonetheless she enjoyed gazing at his rawboned, weathered face. When she could sneak a peek.

He stood and turned to her. "Someone was here not too long ago. Headed toward the List property."

"Saddle up, cowboy. I don't want to miss any more of this dance."

Garcon DePute hopped off the ATV, grabbed his backpack from the vehicle and pushed his way into the cleft in the rocks. Struggling against the mud sucking at his feet, he labored up the hill. Had to be vanished before List's gunmen spotted him again. From the blueprints of List's house they'd pulled off the Internet, this crevice led to a passageway into the mansion.

He gained the tunnel, grateful to be out of the frigging rain and mud. Water leaked through the stony ceiling. He slipped out of his slicker, shouldered his backpack and headed in. Ten steps later, he came to a door. He tried the handle, but it refused to move. *Locked, no problemo. This'll be like cookin' fish sticks.*

Kneeling, he searched the backpack for his pickpocket tools.

Pulling out an LED flashlight the size of his pinky, he turned it on and stuck it in his mouth. Its light shone on the lock. Garcon inserted the pick and pulled it over the pins, imagining the metallic crook of the pick under his manipulations. With his head cocked, he listened for the telltale noises.

With the final whisper of a click, the door swung open. He returned his tools to the knapsack and slung it over his back.

"I have an open door," he said into his mic, "so I'm, like, going into List's palace. Can somebody say, 'That's crazy cool, DePute'?"

"Be careful, Rider," Clark said, her voice evoking no emotion. "Be advised that hostiles are coming down the tunnel."

"Consider me advised."

A moment later, he heard Rye over the headpiece telling Heilo to open the dance.

You go, girl.

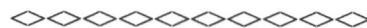

Johnny peered over the crest of rock, pointing his rifle at List's approaching stormtroopers. *Calm your breathing. Wait for them to get closer.* He settled the butt of the rifle against his shoulder, rested his finger alongside the trigger guard, and waited.

Some of List's men vanished from his sight behind a short rocky outcropping and he sighed in frustration. Seconds later, they emerged from behind the stone. He took a deep breath and held it, put his finger on the trigger and sighted the man nearest concealment.

Bam! The gun's recoil jumped against his shoulder as the first man went down.

He sighted a second, who turned to see his companion go down.

Bam! The second man dropped.

The sounds of his gunfire bounced off the canyon walls. List's men spread out to duck behind rocks. In the distance, more gunfire erupted. One weapon fired a long stream of bullets. *Some sort of machine gun.* Then things went silent. He waited. List's men scrambled, bent over, back to the safety of the house.

Johnny stood and shouldered his rifle.

Drawing his Glock 9mm, he held it two-fisted in front of him. *The opening shindig's over. Time to join up with the cop.*

"Eye, this is Crawler Three," Corazón Heilo said into her mic. She kicked a gun away from the hand of one of List's men sprawled on the concrete floor. She touched two fingers to his neck. No pulse. The stench of death permeated the area. "We have secured the garage." Her gun sure chewed the snot out of the place.

Papers from destroyed cardboard boxes floated in the air. The back side of the only car, a Lincoln MKX, had been obliterated, its rear tires shredded. *List won't be driving that for a while.*

Stepping around the pools of blood, Whitewolf grabbed the remaining guns and tossed the weapons out into the rain. "We're ready to roll," he said in an even tone.

The radio crackled in her ear, and Cora thought for a second she lost connection. Then Clark's voice came in clear.

"The garage's entrance into the house leads you into a mud room with laundry facilities. Take the laundry room into a hallway. Be careful. The hallway has several small storage-type rooms. Probably walk-in cupboards."

"Sounds like a good place for an ambush," Heilo said.

"Roger that," Clark said. "Follow the hall. It leads to the living room where Crawler One and Two are currently located. Make your way to them. Crawler One and Two stay put until Three and Four arrive."

No response.

"Crawler One? Two?" Worry tinted Clark's voice.

Whitewolf motioned for Cora to stand next to the door leading from the garage into the house. She nodded her assent. He grabbed the doorknob, mouthed a countdown and flung open the door. Cora filed in and went to her left. Whitewolf followed on her heels and went to the right. The hall and laundry room glowed green fluorescence in her night vision goggles, but revealed no targets.

"Eye," Cora said. "Crawler Three and Four are proceeding to tango-up with Crawlers One and Two."

They stole through the gloom of the laundry room and entered the hall.

Halfway down, they came to the first storage room. Whitewolf nodded to the door, and Cora re-fixed her grip on the HK. Whitewolf flung open the door. The dark room lit up bright with her goggles. Shelves of dry goods, canned foods, office supplies, and various cleaning chemicals lined the walls.

"Something moved back there," Whitewolf whispered, pointing to the far end of the shelving.

"Roger." She brought her gun to bear. "Check it out, Four."

Whitewolf shifted a few feet away from her and aimed his Glock at the stacked boxes along the back. Cora licked her suddenly-dry lips and leveled her machine gun at the corner. She glanced over at him.

He flashed a thumbs-up. "Police," said Cora, rushing the boxes. "Don't move." Whitewolf moved alongside of her.

The faces of three frightened children, pale green in the night goggles, peered back at them. A boy, who looked to be the oldest, and two girls. Hispanic kids.

"Policía," Cora barked then set the HK on the floor, speaking in more reassuring tones.

"Eye, this is Crawler Four," Whitewolf said. "We have a situation. We've found three Latino children. I think Crawler Three is trying to convince them not to be afraid. Suggestions?"

Silence, then Clark spoke, "Take them out of the house and—"

"Drop your guns," said a cold voice from the hallway.

In her headset, Cora heard Clark ask, "Trouble?"

Cora found herself staring down the barrels of several large handguns. "Si."

CHAPTER 21

SUNDAY NOON

"Dawlsen. Paging Rye Dawlsen." A familiar voice blurted in a sing-songy tone into his headset. Rye turned to Reese. Directing two fingers at his eyes, Rye then pointed them around the room: maintain an active watch. Zach nodded his understanding. *Silence*, Rye mouthed. Zach returned a quick thumbs up.

"Who is this?" Rye asked, eyebrows pinching together. With a sickening dread, he knew before he asked. He closed his eyes. *No, God, not this.*

"Dawlsen, this is your old buddy, Richard List. Welcome to my hacienda." List chuckled, but there was no humor in his voice. "You know, the one you've just shot up."

Rye lowered his head. "What have you done with my people?"

"You mean this washed-up Injun and the Cuban tramp?" Rye heard List take a deep exaggerated breath as if he were smelling a flower. "And her hair smells soooo good. We're just getting acquainted."

Rye clenched his teeth so hard, his jaw ached. "If you so much as …"

"Dawlsen, you're in no position to make threats. Either you do what I tell you, or these two cops are dead."

Rye stood still. If he moved right then, he would rampage the house, seeing nothing until List was dead at his feet.

List continued. "And the Haulke woman. Now, she's a looker." A pause. "And your family. I never did understand why such a beautiful woman like your wife would want to spend her life with the likes of you." He laughed. "She won't have to suffer that ignominy much longer."

Rye tasted the bile rising in his throat. "What is it you want?"

"That's more like it. You see, I thought we could converse in amicable tones. What do I want? That's an easy one ... I want you dead. Muerto. Mort. Tot. Guasto."

"Dick. Now that's impressive. I never cease to be amazed by the limits to your knowledge."

"Shut up and listen to me. I know you're in my living room. Stay put." List's voice in the headset went quiet.

"List?" *Nothing.*

"Rye?" Gabby asked with hesitancy.

"Don't say another word. For now, I'm on my own. Cease contact until you hear back from me. I don't have a choice except to play this out List's way."

Rye pulled the headset off his helmet and slammed it to the floor. He glanced at Reese. "But I know someone who doesn't have to."

Zach nodded and scrambled out of the room.

"Chief Dawlsen." With feet propped on his desk, Richard waved a smoking cigar at his prisoner who stood in the office doorway, hands bound behind his back. One of Richard's men shoved him from behind. He stumbled into the office.

"Have a seat," Richard commanded.

"I'd rather stand."

Richard nodded his head once, and Jilt punched Dawlsen in the kidneys, eliciting a satisfactory scream. He remained on his feet only because Richard's men held him up. Richard shook his head in mock disappointment.

"You never learn, do ya? You'll be pissing blood." Richard chuckled then took a drink of whiskey, enjoying its warmth rushing down his throat and into his stomach. "Now, sit down. After tonight, your learning days are over."

Jilt and Junior grabbed Dawlsen's bound arms and forced him into the chair in front of the desk.

Richard took a drawl on his cigar then blew out the smoke, staring at his prisoner through the haze of cigar fumes.

Dawlsen worried him. This do-gooder of an alcoholic cop meant trouble. The man accepted no bribes; would not let go of an investigation even if it meant personal injury. The man was a thorn in his side.

Tonight, Richard stood on the brink of a big money-making deal worth billions. He'd used Amo's cartel to funnel weapons and drugs back and forth across the border. After tonight, he—Richard List, grandson of a penniless rancher—would be worth more than some states. He finished his whiskey in a gulp.

"Dawlsen, Dawlsen, Dawlsen," Richard said, shaking his head as if scolding a child. "You are way out of your league here, boy. You're nothing but a broken-down rooster trying to play with hawks."

"Vultures," Rye grunted, hanging his head low. "I'm playing with vultures." He gasped for air. "And that's an insult to vultures."

Richard laughed, but without humor. "Good. Good. You still got some spunk in you. But you see ... what's going down is much bigger than you can imagine."

He exhaled the cigar smoke in Dawlsen's direction. "Mexico is a land of corruption. Every politician, cop, and soldier on the take. The drug cartels waging war. We're talking third world country. But," he spread his hands wide, "the land is a paradise of natural resources. Just sitting there, waiting for some enterprisin' hombre to take them. And that's what my ... umm ... business partner and I plan to do."

Dawlsen stared up at him. "Why tell me?"

Richard laughed. "I want your little mind to understand what you're missin'. We plan on turning northern Mexico into a prosperous democracy. A strong North Mexico will be good for the US. And you could have been in on it. But nooooo, not the great Rye Dawlsen."

The chief closed his eyes and shook his head. "You're not just nuts, you're a megalomaniac."

Richard nodded to his son standing to Dawlsen's right. Junior wheeled and punched Dawlsen on the cheek, opening a cut just under the damaged eye. Blood oozed down his face.

Dawlsen stared at Junior with his one good eye. "You punch like a girl."

Junior struck Dawlsen in the stomach. Dawlsen bent over gasping for breath. He would have fallen from the chair had Jilt not grabbed him from behind and thrust him back in a sitting position.

"Dawlsen," Richard said with a cold dread, "you can make your last hours of life somewhat pleasant. Or we will enjoy making it a living hell. Your choice."

Dawlsen studied him. "Just being in the same state with you makes my life a living hell."

Junior backhanded the chief across the mouth. Dawlsen's head jerked backward then lowered forward. When he looked up, Dawlsen bled from a swelling lip.

"Don't talk to my daddy that way," Junior said, his face a mask of rage.

"Junior List," Dawlsen said with difficulty, "you are under arrest for striking an officer. Anything you say—"

Junior backhanded the cop a second time. "Whadda ya want done with him?"

Richard looked to the ceiling, considering his options. "Until the transaction is completed tonight, we'll need to keep him as a hostage. Just in case the Feds try to interfere. Take him out to the stables with the others. He can spend his last few hours with his wife. Then ..." a grin spread across List's face. "I will personally kill the SOB, after he watches me enjoy the company of his wife."

Johnny crawled over the uneven tunnel floor towards the firefight. The cold, damp floor conflicted with the hot lead flying overhead. Explosive gunshots numbed his hearing while the flashes lit the tunnel like erratic flares. The pungent smell of gunpowder hung heavy in the air and stung his eyes. He prayed the young cop didn't do anything stupid and get himself shot.

"Hey! WPD! Put down your weapons," screamed DePute.

List's men answered with a barrage of lead.

Johnny hugged the ground, expecting to eat a ricocheting bullet any second.

DePute returned fire. A grunt of pain indicated someone had been shot. From the bursts of light, Johnny watched the young cop rise to his feet.

"NO!" Johnny yelled.

He sprang to his feet and tackled DePute a breath before List's men returned fire. As bullets sang overhead, the cop struggled to free himself. An elbow caught Johnny on the bridge of his nose and stars erupted in his vision.

"Take 'er easy," he said with a string of curses. "It's me, Batts. Johnny Batts."

The cop stared. "Batts? Dude, like, what are you doing at this rodeo?"

"Watching out for your punk hind-side." Johnny pushed on his nose. "Dang it, you 'bout broke my nose."

"Sorry, dude, but you're, like, the one who jumped me, remember."

List's men fired several more rounds their way.

"This tunnel leads into List's house." DePute paused.

"Having some problems breaking through?"

"Yeah. But I've got just the thing." DePute reached into the side-pocket of his pants and pulled out a flash-bang. "I wanted to use this baby later ..." he shrugged. "Just cover your ears and close your eyes." With that, he pulled the pin and tossed it down the dark tunnel.

Seconds later, a bright explosion ripped through the tunnel's gloom.

"Let's get 'em, dude." DePute sprang to his feet, turning on his flashlight.

Johnny shook his head, his ear canals vibrating from the explosion. He pushed up off the tunnel floor.

DePute fished a roll of duct tape from his pack. "Never leave home without it," he said. "No time to secure these dudes any better. We'll come back for them later."

Moving quickly, they taped the prisoners' legs and arms together. Afterwards, Johnny searched the prisoners' pockets while DePute gathered their weapons.

"Gentlemen," Johnny, brushing his hands, said to the prisoners, "me and my partner here are going up to the house to pay our regards to your boss. We'll come back and …"

DePute motioned for quiet. He cupped one hand over one headset speaker. Dropping that arm to his side, he rolled his head back and closed his eyes. "Bad news. List has the Chief and the others."

Johnny patted DePute on the shoulder. "That means it's up to us."

With rain pelting them, Anne and Tex halted their horses in a plot of land overgrown with stunted pine oak and cottonwood. Dusk filled the afternoon. Anne swung off her horse and hobbled the animal. After Tex did likewise, they passed through the tangled land and knelt along the barbed-wire fence. For all his size, Tex moved like a ghost, a skill that never ceased to amaze her. She studied the house, seeing only the top floor and part of the next floor underneath. The adobe walled stables blocked the rest of the house from sight.

"No lights in the stable," Anne said.

While riding down the twisting path of the canyon wall, they heard enough gunshots for a small war. Now, silence hung in the air like an eerie fogbank.

"It's too quiet," Tex whispered.

"I agree. Something's happened. If Chief Dawlsen apprehended List, we would have known."

Tex pointed toward the door at the rear of the stables. "We should make for that."

Annie nodded. "Doesn't look like List owns any horses. There's no evidence. No tracks. No horse smell. No piles. No feed. No hay." She studied Tex's rugged face in the dimming light. She swallowed her smile. He sure was easy on the eyes. "But then ... there's no horses to give away our approach."

"Let's do this." Tex tugged on the brim of his hat.

She drew her handgun and chambered a round, then gave a thumbs-up.

Tex held wide the strands of wire so Anne could step between them without getting caught on the barbs. After she passed through, Tex grabbed the top strand with one hand and leapt the fence.

They sprinted towards the exit at the stables backside. Anne felt chill bumps rise on her skin, the open space triggering her dread of being vulnerable. She waited for the sound of a gunshot, perhaps the last noise she'd ever hear. Fear quickened her pace.

She gained the rear exit of the stables the same time as Tex, and they stood on opposite sides of the door. They waited a few seconds to catch their breath. She nodded when her breathing returned to normal.

This was a routine she and Tex performed many times. She would open the door, and he'd go in first to one side, and she'd follow going to the other. They exchanged signals with their eyes. She took a deep breath, eased it out, and reached for the doorknob.

Just then, the door opened, and she jerked her hand back. A Mexican male dressed in desert fatigues stepped out. He struck a match to light the cigarette hanging from his lips. His eyes went wide when he spotted them and swung his Ak-47 in Anne's direction.

CHAPTER 22

SUNDAY EARLY AFTERNOON

"Doctor!" the nurse screamed.

She sprinted out of the patient's IC room and raced toward the nurses' station. Her lanyard of badges and cards bounced against her dark gray Harley Davidson smock. She reached the station, leaning on the counter and gasping the aseptic air. *Six months pregnant, and I can't run a few yards.*

"Doctor!" She called out a second time, though not as loud.

A gaggle of nurses and orderlies hurried over to her to see what was wrong. Cries of concern for her baby filled the station. A crowd surrounded her, everyone throwing questions at her. She pushed them aside and attempted to capture the attention of the young doctor seated at a computer in the rear of the station. For several seconds he ignored her, hands poised over the keyboard while downloading his notes into the hospital's mainframe. With an angry sigh, he rose out of the chair.

Dr. Dollal, you're a piece of work.

"Nurse—it's Jamie isn't it?—why don't you tell me what's going on?" The doctor's monotone voice with its slight roll of Boston accent hinted at irritation. She took a deep breath and turned to survey the faces of the staff surrounding her.

"The Navajo woman in Room 7. The one from the wreck—" she paused and scanned the faces waiting to hear her report. She turned to Dr. Dollal. *This is going to sound crazy.*

"Go on," said the doctor.

"She's missing. I mean, she's vanished. Her IV, the oxygen tube, all of it, is just lying in her bed. Under the sheets. Her bed is made. It's like she disappeared in thin air."

"Patients don't just disappear." He dismissed her with a wave of his hand. "Someone? Please call security." He stomped towards the patient's room. Jamie followed on his heels. "Are you sure she hadn't died? Or was moved to another floor?"

"She did not code," Jamie retorted at his hint of her professional incompetence. "And no, she wasn't moved out of ICU. Not without me knowing."

They reached Room 7, and the doctor came to an abrupt halt. The bed lay empty with no sign of the patient. Jamie gloated, "Like I said, she's just vanished."

"What?" Richard growled into the radio.

He paused outside his hunting room with trophies of animal heads mounted on the walls alongside guns and compound bows. He relished the times he stood at the entrance and stared at the measures of his manhood. With each head, an image flashed of the hunt, the kill. But right now, other business diminished that enjoyment.

"We'll receive satellite images any moment," came the reply.

"I'll be there." He spun away from the trophy room and headed back to the stairs. Daydreaming about his hunting trips would just have to wait.

"The link is live," said a security agent. Richard hurried down the hall.

"What do you have?" He flung open the door to the stairwell.

"Okay. I'm getting heat signatures throughout the building. Most I can account for: our people and the prisoners. Looks like we've contained the attack. However, I got two large heat sources outside the compound. If I had to guess, I'd say they're … horses?"

"What the … We don't have horses," he shouted. "Can you do one of those zoom things?"

"Yes, sir. Just let me—"

"Anything else?"

"Uh—yeah. There is a fading heat source behind the stables. It's like a C-shaped mound. I can't make it out."

"Zoom in on that first!" *Do I have to tell these geniuses everything?*

"Okay, hold on a second, is that? It is! That's a body!"

Zach zipped from room to room, hiding in rooms whenever he heard patrols getting close. Several things didn't seem right to him. The blueprints of the house indicated this floor had a six-lane bowling alley and an indoor batting cage. But instead, he discovered barrack type rooms. Though the beds had been made with military precision, he found the rooms to be empty. So where was everyone?

At the far end of the hallway, a rusty *errrk* warned of the door opening. Zach halted.

"Report in, SG12," a metallic voice crackled over the radio.

Zach threw glances right and left.

"Beginning to search the third floor," replied the radioman.

"Hurry up, we need more men to load the weapons."

The room on the right yawned open with its lights out. Not hesitating, Zach ducked inside, melting into the darkness. He held his breath and aimed his pistol at the open door, finger alongside the trigger guard. *Try it, mother. Just come in here.*

Two sets of footsteps approached. The men spoke low, the tones of their voices relaxed. Hopefully, they hadn't seen him. Yet.

Don't breathe. Don't move. Don't even blink. Movement attracts attention.

He pointed his handgun at what he thought would be their head height. *One shot, one kill.*

They stopped at the door. One of the guards bragged about doing the Cuban cop, and the other laughed. *Real funny. Reach for the light switch, and I'll make sure you never degrade another woman.*

The door opened, and two silhouettes stood in the doorframe. The one reached a hand into the room to feel for the light. Zach moved his finger to the trigger and squinted against the pending flood of light. *Enjoy your last breath, you son …*

"Hey, amigos." A new voice from down the hall. A Spanish speaker. "Wha'cha doing to my room, man?"

"We're searching for cops," said the guard as he withdrew his weapon. "Wha'cha doing with the girl?"

"Ain't none of your business," replied the newcomer. "I was just here a minute ago, and there weren't no cops in my room."

The other guard, his voice colored with irritation, said. "List has us checking every room in this freaking house. And when the man speaks ..." His voice trailed off.

"Okay. I get it," the newcomer snapped. "I'll check it out, so me and my girl can spend some time together."

The two guards laughed, and Zach could tell they were moving down the hall.

One of the guards said, "Don't take too long, or List'll have your back end. They're moving the weapons to the loading area. Let us know if you see anything, you know, out of the ordinary." More laughter.

A quick search revealed only one hiding place. Zach backed into the closet and eased the doors closed. Watching through the slats, he saw two figures enter the room, silhouetted from the hall's light. A tall male clutching a small woman against her will. She struggled to free herself, but the male maintained a tight grip on her.

"Say nothing, muchacha, and I might let you live," said the male.

The female spat back a slew of angry Spanish, of which Zach caught only a smattering. The man only chuckled. He lifted her and dropped the girl on the bed. The springs protested. Before the girl moved, the man fell upon her.

"You make this fun for José. ¿Si?" Then he backhanded her.

He brought something out of his jacket, but Zach couldn't see what the man had. A moment later, Zach heard the thkkk of duct tape being peeled away and then torn. The man taped her mouth shut.

"To keep you quiet," the man told the girl.

The girl began to struggle, and the man slapped her again. And chuckled.

"I like your aggression." He leaned forward and grabbed her left wrist and bound it to the bedpost with the tape. "*Zorra*," he added and reached for her other wrist.

Zach moved. He eased open the closet doors and rushed upon the man.

When Zach reached the bed, the man must have sensed his presence, for he turned.

"What the ..." the man said, his eyes growing into saucers. Zach raised a fist and pummeled the man's temple. The man's head snapped backward, his eyes rolling back. He collapsed on the edge of the bed, and gravity caused him to slide off.

The girl balled a fist with her free hand and punched Zach in the shoulder.

"Hey! Stop hitting me. I won't hurt you." Zach held his hands out. "Don't scream, por favor," Zach hissed. "No grites." He raised his hands in a surrender position. "Habla Inglés?"

She nodded like a bobble-head doll.

"I'm going to take the tape off your mouth." He watched calm begin to take over her countenance. He pointed to his chest. "Good guy. Bién." He pointed to the unconscious man. "Mal."

After easing the tape from her mouth, he put a hand flat on his chest. "Me llamo Zach. ¿Te llamas ..." he left the question open.

"Amalia," she replied

He pulled his knife free from its sheath and sliced through the duct tape binding her wrist. A quick flip of his wrist, and the knife returned to its sheath.

"I need to get you out of here," he said.

"No," she protested, "I must find the hermanas. And the niñas."

"Hey! Shut up!" the sentry yelled at his prisoners, leveling his AK-47 at them for emphasis. He tapped his feet, anxious for his companion to get back so he could take his smoke break.

"I don't want to hear no more complainin'." He jerked his gun back and forth, aiming at the different stalls.

Rye touched his dog tags under his shirt and felt the square amulet as well. His many bruises ached, his face hurt and his knee throbbed, but he had to get his family out and end this business. *This punk's likely to shoot someone if he doesn't calm down.*

Movement behind the guard caught Rye's attention.

"Drop your weapon." Oakmann's command cut through the stable's gloom.

The guard began to turn. Rye tensed, expecting the sheriff to fire. A shadow dropped from the hayloft and landed on the guard. They fell into a heap, and a struggle ensued. Curses rang from the two as they kicked up dust. Rye moved to help, but the newcomer pinned the guard and twisted one arm behind the punk's back.

"Who ...?" the guard croaked.

"Your judge and jury," Tex said, his voice a growl. "Don't move. Or I'll rip your arm outta its socket and shove it up the first orifice I find. You're under arrest. You have the right to remain silent ..."

Holstering her weapon, Oakmann raced over to Tex. They gagged and handcuffed the guard. Tex dragged him over to a stall and bound him to a pole.

For the next several moments, questions and answers flew among them. Rye let loose with a whistle, and the stable went quiet.

"Time for warm fuzzies later ..." He hobbled on one leg, turning about to see everyone. "This is an ongoing police raid. List and some Mexican drug lord are shipping weapons southward, and we need to stop them."

"But, Rye, you're hurt," said Dee, clutching Manny to her. "Your knee. Your face."

"I appreciate your concern. But this is my fight, and I plan on taking it to List."

A chorus of complaints erupted from the group. Rye waved his hands to quiet everyone, but to no avail. He remained rooted to his spot, eyes closed, waiting for the wall of voices to wear down.

"Dad?" Manny asked.

Everyone turned to the boy.

"Yes."

"I'm scared."

Rye stared everyone down, taking control with just his good eye. "We all are. Bravery is all about being scared but kicking butt anyway." He cleared his throat. "So ... here's how this is going to play out. Oakmann, this cowboy—" he pointed to Tex "—and I are going back into the house. Reese and DePute are still in there. Whitewolf and Heilo, take Dee and Manny back to the cars. Iona and Chee will go with you."

Heilo frowned and gave the briefest of nods. Whitewolf stared at the ground, offering no reply or even a hint to his thoughts.

Iona spoke up, "Do you think just the three of you can take on

List? He's got at least three dozen men stationed here."

Rye shrugged. "No problem. That's only twelve apiece." He said that with much more bravado than he felt. "Whitewolf. Heilo. I want you to watch the front entrance. If any of List's people tries to escape, stop 'em anyway you can. No one escapes." He stared each in turn. "One way or other, this ends tonight."

Manny ran over to Rye and grabbed him around the waist.

"Dad, be careful. I don't want to lose you."

Rye wrapped his arms around the boy as he stuffed back the tears starting to wet his eyes.

"And I prefer you not lose me either."

"Mommy and I prayed for you."

The boy's statement surprised him, but it also filled Rye with a warmth he'd not felt in a long time. His vision went watery. He smiled. They had prayed for him. Even after everything he had put them through.

"Take care of your mother, you hear?" He ruffled his son's hair. "You're her protector until I can come get you. And, Manny ..." He peered into his son's Hershey's-chocolate eyes, seeing his son's love for him. "Whatever you do, don't stop praying. I'm really going to need it."

Manny's face lit up. *The kid should hate me.* But somehow, the boy didn't, and Rye found that amazing.

Rye leaned into Manny and whispered. "I love you ... and Mom."

"People," Oakmann said, "if you exit by the rear door, head straight for the thickets beyond the fence. The stables will prevent anyone in the house from seeing you. Careful crossing the barbed wire. There's two horses out there. I'd take it kindly if you let 'em be."

Rye released Manny when Chee and Iona slid over to him. The Navajo said, "We can fight, too."

Rye studied the two of them. *I don't want to be responsible for any civilians, but … Iona is an ex-cop, and Uncle Chee's been around guns all his life.* He saw the pleading in Iona's eyes and decided.

"Heilo, Whitewolf, when you return to the cars, rearm yourselves. And give Chee and Iona each a handgun and ammo. We're going to need all the help we can get."

Iona winked at Rye. He looked away as his face heated.

Heilo nodded and took over the group, "Time to mount up, girls. Single file. Whitewolf, you lead. The rest follow the nice officer." She bee-lined to Rye and gave him a light hug. "Take care of yourself, Chief."

Surprised by Heilo's unexpected affection, he hesitated before returning the hug. "You take care of yourself. Listen, my family is in your hands. I'm counting on you."

"Me and Whitewolf will take good care of them. Just get that fat SOB mayor." She smiled without humor. "I never cared for the man. He smells like snake oil."

He prowled the grounds, the strength of the wolf spirit surging through him. He felt powerful and wild. A hunter. Deadly. A predator clad in the skins of a wolf that hunted the weak gringos as if they were long-eared prey.

Sounds alerted him to nearby creatures: winged, four-legs, and two-legs. He sensed the storm moving off, and his skin detected the downward shift in temperature. Despite his awkward gait, nature fused with the supernatural in his soul.

He trailed the escaping humans. His animal spirit had alerted him to their presence when they exited the stables. So, he hid and waited for them; watched them hurry out of the stables into the wild land. After the last one had reached the thicket, he glided in behind them.

Each escapee carried their own scent of hope, fear, worry, alertness. Their individual heartbeats informed him of their location like pinging radar. Whenever one of them brushed past foliage, he heard the scuff of plant against cloth.

They will not escape me.

He drew closer to the fleeing group. The anticipation of the kill flowed through his veins. He saw them now, splashes of color in the drab thicket. The group had reached the driveway and raced for the exit. Their labored breathing filled his ears.

Tossing back his head, the Skinwalker howled; primeval, raw, and hungry. Dread-filled shrieks from the group pleased him. Dropping to all fours, he pounced from the undergrowth and onto the gravel path. He stood and drew back his hands, claws out.

The humans stood rooted to the path. He sniffed in their terror as if the scent was a fine wine.

Hunt is over. Time to kill.

His leg muscles prepared for the leap. He opened his mouth and issued a snarl, saliva dripping from his teeth.

He snapped his mouth shut. *What was that?* Something rushed through the underbrush towards him. *Who? No! It can't be! I killed that woman.*

From the undergrowth, this other Skinwalker howled its defiance at him.

She dare challenge me? Where is the she-dog?

Then he saw her stepping onto the gravel.

The female snarled at him, back hunched and clawed hands held out to her sides. She turned to the humans.

"Run," she growled at the group and turned to approach him.

"Time to cowboy up," mumbled Rye as Oakmann and Tex joined him, at the side entrance to the second floor.

He peered into the smoky glass door.

"See anything?" she asked.

Rye shook his head. "Looking through that tinted glass is like peering through a mirror." He turned his gaze back down the way they came, the stairs cutting into the canyon wall.

"The door locked?" Tex said and grabbed the door handle, a large chrome-plated arch. The door opened with a slight tug.

"That would be a nope." Tex flung open the door and stepped inside. "Clear."

Rye followed with his gun pointed downward. Oakmann followed and stood close to her deputy.

The entranceway opened into an unlit hallway. No movement. No sound except for the cool air flowing from the overhead vent.

"Kinda quiet," Rye said. "I don't like quiet."

He nodded for them to move down the hall. Guns poised in double fisted holds, the trio eased their way down the hallway.

Rye's heart pounded in his chest. *Careful here, cowboy.* He fought to maintain a steady breathing pattern. *Don't hyperventilate. Breathe in and out.* Despite the AC, sweat beaded on his forehead. *Just like the search and destroy missions in Iraq. House to house.*

A TV droned from somewhere ahead. With every step, his foot pressed into the soft carpet. The paint on the walls smelled fresh. The swish of their clothing sounded loud in his ears. *Where was everybody?*

They came to the first door, solid wood. Rye tried the doorknob, and it turned in his hand.

"Unlocked," he mouthed. The other two nodded.

Rye flung open the door and stepped inside. Nothing happened. After shining his flashlight about the room, he rejoined the other two.

"These appear to be military style sleeping quarters." Rye cast glances between the two, receiving blank stares in return.

"What are you saying?" Oakmann said, keeping her voice low.

"Looks like we've bitten off a large wad of chew," said Rye, shaking his head. "So, let's see if we can't cut down the size of that chew."

"Whatta we got here?" Johnny said. The two men halted outside the gaping black opening leading off the main tunnel.

He shone his flashlight inside, played the circle of light over a couple dozen gun racks of rifles and pistols. Wooden crates of ammunition sat stacked in the center of the grotto. The scent of gun oil and wood mixed with the dry-dirt smell of the tunnel. DePute whistled.

"Dude," said DePute, drawing out the word. He shifted the rifles he carried on his shoulders. "List's got more AKs and Draco pistols than Hawaii has righteous surfers. That doofus must be getting ready for the Second Mexican War."

"Yeah. Remember the Alamo and all that stuff. Ya know ..." Johnny nodded to the weapons. "Those are the same types of guns walked over the border."

"Wooh! Why store all this?"

"Can't rightly say, 'cepting there's a boat-load of C-4 that's primed to explode."

DePute stepped backwards and examined where Batts shone his flashlight. "Dude, you're right. That's one gnarly boatload. Why?"

"List is up to something more than collecting guns."

"Bro, I'm not liking this setup. Guns walked across the border wired with explosives."

"Think of what'll happen when that C4 goes ..." Johnny gestured a mushroom-like explosion cloud. "Boom."

DePute's eyes widened. "That blows chunks. Let's a move on. I'd rather not be here when that stuff explodes."

"I don't want to be in Arizona when it blows."

A dozen yards further on, their flashlights played across the dull steel of a closed garage door. A security keypad shone like an evil red eye in the dark. DePute spit out a curse. "A dead end. We're like so dunzo."

Johnny flashed his light on the keypad and shook his head with a rueful smile. "No problema." He brandished a credit card sized item. "I got me a free pass in."

He swiped the card in the keypad slot. The red light turned green. Mechanisms to the door rumbled a complaint, and the door began to rise. Johnny turned off his flashlight and stuck it in his back pant's pocket. He removed two of the handguns from his waistband.

"Ready to par-tee?" Johnny grinned.

"Dude, you're freaking nuts-o. I like that." DePute slung one of the rifles from his shoulder. "Partner, this'll be epic. A dance of mayhem, up to death's portal."

They moved to opposite sides of the door while an expanding rectangle of light appeared at their feet. When, the door reached halfway up, the two men ducked under it and raced into the room.

Zach held out a hand, stopping Amalia. Her face paled, and she cringed like a puppy about to be beaten. Two Spanish-sounding voices echoed from the stairwell below them. Zach wrinkled his nose at the acrid stench of their cigarettes. He hated the things, but at least they alerted him to their presence.

He motioned to the girl for silence. He listened to the men's banter for several seconds to appraise his situation. Only two of them. Unfortunately, they blocked the only way out.

When Amalia had babbled about two sisters, Zach figured she had seen the Visser twins. *Nobody can match their Barbie doll meets John Wayne persona.* From Amalia's description—pieced together from her smattering of English and his smaller smattering of Spanish—one of the sisters had suffered a serious injury. That had clinched it for him. If this girl could locate the twins, he planned on getting them outta here.

He eased down the stairwell one cement step at a time. With the guards' conversation drifting up to him, Zach winced at every whisper of noise he generated. Breathing evenly became a struggle. He could have shot them, but that would have set off alarms, so he holstered his weapon. He peered over the edge. One flight down, at the base of the stairs, stood two men dressed in desert-fatigue pants and black shirts. They carried themselves like ex-military. He drew back and stared straight ahead.

Just what I need. Screw it. It's just like executing a play on the football field. Hit your opponent hard and often.

Zach risked another glance downward.

"Hey," one of the guards said.

Zach found himself staring down into the dark eyes of a killer. The blank stare of a person without a conscience. Spitting out a vicious string of Spanish, the guard swung his gun upward. Zach sprang over the railing as a spattering of gunfire rang out.

CHAPTER 23

SUNDAY EARLY AFTERNOON

"Mrs. Dawlsen," Whitewolf said, arms folded across his chest. "You and your son will stay with the cars."

Hands on hips, she returned his glare. She didn't put up with that tone from Rye, and she certainly wasn't going to start now with his subordinate. "I'm a journalist, and I have a right to report what is going on. It's important for the American people to know."

Their eyes stayed locked on each other, both refusing to look away.

"And I'll let you know what happened when it's all over. Now, please, stay with the cars." Whitewolf nodded towards Manny. "I don't want your son in the line of fire. And it's not a good idea to leave him alone out here."

With a grudging scowl, Dee had to admit ... that made sense. If she went with the cops, Manny would have to go as well or stay by himself. It's just that this List creep made her seething mad. She rubbed a hand through her tangled hair. *Calm down, girl.*

Heilo slammed shut the trunk to the Crown Vic and strolled over to them. She carried several handguns and boxes of ammunition.

"Here," Heilo said, thrusting a revolver into Chee's hands with an extra box of bullets. "I assume you know how to use this."

Then she turned to face Iona. For several seconds, the two women glared at each other.

"We had words," Heilo said. "Now's not the time to get into a pissing contest. Here." She handed Iona a revolver and ammo.

"Thank you. And about the other day …" Iona paused. "I was outta line."

"Okay. Me and Whitewolf are trusting you and the uncle to cover our backs."

Iona nodded, and Heilo turned to Dee.

"You're the Chief's ex," she said, "so I hope he's taught you a thing or two about handling weapons."

Dee accepted the revolver and extra ammo. "If you're asking if I know how to shoot one of these, then, yes I do. If you want me to take it apart blindfolded and reassemble it in ten seconds, then, no, I can't do that."

Manny stared at the revolver in Dee's hand. "Cooool. Do I get one?"

Both Dee and Heilo glared a "no" response at him. Heilo turned back to Dee.

"Stay here and stay safe." Heilo turned away from her and motioned to the others. "Let's go babysit the front gate."

A moment later, Dee found herself alone with Manny.

Dee hated to see them go. The sudden isolation weighed heavy on her. The rain … the wind … the gloom brought a surge of melancholy. Like all those nights when Rye went out drinking.

Manny grabbed her hand, and she peered at his anxious face. She smiled, hoping to ease his fears. *Those eyes. The tilt of his head. I never realized that my son is a miniature Rye.* She blinked away the wetness abruptly welling in her eyes. *Oh God, please keep my husband safe.*

She wanted to do her part to help Rye. Yeah, their marriage had serious problems. Yeah, he could be a real jerk at times. Yeah, he hit the bottle way too hard … But she still loved him. And Manny adored his father. She couldn't miss the look in her son's eyes whenever Rye walked into the room.

Whitewolf's right. Staying with Manny is doing my part.

Yet, it didn't feel that way. Then a thought chilled her. *What if List's men succeed? Then we'll be here alone.*

She grabbed Manny's hand and hurried to the SUV. She opened the door.

"Get in and lay on the floor. Don't come out unless you hear my voice or your father's." She slammed the door shut.

"But, Mom," Manny whined, hands and face pressed against the window.

"Don't 'but Mom' me." She raised the handgun toward the estate and sighted down its barrel.

"Where you going?" Manny pounded a fist against the window. Panic colored his tone. Her mother's instinct heard his tears forming.

"I'm not going anywhere, dear."

She spun the cylinder. *Mommy's staying right here.*

Demonio stood with his feet spread wide, his hands clenching and unclenching at his sides. He tilted his head, staring down his opponent. "Ha! The señorita wants a fight."

The woman opened a canvas bag she carried. From its confines, she produced a round leather shield decorated in beads and a solid black feather tied to a black leather cord.

After slipping the feather necklace over her head, she adjusted the shield on her arm and asked, "You were looking for these?" She tossed the canvas bag aside.

Demonio's lips curled into a snarl. "They're mine, thief."

Sunflower shrugged. "I took them to prevent you from getting your hands on them. You came to the museum too late. I got there first." She tensed, positioned to attack.

"I will kill you and take them from you."

"Not if I have anything to say about it." Snarling, she sprang for him.

Demonio turned sideways to meet her rush. Ten yards away, she leapt, hands up by her shoulders. At the last moment, he raised an arm and deflected some of the force as she crashed into him. They both landed hard and rolled away.

Before he could stand, she was on him, arms flailing like a rabid windmill. Some of her jabs, he managed to block. Others struck hard, the talons cutting, searing. Demonio struck back, but the magic in the talismans frustrated his efforts.

Bleeding from several cuts, he shoved her away. Wheeling, he bounded like a canine, her breath on his heels. After a dozen jumps, he whipped back around swinging his fist and caught her on the side of the head. The force of his punch sent her reeling, and she crumpled into a mud puddle face down. But the power of the talismans sent icy shocks down his arm. The limb hung uselessly at his side. He had only momentarily stunned her; time to seize the initiative. Demonio vaulted onto her back, and with his good hand shoved her face into the puddle.

Her arms flailed to free herself, but Demonio only pushed her down harder. A snarl escaped from his lips. He'd kill her, burn her body, and spread her ashes over a refuse dump.

Then, too fast for him to prevent it, she reached up one hand and grabbed his side. Her nails dug in like ice picks. She ripped her hand away, taking a chunk of wolf skin and his flesh. Howling, he pulled back.

With that fleeting respite, she bucked under him. Demonio fell sideways as the she-wolf pushed herself out of the muddy puddle. Thick water streamed off her face.

"Look what you done, *Loba*," he screamed at her. With one hand, he tried to staunch the flow of blood.

"I know who you are." She spat puddle water from her mouth. Rising from the mud, she yelled at him, each word sounding like a gunshot. "Demonio Amo. Drug lord. Killer. Terrorist. May your soul burn for all eternity."

"How you find this out, my name?" *She knows my name. She could kill me with that information.*

"I may be a Navajo. That doesn't mean I'm stupid." She smiled, but her eyes glared at him. "It's called the Internet."

With a bellow, he dove at her. *How dare this insignificant female interfere with my plans! She will pay. I make her suffer long before she dies.*

She rolled away and out of the puddle. Springing to her feet, she fled into the underbrush.

Demonio struggled to his feet. Wincing, he put a hand to his wound. When he drew it away, blood filled his cupped hand. But the bleeding had slowed.

Raising his head, he sniffed the air and detected her scent. She might as well have painted her passage with fluorescent colors. *This will be like finding a long piece of straw in a small stack of short needles.*

Letting loose a long howl, he gave chase.

Junior List found the unmarked cop car bridging the electric fence and stared at it as if he came across a field of primo pot. With both hands gripping his belt, he hoisted his sagging jeans to just under his beer paunch. He patted his stomach.

That there's a history of good beer drinkin'.

He waited and listened to the rain-dripping woods for a sound out of place. Hunting had taught him patience. *I ain't no fool. This thing is going down, but it ain't touching me.* He figured the cop car belonged to the pigs that sought to bring down his daddy. *Well, let 'em. I ain't getting tagged with the old man's crimes.*

Raising his all black .30-06 Remington 740 to his shoulder, Junior peered at the tangled undergrowth through the night scope. He might be running, but he wasn't about to throw caution out the back door. No sir, not Junior List. He scanned his surroundings.

No movement. Nothing out of place.

He emerged from his hiding place and scrambled up the car. Halfway across, his foot slipped on the wet metal. He fell, both knees landing on the roof.

Don't want no fried Junior setting out here like roadkill.

He knelt on the roof, his heart pounding like a galloping horse. Cold fear rooted him there. Yet, he couldn't stay exposed as he was. Inching his way over the car, time crawled past like a snail on ice before he again stood on sodden ground.

Rolling his eyes heavenward and muttering a word of thanks, he pushed his way through the last sliver of brush until he came to the blacktopped road. He planned to cross the road and hide out at the shack they used when branding time came. *Maybe I can come out of this without my record being tarnished. Any further that is.*

With a smile, he dreamed of assuming his daddy's role and taking over the List enterprise. *Sweet!* He wouldn't have to listen to all those insults from the old man anymore.

Then he spotted the other car with Whiskey Police emblazoned on its side. *Just waitin' fer my takin'.* Something moved at the vehicles. Junior sought refuge behind a large rock, rested his jowls against the gunstock and sighted through the scope. The car zoomed into close proximity.

Come on. Come on. Frigging show yourself.

A woman stepped away from the SUV. Dark hair. Attractive. He couldn't see her body, but his mind imagined it and what he'd like to do to her. His excitement grew.

Wait, I've seen her before ... that's Dee Dawlsen!

He grinned. *Time for some REAL fun.* He'd abduct her to the shack, have his way whether she was a willing partner or not. *Hopefully not. Give me an excuse to kill her.* For several minutes, he watched her as his desire hardened. *She's an alert one.* When she ducked back down, he sprinted across the side road carrying his Remington one-handed.

He slipped into the brush and rocks.

Barend Jilt woke to the sound of gunfire. His hand slipped under the pillow and grabbed the Smith & Wesson Model 41. His fingers wrapped around the wood grips. He chambered a round. Though a .22 caliber, he loved its accuracy. Great weapon for up-close wet work.

Taking the extra few moments, he slipped on a pair of desert camo pants and tan military boots. He had slept in a black undershirt. No need to change that. He picked up his Nextel.

"Jilt here. Report."

List's voice came over the device. "Dawlsen got loose somehow."

"Why didn't you wake me?"

"I thought a dozen men could handle it."

"Listen. The man's ex-military. He's been through some tough situations. Now he's here, and you thought you'd let me sleep?"

"Whatever. Get to the Communications Room. I need you there to be my eyes. It's time to evacuate the premises. The copters will be here in short order."

Trying to trap me is what you're doing, telling me to go to the CR. I ain't buying. And I ain't taking the fall for this. "Where's Junior?"

"He's scouting the front."

Yeah. Right. He's running. "I'll be at the CR in three." He cut off transmission before List could reply. "But I ain't staying for long. Just long enough to get intel and find out what's going on."

For a moment, he stared down at the handheld. If Dawlsen was loose, that meant the Feds probably weren't too far behind. The whole plan began to unravel just as it neared completion, and he didn't want to serve time. With a yell, he hurled the Nextel against the glass. The radio shattered; the bullet-proof window wobbled.

Minutes later, he stood outside the CR and typed his password into the keypad. The door slid open. When he entered, the two men at the consoles raised their Colts in his direction.

"Stand down," he commanded.

"Mr. List told us ..." one of the security men said.

"We have a situation that is deteriorating," the other security man cut in. "We had hostages, but they've escaped and set up a guard post at the compound's front exit. Several of Dawlsen's people are inside the building, and we're trying to monitor their ..."

The room plunged into blackness.

"CRAP!" the other tech yelled at the blank monitors.

The emergency exit lights came on, filling the room of lifeless computers with soft light.

"Had to happen sooner or later," said the guard, next to him. "I'm surprised it took them so long. But where's the backup generators? You can't stop them unless ..."

"Unless what?" Jilt gripped one of the man's shoulders, not sure he wanted to hear the reply. "Unless what?" he repeated.

"They've hacked into our system."

Rye peered around the corner into the lounge area. *Empty.*

Numerous TVs sat silent. Racked balls waited on the pool tables. No one sat in any of the many couches. *Just 'cause it looked void of people, didn't mean it was.*

"On my three," he whispered. "Tex you go left. Oakmann, go straight. I'll take the right." They nodded. Rye took a deep breath and breathed out. He held up one finger. Two. Three.

Inching his way around the corner, Rye discovered a couch and several chairs blocking his path. Possible places for a shooter to hide.

He reached the furniture. With finger ready to pull the trigger, he peered over the couch. *No one.* Yet a set of muddy footprints suggested someone had recently been there. He knelt down for a closer look. He'd seen this type of imprint often enough. Military boots.

"Clear," he said. "But someone was here in the last minute or so."

The other two reported their sections cleared.

"Got another room over here," said Tex, standing next to a closed door.

This door did not have the wood finish of the other doors. Rather, it had a dull iron gray color of a metallic utilities office. He would have assumed the architect would have matched the door to the décor. But then, assumptions got good cops killed.

With Rye on one side of the door and Oakmann on the other, Tex tested the doorknob—unlocked—and flung it open. They rushed in. Tex to the left. Oakmann in the middle. Rye to the right.

Empty. Yet, unlike the other barracks, this one contained one unmade bed, a nightstand, a closet, a footlocker, and a shattered walkie-talkie.

Rye stepped into the room and headed towards the footlocker. His hand brushed over the name stenciled on its lid. Barend Jilt.

He opened the footlocker. Several desert and jungle camo uniforms of the Mexican army lay folded in neat stacks. Several army caps sat of top of the stacks. Odd, Jilt was never in the Mexican army. *So what's with all the Mex army duds?*

A pair of muddy footprints stained the carpet next to Jilt's bed. He touched the mud and rubbed it between his forefinger and thumb. Moist. He raised his fingers to his nose and rubbed it again while sniffing. It smelled of … *stables.*

Rye rose to his feet. "We just missed Jilt by a minute. Get this. His footlocker has several army uniforms. Mexican army uniforms."

"Makes no sense to me," Oakmann said. "I've read Jilt's rap sheet. He hates Mexicans."

Tex cleared his throat. "We've seen this along the Texas border. Some less than patriotic US citizens working with the cartels by posing as Mexican army."

They exited Jilt's room, crossed the lounge, and headed down the next hallway. At the next room, Rye opened the door and stared into darkness. He held out his handgun and flicked on the flashlight. He pointed its beam into the room.

"What the—"

Jumping backwards, he let out a curse. A grizzly bear stood in the back of the room, mouth frozen open and paw raised ready to strike.

Rye aimed his handgun at the creature, laser beam dotting the bear's chest. His finger itched the trigger. The animal just stood there. With a wry grin, Rye shook his head in embarrassed understanding and lowered his gun. This was one of List's hunting trophies.

"Don't feel bad," said Oakmann, Hand over her mouth to suppress the mirth beginning to spill out. "I'd have blasted the thing."

"I just about peed on myself," Rye said.

"In Texas," Tex said, "our Chihuahuas are bigger than that."

Flashing his light around the room, Rye observed the many creatures whose heads decorated the walls: wolves, antelopes, longhorn sheep, and a moose. Their glassy eyes stared back at him in their death gaze. Hunting rifles bid their time in racks, stocks gleaning with meticulous care. His beam crossed over a hunting bow, and he stopped.

He stared at it for a moment, breaking into a smile.

"Now that's what I'm talking about," he murmured then fetched it off the wall. "A Hoyt ProElite with XT 3500 limbs and the C2 Cam. Consider this baby recompensed."

"Hey, Dawlsen," Oakmann said, standing next to him. "What are these?"

She held up a box of cone shaped devices.

"Those, my dear, are explosive arrowheads. As is, they're not armed. But you take one of these arrow shafts," he held up one without the head, "and screw the arrowhead onto the shaft," which he demonstrated, "and you have created one very lethal weapon. I'm going to assemble me a few of these."

After he finished, he spotted a leather quiver decorated with beaded Native American designs and beaded fringe. Taking it off the wall, Rye stuffed it with over a dozen arrows.

Slinging it over his head, he joined the others waiting for him in the hallway.

That's when the gunfire erupted.

CHAPTER 24

SUNDAY MID-AFTERNOON

Zach hopped the railing and plummeted into one of the guards. Gunfire exploded in his ears, and bullets whistled past his face. His upper back struck the cement floor just as the lights went out.

In the sudden cave-like darkness, Zach rolled away from the guards. He hoped. Backing into the corner, he pushed to his feet and waited for his eyes to adjust. Pale light leaked from under the door. He reached for his gun and realized he'd dropped it.

The light from the exit sign came on.

One guard lay still on the floor. The other man, bigger than Zach, spat out a stream of tobacco. He wore the brown and tan desert camo of the Mexican army. Zach noticed the prison tat of an Aztec bird on the back of his hand. *So we got a tattoo-wearing member of the Mexican drug Cartel, el Águila. The Eagle.*

"You kill mi hermano, cerdo." *Pig.* The man rotated his head back and forth, neck cracking at every move.

Zach shot a glance at the man's "brother" on the floor and noticed the odd angle of the guy's head.

"Now, you die. Lentamente." *Slowly.* He tossed his pistol with a clatter to the floor and drew a 12" long Bowie knife. The rasp of steel blade against steel sheath sounded ominous echoing up the stairwell.

Zach reached for his duty belt and grabbed his ASP, the expandable wand. Mr. Aztec Tat stepped over his companion to trap Zach in the corner.

"You think you hurt me with little stick."

"No, I think to hurt you with big stick." Zach whipped his hand back over his shoulder. With a crack, the ASP extended its full length. Before the other could take a breath, Zach whipped the wand against the outside of the man's thigh. Yelping, the Águila dropped to the floor, aiming a weak jab with his Bowie. Zach dodged the blade and lashed the wand down on the man's collarbone. A scream followed a snap of breaking bone, and his knife arm hung useless.

"Stay down," Zach said. "I'm WPD."

"If I get my hand on you, you're DOA." His face transformed into a mask of agony-filled rage.

A scraping noise sounded on the stairs.

Mr. Aztec Tat peered upward. Zach, not waiting to find out the source of the noise, flicked the ASP across the man's nose. An enflamed welt rose across his face.

The man let loose a string of profanity intertwining English and Spanish.

"Drop the knife," Zach said.

They exchanged glacial stares.

"Next swing," Zach threatened by pointing the ASP at the man's face, "and your nose will be a bloody smear."

Zach watched the fight go out of the man's eyes, and he dropped the blade, the weapon ringing on the cement floor. He grasped his injured shoulder.

Whipping his gaze upward, Zach called out, "Who's there?"

"Just me," said Amalia, her voice a blend of tears and terror.

"Stay put."

Zach grabbed the injured man by the collar. With the prisoner screaming, Zach forced him over to the stairs. Though the man whimpered pleas, he handcuffed his prisoner's uninjured arm to the railing. Zach made sure no weapon lay within the man's reach before turning his attention to the man he had crashed into. Bending over, he checked the guy's pulse and found none.

"All secure," Zach called up the stairwell to Amalia. While listening to her feet slap against the metal stairs, he gathered his gun and the two guns dropped by the guards.

When Amaila neared the bottom, Zach said, "You might want to shield your ..."

The girl poised on the last step, eyes fixated on the dead man. She snorted. "You think I not see dead men before." With hands on hips, she leveled her gaze at Zach. "I live in Mexico. When gangs fight, they leave many dead bodies. Beinvenida para mi mundo." *Welcome to my world.*

"Okay ... then," Zach drew out his words. "Wait there." He motioned for her to stay at the stairs then nodded at the door. "I'm going to check it out."

The injured man moaned for the girl to help him.

"I hope you die many slow deaths," she said in Spanish, her eyes narrowed into angry slits. She spat at him.

Zach raised an eyebrow. *Sticky note to me, never make a Mexican chick mad.* He eased open the door and peered through the crack. The stairs led to a utility room with a boiler and AC units.

"It's clear," Zach called over his shoulder.

"This I know. Follow me," Amalia brushed past him and marched into the room. An open seven-foot wide roll-up door cast dim illumination from the last throes of sundown.

Zach slinked behind the girl in a low crouch. His gaze swept across the room.

"This way," the girl said, motioning with an index finger.

"Wait," Zach called out to her, but she ignored his soft cry.

Muttering, he grabbed her arm. "Hold up, there."

She jerked her arm free of his grasp and started to say something. Zach clamped a hand over her mouth.

She tried to bite him.

"Be quiet," he hissed. "Callate. Mal hombres." He pulled her into the shadows behind a tractor just as two guards strolled past.

Her soft, brown eyes went wide. She nodded.

Zach eased his hand from her mouth. "¿Donde estan las muchachas?" *Where are the girls?*

Amalia pointed at a door secured. A steel bar across the door ensured no one from the room would escape. "Allí." *There.*

They crossed the grease-stained cement floor, skirting around a pallet with a discarded boiler and HVAC apparatus. Lawn care equipment and yard decorations sat along one wall. In the center of the wall, between racks of tools, the door awaited them.

"Esconde te." *Hide.* Zach pointed to a hidden and secluded spot.

He waited until Amalia crammed her body into the hiding place, and then motioned for silence. She nodded again.

With both hands, he strained to lift the steel bar. Muscles tensed at the weight of the metal, but Zach set it down against the wall without making a sound. *Man, is that thing ever heavy. It must weigh over sixty pounds. Closer to seventy. Maybe even eighty.*

He opened the door an inch and said into the opening, "WPD. Don't move." Then he flung open the door the rest of the way.

Garcon DePute followed Johnny Batts, guns pointing down. They ducked under the door rolling upwards, exiting the tunnel, and dashed into an indoor pool area. The room's moist heat smacked DePute like a girl-slap, sweat immediately beading on his forehead. An indoor Olympic-sized pool spread out before him. Lights from the pool sent dancing circles of illumination onto the walls and ceiling. Arrangements of plants and a manmade waterfall in the back of the room created a jungle-like atmosphere. Lounge chairs and wicker tables formed perfect military lines besides the pool.

A dozen armed men, smoking cigarettes and lounging at the bar near the glass wall, spotted them at once.

Holy Ungnarly.

DePute dodged in one direction, failing to see where Batts went. Several shots rang out, bullets whistling overhead. He scrambled behind a bar with a shiny metallic front and tucked the handgun between his belt and his lower back. He lowered the rifles from his shoulders, laying them out before him. The clips of ammo he dropped beside the guns.

He snatched one of the rifles and jammed home a clip. More

bullets pinged the metallic surface of the bar. One struck a metal pole behind him and ricocheted off with a zing.

He raised the rifle over the bar and, aiming at the shooters, emptied the clip in three burst spreads. A strangled cry acknowledged he hit someone.

Maybe that'll slow 'em down.

A dozen bullets smacked against the bar.

Then again, this is jacked.

He leaned to peer around the side of the bar when the lights went out.

Cora Heilo heard them first.

Kneeling next to Whitewolf, she noticed no fresh tracks cut through the muck. She patted Whitewolf on the shoulder.

"No one's been through here," she whispered.

He nodded.

The first storm had passed into the eastern night. A new one approached from the western sunset, flashes of lightning on the horizon. A distant rumble of thunder registered in her mind. Frowning, she tilted her head to listen better.

What the … that's not thunder. She tilted her head, listening. "Hey, listen. Helicopters. We've got incoming birds."

Whitewolf glanced up at her. "They ours?"

"How should I know?"

"If they're List's … we're like Custer." Whitewolf shook his head. "I don't like this."

"Oh. No. No no no no ..." She threw looks between Whitewolf and the direction of the house.

"Now what?"

"The explosives in the truck," she said, her eyes going wide.

"Huh?"

"Don't interrupt." Cora held up a hand to stop him. "I'm thinking here."

Whitewolf ignored her comment. "I been wondering over the amount of resistance we've experienced here. I expected more. Much more. So far, the resistance's been little more than token. Almost as if—"

The thump-thump-thump of the helicopters' rotors drew closer.

"Hey!"

Cora and Whitewolf spun around, raising their weapons, only to see Chee and Iona hurrying down the driveway.

"Get back to the gate," Whitewolf said.

"No, wait—" Chee began.

"You heard the man," Cora added.

Iona shouted, "Will you listen to him?"

"I heard a strange thing when we were prisoners," Chee said. He paused and looked at each of them in turn. "One of the guards said something about some wiring's done. The other mentioned going home tonight. I had trouble understanding their Spanish accent. But I think they mentioned fireworks."

"Oh my sweet mercy." Cora held her palms against her temples. "List's wired the house with explosives. It's a trap. We have to warn the Chief and the others."

CHAPTER 25

SUNDAY MID-AFTERNOON

The scent of the female Skinwalker dominated the earthy odors. She had the shield and the feather, and all he had to do was take them from her dead body. With the thought of gaining ownership of the totems, jubilation coursed through his veins.

Sounds flooded his ears—the raindrops, the thunder in the east, the cops running up the driveway, the helicopters, the rabbit scurrying away. And the witch's ragged breathing. She stopped. So did he. Moments later, she moved like a glider. Though muted, her footsteps exposed her exact location to him.

When she turned, so did he. He raced to intersect her. He longed to breathe in the exhilarating scent of her spilt blood. *The more blood the better*. To watch her draw her last breath. To hear that final exhale of air. To sense her soul exiting.

Then he'd finish off that Whiskey pig. Rage seethed through his veins at the mere thought of the man. Perhaps he'd take him back over the border. *Make him suffer. Skin him slow*.

Through the undergrowth, he caught a flash of movement. The

witch. Her accelerated heartbeat sounded loud in his head. He dashed across a patch of bare earth, gaining on her.

What's that?

A breeze carried the scent of the car and its warm engine. Along with a taste of perfume. *Dawlsen's wife.* Another opportunity presenting itself. He could barely believe his good luck.

Take down the witch. Get the artifacts. Kill the Dawlsen woman. Then start my war. The squaw's headed for the car. Must stop her.

She changed course again. Demonio raced into the clearing mere seconds behind the woman. Steeling his legs, he sprang and tackled her. They fell to the wet ground together. She grunted as he slammed on top of her. He rolled off her and leapt to his feet.

The Navajo rose to kneel on all fours, gasping for air. She turned her head towards him. Loathing oozed from her eyes.

"You are not Diné," she said. "You are Nakai. You desecrate my people."

"Screw you, Injun," Demonio said, and kicked her in the side. Pain shot up his leg. *She wears the feather. Its magic protects her.*

He spoke her name in Navajo. "I take my magic back." He reached down but she clawed his hand. He stepped back clutching his bloody wound, and she rose to her feet. With a curse, he attacked. They traded punches in a furious exchange. She swung her claws at his face, but he blocked it and returned a solid blow to her chin. Her eyes rolled back up into her head, and she collapsed. Reaching down, he tore the shield and feather from her. Their shamanistic power coursed through his veins and charged his muscles.

He snapped a two-inch thick dead branch from a tree. Swishing the heavy limb back and forth, he relished his newfound power.

She watched the limb, her eyes widening. The scent of her fear overwhelmed his nostrils, and he smiled. "I will kill the Dawlsen woman and return for you. If you survive this."

He swung the branch like a baseball bat, enjoying the smack of wood against her skull.

Junior lurked in the undergrowth, slithering like a freshly fed viper towards the car.

Through the foliage, he spotted the pastel color of her blouse. The faint fragrance of her perfume danced on the breezes. He loved pretty-smelling women. Not like the ones he took in Phoenix or Tucson and their cheap perfume. Heavy Mexican twenty-somethings or scrawny white runaways. Though he did enjoy beating them.

Taking a couple of deep breaths, he waited. When the pounding of arousal slowed, he eased through a wide opening in the brush. A dozen more steps, and he'd be clear of the undergrowth. He estimated three more would take him to the car.

She turned like she sensed something, and he stopped in mid-step. *Don't move. Movement gets you noticed.* She peered into the underbrush, staring directly at him but didn't see him. Junior didn't blink. He held his breath and ignored the trickle of sweat rolling across his cheek.

Her gaze swept on. If she saw him, she gave no indication. Then Junior spotted her gun and the practiced way she held it. *She's prepared to shoot. Too bad she's looking the wrong way.*

He pushed the rest of the way through the copse, making no

sound, and emerged into the open. Too late, Junior realized there was a kid in the car. The twerp stared right at him.

"MOM!" the kid screamed, pounding on the glass.

The Dawlsen woman wheeled, but Junior swept upon her. Before she could bring the gun into play, he punched her in the mouth. She collapsed, blood pouring from her split lip. Junior stood over her a moment, gleeful he had knocked her unconscious. He ignored the kid pounding on the car window, yelling at him.

Junior bent over to take the gun from her. As his hand started to close on the barrel, she opened her eyes to stare right into his.

"Eat lead, Junior," she said and pulled the trigger. The gun exploded.

Junior screamed as the bullet tore through the GSR-blackened skin between forefinger and thumb. He raised his arm to see half his hand was gone. The shock kept the pain at bay. He flung out a string of curses.

The Dawlsen woman let loose with a feral yell. He glimpsed her swinging the weapon a moment before it caught him on the cheekbone.

Stars exploded in his skull. He staggered backwards. Touching his good hand up to his cheek, he found the wound already swelling. A sticky wetness covered his fingers. He stared at the crimson dripping from his fingertips. His mouth formed a snarl.

The Dawlsen woman moved backwards, keeping a firm grasp on the gun.

Junior stumbled after her, intent in stripping the gun from her.

"Mister."

The kid's voice came from right behind him.

"No!" screamed the woman, "Run, Manny!"

Junior spun and saw the kid just a few steps away. He pounced on the boy, seizing his thin shoulders. Pain shot through his wounded hand. The kid went limp. Junior lost his hold at the sudden dead weight.

Junior cursed and cradled his damaged hand.

Lying on his back, the boy drew a leg towards his chest then lashed out. The foot caught Junior in his groin. Shock engulfed him. Anguish paralyzed him. Then he heard a gun blast the same moment a hot searing spasm struck him in the back.

Junior remembered spinning and falling. Then blackness.

Gunfire roared in the hallway. Rye dropped to the floor. Bullets smacked the wall above him. Dry wall and splinters rained upon him. The acrid smell of gunpowder hung like a heavy cloud. Rye's senses tunneled down the hallway.

"Police!" he shouted. "Put down your weapons."

Another round of automatic gunfire answered his request. Rye spotted movement down the hall and fired several shots, spent shells pinging off the wall.

Silence. Except for the ringing in his ears.

"I'm hit," said Tex through clenched teeth. Rye glanced his way and saw blood soaking the man's shirt at the shoulder. "Can't move my arm. Hurts like a son ..."

"Shhh," said Oakmann, kneeling besides him, her hand pressed against the wound. Tears moistened her eyes.

Rye heard a distant rumble, one he'd recognize anywhere. *Copters. Several.* He rubbed a knuckle across his lips.

"Watch the hallway," Rye told Oakmann. They switched places as Rye knelt next to the wounded man. "Anyone got a knife? List took mine."

She fetched a Schrade knife from her pocket and handed it to him. Rye cut open Tex's shirt at the wound. The bullet had left a deep furrow across his outer shoulder. *Bloody and painful, but not fatal if the vic didn't bleed out.* Fortunately for Tex, the bleeding had slowed, only oozing from the wound. *Dangerous enough if not taken care of.*

"Oakmann," Rye said, "hurry over here. I need some material to make a dressing. His bleeding's slowed, but I need to staunch the blood loss."

Keeping an eye on the hallway, she backed towards Rye. He pulled her shirttail out.

"Hey," she complained.

Rye sliced off two widths from her shirt.

"Nice abs," he said.

"Dawlsen, you're such a pig," she said.

"I've been told that."

He finished bandaging the wound. It wasn't pretty, and it'd need to be redressed soon. However, for the immediate time, it'd do the job.

"Thanks," mumbled Tex.

Rye helped him to his feet. "No problem. Tex, were you in the service?"

"Yep. The Corp. Hoo-Rah." Tex held his injured arm close to his body.

"Oakmann?"

"Army Ranger," she said over her shoulder.

Drawing out his words with a suspicious tone, Rye asked, "Does the actions of List's men strike you as a familiar tactic?"

Tex studied Rye for several seconds. "As a matter of fact, it does. We used similar methods to extract troops out of a hot zone." Understanding spread across his countenance. "Y'all might be on to something there, Dawlsen."

"So. List is abandoning his house?" said Oakmann. "That doesn't make sense."

"I agree," Rye told them. "But I can't shake the feeling that List and his men aren't fighting to keep us out."

"They're fighting to keep us in," added Tex.

"Whatever. We got copters coming in," said Oakmann.

Rye said, "We don't have much time. Once List leaves the state, it becomes an FBI case. And if he flees to Mexico ..." He left the implication unspoken.

Rye and Oakmann proceeded down the darkened hallway, pistols held in front of them. Rye fired a glance over his shoulder. Tex languished behind, his gun hand hanging straight down as if the weapon weighed too much for him to lift. Rye thought the Texan looked too pale. Like he was going into shock. *We need to get him medical attention. Soon.*

Rye refocused on the 8x4 opening in front of him. Any movement in the hallway, he was prepared to shoot.

They reached the intersection where the shooter had hidden. In the small circles of light provided by their flashlights, they found a substantial pool of blood on the carpet. Blood splatter decorated the wall.

"We got at least one of 'em," said Rye.

"Yeah," said Tex with a wince. "So did they."

They eased down the dark hallway. Sweat beaded on Rye's forehead and his mouth dried to where he could spit sand. This was too much like doing a building search in Iraq. The helicopters grew louder, and Rye cursed under his breath. The birds drowned out any slight noise that might warn them of the presence of List's slimeballs.

The hall emptied into a lounge larger than most buildings in Whiskey. The ceiling must have reached two stories in height. Western paintings, buffalo skulls, furniture with Native patterns, and pillars made of river stone radiated the aura of a wealthy cattleman. Half a dozen groupings of lights revealed the approach of the copters. The lead copter turned on a searchlight. Its beam searched the lounge.

"Get down!" yelled Rye.

Just then, the side door to the copter opened, and a man with a large caliber machine gun commenced firing into the lounge. For several moments, the bulletproof windows resisted the pounding of large rounds. Rye watched fractures spiderweb across the glass. A hole blew in shards of glass seconds before the window exploded under the impact. Hot lead chewed up furniture, sending up plumes of stuffing. Bullets tore holes into the walls. More glass shattered. Things fell.

All the while, Rye heard someone screaming, then realized it was him.

The gun stopped firing. Over ear-numbing quiet, Rye heard shattered items tumbling to the floor and the *thump-thump-thump* of helicopter blades. With bow in hand, he sprang to his feet and, nocking an arrow, stepped into the remains of the lounge. Someone from the copter played a searchlight about the room. Papers from shot-up magazines fluttered about in the backwash of the helicopter blades.

Rye dodged the light until he reached the center of the room, where he had a clear shot of the helicopter through the shattered windows. He took a few moments to get in the correct stance. He calmed his breathing with a quick inhalation exercise. He pulled back on the string and aimed at the gunner.

Everything else faded away until he saw only the figure in the open side door of the copter.

"There," someone in the copter yelled when the searchlight found Rye.

"Eat this," Rye said, and he released his fingers from the string.

When Amalia had told Zach "niñas," he'd never expected this.

Zach held his flashlight by his ear as if he were going to stab someone. Within its beam, Missy sat with her unconscious sister, Mel's head in her lap. Bloody rags wrapped the girl's legs, arms, and torso. She appeared feverish and sipped in breaths of air. Her skin reminded him of desert sands bleached white by the sun.

Getting Mel out of here—alive—became his number one priority. Everything else took a back seat.

He shone the light beyond the twins. A dozen or so Latino pre-to-early teens dressed in rags, huddled in a group against the back wall, their eyes wide in fear. *Just like abused kids.*

"¿Usted bueno o malo?" asked a rail-thin boy. *Are you good or bad?*

"He's good," answered Missy. "Bueno. He's a friend. An amigo."

Amalia pushed past Zach and knelt beside the wounded girl. She rubbed Mel's forehead and shot a look at Missy. Spanish flew between the two girls like staccato automatic arms fire.

"Hate to interrupt you two," said Zach, sensing an urgency to get everyone to safety, "but we need to evacuate the premises."

"Mel shouldn't be moved," Missy said, sadness coloring her voice.

"Right. But she also needs immediate medical care ... in an ER. And I mean like yesterday." He handed the flashlight to Amalia and held out his arms. "I'll carry her. You'll have to watch my back."

"I take you to road," said Amalia. "I know way."

"What's that noise?" asked Missy.

Zach listened. "My guess: copters. I'll take her now." Zach scooped up the wounded girl as if she were a loose sleeping bag. He eyed Amalia. "Tell the kids to follow us. And to be quiet."

With everyone gathered around him, Zach balanced Mel in his arms so he could open the door.

"Quiet," he repeated, and the room turned to silence. He grabbed the doorknob, eased the door open a crack, and peered out. He dropped his head and eased the door closed with a foot. Taking a deep breath, he released his breath slowly. "We have to wait a minute. There's a couple of bad guys out there." *A couple dozen to be more accurate.*

Richard List directed the stacking of munitions on the outside patio. Every box represented more wealth in his offshore accounts. To him, they weren't cartons carrying death; they were a means to a fortune beyond his wildest expectations. A ticket away from this sandy pit. If he never saw another cactus again, it'd be too soon.

Mentally checking off the remaining tasks, he ordered Demonio's men where to set the final boxes of weapons and ammo. Men ferried supplies from their storage area. Whenever someone exited the patio doors, the chlorine from his indoor pool washed over him.

"Start a new stack," he ordered the men dragging the latest boxes. "Over there." He pointed.

Richard stared up at the three-story expanse of glass. Despite the appearance of luxury oozing from every wall of the house, he never cared for it. He built the house years ago for that nag he had married. Here she had died—no loss there. And here his worthless son grew up.

The lights went out. Curses spewed from his lips, but it was something they had planned on.

Scattering gunfire erupted in the pool area. *What the ...*

A security guard rushed over to him.

"Señior List," the man said. "We have two of Dawlsen's anglos penned down by the pool. They're not going anywhere."

"Keep 'em there. The explosion'll take care of them."

He scanned the canyon. The copters would arrive soon. He'd evacuate, then blow the place. And forget this godforsaken desert. By the time the Feds got a handle on things, evidence would point to a Mexican army base in Arizona. The thought of the fallout between the two countries brought a smile to his lips. *Sweet.*

But it was none of his concern. Once he got his money, he could care less.

Jilt arrived, looking bent out of shape three ways from Kansas. Richard's old man used to say that, and Richard never understood what it meant. But somehow Jilt's mood reminded him of that saying.

"What?" said Richard, frowning in anticipation of bad news.

"We got trouble," Jilt said, staring at the ground between his feet.

"I don't like trouble. Explain."

"Our electricity was cut prematurely. Dawlsen and his people have escaped the stables. I found tracks of two more possible intruders. Might be backup." Jilt shook his head and paused.

"Go on." *I hate the way this fool takes his time to lay out situations.*

"From reports I received, we got Dawlsen's men out along the driveway. Probably think they're cutting off our exit."

"What else?"

"Dawlsen is now searching the house," Jilt looked up at his boss. "I've posted men to engage. Slow 'em down."

Richard turned around, walking a few steps. He removed his hat and rubbed a hand over his stubbled haircut. He made his decision and returned the hat to its position. "Okay. Okay. None of it makes any difference. The copters are on the way. I'll proceed with the operations here. Make life miserable for Dawlsen. And make sure he's in the building when it blows."

In the distance, lightning flickered with another storm moving in. Thunder rumbled far away. Then Richard heard them, the helicopters. Their *thump-thump-thump* blending in with the thunder.

Jilt marched away, signaling a group of men to follow him into the house.

Richard yelled at the remainder, "Hurry up and get the rest of the weapons. Apresurarse." A spate of gunfire erupted in the pool area. A bullet whined past him. "And will someone kill those two?"

One of the communications personnel strode up to Richard and handed him a headset. "Incoming is on the line."

Richard snatched the device from the man and put it on. He adjusted the mic. "This is Base Chief, come in."

Crackly noise sounded in the ear pieces, then a voice came through the headset, "Base, this is Incoming Main. We are one minute out. Are you ready? Over."

"We're ready for evac to proceed. Be advised, we have a situation with local law. We are in the process of containing them. The zone may be hot. They are on the second floor, over the patio area. Over."

"Roger."

"And if you happen to spot suspicious activity in the house, make sure it ceases.'

"Roger that."

The helicopters flew into the landing site, their props creating a backdraft strong enough to knock a couple of men off their feet. One of the copters zoomed in close to the house, shining a floodlight into the second floor windows. From its side, a machinegun opened fire. Glass and expended shells fell like hail onto the patio. The gunner stopped, and the searchlight flashed through the damaged windows.

Just then, something flickered from the house straight towards the closest helicopter. The gunner screamed. A second later, an orange ball of fire engulfed the copter. It buckled, almost torn in two, dropping orange liquid.

"Yes." Rye pumped a fist in victory, gawking as the fiery helicopter slammed into the ground. Blistering flames hip-hopped from the heap of metal. Oily smoke coagulated the air with its reek. The rending of twisting metal blended with the screams of men running away from the wreckage.

"Get those men out of there," he heard List yell. "Spray that bird down with foam. Bring that truck over here and drag that thing out of the way. I want those copters landing in two."

Rye smiled in acknowledgement that his attack prevented the other helicopters from landing. At least for the moment, he bought his people some time.

He hobbled over to the window and risked a quick peek.

List stood amid the burning twisted metal, pushing his men to clear the mess. The mayor stopped what he was doing, turned, and looked up at the ruined windows. His lips curled in disgust. "Dawlsen," he screamed. "You're a dead man."

The copter exploded and rammed into List like a giant's fist. It flung the man a dozen feet into a stack of transport boxes. For seconds, he lay still, and Rye thought the evil of Richard List had passed from this earth. Then, the man's arms twitched, and moments later, he eased himself into a sitting position.

Rye caught movement from his peripheral vision and glanced that way to see Demonio Amo, dressed in a black wolf skin, carrying a woman over each shoulder. The drug lord came around the corner of the building and headed for the stack of munitions. Rye clenched his fists so tight his knuckles turned white.

"No," he moaned, pounding an unbroken window pane with the meaty side of his hand. "Why, God?" He pounded the window again. "Why did you let this happen?"

One of the paramilitary types hurried over to the mayor and

offered List a hand up. List reached for the man's hand.

Behind Rye, running footsteps pounded the wooden floor combined with a roar ripping from a man's throat. Rye swiveled on his good leg when a huge weight blindsided him. The assailant drove him into a bullet-ruined chair, which disintegrated under their impact. Stunned, Rye crowned in shreds of stuffing, fabric, and wood. Before he could recover, a hand grabbed him by the back of the collar and lifted him partway off the floor. Rye gasped a breath of air before a fist pounded him in the kidneys. His vision wavered under a hot explosion.

The hand on his collar released him, and Rye found himself face down in the debris of the chair. A boot kicked his bad knee, and bolts of torture shot through his leg.

A ragged groan tore from his throat.

In the same moment, his left hand touched a length of wood from the chair, his fingers curled around its smooth roundness, a muffled voice snarled something at him, and the pointy toe of a western boot came into his limited view.

Rye stabbed above the boot with the length of wood.

It connected and someone yelled. That someone smacked the wood from his hands, and it landed several yards away. Rye rolled onto his back and opened his eyes, his vision swimming in vertigo.

"Barend Jilt," Rye mumbled.

"That's right, pig. I'm going to finish what I started back in the Phoenix garage. And I'm gonna enjoy it."

Jilt bent down to grab the front of Rye's shirt. With all the force he had left, Rye kicked upward with his good leg, driving the point of his boot in between Jilt's legs.

Air exploded from Jilt's lungs, and his eyes bulged. The ex-cop crumbled into an apostrophe shape, hands groping the source of his pain.

Rye struggled to his feet, keeping his wounded knee stiff. He leaned against a splintered pillar, his breathing coming in ragged gasps.

Just as he rested his head on the pillar and closed his eyes, several gunshots rang out.

CHAPTER 26

SUNDAY EARLY EVENING

Rye dove to the floor behind the remains of a couch and grabbed the pistol from the holster at his back. Bullets tore into the fabric of the furniture. He swung the weapon in the direction of the shooter and fired. The man stared at the circle of crimson on his shirt and dropped to the floor.

Hearing a grunt, he turned to see Oakmann struggling with one of List's men. The sleeve of her left forearm had transformed to blood red. Her opponent swung a ka-bar knife at her, but she dodged and the blade whistled past her by a hair's breath. Rye aimed at them but hesitated to fire for fear of hitting her.

Using the man's momentum, she pushed him away from her. Seeing his chance, Rye fired several shots into him. The bloody knife fell from the man's lifeless hand and hit the floor as he did. Grimacing, Rye stood and limped over to the injured sheriff.

"Thanks," she said.

"You okay? Your arm?"

"It hurts like a—" She glanced down at the blood-soaked sleeve.

She moved her arm and grimaced. "Still attached. He cut me when I blocked a jab. I really hate knives."

"Let me have a look at it." Rye knelt next to her. "It'll need stitches. The best I can do right now is to wrap it up. Can't use your shirt, there's not enough left after Tex's dressing."

Oakmann smiled at his attempt at humor. "Go ahead. I've got my vest on. Won't be indecent."

From the hallway opposite the stairs, an ashen Tex ambled zombie-like into the room, dragging his assailant by the collar. One look at the unnatural angle of the captive's head, and Rye knew the bad guy was dead. Tex stopped and let loose of the collar. The body hit the floor. Tex opened his mouth to say something and collapsed face first. A wet crimson stain covered the back of his shirt.

"Noooooooooo!" Oakmann pushed Rye away and stumbled over to where Tex lay.

The powder burns around the bullet hole under his shoulder blade indicated a gunshot at close range. Oakmann collapsed next to Tex and rolled him. Blood dribbled out the corner of his mouth when he tried to talk. Rye joined them and bent over to hear.

"He's killed me, Rye," the whispered words seeped out. "But I got him ... Anne ... I love you ..." A last soft sigh escaped from Tex's mouth, and he was gone.

Oakmann wailed, tears staining her face.

The agony of the passing of another brother-in-arms overwhelmed him. Rye lowered his head to hide his tears. Why did one more good cop have to die? He thought of Jilt and the tales of horror when that man ruled as Police Chief. Why do bad cops live?

Heilo, Whitewolf, and Iona burst through the stairwell door.

"Oh, no," Iona said, stopping when she spotted Oakmann cuddling Tex's body.

Whitewolf took off his hat and lowered his head. He started a low chant in his native language.

Heilo's hand covered her mouth. Without making a comment, she walked over and handed her headset to Rye.

He took it from her. Glancing down at the grief-stricken Oakmann, Rye swiped away his tears. *Time enough to grieve later.* "Thanks," he said, taking the headpiece. "Keep it together, people," he said, louder. "We still got a job to do."

He put on the headset and adjusted the mic to his comfort. "This is Crawler One."

"Oh, Rye, you're alive," gushed Gabby.

"Crawler One this is Eye." *Agent Clark.* "Glad to see you're still with us."

"Me too. But we just lost an officer. A sheriff's deputy named Tex. No last name." He heard a gasp. "What is it, Agent Clark?"

She struggled with her words. "Tex ... Tex is my step-brother." She took a long breath and paused. Rye sensed her sorrow over the headset. "I will have to deal with this later. Now we need to get you out of there. Officers Heilo and Whitewolf have found evidence that List plans to detonate the house. They spotted C-4 charges."

"We gotta get you guys outta there," Gabby broke in. "The house could blow any minute."

"Roger that. Me and the sheriff," he said, "have found uniforms from the Mexican army scattered throughout the house. List is planning something big."

"We read you on that." *Clark's back in control.* "First things first, we need to extract you and your people. With the break in the weather, our helicopters have left out of the Phoenix office and are on their way …" A long sigh followed a deep breath. "They should arrive in five."

Rye hobbled over to the windows. Hiding behind the wall, he peered into the activity swirling below him. Men loaded boxes of weapons and munitions into the copters at a furious rate. List shouted out directions. The man did not yet know of Jilt's failure. Only a few cartons of ammo remained.

Rye adjusted his mouthpiece. "You better tell them to hurry. I don't think we have five minutes until List's crew departs. Evidence points to him fleeing the country in minutes. For good."

Just then, the man wearing the wolf skin stepped up to the last helicopter. He carried the two forms over his shoulders like they were sacks of potting soil. One after the other, he handed the two unconscious women to someone in the copter

In one gut wrenching moment, Rye recognized them. *Dee and Sunflower.*

DePute shoved several planters under the bar. Not much protection, but it beat being cranked into Swiss cheese. He peered through the bullet holes decorating the bar's metallic skin and spotted several of List's men moving ghost-like through the thick haze of expended gunpowder. With so little of the bar remaining, he needed to cruise to another locale.

However, every attempt to reposition brought a hail of hot lead his way. Smoke from outside thickened the air like a London fog, and tracer ammunition cut through it with eerie streaks.

"Kid," Batts yelled. "You okay?"

"Dude, this is, like, so bogus. How do you want to handle this?"

"Plan A and B didn't work out so well."

Several shots rang out, and a number of bullets smacked into the wall and furniture around him. DePute cringed into the smallest fetal position for protection. When the firing ceased, he glanced over to see Batts peering at him.

DePute nodded in the direction of their assailants. "I know, Bro. Let's, like, order out some pizza. It's on my dime."

He heard Batts chuckle. "No anchovies. I hate those things."

DePute wanted to ask him about the explosion he heard a few minutes ago. From the orange light dancing on the walls, he figured a big fire raged just outside the house.

List's men yelled back and forth in rapid Spanish. They moved like pale specters within the smoke. The whine of rotors from waiting copters swelled. Not good.

"Batts," he called out. "I'm getting hammered here. We're going to have to boogie on out of here."

"I hear that. I ain't waitin' around for this house to be blowed up and me in it like some skunkin' coward."

"Roger that—"

Another hail of bullets interrupted their conversation.

"Shut up, pigs," yelled one of List's Latino thugs.

"Bite me," DePute yelled back. He raised a rifle above the wreckage of the bar and blindly sprayed bullets in the direction of the voice.

Another round of slugs slapped around him. This time, the

metallic wet bar, so riddled with holes, wobbled and came near to disintegrating. *Dude, you so gotta get outta here*. He searched the pool area for another place to hide.

Behind him, a planter crashed to the floor. His head spun in that direction. Beyond the clump of dirt and vegetation, DePute spotted what appeared to be ... *what? Rocks?* He had seen these before, but what ... then it dawned on him. The rock waterfall for the pool.

He loaded his last clip into the rifle and raised it above the bar. Taking aim in the general direction of List's shooters, he pulled the trigger and emptied the clip. Spanish curses followed. Leaving the weapons, he sprang to his feet and raced to the waterfall. More tracer shots rang out as he leapt over it.

Bullets smacked into the wet bar, and it collapsed into a heap of twisted metal. Other bullets pinged off the rocks to the waterfall.

"Good move," Batts said from his cover.

"Except I'm further from the exit." DePute's breathing came ragged. "How jacked up is that?"

"Can't have everything."

"I figure, if I'm, like, dead, the exit is just bogus."

"You might be on to something there."

"Batts, listen."

It sounded like the workers outside had halted in their progress. Another droning noise rumbled in the distance.

"I hear it," Batts said. "Sounds like more copters comin' in. We're screwed. If List has more men, they'll flush us right out of here."

"No. I don't think that's it. These copters sound different." DePute risked a glance over the stones to see the ghostly shapes of List's men backing out of the pool area. "Hey, they're pulling back. They're leaving."

"Let's make a go of it." Batts started to rise.

DePute heard the clink of metal canisters being tossed in their general direction. He knew in a heartbeat what those things were.

"Batts. Get down!"

As he finished saying it, several grenades exploded.

Zach peered out the crack between door and frame. Several men, black silhouettes against the burning equipment, moved materials into helicopters. The mayor barked orders. The stench of burnt metal lingered in the storage room.

"Are they gone?" whispered Mel.

Zach shook his head.

"What's going on?" she whispered, her hand resting on Zach's bicep.

"Quiet," he replied. Sporadic gunfire echoed, but he couldn't tell where it came from. Then Heilo's voice came over the headset. His blood chilled when she described the C-4 set to go off. He closed the door without making a sound.

"Eye," he said, "this is Crawler Two."

"Zach!" Gabby's voice, a joyful shriek in his earpiece. "Where are you?" Her reception came over broken and static-filled.

"A storage area on the bottom floor. Where is everybody?"

"Crawler Two, this is Agent Clark. You're breaking up. Can you repeat that?" Zach did so. "Crawler One, Three, and Four are on the second floor. We have copters coming in. Are you ready for extraction?"

"Roger. Note, I have the Visser twins, and one is hurt in a bad way. Needs immediate medical attention. Plus I've got me a dozen Mexican kids between the ages of eleven and fourteen. They're scared and hungry. And abused."

"Roger that. Stay put until ..." The rest of her words came through garbled.

He frowned. "The reception is bad. I have to move to where I can hear."

The headset crackled in response, and then went dead.

CHAPTER 27

SUNDAY EVENING

Cold fury coursed through Rye as he watched the callous way Demonio Amo dumped Dee and Sunflower into the helicopter furthest from the house. For a moment, he considered taking him down with an arrow, but estimated the distance to be around 400 yards. With the backdraft from the helicopters' rotors, he doubted his accuracy with the bow.

Demonio jumped into the copter, and shooting him became a moot point. Rye would not risk firing gun or bow if it meant he might hit Dee. Struggling to come up with Plan B rattled around in his mind, but the plan failed to materialize.

His eyes narrowed into slits of ice. The primal urge to kill those who endangered his family pervaded him.

"Heilo," he barked, "can you read what's written on those boxes? Your 15/20 vision is better'n mine." He pointed to where a group of men bustled around the last stack of wooden crates.

She stepped up next to him and followed the direction he pointed. "It's hard to read ... can't tell with all the bad hombres in the way, but it looks like ... RPG. That's enough to do a world of hurt."

"Clark," Rye said into the mic. "How far out is the cavalry?"

Below them, the helicopters' rotors spun with incrementally increasing speed.

"About two minutes," came her reply. "The new storm to the west is causing turbulence. Slowing them down."

The top rotors on several helicopters whined as they approached take off speed. List's men began to climb into the birds.

Rye jerked his head to the beat of a string of curses. "Clark, I'll get back to you." He motioned with his arms. "Everyone over here. On my count, I want everyone to shoot at those boxes." He pointed at the remaining few. "And be ready for the explosion. Don't worry about List's men. They're not targets, but if they're in the way ..." He paused. "It sucks to be them."

The rotors of several of the helicopters reached traveling speed.

"Three."

List waddled to the last bird and climbed in.

"Two."

Demonio tapped the pilot on his helmet. The rotor to the last helicopter began to pick up speed.

"One."

They opened fire. Several of List's men fell under the torrent of bullets. Others fled to the copters to escape the maelstrom. Two stood petrified, gripping a crate, watching lead chew it into splinters.

Gaping holes had appeared in the boxes. Rye aimed an explosive arrow at a crate and pulled back on the bowstring. The string creaked ominously.

"Ya'll might want to step back. Pronto." He loosed the arrow and ducked behind the outside wall.

Moments later, a fireball erupted. The percussive wave from the blast pounded the house, knocking Rye over in a heap on the floor. A scream ripped from his throat, hands covering his twisted knee.

Check on Dee. She's got to be okay.

He rolled over rubble to reach the window. Searing flames engulfed the closest helicopter. That bird exploded, sending it crashing into the bird beside it. Both crashed into yet a third. Debris rained down on the inferno.

Below, smoky fires raged in the wreckage of crumpled helicopters. The air stank of oily smoke and charred flesh. Winds caused by those fires tore at his clothes and hair. His hearing returned to the screams of wounded. Bodies lay scattered about.

The last helicopter—the one with Dee—struggled to make its getaway. Black smoke streamed from its underbelly. Through the heat waves emitted by the flames, Rye spotted Dee leaning out of the opened side of the helicopter. She stared at him in wide-eyed panic. Someone in the copter grabbed her and pulled her back in. He clenched his fists, watching the copter disappear over the ridge.

Manny hid in the SUV. But he had to pee … bad. When that man dressed in wolf skins had kidnapped his mother, twilight allowed him to witness it. Now, it was dark.

He waited. Time dragged on. With growing curiosity, he risked peering out the car window. He didn't see anybody, but the dark made that difficult. Manny sank back onto the back seat.

Now what?

From the direction of the big house, an explosion shook the ground, rattling the car windows. He watched the sky turn orange. *That does it. I'm looking for Mom.*

Manny scrambled into the driver's seat and moved the seat forward until his toes touched the gas pedal. Strapping on the seat belt, he reviewed the driving lessons his father gave him last summer.

Keys dangled from the steering column. He fired up the engine and slipped the transmission into drive. He pushed down on the gas pedal with his toes, and the vehicle inched forward followed by a dinging noise. Staring at a red light flashing on the dashboard, he pondered for a few seconds the meaning of that light. He was doing something wrong. *Come on, come on, it's got to mean something.*

Then he remembered. The parking brake. He found it and released it. Giving the SUV gas, he inched towards List's driveway.

DePute dared a peek over the waterfall's fake rocks. The gunmen had boogied out the pool area and headed for the copters. He watched the frenzied scene outside. Helicopters started to lift off the ground. Men scrambled to load the last of the munitions. Two men hefted a crate labeled RPG. That could only mean …

Gunfire coming from some floor above them shredded the side of the RPG crate.

Batts raised his head. "What's happenin'?"

"Get down!" DePute screamed.

A massive explosion sent a ball of fire into the glass wall.

Gritting his teeth, Rye spun away from the ruined window. *List has Dee. He's evacuating his personnel, and this building's primed to detonate.*

"Heilo," he yelled, "help Sheriff Oakmann." He pointed to the dead deputy. "Whitewolf, can you handle Tex's body? We need to locate DePute and Reese. I want everyone out of this building ASAP. No one gets left behind."

"Nephew," said Chee, clamping him on the shoulder. "Get your wife. And Sunflower. We'll take care of this." He pointed with his chin toward the stairs. "Go."

Rye grabbed the bow and quiver of arrows he'd dropped in the explosions. He limp-ran to the stairs and hobbled down cursing at his knee but grateful the brace offered some support.

No one moved in the pool area. Wherever he stepped, his boots crunched on shards of glass. Debris floated in the pool's water, along with bodies of List's men. *Just like Iraq.* He heard a moan and saw a hand push through a pile of wreckage. In the dancing light coming from the burning ruins outside, the hand resembled a desperate escape from hell.

Rye nocked an arrow and aimed at the emerging person. A body followed the hand, and Rye raised his bow and sighted along the arrow, prepared to unloose the bolt.

"WPD!" Rye yelled. "Put your hands in the air!" The next second would be critical. He took a deep breath and held it.

"Chief?" replied the figure, scraps of drywall falling off him. "It's DePute. I got Batts with me. Though it feels like I got pounded by a monster wave, I'm not hurt more'n a few scratches."

"DePute? You have to evacuate immediately," Rye ordered. He watched Batts rise from the ruins. "Batts. You need assistance?"

"Naw," said DePute, "we're good."

Rye said, "Our people'll be coming down these stairs in a few. Hook up with them and get out." *Now, where's Zach?*

Rye skirted the fiery wrecks of helicopters, bypassed the torn and burnt bodies, while ignoring the pleas of the wounded. Pressing his lips together, he gazed at the ridge where the helicopter with Dee had disappeared. He'd heard no crash, so he assumed they were okay.

If List so much as harms one hair …

He started toward the ridge. If only he had the means to travel faster. They already had too much of a head start. How was he going to catch up? He snapped his fingers. *Oakmann's horses.* Using the stable as a compass, he headed in that direction.

Not more than a dozen steps later, his knee buckled. On all fours—his injured leg straight out—Rye studied the fence. He'd never make it. Not with his bum knee. He had to come up with another idea pronto, or Dee was in for a world of hurt.

A car horn blasted. Rye glanced over his shoulder to see a car's headlights breeching the same ridge List's helicopter had disappeared over. An SUV followed after the lights and skittered an erratic path across the canyon floor towards him. Tires whined against the mud seeking to suck the vehicle into stopping. The car's lights played across him, blinding Rye. He pulled a gun out of his waistband.

"Stop the car," Rye commanded, gun pointed at a spot above the headlights.

The vehicle careened to a stop, then slid a few feet in the sodden ground. The driver leaned out the window.

"Dad!" the driver yelled.

Manny?

Slamming his gun back into its holster, Rye limped over to the SUV.

"The wolf man's got Mom." The words poured in a torrent from Manny's mouth. Wetness welled in his boy's eyes.

"Scoot over, partner." Rye eased into the driver's seat. "We're going after Mom."

CHAPTER 28

SUNDAY NIGHT

Thick, black smoke gushed into the helicopter. Struggling to breathe, Dee cupped her hands over her nose and mouth. Tears blinded her eyes and flooded her cheeks. Despite these discomforts, at least it choked off List's rampaging curses.

Her thoughts went to Manny and Rye. The desire to clutch her son and hold him close overwhelmed her heart. The thought she might never see him again brought fresh tears. And Rye. He was trying so hard to gain her approval. To win her heart again. He wasn't perfect, but no one was. Least of all her. He remembered important dates like birthdays better'n most husbands. Manny still adored him.

And I keep shoving him away.

Dee began to pray out loud, though she couldn't hear her own voice.

The helicopter's engine sputtered, and it kicked like a bronco with a bear on its tail. They swiveled back and forth in half circles. Her stomach turned gushy, and she thought she was going to vomit.

A semi-conscious Sunflower sat next to her on the metal bench.

The woman coughed, so Dee, fearing the other would suffer smoke inhalation, cupped a hand over Sunflower's nose. Unable to brace herself, the helicopter's rocking repeatedly flung Dee into the metal wall with bruising agony.

"Sir," yelled the pilot to List, "I can't control this thing."

"You're a pilot. Fly this piece of—" List shouted, his face an ugly sneer.

"No, sir," the pilot interrupted calmly. "The oil light's on. I'm losing fuel quickly. I'll need to put this bird down in less than a minute, or we'll crash."

Transfixed, Dee gaped at the transformation on List's face. One second he snarled like a madman, and now he smiled like a kid at Christmas. Like he resolved something in his mind.

"How far will she go?" List yelled back.

"Maybe a mile or two."

List peered out the open side. Leaning back toward the pilot he pointed and said, "Go about 1000 yards that way and set her down."

"Yes, sir," said the pilot.

"Just park this baby by those rocks," he yelled at the pilot.

List turned to Dee. "Ready to go for an ATV ride?"

When the helicopter touched down, List pulled out a large black handgun from the back of his waistband and pointed it at the back of the pilot's head.

"Look out," yelled Dee.

List pulled the trigger.

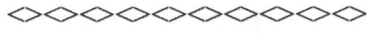

Rye stopped the SUV after crashing into and running over the barb-wire fence, leaving a gaping hole in the fence line. He flicked on the high beams and scrutinized the scrub trees beyond the fence. Bugs twirled inside the beams, and several pairs of eyes stared at him before the small animals scurried away. Oakmann had hobbled their horses somewhere in this area. Hopefully, the animals hadn't wandered.

Opening the car door, Rye tilted his head to listen. He only heard the typical night sounds and the oncoming thunder. But no helicopter. The bird had been in bad shape, so it couldn't have gone far. Glancing at the glass-enclosed backside of List's house and the fire reflecting off its remaining windows, Rye figured List wouldn't wait much longer to detonate the building.

"Dad, look," Manny said, pointing.

Following his son's gaze, he spotted the flashing lights of the incoming Bell copters. Seconds later, he spotted the white letters under a side window: FBI. *'Bout time.*

"Son," he shifted in his seat to face Manny, "open that glove box. There should be a handgun in there. I make sure all WPD vehicles keep one. Be careful."

Manny reached in, pulled the weapon out, and held it up.

Rye breathed in deeply and released the air. *God, I don't want to do this. But I really don't have a choice.* "Nope. You take it. I need you to cover my back."

"But," Manny started to protest.

"I was thinking of making you stay in the car. But I know you'd just get on the horse after I leave and trail behind me. Therefore, I'd rather have you ride with me."

"Mom'll kill me if I get hurt," Manny said with some hesitancy.

"She'll kill me for bringing you along." Rye gave his son a half grin.

"She told me to stay in the car."

"And you did. Until I said otherwise." Rye smiled and said with a comical imitation, "I'm the law in this here town. And what I says, goes." Father and son laughed. "¿Comprende?" Rye studied his son for moment. "Come on," he said, sliding out of the car. "We got horses to find and a bad guy to chase."

"And a mom to rescue."

Standing at the front of the SUV, Rye considered which direction to take to look for the horses. Any sign of tracks would have been washed away by the storm. Beyond the beams of light, a horse whinnied. Rye pointed toward the sound, and Manny nodded. With Rye in the lead, they entered the thicket. Moments later, they found Oakmann's Appaloosa and Piebald munching on some low vegetation. The Appaloosa raised its head while still chomping on grasses and eyed them.

"They're probably spooked," Rye whispered and motioned for Manny to stay put. Speaking in soothing tones, Rye approached them. He reached the closest, the Piebald, grabbed its halter, and rubbed its neck.

"Good boy," Rye repeated in soothing tones. He motioned for Manny to take him. Approaching the Appaloosa, Rye repeated his performance. He rubbed the animal's forehead and spoke silly nothings in soft tones.

"Check the cinches," Rye said after wiping the rainwater off the saddle.

The FBI birds hovered in the background while Rye rushed through a checklist of the horses' equipment. With leather creaking, he swung up into the saddle of the Appaloosa. Nodding in approval, he heard the copters taking off. *Good. Now fly like the Devil's after you.* He patted the horse's neck, glad to see Manny already seated on his horse.

The house exploded. A fiery ball gushed skyward like an orange geyser. A shower of debris from the building began to crash down on them. Rye's horse reared, hooves clawing the air. The Appaloosa twisted in circles, snorting and bucking. Its eyes opened wide, showing white. Rye held tight with his knees and gripped the reins.

He called out in soothing tones in an attempt to quiet the beast. After half a minute, the horse stopped fighting and began to settle. Rye continued talking in a relaxing tone. The horse shook his head up and down a few times and then calmed.

"That was soooo cool, dad," Manny said, hands resting on the saddle horn. "Just like in the movies."

"How'd your horse do?" he said gasping.

Manny shrugged. "He flinched some."

I'm just one happy horned lizard that Manny didn't get this crazy beast.

Rye gazed at the blinking lights of the FBI's helicopters disappearing into the night. Fire raged at the former List home, filling the canyon with garish smoke and hellfire light.

He turned his horse toward the approximate direction of List's exit tunnel.

"Manny, let's ride." Rye spurred his horse.

CHAPTER 29

MONDAY SUNRISE

Dawn approached like a sniper stalking a target. Black faded into a leaden overcast, remnant from the second storm. Fog hovered over the ground like dirty cotton. During the night, Rye rode in the pounding rain at a slow pace, not willing to risk the horses slipping on the muddy trail along the creek bank. The creek still roared with flash flood waters.

Stopping to give the horses a breather, he leaned over in his saddle to read the story left by tire tracks and footprints. The extra depth of the tracks indicated the ATV stopped here. A set of small footprints—probably a woman's—headed off behind a rock and returned. The tracks appeared to be fresh. Definitely after the storm, and most probably, less than an hour.

He sat up straight in his saddle, the leather creaking. He figured they were nearing I-8 where this creek went under the expressway. *Where would they go when they reach the interstate?*

"Dad?" Manny rode up beside him with a quizzical look.

"What is it, son?"

"Could they be going down to Goldwater?"

"The Air Force Range? Why'd they do that?"

"The Sand Tank Mountains."

Rye bit his lower lip and thought a moment. "We'll check it out when we reach the highway." Rye held out his fist to his son and they bumped their knuckles together. "This creek heads towards the Sands. Some tough going in there. No real trails to speak of. But there's catchments with water and caves to hole up in." He looked off to the south. "Bet he didn't get a camping permit."

"C'mon, dad. Stop with your stupid jokes."

"What? I'm not funny?" Rye turned serious. "Let's see where the trail leads us."

Within a half hour, they reached I-8. Standing water submerged sections of the road. Allowing the horses to slurp up some water, Rye studied the mountains rearing up over 2000 feet.

"Wait here," Rye said.

He rode to the other side of 8, the horse's hooves clip-clopping on the pavement. Ten feet from the road, Rye leaned over in the saddle to discover no tire tracks. *That's odd.* He sat upright and looked right and left and back and drew a hand across his mouth. He rode on for another fifty feet and still found nothing. After riding in ever-expanding concentric circles, Rye concluded they never came this way.

He crossed back over I-8 and rejoined with Manny.

"Trail's gone cold," Rye said. He rushed a hand through his hair.

"It was boring watching you over there," Manny said. "So, I kinda looked around over here." Rye raised an eyebrow. "And I found something." Rye noted the hint of pride in his son's voice.

Manny spurred his horse, moving towards the curb. Rye followed.

Manny tugged on the reins to stop the horse and pointed to the ground. "This."

The ATV's tire tracks had splashed through a puddle, leaving ruts in the rain-soaked ground.

"Nice detective work," Rye complimented his son.

Without warning, the edges of his sight went dark, and he fought off the vertigo threatening to overtake him. One of his visions. Eyes closed, he licked his lips. An image of Whiskey's only Baptist church came unbidden into his head.

"Dad?" Manny's hesitant voice broke into his dreamscape, and Rye blinked his eyes open. "Dad, you okay?"

"Yeah. It's some Navajo thing. But I think I know where Mom is," Rye said, fiddling with his dog tags under his shirt. "Let's go get her." He rotated his horse towards Whiskey and urged his horse into a gallop.

Rye lay on the wet ground atop a small rise, moisture soaking into his uniform. Using binoculars procured from the Appaloosa's saddlebags, he pressed them gingerly against his battered face and studied the basin below. Nothing moved around the small white-clapboard church. It lay atop the exposed knoll like bleached bones.

He had to smile in spite of himself. He often cursed his vision-thing, but this time he welcomed it. Parked in the church's parking lot, the WPD ATV waited by the building's side door. The *opened* side door.

Rye sighed and swung the field glasses to study the ground behind the church. Rocky with evergreen shrubs. A covered patio with a brick grill, which Rye estimated to be seventy-five yards from the church. Seventy-five OPEN yards. It couldn't be helped. That was the closest protection to the building. He crawled backwards through the thicket. When he cleared the ridge, he stood and headed for Manny waiting with the horses, a plan percolating in his mind.

Rye looked skyward. Heavy clouds rolled overhead, squelching dawn's light. He and Manny sat with their backs against the brick grill, hidden from any inquisitive eyes in the church.

Rye cleared his throat. "Manny, I'm gonna ask you to do something, I wish I didn't have to."

"Okay." Manny's voice quivered. "Anything to help Mom."

"That's good. Mom needs our help." Noting the fear in Manny's eyes, Rye mussed his hair. "I need you to take this rifle and use the scope to watch the windows. I'm going to have to cross the parking lot to get to the church. If List or his Mexican buddies glance out, I'll be an easy target. They will attempt to kill me. I'm depending on you to have my back." Rye held his son's gaze. "That means ... shoot to kill."

"You mean ... I'll get to be like a SWAT member or something?"

Rye suppressed an emerging smile. "That's right. I now deputize you to be the official Whiskey Police Department SWAT Captain. All that target practice we used to do is going to come in handy."

"I miss that ... I miss you, Dad. I mean, living with Mom is cool and everything. But I miss having you around to do, you know, like guy stuff." He laughed. "Mom tries, but she's not very good at throwing a football."

"I want to be a family again. I'd really love to have that happen. But right now, we got to focus on rescuing the captives." Rye changed his voice to command mode. "You got that, Captain?"

"Yes sir."

"This here rifle is a Smith and Wesson M&P15. It holds 30 rounds. I hope you won't need more than that." The rifle had been in a sleeve on the Piebald's saddle. "Can you handle this weapon?"

Manny leveled an exasperated blank stare. "Dad, you know I can."

Rye set the bow and quiver next to his son. "Take care of this for me. And, Manny, one last thing." He removed his gun from his holster and stared into his son's eyes. He chambered a round into the gun. "I love you."

Using his arms and good leg, Rye rose from behind the grill and limp-ran for the ATV. Any second he expected to hear a shot ring out and feel hot lead smack into his body. Each puddle felt like muck grabbing his ankles. The splashes sounded too loud in his ears. Like a herd of mustangs. The closer he came to the ATV, the further away it seemed.

Then he reached it and lowered himself to the pavement. Breath came in ragged gasps. He peered into every church window, one at a time, studying each for any untoward movements. He saw nothing suspicious. *Did I make it without being noticed?* He made a conscious effort to slow his breathing. One last quick dash, and he'd be inside the building.

Stay alive, Dee. No matter what you have to do. Stay alive.

Manny sighted down the rifle barrel, searching from window to window. Closed blinds hung in each, except for the stained glass in the white clapboard section. Manny decided to ignore those windows, unless one of the lower panes opened.

He breathed a sigh of relief when his dad reached the ATV. Moments later, he watched his dad disappear inside the building.

"Oh, God, protect my mom and dad. I don't want to lose them." He pointed the rifle at another window.

Inside the church, Rye leaned against the wall beside the side door, allowing his eyes to adjust to the thicker darkness. It didn't take a forensic genius to tell, by the destruction of the doorjamb at the strike plate, that the side door had been forced open. List and his cronies were here. The building smelled closed up, the air, stale. An air conditioner hummed, struggling to maintain the inside temperature to what felt like 80 degrees. He heard no other sound. He clenched the P226, ready to use it.

In one direction, the hallway went about fifteen feet to three stairs that led to a closed door at the top landing. Rye tiptoed that way. On the top step, he tried the door. *Locked.* He peered through the window in the door. It led to the sanctuary. A tiny platform. A piano. An altar railing separated the stage from twenty-five or so rows of hard wooden benches. *No one's there.*

He eased back down the hallway and passed the side entrance. Five steps further, an alcove intersected with the corridor. He stopped, hugging the wall. Signs indicated the restrooms were located in the recess. He risked a quick glance. No one. With head cocked, he strained to listen. Seconds ticked away. Hearing only the wind whistling through an unlocked window, he figured the restrooms were empty. The hallway ended in several steps at another doorway. He tried the doorknob ...

Whistling came from the men's restroom.

I gotta take this guy out. Can't have him coming up behind me.

In the alcove to the bathrooms, Rye stopped outside the men's. Gun in hand, he eased open the door. A sink cabinet. A urinal. And a restroom partition hiding the toilet. A sheet of plastic held up with duct tape covered the broken window. The man stood at the urinal. In two steps, Rye stood behind him.

"¿Quién está alli?" the man asked. *Who's there?*

Rye pressed the barrel of the gun into the small of the man's back. "Make a wrong move, and I'll blow away your lower spinal cord."

The man's water stopped flowing. "No hablo Inglés, señor."

"You better learn fast." Rye pressed the gun harder into the man's back. Spotting the shape of a handgun under the man's shirt, Rye took the weapon, slipping it into his own waistband. "How many hombres are there?"

"Just me and a friend. We're landscapers."

Rye slammed the handle of his handgun into the man's kidneys. He groaned and almost went down.

"That's your last wrong answer! *¿Comprende?*" When the man didn't answer, Rye shoved the gun barrel into the man's back. "That's my wife in there. Mi espousa. I'm one pissed off hombre, and I'll kill you in a heartbeat. We got an understanding?"

343

"Si, señor. An understanding. But after this is over. I come back for you."

"I'll be waiting. Now how many men are with you?"

"Seis. Plus Señors List and Amo."

"What are you doing here?"

The man said nothing.

"Contesta," Rye snarled. *Answer me.* He jammed the handgun into the small of his prisoner's back.

"Taking a leak."

"I mean, what are you doing here at the church?"

The man waited for several long seconds before answering. "We wait for trucks."

"What trucks?"

The man laughed. "You think you destroyed all our merchandize at List's house? Nada. That was just—how you say—the iceberg tip."

With sudden clarity, it all made sense to Rye. The fandango at List's residence was only part of the shipment. List trafficked drugs and guns back and forth across the border. But he never put all his pills and bullets in one basket. The shipment they stopped last night would have been flown in under the cover of a stormy night. The rest would be trucked over the border. Chances are, both shipments would not fail to cross. List might be a crook, but he was a clever one.

"Don't move," Rye said with a growl. He glanced down at the cabinet below the sink. Without removing the gun from the man's back, Rye reached over and swung open the cabinet door. Cleaning supplies, toilet paper, garbage bags ... yes! A couple rolls of duct tape among some sponges in a bucket. Maybe Dee was right after all, and there really was a God in heaven.

He snatched up the tape.

"Put your hands behind your back," Rye commanded.

"At least let me tuck myself back into my pants."

"Better yet, drop them drawers. Remember, no false moves."

"How can I forget with your gun in my back?" the man snapped, letting his pants fall around his ankles.

"See, your English is improving already."

The man put his hands behind his back. Rye wrapped the tape around his wrists several times and secured a piece over the man's mouth. Then he bound the prisoner's ankles making sure to include the hairy legs. *That'll hurt coming off.* Rye turned him around to face the door and taped the prisoner's arms to the urinal's plumbing.

Bending over and not taking his eyes off his prisoner, Rye searched his pockets. The guy carried some loose change, a well-worn wallet, and a cell phone.

"I'm going to borrow the phone." He held it in front of the man. "Don't go anywhere," Rye said. "I'll be back."

Rye peeked out the door. *One down.* Stepping out the bathroom, he pushed three numbers on the cell.

"911. What's your emergency?"

"Gabs, this is Rye." She started to say something. "Don't interrupt, I just have a second. I'm at the Whiskey Baptist church. Send backup ASAP." He hung up.

Rye glanced through the window of the door that led to the dining area. What did churches call this room? *Fellowship Halls.* By the dim light leaking through the outside windows, he spotted several folding tables lining the wall like ordered soldiers. Chairs were packed into some kind of cart. Falling ice cubes clunked in an icemaker he couldn't see. A Coke machine had been unplugged from the wall and angled as if someone was doing repairs and hadn't finished.

Telling evidence of non-church activity lay with the empty bags of junk food and beer cans that littered the floor in a circle of chairs. The rubbish bothered Rye. Church people wouldn't leave their room trashed like this. Especially the beer cans. *Someone's been naughty.*

At the far end of the dining room, another door beckoned.

He opened the door and stepped into the dining area. Muffled talking came from the direction of the other egress.

Rye hurried across the dining area to the far door. This led down another unlit hallway which dead-ended at a door with "Music Department" stenciled on its frosted window.

Suddenly, a scream came out of nowhere that sent shivers down his spine.

Dee!

Rye never expected this. But, he figured, with Dee involved, unexpected things just happen.

From the last room, an angry shout followed the crash of falling drums and cymbals. Someone cursed in Spanish, then someone else in English. A fist punched the wall. He smiled. *Only Dee can make a man that mad.*

Leaning against the wall, Rye pondered his best approach. How to free Dee and Sunflower? How to capture List and the others? How to keep their guns outta the warzone called northern Mexico? How to do all that ... and come out alive at the other end.

Then he remembered the supplies on the ATV.

"Police! Don't anybody move."

Rye's words cut through the cacophony in the music room. He stood in the doorway, holding a flash-bang for everyone to see as he aimed a P266 at List.

"That's right," Rye snarled. "You move, you die."

Silence so overtook the room, dust bunnies could have been heard. List's men studied him with cold eyes while the mayor sat on the piano bench. Both his hands clenched in white-knuckled fists. A dozen Latino males, decorated with various martial accouterments, lounged in chairs or on the floor. Rye could read in their eyes that they itched to reach for their weapons.

"Can't you just feel the love in this place?" Rye said.

Dee and Sunflower were slumped on the floor, away from the men. Dee gave him a slight nod, and Rye understood she recognized what he held. *Good. She'll know what to do if I have to set this off.*

One of the men reached for a handgun at his waist. Rye swung the P226 in his direction, his focus drilled into the man. "You ready to die? Then do it. Hell waits for you."

For several long heartbeats, Rye's focus zeroed in on the man's hand hovering over the handgrip. Nothing else mattered. The man's fingers twitched, began to reach for the gun, then he lowered his arm away from the weapon. Rye sighed in relief. His gaze bore into the man's eyes, the twin pools of hate rippling there. Given a chance, the Latino would kill him without thought or regard.

Rye heard a rustling of cloth. He swung his gun in that direction. One of List's men had pulled a revolver and sought to bring it to play. Rye moved faster.

Rye fired three rounds at the gunman.

List's man screamed, flowers of crimson appearing on his chest. He looked at his chest, then at Rye and collapsed.

A second ticked past.

"KILL HIM!" List yelled and pounded the keyboard with a fist.

As one, List's men moved for their weapons.

Rye tossed the flash-bang in List's direction. He dove out of the room just as several gunshots tore chunks into the closing door.

The flash-bang exploded with a luminous burst.

Rye pushed off the floor and limp-ran back into the music room.

Pungent smoke choked the area.

Men lay on the floor, stunned by the explosion.

Their eyes leaked tears.

Several moaned.

In rapid fashion, Rye bound the gunmen, using duct tape to secure their wrists and ankles. The man he shot lay unmoving.

With no means of dissipation, the cloud of smoke lingered in the room. Rye's eyes watered as he struggled to see through the smoke. Breathing became difficult. He forced aside his desire to rush over to Dee and hold her.

Secure the area first.

When he reached the piano, he found the bench overturned but no Richard List. He stared out into the smoke. "Dick List, you're under arrest. Give it up."

A roar came out of the fog. The mayor steamrolled into Rye,

crashing him against a chair and onto the floor. His weak knee buckled and twisted. A shriek ripped from his throat.

With one massive hand, List grabbed Rye by the front of the shirt and lifted him bodily off the floor.

"Richard List," Rye's voice choked, "you have the right to—"

"I'll show you my rights," List snarled and smashed Rye against a wall. "I have the right to kill anyone who interferes."

Rye grasped for a breath of air, but failed. With his head swirling, Rye croaked out, "... to remain silent."

"Listen, smartass." List slapped Rye across the face and dropped him to the floor. Rye sucked in precious air through his ragged throat. List leaned over him and continued, "I'm going to mess you up real bad. Then I'm going to take your woman and do her right in front of you. I've been waiting for—"

"That the only way you get women?"

"I hate your sarcasm." List slapped Rye again. "See how you like this." He lifted Rye off the floor and shoved him into a window hard enough to crack it. Broken glass sliced his back. Rye grimaced at the warm stickiness of blood flowing down his back.

Don't shoot, Manny. It's me.

List tossed him aside like a bale of chaff.

Got to do something. Darkness swirled to overcome him. *I can't take much more of this.*

Just then, the broken window shattered, glass shards flying inward, followed a split second later by a gunshot.

List grunted a curse and collapsed to the floor.

Rye forced himself to stand. Red spread from List's shoulder, soaking his shirt, and pooling on the floor.

Rye muttered a faint, "Thanks, son. Good shooting."

Using the overturned piano bench, List rose to his feet. His good hand clenched his wounded shoulder. Blood leaked from the wound and around the fingers.

"I've been shot!" he yelled. "I can't move my fingers."

"Too bad." Rye grabbed List by the wounded arm, and struck him hard above the chest with the flat of his other hand, fingers grabbing a handful of shirt. Yanking forward, Rye swept List's leg out from under him. His knee again exploded in anguish. When the big man fell, Rye rode him to the floor. List crashed, face first, into the hardwood, his nose popping with a loud snap. Rye, on top, punched the man several times in the kidneys.

"Rye," Dee called. When he looked up, she tossed him the roll of duct tape.

In swift motions, he bound List's feet and hands. "I guess this means you won't be sending me any Christmas cards this year."

"My nose is broken," List cried into the growing circle of blood.

"Stay down," Rye said, "or that won't be the last thing that gets broken."

"Rye?"

He peered upwards to see Dee offering him a hand up. She wiggled her fingers. He took her hand and rose on one leg as she pulled. He drew her into his arms and stroked her hair. Whispering soothing words in her ear, he closed eyes already welling with tears.

Click!

Rye' eyes snapped open at the chambering of a pistol.

"You forget me, amigo?" Demonio stood in the doorway. Rye stared down the barrel of a very large handgun held by a very ugly Skinwalker.

Rye loosened his grip on Dee and eased her behind him. His throbbing knee forced him to hobble on one leg. Demonio glared at them through the empty sockets of the wolf-head. Yet, Rye could not remove his gaze from the gun barrel pointing at his chest. *At this range, a round of that caliber would go through me and hit Dee.*

"You are one persistent hombre," Demonio said, his voice tone-dead.

"And you're one ugly effing wolf." Rye spotted the leather shield worn on the wolfman's arm and the feather stuck in the wolf's fur. *From the museum.*

"Ahhh, Chief Dawlsen, don't be crude. Okay?" Demonio Amo stepped into the room and held up a radio. "My trucks are almost here. I will kill you and the women when we leave. That's your penalty for all the trouble you cause me."

"Let the women go, they have nothing to do with this."

"How noble." Demonio laughed. "First I shoot squaw. Then your wife. But you … I kill you not right away. No, I make you hurt. Now call in your man that's outside. Him I kill first."

No, not Manny! Think, Dawlsen, stall him.

"You'll not reach the border. FBI has helicopters swarming this area. You might kill me, but they'll get you."

"Tsk, tsk, you Americanos always with the idle threats. Now call in your man, or," and he pointed his gun at Sunflower. "Or I kill her right now."

"How dare you," Sunflower spoke, her voice diminished and weak, "wear the amulets you stole from me?"

"They are mine," Amo said.

"Just like a Nakai to steal from Navajo." She pushed herself off the floor.

He slashed the pistol across her cheek, tearing a bloody gash. "Shut up."

The Navajo woman touched her cheek and stared at the blood on her fingers. She lowered her head so her long black hair covered her face. She let out a long sigh and lifted her head.

Her eyes glowed with a golden color, and her mouth turned into a snarl. A grumbled noise escaped from her throat. In a swift move, she grabbed Demonio's gun hand. Her fingernails dug into his skin. Rivulets of blood leaked between her fingers.

The handgun clattered to the floor.

Amo screamed and tore his hand from her grasp. Sunflower roared, an angry she-wolf, shoving Demonio towards the ruined window.

"How?" he asked holding up his arm. "I have the shield and feather. They're supposed to protect me."

"I took those from the museum to make you think you'd want their power. You Nakai don't understand. Only Navajo receive their power. They don't give you power, they steal your power."

From halfway across the room, Sunflower leapt like a wild beast. The moment she struck Demonio, a rifle shot rang from outside.

Sunflower's leap carried them through the shattered window, both growling as they fell from sight. For a moment, a bloody mist lingered in air where Demonio had stood.

"Sunflower," Dee screamed. She started towards the window, but Rye grabbed her arm.

"No," he said. "Stay. It might be dangerous."

Without waiting to see if she listened, Rye limped to the window, grimacing with each step. He spotted Manny and waved. His son returned a salute. Rye glanced down at the ground below the window. A stunned Sunflower lay in a cacti bed ... alone. Her body twisted in an unnatural way. Next to her lay the two amulets, the feather and the shield.

Dee came alongside him. "Is she ...?"

Rye took her by the hand. "C'mon."

They hurried outside as fast as Rye's leg would allow. When they reached the injured woman, Dee knelt beside her.

"Dad!"

Rye spotted Manny running up to him.

"The weird guy wearing wolf skins ran that way." Manny pointed. "He just snuck behind those rocks." Rye squinted and noticed the tan conical rock jutting out of the desert floor.

"Give me the bow." Manny handed over the bow and quiver. Rye figured the outcropping of rocks hiding Demonio had to be at the edge of the bow's range. But with the explosive arrow head, he only had to get close. With his bum knee, he obviously wasn't going to sprint after him. His only hope in preventing Demonio's escape lay in his marksmanship.

Rye nocked an arrow. Gauging the distance, he angled the bow above the horizon and loosed the arrow. Demonio stepped out from behind the rocks just as the arrow struck the base of the outcropping. The rocks exploded into a cloud of dust and stony projectiles. When the dust cleared, Demonio had disappeared.

The church's parking lot drowned in a flood of vehicles from various law enforcement agencies. Crown Vics and SUVs marked with WPD on their doors mixed with black FBI Ford Expeditions, white county sheriff cars, I.C.E trucks, and Homeland Security black sedans. All had their lights flashing. FBI helicopters waited off the parking lot while others flew in search patterns looking for the escaped cartel head. A man in a sheriff's parka led the two horses towards a horse trailer.

Crime Scene people swarmed over the church lot, documenting every detail of discovery. Officers stood in groups, some smoking others, not. The sound of so many voices turned all sound into a blur.

Dee sat on the hot muddy ground, stroking Sunflower's hair for there was not much else she could do. Sunflower was dying and had refused any medical assistance. Probably wouldn't have done any good. Dee listened as Sunflower, with a weakening voice, spoke about being a Navajo witch.

Switching topics, Sunflower said, "I'm glad I'm not in the building of the Jesus People. I don't want to infest their place with my ghost sickness. When I die, all that is good in me will return to the gods, but my evil will roam the earth."

"You have much less evil in you than most," Dee said in a comforting tone. "You won't leave much to walk around."

"Thank you, wife of Rye." Sunflower closed her eyes and loosed a weary breath. Dee studied the woman's coppery and lined face wondering if she would speak again. Then Sunflower's eyes fluttered open and focused on Dee. In a low, raspy voice, Sunflower said, "Why are you being kind to this Navajo witch? My own Diné clan spurns me. My father disowned me. I am just a nothing Navajo."

"You are not a nothing. You are my new friend, and I wish I had more time to walk on the road of our friendship. But why am I kind to you? I am a," Dee paused for a moment while a spasm shook her new friend. "I am a Jesus Person. I walk the Jesus Path."

Sunflower managed a weak laugh. "Thought so. Tell me," she coughed and her gaze went to a distant land. With a sigh, Sunflower refocused on Dee. "Why do you walk this path of Jesus?"

For several minutes, Dee spoke of why she loved being a Jesus person. About the change in her heart. How she could love her new friend. How she could even forgive ... Rye.

Sunflower shook again with spasms. "I'm growing cold. Ever since I was ... a little girl, I wanted to have ... someone sing me to sleep." She coughed and blood touched her lips. "Sing me your ... your favorite Jesus song."

Dee closed her eyes. She knew the song to sing, but she had to choke back her emotions. *Lord, let my song bless this woman and honor You.*

She opened her eyes and began to sing.

"Amazing grace, how sweet the sound,

That saved a wretch like me."

She sang and stroked Sunflower's hair. Dee smiled to see Manny, a supportive arm around Rye, approaching. She swiped away the tears threatening to dissolve her singing and sang louder. Some law officers heard her and came over, joining in her singing.

Sometime during the song, an owl circled overhead and landed on the roof of the church. It did not wait long before it flew off.

When Dee finished the song, she looked down at her new friend. Sunflower had stopped breathing, her eyes open and her lips smiling.

CHAPTER 30

EPILOGUE

"Dad!" Manny rushed into the hospital room.

Rye sat propped up in a hospital bed, his injured leg immobilized in a cast. He wore a sleeveless t-shirt and Diamondback running shorts in lieu of the hospital gown.

Manny pushed through the well-wishers to reach the bed. Rye reached out and gave his son a one-armed hug.

"Me and Mom got you something," Manny said in rapid excitement.

"More flowers and balloons?"

"Naw, that's sissy stuff."

The crowd chuckled.

"Hope you like it," Dee said when she joined them at the bedside. She planted a lingering kiss on his lips—amid the catcalls of those in the room—and handed him a small box.

Rye shook the box. "I don't think it's a new mobile home." He unwrapped the gift, making dramatic gestures to slow the process.

"Come on, Dad." Manny motioned with his hand. "Hurry up and open it."

Rye undid the wrapping paper and opened the box. He gazed upon a graduation styled ring with a green stone and two crossed gold flintlock pistols, the insignia of the military police. Engraved on one side was the motto: "Assist, Protect, Defend." The MP motto. The other side displayed his regimental coat of arms.

He didn't know what to say. He had wanted one for years, but they had struggled with finances. Her schooling. His knee. His drinking. Somewhere along the way, he had given up on getting one.

Rye glanced up at Dee. "Thanks, hon. I love it." He slid the ring on his finger. "It's a perfect fit."

"I thought ... you know," she stammered, "since we ... like ... couldn't afford the ring before ..." Her voice trailed off. "I know your service as an MP really meant a lot to you."

He held up his hand with the ring. "This," Rye said, emphasizing the word, "is perfect. It's the best gift ever."

He took hold of her hand. He squeezed and let go. Then he looked at Manny. "Thanks, bud."

"I talked to Chee," said Dee. "He's headed back to the reservation with Sunflower's body. They want to do a proper Navajo burial ceremony ... with you there."

"I'd like that." He glanced down at his leg and then back at Dee. "Um, I might have some trouble driving ..."

Dee smiled and squeezed his hand.

"Okay. Okay," said Heilo. "This is turning into a freaking Kodak moment. Let's see that sucker." She nodded at the ring.

Rye held up his hand. She tilted her head as she looked at the jewelry. She slapped him on the shoulder.

"Dude, check that out," said DePute, sliding in next to Heilo.

"That's, like, bangin'."

"DePute, don't call me dude." But Rye held the ring out for him to see.

Reese stood at the base of the bed with his girlfriend from the Drivin' Diner, Auborne, at his side. "I don't need to see no stinking ring. Just need you to get your rear end better so you can get back. These two," he said, pointing to Heilo and DePute, "can be a real pain sometimes."

"Sometimes?" Rye questioned.

"By the way." Zach continued, "me and Aub checked in on the Vissers. Mel is still in ICU. They're still not sure if she's going to make it."

"But they said," added Auborne, "the prognosis looks … better. List's pigs didn't treat her wounds properly. They're infected, red, and leaking pus. She's got a fever and nausea. But she's made improvements. Poor Missy. She won't leave her sister's side."

Dee reached out and took Aub's hand. "Tell them, I'll be praying for them. And if there's anything I can do …" Dee's voice trailed away seeing the anguish in the girl's eyes. "You were close to them, weren't you?"

Auborne nodded and swiped away her tears.

"We still need to investigate the drugs in their apartment." Rye looked at his officers. "But that can wait."

Three familiar voices chattered at the doorway.

"We finally found the room," said Iona. "I swear architects who design hospitals are just plain demented."

"Probably done by a white man," Whitewolf said. "No self-respecting Indian would design this."

"Just look at all these flowers," said Gabby, following them. "No wonder the Whiskey Flower Shop was out. They said orders for some injured cop had run them dry. All they had left in balloons were SpongeBob and Justin Bieber. Can't imagine who'd be that popular in Whiskey. Hey, Chief, how you doing?"

Gabby pushed her way through the crowd and gave Rye a hug.

"Good to see you," she said. "We came bearing gifts." Iona appeared behind her and held up a Wendy's bag.

"Thought you might like some real food," she said, handing him the bag. "Imported all the way from Yuma in a heat-sealed package to make sure it lost none of its flavor."

"Gimme that." He took the bag, opened it, and inhaled the aroma like a greedy man sniffing newly printed money. "Thanks."

"Eat up," Gabby said. "It's got to be better than hospital food."

"Thanks, Gab. Iona." He nodded at Whitewolf.

In minutes, he'd wolfed down the double cheeseburger and fries.

While he ate, conversation drifted along. About the Diamondbacks trade for an infielder. The Cardinals training camp. Another hurricane headed straight for Baja. The two tourists kidnapped in Phoenix.

A nurse came in to give Rye his medicine. She pretended not to notice the crumpled Wendy's bag on his lap or the lingering smell. When she finished and headed back to the nurse's station, DePute started to follow the nurse. Heilo grabbed his arm.

"What?"

She gestured with a questioning look.

"She's smoking hot."

Heilo rolled her eyes.

"Is there a Chief Rye Dawlsen somewhere in this room full of reprobates?" someone called from the doorway.

"Agent Clark?" Rye asked, recognizing the voice. "Is that you?"

"Yes, sir." Stepping into the room, the tall, fit blonde slipped out of her navy blue windbreaker.

Those standing around the bed cleared a place for the agent to join them. She laid the windbreaker on the bed.

"That's for you, if you ever feel the need to go running around during a monsoon. But, I'm heading back to Phoenix, so I thought I'd come by and say my howdy before I took off."

"Appreciate that," Rye told her with a nod. "Heard any news?"

"Yeah, I've got plenty. But first, let me ask you a question." Rye tilted his head and she continued. "Why did you tell my men follow the owl? It seemed like an odd request at the time … and it's only gotten odder."

"An old Navajo tradition. When a person dies, they take on the form of an owl. When Sunflower passed, that owl landed on the church then took off. I figured, you know, what the heck, it might be Sunflower searching for her killer."

"Thanks to the owl, we located a blood trail near the point of your archery explosion and followed it for several miles." She paused, and her voice grew hesitant as if unsure what to say next. "It ran cold. All we found were animal tracks. Wolf tracks to be exact."

Rye, his officers, and Dee exchanged looks.

She held up her hand. "I don't want to hear anything about Navajo Skinwalking witch mumbo-jumbo. We'll find him eventually. Either in Mexico, or his bones bleaching in the desert."

"Yeah, that's the way I see it," Rye said.

Clark paused and gazed with eyes unfocused across the ICU unit.

She sighed and said, "We received a tox report on the body of your officer ..."

"Juan. A good man."

"Yeah. Well, he had been contaminated with some sort of chemical comp. Our lab is still working on the exact formula. Whatever's in it prevented death's favorite insects from ... you know. I don't need to paint a picture."

"That's weird." Rye rubbed his forehead. "Makes no sense."

"Okay then," Clark said drawing out the words. "You need to know about Johnny Batts. He's been working undercover for some Washington agency. He's a former CIA operative. Retired to his family mining site to live quietly. With all the UDAs entering the country, the government pressed him into service. He's been instrumental in sending some big time bad guys back home. Including a couple of al-Qaeda terrorists."

Everyone stared at her, each with their own interpretation of incredulous stamped on their face. Rye broke the silence, "Who'd a thunk it? Batts. A spook. But it explains some of his nutty behavior."

"What we've uncovered so far in investigating Mayor Richard List," Clark continued, "reveals a Medusa-like smuggling operation. He had operatives stealing military grade weapons. He'd trade these to Mr. Amo for drug shipments. List would turn around and sell the drugs for profit and purchase more weapons."

"Figures." Rye grimaced as he moved his leg into a more comfortable position.

"There's more. He just purchased some island in the Caribbean. We figure he was fleeing the states. There's evidence indicating his involvement in smuggling young Mexican girls to be used as sex toys.

One girl, Amalia, is providing us with some interesting details. One of our agents has uncovered a money-laundering scheme. We've seized his assets, and your department will benefit from that seizure."

"Good," said Rye. "We can use a little help."

"The judge ordered him held without bond. But he's got his lawyers ..."

"Great." Rye frowned.

"I never cared for the man," said Dee. "You could see evil in his eyes."

"And I just thought he smelled bad," said Heilo.

"We also have Mr. Barend Jilt in custody—in a Phoenix hospital due to his injuries—along with several of List's men. So far, we haven't located List's son. We have an BOLO out on him."

Rye laughed. "Junior's not the sharpest cactus in the desert. He'll stumble into a gas station to pick up some beer, and there'll be a cop."

"I ... uh ..." Dee stammered for the right word. "Junior tried to rape me. I've tried to put it out of my memory, but I can't do it. And, well, I shot him." Dee's words tumbled out. "I didn't kill him. Demonio captured me before I could." Tears welled in her eyes. "I ... I ..." and the tears came. Rye took her in his arms.

"Do you know where is he, ma'am?" Clark asked.

Dee's shoulders drooped. "Last time I saw him, he was lying in the roadside ditch by the List residence."

"It's alright, hon," Rye whispered in her ear. "It wasn't your fault."

Auborne added, "He's probably hiding in some mountain shack. Or camping on a mesa. If he's alive."

Dee shook her head. "But Manny saved me." She rubbed her son's head. "Junior'll be singing soprano for a little while."

"Hi-yah," Manny said and swung into a karate form. Everyone laughed.

Rye held Clark's gaze in his. "Agent, your team did good work."

She smiled. "Yours too. Stay safe." Clark patted him on the shoulder and left the room. A shower of byes followed her.

A sudden tiredness swept over Rye. He fought to keep his eyelids open. He stifled a yawn and said, "Isn't there anybody at the station? What are my best officers doing lingering around a hospital room?" His voice faded as he spoke.

The cops started babbling about getting back to work, filling out reports, running checks on various investigations. They mumbled their good-byes and filed out one after another.

Iona came over to the bed and leaned over to whisper into Rye's ear, "I love you, Rye Dawlsen. But I've never been one to go after another woman's man. You take good care of her, you hear me. She loves you, you know."

Rye smiled. "Thanks, Iona. You're one special woman."

"But if you two don't work out …" She kissed him on the forehead. "Get some rest," she said after standing upright.

Rye closed his eyes for a moment and felt the mattress settle. He cracked open one eye to see Dee sitting on the bed. She reached out and took his hand. She smiled. How long had he waited to see that smile? He squeezed her hand, and she returned the squeeze.

"I called my story into the paper," she said. "My editor wants me here a few more weeks. You know … reporting on the loose ends. I'd like to spend …" Her voice trailed away to an awkward silence.

"I'd like that," he mumbled. He struggled to keep his thoughts from fading into the sleep he desired. *Just a few more minutes with her.*

"I didn't tell you. The pastor of that Baptist church came by while you were asleep."

"Okay? Why? Was he looking to preach to me?"

"No. He said he appreciates your efforts to keep Whiskey safe. He heard you were in need of living quarters. It seems one of his parishioners has an empty rental house he's offering to you. Says you can use it rent free until you get another trailer."

"That's nice of him," Rye mumbled, his eyelids drooping. "Tell ... him ... thanks."

"Good night, Dad," Manny said, his voice sounding far away.

"Thanks," Rye replied, his voice hovering above inaudible. He reached up and touched his dog tags.

"One last thing," Dee said. "The President called to wish you well."

"Tell him ..." He succumbed to the realm of sleep.

Demonio reached the tunnel just after midnight. High clouds partially hid the moon. Shrubs and rocks hid in the dark. Looming overhead like a sheer black mountain, the border wall blocked further travel overland. *No problemo, I got my own way across.* He scanned the dark desert, glad to be returning home to Mexico. But, he'd be returning real soon to the US of stinking A. Unfinished business.

A creaking noise interrupted the desert quiet. A few feet away, the ground shook, and a square piece of land swung upward. Issuing from below, a soft blue light hinted at the tunnel opening. A featureless head-shaped oval raised above the lip of the entrance.

"¿Filino?" The head whispered the soft question in the breeze.

"No. Canino." Demonio replied, moving towards the tunnel.

"Demonio," the man said, "Good to see you, mi amigo. I hear you had some tough times in Whiskey. I have news. Bueno and mal."

Demonio stood on the edge of the tunnel. The light from the tunnel revealed a yawning pit.

"Tell me," Demonio snapped.

"The bad news …" the man paused. "Your wife has disappeared. We had her detained. But she vanished last night."

Demonio spat a string of curses.

"Good news?" said the man in a rush to appease his boss. "The shipments arrived. We received many guns. And the radioactive material."

"Bueno. Forget mi espousa. Plans for the revolution move forward. But I have one thing I need to do before that. A man I need to kill with a very ugly death."

"And who is this unfortunate hombre?"

"Rye Dawlsen."

The End

As we wait for the sequel, enjoy another Brimstone Fiction book, *Crossing into the Mystic*, by DL Koontz.

Crossing into the Mystic

DL Koontz

Brimstone
Fiction

Chapter 1

All of it became mine that day: the hefty trust fund, my mother's red SUV, and my stepfather's ancestral estate isolated amidst the caverns of the Blue Ridge Mountains. I was embarking on a 500-mile journey to make solo use of all three.

As long as I remained in Boston, I would continue to live my life backward—dwelling on the past and longing for the parents and sister who were dead. Buried. Gone. There was no way I could have known that by turning away from death I would be running into it.

That day seemed like the perfect time to launch my escape. The rising sun shot beguiling streaks of crimson through the divisions of the massive brownstones on Boston's Beacon Hill, teasing away any threat of "Red sky at morning, sailor take warning."

In the stillness of the morning, I heard a house door latch, then a husky voice grumble. "Ouch ... ouch ... dang!"

My cousin, Michael, barefoot and clad only in gym trunks and a T-shirt, pranced between stones as he hurried up the steep three-block incline toward me. He was carrying travel snacks, but what I hoped he was bringing me was reassurance of our individual escapes.

"Grace, go! Go! Go! Click your heels and get the Sam Hill out of Oz before she changes her mind!"

Though Michael's words echoed my resolve, I laughed. He was four inches taller and eight years older, but a million times more sociable and often reminded me of an oversized little boy.

"Auck, Dorothy." He reached my car, glanced back toward our house, and handed me a zip-locked bag stuffed with trail mix. "You're too late. You'll never get to Kansas now."

I turned to see the subject of his wicked witch allusion exit through the oversized front door of our ivy-covered brownstone and begin her march up the sidewalk with Uncle Phil dawdling behind. Aunt Tish wasn't toting a flying broom, but she was storming along, face scowling, hands fisted.

Michael grinned. "I guess she's saving the flying monkeys for me."

"Maybe. She wasn't very happy about you leaving tonight for Chile. You sure you're tough enough to stand up to her?" I elbowed him, knowing he wouldn't feel the jab. Despite his baby face and wire-rimmed glasses, he had the abs of a bodybuilder.

"No problem. She can't control me anymore. It's you who better leave quickly."

"I'm going. Don't worry about that." I tossed the trail mix on the back seat. From the front, my dog, Tramp, watched it land and turned back to the front window, more excited about going somewhere than the goodies. He barked twice. *Let's go.*

"Good. It will be two years before you'll get another chance," Michael warned in a whisper. "I won't be here this summer to save you like I have before."

"Which is exactly why I'm leaving today. Thanks for coming home to see me off. She's not that bad you know." Maybe voicing such hope would make it so.

Eyes wide, he said, "What? She's an unstable, soul-sucking—"

"Shush." I stifled laughter. "She'll hear you."

He sobered and leaned against my car, crossing his arms. "You're sure about this?"

"The trip? Of course."

He shook his head. "The house. It sounds … weird. Like Norman Bates lives there."

I looked at him, startled. Michael was generally carefree and titillated by the unknown. He loved the notion that people held secrets within themselves.

"That's crazy," I affirmed, lest his uncharacteristic concern unnerve me.

"Is it? Jack was so close-mouthed about the place."

"Michael, stop it! It's only a house. Jack was there three years ago. How bad could it be?"

"Remember. I'm only a phone call away. You have to live there what— three months?"

"That's what the will says. Then it's mine to do what I want. Including selling it. And, of course, that's exactly what Aunt Tish expects me to do."

"We'll work that out later. Stick with this charade that you're fixing it for your senior project, then selling it and moving back to Boston. By the end of summer, my new company will transfer me back to the states, and you can live with me. Just don't come back here."

"I know, I know."

"And keep Tramp close by."

I shook my head to indicate his concern was unnecessary. But inside, I couldn't help but wonder if Tramp would be able to stop *all* threats that I might encounter.

* * *

After stopping to assess her own vehicle and bark orders at my Uncle Phil to take it to the car wash, Aunt Tish reached us. As her eyes scanned my car, Uncle Phil plodded up behind.

Beside me, Michael murmured, "Shoulda' tied garlic around our necks," then he donned a Cheshire grin and bellowed, "Good morning, Mother dearest."

"Nice of you to grace us with your company, darling," Aunt Tish clucked with saccharin sarcasm and crossed her arms. Her face was stern, her eyes leveled. "If I didn't know better, I'd think you were trying to sleep your way through the day until your flight leaves."

"Got in late, Mom."

She arched a skeptical brow. "If you're turning right around and leaving for that ridiculous job in Chile, why did you even bother coming home? You could have been working at MacGruder's, you know. They *are* the most prestigious firm in Boston."

"Yeah, Mom, I know."

"They certainly would have paid better. Must be nice to have no concerns about money."

"I haven't cost you a cent since I turned twenty-one. And if you're so worried about money, why do you live in this pretentious place? How can you afford it anyway?" He clicked his thumb and middle finger. "Oh, that's right. You used Grace's education fund."

She exhaled into a pout. "You kids are so disrespectful. Why do you do these things to me? Haven't I suffered enough?"

"Here we go." Michael rubbed his forehead.

"And look at you. Go put on some clothes. What will the neighbors think?" Her eyes darted to the windows of the lofty brownstones shadowing the street.

"Yeah, Mom. They'll probably think I feed nails to little children since I don't wear shoes." He turned his back to her and smiled at me, then withdrew to the back of the car and shook my bike as though to make sure it was tethered securely. I could see his grin from the corner of my eye.

"We'll talk later about you arriving home one day just to leave the next."

She turned to me, swapping irritation with sadness as easily as if she'd replaced a straw hat with a ball cap. Wiping at invisible tears, she sniffled and brushed back a lock of frizzled hair, causing her peace sign earrings to sway to and fro. With characteristic dramatic flourish, she took one of my hands and pressed an object into my palm.

"Your keys. Why your mother insisted you keep this atrocious gas-guzzler, I'll never know. I never did understand her."

I wrapped my fingers around the keys, feeling the shape of independence. "Thank you."

It was expected of me to treat this as a heart-rending gesture on her part, even though she had readily agreed to the trip because she wanted the house to be sold as quickly as possible, thereby placing more money into my accounts, to which *she* had access.

Aunt Tish pouted. "You selfish kids are breaking my heart with these trips."

I kept quiet. Best not to acknowledge her fabricated sadness or her varnished insult.

Receiving no response from her selfish kids, she turned to my uncle. "Philip, I must be crazy. I'm going to be thrown in jail for letting a 16-year-old live by herself ... in some creepy house in a ... a ... redneck wilderness."

From the back of the car, Michael groaned.

"Aunt Tish—" I began.

Uncle Phil cleared his throat and stood tall, looking for a moment more like the commanding professor he was when teaching Chaucer at Boston College than the ventriloquist's dummy he played at home for his formidable wife. "Tish, she'll be fine. It's only for the summer."

"But it's so far away from Beacon Hill and civilized society, for bloody sake," she responded stiffly. "She won't be around our kind. Those people are so provincial. What will my friends think? And that house ..."

Uncle Phil sighed. "The house is fine. The management company said so."

"Yeah, Mom," Michael scolded from his retreat, "just because the place is old doesn't make it creepy. Heck, our house is old."

Uncle Phil shot his son a quelling look. "Jack loved the place. He spent a lot of time there. It must be in good shape. And if it's not, then Grace will fix it up. That's the whole point of this trip anyway." He frowned. "Besides, by the time you were sixteen, you had already been arrested for disturbing the peace and indecent exposure."

"Oh gawd, Pops." Michael cringed and reached up to rub his temples. "Too much information."

Uncle Phil continued. "You already set up a bank account for her. She has a credit card. She's got everything she needs. If anyone can take care of herself, it's Grace."

"Yeah, Mom," Michael chimed from behind the car. "Crimeny, she's been taking care of you for the past three years."

Aunt Tish pushed her tangled hair behind her ears and huffed. "Fine. Obviously no one cares what I think. Just go, Grace. But stay out of trouble. I don't want any calls from the police."

I mouthed a "thank you," to Uncle Phil, shoved my backpack on the heap of boxes lining my back seat, and shut the door. Tramp sat waiting on the passenger seat. On the floor, my cat Chubbs crouched in his carrier, obviously annoyed. On the console sat an envelope containing $5,000 in cash, covered with road maps graphing my way from Massachusetts to West Virginia.

"Aunt Tish, I'll be fine." I pulled her into a sideways embrace as I rounded to the driver's side and opened the door. She was my only aunt and despite her opinions of me, I wanted to believe her capable of feeling genuine concern. "I promise to call every day."

"Be careful. If something goes wrong, it's a reflection on me." As she pulled away, she flicked at my hair. "And for pity's sake, Grace, do something with that ridiculous hair while you're there."

I ignored her. "Remember your dentist appointment tomorrow. I left a note on the fridge."

She waved that away with a *Yes, yes, I know all this* dismissal, but I knew she would forget.

Then, because I felt it was expected of me, I looked back toward the house and lied, "I'll miss this place."

I voiced some inane comment about what I'd miss, but my thoughts were on the excitement of being *me*, rather than a dead couple's orphaned child or Tish Rosenburg's ungrateful niece.

The goodbyes complete, I climbed into my car and pulled away. I could see Michael standing behind my aunt and uncle, flailing his arms in a dramatic *don't-stop-keep-going wave*.

"Call your Grandma Sadie, she's not doing so well," was the last thing I heard Aunt Tish bark as I descended the hill and rounded the corner onto Beacon Street, took a final glance at Boston Common, and headed toward I-95 South.

The trip underway, I exhaled deeply. I'd loved to have driven into the future without looking back, to have fast-forwarded to summer's end when Michael and I could plant roots somewhere together. But, there was no shortcut to that time, and I felt dread press in on me as if each accumulated mile were adding a hole to the safety net I hadn't yet hung in place.